THE WHISPERING MUSE

THE
WHISPERING
MUSE

LAURA PURCELL

R A V E N ❧ B O O K S

LONDON · OXFORD · NEW YORK · NEW DELHI · SYDNEY

RAVEN BOOKS
Bloomsbury Publishing Plc
50 Bedford Square, London, WC1B 3DP, UK
29 Earlsfort Terrace, Dublin 2, Ireland

BLOOMSBURY, RAVEN BOOKS and the Raven Books logo are
trademarks of Bloomsbury Publishing Plc

First published in Great Britain 2023

A catalogue record for this book is available from the British Library

ISBN: HB: 978-1-5266-2718-6; TPB: 978-1-5266-2719-3;
EBOOK: 978-1-5266-2721-6; EPDF: 978-1-5266-5126-6;
WATERSTONES SPECIAL EDITION: 978-1-5266-6181-4

2 4 6 8 10 9 7 5 3 1

Typeset by Integra Software Services Pvt. Ltd.
Printed and bound in Great Britain by CPI Group (UK) Ltd, Croydon CR0 4YY

To find out more about our authors and books visit www.bloomsbury.com
and sign up for our newsletters

For Katie

ACT I

Macbeth

'A false face must hide what the false heart doth know.'

CHAPTER 1

The offer was too good to be true. I knew that from the start. Opportunities don't fall into your lap from the sky; they must be fought for, tooth and nail. I *knew*. But I wanted her to prove me wrong.

It rained stubbornly that morning, on and on like an infant that won't hush. I didn't have an umbrella. The omnibus could only carry me part of the way, and so by the time I turned into the square of tall, white townhouses, I was soaked through to my petticoats.

My left boot squelched from where I'd stepped in a puddle earlier. Pausing, I checked the direction again, but it was difficult to see house numbers through the drizzle. For a while I floundered there, listening to the water tinkling from the eaves, and toyed with the idea of going home again. But my family couldn't afford to offend these people any more than we already had. Better to see the lady and possibly receive some refreshments than return to the cramped room with its mountain of chores.

When at last I found Number 13, it looked exactly like its neighbouring houses: three storeys of white brick with a slate roof and dormer windows. A cherubic girl of about six years peered down at me from her nursery in the attic. At that distance, the raindrops sliding across the window might have been tears, running down her plump cheeks. I waved. Before she could return my greeting, a hand appeared over her shoulder and drew the curtain firmly shut.

I wasn't surprised. The gentry taught their little ones reserve from a young age, and perhaps they were right to do so.

The front door shone as black as a freshly polished boot. It wasn't intended for the likes of me. Instead, I gripped the slick iron rail and took the area stairs to the basement. I can't say I was nervous, exactly; nerves imply hope of a happy outcome. I trod wearily, a broken-winded horse on its way to the knacker's yard. Mrs Dyer might have dressed her summons up as an invitation to tea, but that was the veneer of good breeding. She could have nothing pleasant to say. The only reason for her to seek me out would be to deliver more bad news.

I knocked on the trade door. After a long wait, a pimple-faced youth answered. 'What d'you want?'

'I'm here to see Mrs Dyer.'

His eyes raked me up and down, from my limp capote hat to my mud-splashed skirts. 'Not likely.'

My cheeks flushed, more from anger than embarrassment. I had twice this boy's training in service – and I knew how to answer a door with good manners. 'Well go and ask her, then. Tell her Jenny Wilcox is here.'

He looked me over again. 'I suppose you can come in from the rain. But I'll be watching you.'

He let me into a smoky kitchen with soot-stained walls and sat back down at a long deal table. A pot bubbled over an open range. I'd expected to see a bevy of servants, like at Mrs Fielding's house, but there was only the youth there, sharpening knives and polishing silverware.

I stood in front of the fire to dry myself off. My clothes started to steam and I could feel my hair frizzing at my ears, as it always did in the damp. I would look a mess. Still, perhaps that was good. Mrs Dyer might pity a bedraggled waif.

A bell chimed the hour from somewhere inside the house. Ten o'clock, the exact time of my appointment. As if by magic a footman appeared, dressed in an old-fashioned livery and powdered wig.

'This way, please.'

Rain murmured on in the background as he led me out of the servants' quarters and into a long corridor. Everything seemed smart and well kept. Pier tables displayed vases of fresh flowers and a mirror gleamed from the wall. Months of absence had served to make me feel out of place in a gentrified environment. Had I ever really enjoyed so much space?

The footman glided to a door at the very end of the hallway, beside a grandfather clock. He knocked once and counted to five under his breath before pushing the door open.

The parlour inside was decorated in pale green chintz. Ferns and a cage of lovebirds hung over the window. No fire burned in the grate – it was August, after all – and the space was occupied by a pair of matching china dogs instead.

A lady sat on the sofa, staring at them. Caramel hair was piled on top of her head and held in place with combs. She wore a high-necked teal gown with fashionable pagoda sleeves. So this was Mrs Dyer, my correspondent. Wife to the owner of the Mercury theatre.

The footman cleared his throat. 'Miss Wilcox for you, madam.'

Her head turned slowly in my direction. She was handsome, a little past the age of forty. 'Ah,' she said, smiling with cochineal-stained lips. 'Do come in. Sit down.'

She slid forward and began to busy herself with the silver tea-tray on the table in front of her. Her hands trembled as she worked. The cup rattled against its saucer, the porcelain chattering together like teeth in the cold.

But why? Mrs Dyer was at home. She'd asked me here. Surely there was no cause for *her* to be nervous?

Warily, I perched on the edge of my seat, trying not to leave a water mark. I didn't know what to say, so I kept my mouth shut.

'That will be all, James,' she told the footman.

He made a low bow and retreated backwards, as though leaving the presence of a queen.

Mrs Dyer stirred milk into the tea. 'I am so glad you received my letter, Jennifer – may I call you Jennifer?'

I took the cup from her perfectly manicured hands. 'If you like.' It was the only reasonable answer, but I'd rather she didn't. Using my Christian name implied a level of familiarity. I didn't know her from Adam. For the first time, she met my eyes. Hers were green like absinthe. 'I can detect the family resemblance. You favour your brother.'

My fingers curled around the handle. 'Forgive me, madam, but ... I'm not sure exactly why you've asked me here. If Greg left the theatre owing you money, I can't ... I don't have ...'

Mrs Dyer assessed me over the rim of her cup and took a careful sip. She must have seen the truth of my words. He'd left us with barely tuppence to rub together. 'As a matter of fact, Mr Wilcox *did* take more than he was owed. His wages were paid up until the next quarter day. But please do not imagine I invited you here to collect a debt. I wish to speak to you on a more ... delicate subject.'

My pulse quickened. Every time I thought I'd cleaned up my brother's mess, fresh sewage bobbed to the surface. Had he stolen something from his former employer, too? Maybe Mrs Dyer's hands were trembling for the same reason as my own; maybe it was the effort of holding back all that wounded rage.

I drank to buy myself some time.

'Do you enjoy the theatre, Jennifer?'

Her question took me by surprise. 'I do, very much, when I have a chance to go. It's been a while since I saw anything ... Greg took me to the gallery once or twice, when he first started working for you. We saw *East Lynne* and *The Corsican Brothers*.' Those happy memories were galling now.

'Ah, yes. Such touching pieces.' Her expression softened. 'I do not recollect seeing you at the time. I should not have been aware of your existence, yet I am afraid gossip has spread rather rapidly through the theatre since your brother absconded. As a philanthropist, I was naturally concerned to hear that Mr Wilcox had left behind a family in need. We have lost a painter and a soubrette at the Mercury, but I fear you have lost even more from these sad events.'

She didn't know the half of it. 'What's a sou — sub —'

'A soubrette? That is what we call young actresses that play supporting roles. Actresses like Georgiana Mildmay.'

I could think of one or two other names for her.

The rain pattered on. One of the lovebirds chirped. Mrs Dyer took another sip.

What could she want with me? She seemed a kinder sort of lady than my mistress had been. There was no reason to think she'd help me, but it was worth asking whilst I was here. We were running too low on money for subtlety. 'I'm not overly familiar with the theatre terms,' I admitted. 'My work's all been in service. In houses like this. I don't suppose ... Forgive me for asking, but we've been left rather short. None of your acquaintance need a char, do they, madam?'

Mrs Dyer nursed her cup in her palms. She seemed to be weighing it, weighing me. 'I *had* heard it said that you were seeking a new position, following your brother's departure. Tell me, what was your previous role?'

I liked how she said *role*, as if I'd taken a part in a play. I'd certainly worked hard enough for it. Years of auditions in the scullery, clawing my way up the servants' hierarchy, and all of it blown away in a moment. 'I was lady's maid to Mrs Fielding and her two daughters.'

She frowned. 'Excuse me for speaking candidly. But would it not be a shame for an accomplished young woman like yourself to spend her time cleaning houses? As a lady's maid, you must have possessed other talents. I am sure you can care for garments, style hair and sew perfectly. Life as a charwoman may prove somewhat ... demeaning to you.'

I swallowed a ball of pride. Mrs Fielding hadn't given me a reference. Without one, I'd be lucky to secure work sweeping carpets. 'I'll do what I must.'

'What if,' Mrs Dyer said slowly, her green eyes flicking back to the china dogs, 'there were another option? A position more suited to your talents? Should you be willing to take that up instead?'

Hope sparked, painful in my chest. 'Do you mean ... something at your theatre? Is there an opening?'

'Precisely.' She flashed a smile. 'My husband has taken a select group of actors on tour to Southend-on-Sea for the summer, but when he returns we shall be busy – very busy indeed. I must prepare by taking on more staff. I invited you here hoping that you would agree to be one of the number.'

I placed my cup down on the table before I could drop it. Relief made me weak. After so much misery over the last few months, I hardly dared trust what I was hearing. 'Mrs Dyer ... I don't know what to say. It's so kind of you to think of me! I'm sure you have other women eager for the place.'

'I do. But the position calls for a very particular worker. One in whom I will place a great deal of trust.'

Anything. I'd do practically anything to help winch my family back to the place it'd fallen from. 'Yes, madam. Of course, I'll do my utmost to deserve your kindness. I'll pay back what my brother owes you and be the best – the best in the position that I can be.' I stumbled, realising I was babbling. 'I'm sorry – what exactly *is* the position?'

She looked indulgently on my fluster. 'We call it a "dresser". A person who arranges costumes, hair, and applies stage paint to the actresses.'

I hadn't dared expect work at all, let alone an interesting prospect like this. It would be something, to dress a character. I'd grown bored of tweaking my mistress and her daughters for the same old society balls, arranging fashionable hairstyles that didn't suit them, fastening pastel-coloured gowns.

'I could do that, Mrs Dyer. I'd be happy to do that.'

'I am glad to hear it.' Her throat worked beneath the high collar of her gown. 'Yet do not let your gratitude run away with you. I will not engage you under false pretences. You must understand, the actress you shall be dressing ... She is not a good woman, Jennifer. She needs to be watched.'

Surely she could be describing any actress. None of them were trustworthy. Look what Georgiana Mildmay had done! Mrs Dyer's warning didn't put me off. I hadn't exactly liked my former mistress, either.

'How do you mean, watched?' I queried.

Mrs Dyer set her cup down beside mine on the table. A pink crescent marked the rim of hers. 'Allow me to explain the situation. Our leading lady of many years retired in the spring and Mr Dyer promoted an actress of our company in her place. She calls herself Lilith Erikson. A stage name.' Thunder purred outside. The light was growing dimmer by the second. 'There is something not right about her, Jennifer. You will sense it the moment you meet her. My husband is convinced she has "untapped talent" and perhaps that is true. But I do not like the cut of her jib. You see, we are investing a great deal of capital in bringing her forward, the reputation of our theatre is at stake. Georgiana has already deserted us, and I should feel much happier knowing there was someone keeping an eye upon Lilith.'

'I'd be glad to oblige. But surely you don't need to worry so much? Your husband must trust Lilith, to give her this big chance?'

She looked me dead in the face. 'Mr Dyer,' she said levelly, 'is bewitched. I mean that quite literally. My husband is a good man, but not a strong one. He is not proof against Lilith Erikson's tricks.'

I lowered my gaze. Was there more to this than Mrs Dyer was letting on? Actresses had a reputation for loose morals. Maybe it wasn't just her husband's money she wanted to keep safe. His fidelity might be in question.

Well, I wasn't above watching him for her. If she needed a sneak and a tattletale, I'd do that too. There wasn't much choice.

'Of course, I should be willing to pay for your discretion,' Mrs Dyer continued, her hands quaking softly in her lap. 'You would have forty-five pounds a year in this role.'

I blinked at her, certain I'd misheard. Forty-five pounds! That was more than even the manservants earned at my last place. It wasn't the kind of wage I ever dreamed I'd see.

And what I could do with that fortune ... I could save for Bertie's operation again. Move us to better lodgings. With this job I'd have enough to keep us all safe.

'You're certain it's that much? There hasn't been some kind of mistake?'

Mrs Dyer gave a rueful smile. 'You will learn, Jennifer, that I am good to those who are good to me. It is only a shame your brother did not count himself amongst that number.'

I took a fortifying sip of tea. Greg had never earned anywhere near that money. Mrs Dyer cared deeply to stump up so much cash. 'Could you teach me, madam? About working in a theatre? I know a bit from my brother, but I'd need some help.'

'Of course!' she said warmly. 'Never fear, I will verse you in all our ways.' Mrs Dyer rose to her feet and unlocked a drawer in one of the cabinets. She returned with a purse and a leatherbound book. '*The Complete Works of Shakespeare*. Consider it a gift. Read it all, but pay close attention to *Macbeth*. That is the play we will open with, come September. You will be dressing Lilith as Lady Macbeth.'

It was a thick slab of a book. I flicked through the pages, surprised to see they were as thin as onion skin and packed with small, close print. It would take me ages to plough through it. I'd never read a book this big.

'Thank you, madam. I've heard of Macbeth. Isn't he a great villain?'

'Indeed he is. Ghastly. Yet I consider his wife to be even worse.' She stroked her chin, thoughtful. 'What else may assist you? I am sure it would be helpful to see one or two productions at other theatres before you start – they will not be *Macbeth*, of course, but we are not above borrowing elements of costume from other companies. My wardrobe mistress, Mrs Nettles, is always scouting for inspiration.'

I didn't have the money to spare for theatre tickets. It felt like pushing my luck to ask for an advance. 'But ... it's summer,' I said as an excuse. 'Aren't the London theatres shut right now?'

'All but one.' She paused. A strange, wistful smile took possession of her lips. 'One very special playhouse remains open all year round, devoted to its art. The Helicon.' Her voice hushed, as if she were imparting a sacred secret. 'It belongs to the most splendid actor I have ever known. His name is Eugene Grieves. Have you heard of him?'

'The name sounds familiar, but ...'

'I must confess to being something of a devotee.' She unclasped her purse and released a spill of coins. Not worn and dull like the coins I traded with, but shiny, a dragon's hoard. 'Mr Dyer says that Lilith Erikson has talent, but you may judge between us when you have seen *my* conception of a brilliant actor. Here.' Taking my hand, she opened it and let pennies shower in.

I cleared my throat. 'Mrs Dyer, that's more than enough for a single ticket!'

'Take it all,' she urged. 'I believe you have younger brothers and sisters at home? Perhaps the children should like to go too?'

There it was: the crack in my defence. Kindness to me was one thing, but showing consideration for my siblings warmed my heart. I tried to hush my misgivings. This was the luck I'd prayed for. Maybe some rich ladies simply liked to help people of my class? To show themselves as virtuous and charitable Christians?

'Thank you, madam,' I said earnestly, closing my fingers over the treasure. It felt heavy, reliable. 'I appreciate that. I'm sure they'll be delighted to come. What's the play?'

'A great classic. You will see Eugene Grieves portray Doctor Faustus!'

It meant nothing to me. My ignorance made me ashamed, but she'd promised to be my teacher. 'And what's that about?'

Her lips parted in surprise. 'Why, it is a famous legend! Faust. The foolish man who made a deal with the Devil.'

CHAPTER 2

I'd never seen Philip so excited. He stood on tiptoes before the mirror, combing his hair back with water.

Dorcas winked at me. 'He wants to look nice for the ladies.'

Philip blushed a deep red. He was only thirteen. 'Leave me alone! I've never been to the theatre before. Greg always said I had to stay at home and be the man of the house.'

I flinched to hear him speak Greg's name. 'You'll love the theatre, Phil,' I replied high and bright, as if I could bury the mention of our brother with the tone of my voice. 'You're right there inside the story. When there's thunder, you feel it in your ribcage.'

Bertie set up a whine and pushed his uneaten supper across the table. 'I want to go too!'

I cursed myself. I should have foreseen this. I wrapped my arms around his thin shoulders. 'I know you do, love. But there are too many steps up to the gallery for your poorly foot. You wouldn't make it.' Bertie's lower lip poked out, trembling. 'I'll take you when you're older,' I tried. 'And remember, Mrs Khan from downstairs is coming to sit with you. She'll tell you lots of stories, probably better stories than the one we're seeing.'

Bertie was nine now, but his tears still caused the same surge of panic in me as his infant cries had done. I didn't suppose that would ever go away.

Just then the watchman called the hour from the street. Dorcas grabbed Philip's collar and pulled him away from the mirror. 'Time to go. You ain't getting any prettier.'

I sighed. It cut me to leave Bertie, but the three of us deserved one night off, at least. I kissed his hot, tear-stained cheek. 'See you in a few hours.'

It was impossible to feel guilty for long. The evening was perfect, warm with a gentle breeze, and the sun had only just started to dip. People spilled into the streets, eager for amusement after a hard day's toil. Ragged boys tumbled and turned cartwheels for pennies. A man set up his hurdy-gurdy and began to play for a troupe of dancing dogs.

Philip grinned. My spirits lifted to see joy on his freckled face. It had been sadly lacking since Gregory took off.

'Who wrote this play?' Philip asked me suddenly.

'I don't know. I never saw this one before.'

'Is it Shakespeare?'

'No. Someone else. Another dead writer.'

Dorcas laughed. 'Don't quiz her, Phil. She's only paid to care about the clothes.'

I *was* interested in the plays too; I just struggled to make sense of them. My schooling hadn't been heavy on literature or history. I kept having to read the pages of *Macbeth* over again, to make sure I understood what had happened. Thankfully Mrs Dyer was patient and explained everything. The more I visited her for instruction, the more I warmed to her. She was articulate and generous, fond of her little girl, whose name I learnt was Rachel.

As we neared Covent Garden, the streets filled with traffic. Stalls steamed on the corners, offering saloop, chestnuts and brandy balls. I bought a bottle of ginger beer before joining the queue: we passed it between us, glad of refreshment in the heat. Ladies glided into the Helicon through the subscribers' door without having to wait.

'Get an eyeful of them,' Dorcas marvelled. 'How do they manage to look so fresh and keep their skirts clean in all this dust?'

'Money,' I said.

At last it was our turn to push ninepence through the hole in the wall and receive our metal tokens. The crowd moved forward in a rush, treading on my skirts as they propelled me inside. I'd been right when I told Bertie about the steps. He never would have made it up to the gallery. Hundreds of stairs led higher and higher, with no landings to stop and rest in between. By the time we reached the top, the muscles in my legs were screaming.

But it was worth the climb to hear Philip's intake of breath as the auditorium unfolded before him.

Up in the gods we could see each drop of the crystal chandelier. Lines of benches raked steeply from the back down to the front, where a protective rail stopped people from toppling over into the dress circle below. Dorcas grabbed our hands and made a dash for the lowest bench. We gained it just before a group of costermonger lads. Poking out her tongue at them, Dorcas removed her bonnet and tied it to the rail by its strings.

Philip grinned. 'The best seats in the whole gallery!'

Already the air was thick with orange peel and sweat. Voices buzzed, feet stamped. Someone behind us cracked nuts.

Was it really possible that I was swapping my drab maid's existence to work in an exciting place like this? I hardly dared trust my good fortune. Happiness was a beast to be kept on a short rein – in case it bolted and threw me into a ditch. Better to keep wary and guarded in a world where anyone could betray you – even your da, even your eldest brother.

But I couldn't resist peering under the railing for a glimpse of the stage. It looked tiny. The swells sitting in the orchestra stalls were like ants: some of their heads shone with bear's grease; others had their hair piled up in ribbons and feathers. Their finery sat at odds with the rather worn auditorium. The Helicon had definitely seen better days. When I let go of the rail, it left rust on my gloves. The safety curtain looked moth-eaten, its velvet sheen dulled by dust.

Glancing up, I noticed one side of the chandelier was tarnished. A cobweb stretched between the discoloured crystals, waving gently. Once, the ceiling had been painted with a fresco of nine women in ancient garb, but they were faded now. One figure had weathered better than the others: she held a club and some kind of mask in her hand.

'I can't believe you're going to work here,' Philip gasped.

Excitement stirred in spite of me. 'Well, not here. Another theatre. I haven't been inside the Mercury for years, it might not be as fancy.'

'It might be better!'

The theatre had always been Greg's domain. He'd been the one who got to experiment with colours and flights of imagination – the prerogative of the eldest, perhaps. My duty had been to leave the others behind as soon as Bertie was weaned and earn a decent wage, sending money back to the home I rarely saw. There was a kind of savage joy in thinking I might finally seize this fantasy world for myself. Greg owed me something, in return for all he'd taken.

Finally, a bell rang. The chatter subsided and a shushing ran through the audience. The conductor raised his baton.

Philip gripped my hand as a bold, strident overture boomed through the auditorium. I felt it right in my bones; music so powerful it could sweep you away, make you leave all you knew behind.

The curtain raised to reveal a ghostly chorus wearing white masks and black robes. As one, they began to chant in old-fashioned language. The scenery wasn't impressive; perhaps that was the point, for all eyes were instantly drawn to the actor Mrs Dyer had enthused about, Eugene Grieves, as he stalked on stage dressed in a scholar's robe and cap. That simple costume made him stand out, showcased his high, sharp cheekbones and the pallor of his face. A watch swung from a chain at his hip, glinting in the limelight. I don't know what it was about him, but he had a presence, something shimmering in the air around him like mist.

The winnowing machine turned, releasing a throaty howl as Doctor Faustus vowed to call up powers from Hell. He began to spout some other language, gruff and demonic.

'What's he saying?' Philip's voice was small and scared.

Mrs Dyer had warned me that Doctor Faustus made a deal with the Devil, but I hadn't expected it to be so visceral.

'Don't look, Phil. This bit will be over soon.'

A stinger chord and a clash of cymbals. Resin flashed and a shadow loomed over the backdrop. Slowly, the shape dwindled into a puff of smoke and a man emerged, dressed in red. Mephistopheles, the demon.

Balls rumbled down the thunder run and the music gave a dizzying plunge.

'*Go bear these tidings to great Lucifer: say Faustus surrenders up to him his soul, so he will spare him four and twenty years, letting him live in all voluptuousness, having thee ever to attend on me.*'

Dorcas sat deadly still. 'That's a bad idea,' she whispered.

Eugene Grieves rolled up his sleeve, took a dagger and tore it across his flesh. Something splattered over the boards. In other plays, I'd seen a red handkerchief produced to signify blood. This was some new effect.

'Did he really do that?' Philip hissed. 'Did he just cut himself?'

'Of course not,' Dorcas snapped back.

But I wasn't sure. Nausea pushed at the back of my throat.

'*And Faustus hath bequeath'd his soul to Lucifer – But what is this inscription on mine arm? Homo, fuge! Whither should I fly? My senses are deceiv'd; I see it plain; here in this place is writ Homo, fuge!*'

Maybe it was my imagination. I suppose I was too far away to see. Yet I could have sworn the blood began to congeal and make letters on his arm, just as the character was saying.

There was something wrong here, it didn't feel safe. I'd promised Philip the story would come alive, and it had. It was a hellfire and brimstone sermon made flesh. How could Mrs Dyer encourage me to take children to this? She'd been right about one thing though: Eugene Grieves was an astonishing actor; for he made me believe, without a shadow of a doubt, that he'd just made a pact with the Devil.

I sat on the edge of the bench, gripping Philip's hand, focusing on the flaking rail rather than the action on stage. I kept anticipating the end. What would happen when the twenty-four years passed and Faustus had to pay the price?

There was no twist of the plot to save him. He sensed his time grow short. There were speeches of remorse that seemed to rip inside my chest.

'For vain pleasure of twenty-four years hath Faustus lost eternal joy and felicity. I writ them a bill with mine own blood; the date is expired; the time will come, and he will fetch me.'

He clutched at the watch that hung from his waist. The lights turned blood red. Flames capered, smoke belched and a scent like sulphur filled the house.

I could feel his fear, choking me. I didn't know a play could frighten me like this. I tried to hold myself steady and be brave for the others.

A bell tolled. Midnight had arrived and with it the bill was due. Eugene Grieves scurried about the stage in terror. He would have left through the wings, jumped into the orchestra pit, but each time a devil barred his way with a pitchfork.

At last he crumpled to his knees, gasping. *'Adders and serpents, let me breathe awhile!'*

And then it happened.

I knew at once that it was no theatrical trick. As he spluttered for air, blood gushed from his lips.

A lady in the stalls screamed.

We were up high, a good distance from the stage, but it looked like his tears had also turned to gore. The violins screeched to a halt.

Eugene Grieves dropped and began to twitch. It was some sort of fit, hideous to behold, like a puppet jerked on its strings. The sound he made – the liquid, tortured moans. I covered Philip's eyes, but it was too late.

The man playing Mephistopheles called out, 'Merciful God!' Other actors ran on stage and tried to revive him. Then the green curtain fell abruptly.

There was no national anthem. Whispers shivered through the gallery. A man wearing a forage cap crossed himself and rushed to leave, followed by an elderly woman. I was too stunned to move.

'Did that really happen, Jenny?' Philip gabbled. 'Did the Devil come and carry that man off to Hell?'

I didn't know how to answer him. What unholy thing had just taken place? I'd never rid myself of that awful sight.

'I think it was an accident,' Dorcas said uncertainly. 'I think the actor just … died.'

But what a hideous way to go. Eugene Grieves had looked so afraid …

Eventually, a flustered-looking gent was thrust out on stage; he must have been the manager. He stumbled an apology that Mr Grieves was 'indisposed'. Who did he think he was fooling?

'I would ask you to kindly vacate the theatre as soon as possible, to allow us to deal with this … unfortunate event.'

Someone at the back of the house demanded a refund. The manager didn't respond, only whisked himself behind the curtain.

Chaos must be reigning backstage. Did Eugene Grieves have a man who dressed him, as I would dress Lilith? Had someone carefully arranged the actor's hair and put those clothes on him before they were drenched in blood? Imagining it made me want to weep.

I thought I'd feel better in the night air, but I didn't. Covent Garden was as lively as ever and every object recalled that hellish scene: the fug of cigars, sparks flying from a barrow's wheels as it rolled over the cobbles.

Philip was ashen. 'I don't want you working at a theatre any more, Jenny. I thought it would be a magical place, but it isn't. It's … wicked.'

If I was honest, I felt the same. The prospect of my new job had soured like a pail of milk in the sun. Yet still, it was work. Work we desperately needed. I tried to shake Philip's words off and be rational. 'Only that play. They're not all horrible like that.'

Then I remembered there was plenty of blood in *Macbeth*, as well.

Crimson light spilled from the baked chestnut stall, turning its patrons into demons.

'Not a word of this to Bertie,' Dorcas ordered. 'He'd have nightmares for weeks.'

I thought that I would, too.

CHAPTER 3

I didn't want to tell Mrs Dyer what I'd seen, not when she was so fond of the actor who'd died. Although *died* seemed a paltry word for an ending like that. The way he shrieked, the tracks of scarlet oozing down his cheeks ... I wished I could forget it.

But when I turned up at Mrs Dyer's house for my next lesson, I worried that something even worse had befallen her. All the shutters were closed. Straw coated the cobbles outside and there was a black ribbon muffling the door-knocker. Her husband was due to travel back from Southend imminently. Surely he hadn't died? What would that mean for me, for the theatre?

Buzzing with anxiety, I tapped on the trade door, but it opened swiftly. 'Is Mrs Dyer receiving—' I began. Before I could finish, James the footman beckoned me in. He didn't speak as he escorted me on the familiar route towards the parlour. Mrs Dyer sat on her sofa, clothed from head to toe in black.

My heart dropped. 'Oh, madam! I'm sorry ... I didn't realise. Have you lost a relative?'

She offered me a wan smile. 'It certainly feels like I have.'

'I'll come another day—'

'No, stay.' Waving a hand, she dismissed James and encouraged me to sit beside her on the sofa. 'Please tell me you saw him. Say you glimpsed the brightest star in the firmament before it burned out.'

I faltered. She was a lady of the theatre – she tended to be dramatic, but I couldn't think what on earth she meant by this. 'Saw ...?'

'Saw Eugene Grieves, of course. Who else would I mourn?'

Her gown was made of the finest bombazine. A jet brooch rode at her collarbone. Attached to the brim of her hat was a netted veil, to be pulled down to hide her tears. Was all of this really for an actor?

'I ... yes, I saw him, Mrs Dyer. I hadn't understood that he was a friend of yours.'

She shook her head. The veil fluttered. 'I only spoke to Eugene Grieves a handful of times, yet for me he represented ...' She started again. 'You are young, Jennifer. Barely more than twenty, I think.'

'I was two-and-twenty this summer, madam.'

It looked as if the number caused her pain. 'Then you may find it hard to understand my grief. I am mourning a period in time, as much as a person. His death really is the end of an era.'

I fought to keep my expression neutral. Clearly, it mattered to her, and I should be sympathetic, but I kept remembering the days after Ma died. I hadn't had the time to sit around in a costume of grief like this; we were trying to keep baby Bertie alive, trying to scrape together the money for a burial.

Mrs Dyer didn't notice my discomfort. 'The first time I saw Eugene Grieves perform ... well.' Her eyes kindled with the memory. 'I was younger than you are now. Not such a good and dutiful daughter though, I am afraid. My parents ... to be frank with you, my parents bored me to death. Their world was so respectable and ordered. Ennui plagued my days. But when I saw Eugene Grieves perform ... I thought it a miracle. I seemed to wake from a long and terrible sleep. I could not sate myself. Going to the theatre was the only activity that made me feel alive.'

I couldn't imagine that kind of childhood: being rich enough to grow tired of your own security. But I supposed if you were born to it, you simply didn't notice your good luck.

'I spent a fortune on theatre tickets. I fear I made myself something of a nuisance. But you have sat in that presence now. You understand what a magnet he was, especially when he was a young man and even more spirited.'

It was necessary to say something now. 'He was handsome, too,' I offered.

She dabbed a handkerchief to her eyes, smiling fondly. 'Heavens, yes. Not a word of that to Mr Dyer, of course. You can comprehend how deeply that actor affected me, as a young girl.'

It still didn't explain the overt mourning. I wondered what her husband would say, if he was at home. 'But ... everything's going on as usual, despite this tragedy? The Mercury's opening up and Mr Dyer's coming back soon?'

'Yes, very soon. Bringing the dreaded Lady Macbeth with him.' She reached out and touched the small, pewter cross I wore about my neck, nodding gravely. 'I am glad you have that. You will need protection against Lilith's wiles.'

As though Lilith Erikson were a vampire to be repelled! Did I dare laugh? Was I supposed to? She was so strange this morning.

At a loss for a response, I inspected her jewellery in turn. The brooch beneath her throat showed a female figure picked out in white against the black background.

Seeing me looking, she unpinned it. 'Ah, here is another theatrical lesson for you, Jennifer. Who do you think that is?'

I thought she must be a goddess of some sort; she wore a toga, sandals on her feet and laurel in her hair. In one hand she held a club, in the other, a gaping mask.

'I know this,' I realised. 'I saw a painting of this lady on the ceiling, at Eugene Grieves's playhouse.'

'Oh yes, you would have done. Perhaps you also recognise that mask she holds? You might have glimpsed it above the stage, beside a smiling one. This is Melpomene, the tragic Muse. I always said she must have paid a visit to Eugene Grieves and inspired him. He has been *the* tragic actor for ... well, over two decades now. I cannot think who shall ever replace him.'

I ran my thumb over the brooch. Melpomene looked stern, timeless in her sorrow.

'Mr Grieves owned a watch,' she went on, 'with Melpomene engraved on the front. I had this brooch made in imitation of it.'

Memory flashed. I saw him clutching that watch, his eyes wide in terror. 'It's so sad, madam. But maybe some good will come of this? Things might work out well for your theatre. The Mercury specialises in tragedy plays, doesn't it?'

'Well, yes.'

'And aren't we trying to launch Lilith Erikson as a tragic actress?'

Her mouth puckered. 'Yes, I suppose we are. It would go against the grain for me to see such a woman take Eugene Grieves's crown ... But as you say, it would be good for the Mercury. A real opportunity. It is more important than ever that you pay close attention to what Lilith is doing and send me a report of anything suspicious each week.'

I gave the brooch back. A weekly report? What exactly did she expect this actress to get up to?

There was a tap at the door and little Rachel, escaped from the governess, poked her head around. 'May I see the birdies, Mama?'

The lovebirds chirruped at her voice. Mrs Dyer's face smoothed from its sadness for an instant. 'Of course, darling.'

Rachel gave a delighted squeal and trotted in, her short skirts frothing. She was a sweet, tow-headed thing. Mrs Dyer had never mentioned brothers or sisters. I would have expected a woman of her years to have more children, but maybe there was a medical cause. It struck me now that I had never seen any calling cards on the mantelpiece in the townhouse, never caught a friend just leaving. Compared to my family, this one felt small and isolated.

Mrs Dyer stood and lifted her daughter up so she could see the cage. The birds twittered and cocked their heads. 'I do not believe there is much left for me to say, Jennifer. You have proven an apt pupil. I consider you quite ready to start next week. I shall send the carriage to collect you.'

'There's no need for that, madam,' I began.

She smiled. 'Only on your first day. Go straight up to the wardrobe room and ask for Mrs Nettles. She will be expecting you.'

It felt very final all of a sudden. From now on, the play and Lilith Erikson herself would be real, not vague concepts in my mind. 'Thank you.'

'Keep your observations and wait to receive my note. I shall allow you some time to learn your new position. We will reconvene ... say, near the end of the week?'

I nodded. 'Yes, Mrs Dyer.'

'May God watch over you, Jennifer Wilcox.'

I gathered my belongings, trying not to shake my head in disbelief. Had she always been this melodramatic? Perhaps I'd been too distracted by the glitter of her money to realise Mrs Dyer was a woman of fancy and romance. No doubt her fears were exaggerated in a similar way. Lilith Erikson couldn't be so bad that I needed a benediction and a cross to protect me.

But my memory kept showing me that night at the Helicon, Philip's face bathed red by the light of the chestnut stall, calling the theatre wicked.

The theatre had corrupted Greg. Surely it couldn't change me, too?

———

Between them, *Doctor Faustus* and Mrs Dyer's extravagance had caused my excitement to wither away. It was with a pang of dread that I saw the carriage come to a halt on the street outside, ready to take me to the Mercury theatre for the first time. But there was no terror like the prospect of not being able to pay the rent, so I gave myself a stern talking to as I pulled on my gloves and bonnet.

Bertie sat at the table, pasting together matchboxes. It didn't bring in much money, but it was something. The hat factory where Philip worked had declined to take Bertie on because of his bad foot. 'I wish you didn't have to go,' he sighed. 'I'd just got used to having you here again.'

'I won't be too long. The play doesn't open for a while yet. Back before supper, I promise.'

He watched me, his eyes hazel like Greg's. 'Cross your heart?'

'I'm coming back, Bertie. I'll always come back.' I could see he was struggling to believe that, to trust I wouldn't disappear too. It pierced me. 'I love you. And I'm going to make our fortunes. You'll see.'

Mrs Dyer's vehicle was a growler with polished doors and gleaming wheel spokes, drawn by a single black horse. It was a great compliment to be conveyed personally. The same footman

I'd seen at the house sprang down to open the carriage door, revealing claret upholstery. Awkwardly, I climbed in. The door shut behind me and a whip cracked. We lurched into motion.

It wasn't often I took a journey in silence. I was used to the crush of the omnibus or, on the rare occasions we were flush, sharing a cab with Dorcas. What would the servants at Mrs Fielding's say if they could see me now?

Traffic began to slow as we reached the fashionable part of town. Peering out, I had leisure to read the bills plastered on the walls. There was one for *Macbeth*. Seeing it made me feel queer, like recognising my own face unexpectedly in the reflection of a shop window. For the first time I was about to be part of something bigger than myself.

Gradually, we approached the Mercury theatre. Of course I'd seen the building before, an eye-catching blend of red bricks and terracotta tiles, but I'd never observed the details. At the top was a pediment, bearing a statue of the Roman god Mercury. Mrs Dyer said he was an appropriate patron for a tragic theatre, because he guided souls to the Underworld. Three arched windows glimmered beneath him, each separated by a column. Below ran a balcony, and lower still three square, gated doorways: one for subscribers, one for occupants of the gallery and the pit, and one for the box office.

The carriage pulled round the back, beside a yard that was much less impressive. Bird droppings and lichen hazed the brickwork, whilst the railings were eaten up with rust. This must be where the magic of the theatre came to die: the worn-out bales of canvas, fraying coils of rope and chipped scenery flats that had amassed from former plays.

I climbed out and thanked the driver. He didn't respond. Half a dozen men, wearing corduroy trousers and with their shirt sleeves rolled up, were milling around the yard. It seemed to adjoin a carpenter's workshop. Maybe I should ask one how to get inside the theatre, but they barely seemed to notice as I stole across the cobbles, they were so focussed on their work.

Then I saw a face I recognised. A girlish fancy I thought long dead kicked alive in my chest. 'Oscar?'

He was older and even more handsome than I remembered him, although the paintbrush stuck behind his ear and the smudge of yellow across his cheek offset that. It took him a moment to realise who I was. 'Miss Wilcox. What are you doing here?'

The young man I'd known had a ready smile, a jaunty step and whistled catch-penny tunes. Now he looked as if the sight of me made him sick.

I floundered. 'I work here. Mrs Dyer gave me a place.'

'I thought you were a maid. What's she got you doing, cleaning the stalls?'

Another of the men looked over his shoulder and whispered to his friend. I glimpsed a carpenter in the workshop glowering. In all my preparations for the job, it hadn't once struck me that I'd have to deal with any wrath my brother had incurred. Maybe Greg had treated his scene-painter friends every bit as badly as us. I remembered what Mrs Dyer had said about me favouring Gregory and wished I could scrub off my features, like stage paint.

'No, actually,' I said with all the dignity I could muster. 'I'm going to be a dresser. I'm dressing the leading lady.'

A strand of rich mahogany hair fell over Oscar's forehead. 'You?' he said, incredulous. 'You're going to be dressing Lilith Erikson?'

'Yes. That's why I came over to see you. I was going to ask where I might find Mrs Nettles?'

He scowled. It didn't suit him. I wanted him to be Greg's bright and chirpy friend again. A man like that would have proved invaluable: someone who might help me find my feet in the theatre and get information about Lilith Erikson on the sly. Instead I had to deal with this sour face. What reason could he have to be so pettish? He still hadn't answered my question.

'Never mind—' I sighed, but then he started to move.

'I'm going back up to the paint frame anyway,' he admitted. 'Wardrobe's just next door. You might as well follow me.'

'Thanks.'

The other men watched us go. One started to chuckle and I shot him an icy glare.

Oscar led me past the workshop to another door that squealed on its hinges and admitted us to a dark, musty-smelling corridor.

There was no finery, only practical limewashed walls and wooden cladding. We took a path to the right, clogged by ladders, crates and bags of sand. A hammer pounded somewhere in the distance.

'I haven't seen you in years,' I tried. 'I nearly didn't recognise you.'

He didn't look round, just lengthened his stride.

Had it been anyone else, I might have shrugged it off and dismissed him as a miserable sod, yet the memory of the young man I'd met before made his rejection sting. We hadn't known each other well, he was always Greg's friend, someone I saw fleetingly, but the impression he'd made had caused me to dream of him on more than one occasion in my narrow maid's bed.

Oscar turned left and began to climb a ladder. I tucked up my skirts and clambered after him, making the rungs creak.

We emerged into the fly gallery. It was like being in the rigging of a ship. Ropes and catwalks ran in all directions, dizzyingly high above the stage.

'I thought the wardrobe room would be downstairs,' I gasped.

'It isn't,' he said bluntly. 'But you'll get used to the height. Try not to look down. We're going there, across the bridge, see?'

A long, wide platform stretched from stage right to stage left. Strips of painted cloth screened it from the audience's view. There was no real danger of falling, but I found myself planting each foot with caution. I'd seen a man die on stage. I wasn't about to plummet down there and do the same.

'I told you not to look down.' At least he was talking to me, now.

The machinery around us was vast and complex. We passed cables, chains, drums and counterweights, all with some mysterious purpose of their own. Oscar brushed the wind machine with his hand as we walked by.

'*What beast was't, then, that made you break this enterprise to me? When you durst do it, then you were a man.*'

Oscar stopped, cocked his head. 'That's her,' he said. 'Hers is the strongest voice. It's the only one that carries up to the paint frame. Listen.'

The actress continued her speech from the stage below. She had a warm, rich voice with a slight rasp. It put me in mind of a cat's tongue. 'That's Lilith Erikson?'

He nodded.

I peered down over the edge of the bridge. All I could see was the top of Lilith's head, blue-black like the plumage of a crow.

'What's she like?' I asked Oscar.

'Like? She's promising. The Guvnor was right to promote her, there's talent there. It just needs coaxing out.'

'No, but ... off the stage. How is she as a person?'

He shrugged. Something crossed his face that I couldn't decipher. 'Don't know. We move in ... different circles.'

Once we'd crossed the bridge, we came to a case of rickety stairs with ropes for banisters. I wrinkled my nose at the fug of paint and turpentine.

'You'll need to get used to the fumes, too,' Oscar told me. Removing the paintbrush from behind his ear, he pointed to a door. 'You work right there.'

'Thanks for showing me.'

'Well, I was going this way anyhow. Better get back to it.' I watched as he trudged up to the paint frame. The canvas stretched over the back wall suited his demeanour: a blasted heath in dull purples, blues and greens.

I'd always thought the theatre a jolly place before *Doctor Faustus*. Now it was full of misery, devils and death. But it paid the bills. I had to remember that.

There was no reply when I knocked for admittance to the wardrobe room. I opened the door to a wave of heat. Steam moved through the air like an unquiet spirit. A woman with a flat iron was pressing the creases from a long, black cloak, which hissed as though in pain.

Rails of costumes bordered her on three sides, such a variety of colours and textures as I'd never seen before: some spangled, some beaded, still others shot through with golden thread. A shelf of blank, faceless heads supported wigs and hats.

A long table occupied the centre of the room. Seated at it was a pretty, dark-haired girl. Despite the sewing machines beside her, she was stitching by hand – and often did, to judge from the bandages wrapped round her wrist.

I cleared my throat. 'Hello?' Their hands kept moving. 'Jenny Wilcox?' Somehow I made my own name sound like a question.

The woman put down her iron. 'I expected you ten minutes ago. Come in, close the door behind you. Hang your hat up if you can find a space.'

She was thin and flat-chested, dressed in the aesthetic style: a simple russet gown that fell in a Watteau pleat at the back. It suited her, as did the Titian hair caught up at the nape of her neck. I'd expected something flashier from a wardrobe mistress, but her style was simple and elegant.

'I'm Mrs Nettles. You know that already. This is Polly.'

The sewing girl gave a nod. Her focus had already returned to her work.

'Pleased to meet you both.'

'Mrs Dyer told me you were lately in service,' Mrs Nettles observed. 'That's a help, actually. Most young people don't know how to take orders these days.'

The wall behind me was plastered with sketches and swatches of material. For the first time, my spirits lifted. I wanted to be here, I wanted to know more about these designs. But now wasn't the time for idle questions.

'What can I do to be useful?' I asked.

Mrs Nettles glanced at the clock. 'They'll be rehearsing for a few hours yet. Polly, have you anything that needs mending?'

Nodding, Polly set down her needle and consulted the costume rails. Her quick hands pulled down a dozen garments without checking them first. She must have memorised where they hung.

I sat on a stool beside her and took up a needle of my own. It was a relief to follow the rise and dip of my thread, listening to the iron hiss in the background. There was nothing sinister in that. The room was as hot as Hell – but that was the only link to *Doctor Faustus*.

'Heard from your brother?' Mrs Nettles asked suddenly.

I looked up, startled. 'No. I don't want to, either. I thought Mrs Dyer would've told you. He abandoned us.'

She nodded. 'Yes, she did say something of the sort. But it's been months. We figured maybe he would have written to you for help by now.'

I pulled my thread cautiously. 'Help?'

'I said it when she took up with that lad she jilted, and I'll say it again. A painter will never be enough for the likes of Georgiana Mildmay. She'll give your brother cause to regret going to America and I doubt she'll pay his passage home.'

My mind was spinning. Of course I'd known Greg had run off with a young actress. I'd blamed her for being a bad influence on him, but I had no idea she was engaged to someone else at the time.

'I only met her once,' I admitted, remembering the dimpled cheeks and the neat button nose. 'I thought she was dreadful.'

Mrs Nettles harrumphed. 'Challenging. That's what we call the players who give us trouble.'

'Nothing we did was good enough for her,' Polly burst out. 'She wanted to work in one of them showy theatres what hire painters to design their costumes, or get them run up by the House of Worth.'

Mrs Nettles was right – such a woman would never be satisfied with what Greg could provide. Was that why he took our savings and stole that jewellery? To please his lover?

'She sounds like a right handful,' was all I trusted myself to say.

Mrs Nettles pressed down with her iron. 'Hardly surprising the painters should take to her. That sort are always after a muse, but it all ends in tears. How stupid that boy looks now! He gave himself so many airs, saying he was going to marry a star. Thought himself better than the rest of them.' She sighed. 'And here's you, Miss Wilcox, forced to change employment. It's a sorry affair.'

I didn't want to hear any more about Georgiana Mildmay. 'What about the actress I'm going to dress, Lilith Erikson? What's she like?'

Polly bit her lip. Mrs Nettles pulled her shoulders back and considered. 'She's … different. There's more to that one. Keeps herself to herself. What I need you to get from her are measurements. I have a devil of a time fitting her.' She nodded to the wall by the door. 'Those charts are all I've got but they're at least a year out of date. We could make do while she played small parts – a leading lady's a different matter.'

I let my eyes drift to the sketches. These were garments of Shakespeare's time: velvet tunics, slashed doublets and feathered caps. Swatches of tartan hung beside scraps of lace, materials more beautiful than any I'd had the chance to work with. I found myself trying to guess the character without looking at the name.

'Which are Lilith's costumes?'

Polly set her needle down and untacked the papers from the wall. I grinned as she spread them before me. They'd found fabrics to match Lady Macbeth's slippery nature: taffeta that shifted between moss and mustard hues; webs of black lace; sequins like snake scales.

'They're perfect,' I said honestly. 'Do you draw them, Mrs Nettles?'

'I do. Everything's planned and made in this room. You'll be obliged to pitch in.'

'Gladly.' Here, at least, was something I could love. The actresses sounded like a nightmare, but I was used to that – ladies of quality weren't easy to please, either. If I could spend most of my time up here in the wardrobe room making beautiful things, I might actually enjoy my work.

Just then the door banged open. A middle-aged man walked in with his hand held dramatically to his forehead. He fitted the bill for the kind of person I'd expected to see inside a theatre, with his immaculately dressed frame, pomaded hair and curled moustache.

'Silas! We wondered what had become of you.'

The dandy flung himself onto a stool. 'I am not late, my dear Polly. I have been down there, suffering for my art.'

Polly rolled her eyes at me. 'Silas dresses Anthony Frost, our leading man. Silas, this is Miss Jennifer Wilcox. She'll be dressing Lilith Erikson from now on.'

He turned to me, aghast. 'Why, she's the facsimile of that dastardly painter Gregory! Were the two of you twins?'

'No, sir.'

'Well, I'd be obliged if you'll resemble your brother in another respect. Please take that actress and carry her far away!'

So maybe it wasn't all Mrs Dyer's imagination; Lilith wasn't popular in the wardrobe room. I saw my chance to glean some gossip to report. 'Why would you want to get rid of Lilith?'

Mrs Nettles shook her head, as if warning me off, but it was too late now. Silas inhaled deeply. 'The first day of rehearsal, and she has already set her cap at Anthony. You should have seen her, down there, touching him every five seconds, hanging on his arm as if her character was a loving wife full of affection!'

'I think,' Mrs Nettles said haltingly, 'that Lilith knows better than to try her luck in that quarter, Silas.'

'You give her too much credit. You know what these actresses are. They won't lose anything for want of trying. She'll have them eating out of the palm of her hand. Well, she won't fool me. An amateur like that, unfit to play opposite poor dear Anthony!'

I cocked my head with interest. 'So Anthony Frost will be the one playing Macbeth? What are his costumes like?'

Everyone stopped. Silas's face turned puce, as though I'd uttered an obscenity. 'Miss Wilcox! You must never, ever say that!'

'Say what? What have I done wrong?'

Mrs Nettles tutted. 'Come now, Silas, go easy on the poor girl, she's new.'

'She's blighted the whole production!'

'It's not as bad as all that,' Mrs Nettles soothed. 'We consider it unlucky to say the title of this play inside of a theatre, Miss Wilcox. You'll kindly refer to it as "the Scottish Play" while at the Mercury.'

My bafflement must have shown on my face. 'But ... why?'

'It's a curse,' Silas declared. 'The play is cursed. Don't you realise what you've done? There could be all manner of disasters unleashed by your loose tongue!'

Doctor Faustus was fresh in my mind. Was this what happened to Eugene Grieves? Did he die in agony because some careless dresser murmured the name 'Macbeth'?

It couldn't be true.

'I don't ... I don't believe in curses,' I told Silas as calmly as I could. 'And if this play is so dangerous ... why are they putting it on?'

'Get out,' Silas said.

I blinked at him. Surely he didn't have the authority to sack me over something so trivial? 'I beg your pardon?'

'Leave the room. Spin around three times on the landing, then spit and swear for all you're worth. Knock to come back in here. It's the only way to remove the curse.'

He couldn't be serious. I started to laugh, but then I saw all three pairs of eyes were trained expectantly on me. 'Mrs Nettles …'

'You had better do it, Miss Wilcox.'

Burning with shame, I pushed back my stool, exited and shut the door behind me. I felt like a misbehaving child. Luckily, no one was around.

What did Silas say? Spin three times, spit and swear? I couldn't. It felt too stupid.

I just stood there, trying to estimate how long the charade should take. People didn't die because someone said the name of a play!

At least I could comply with one part of the ritual. I was able to swear.

'These people are bloody cracked,' I muttered to myself before knocking on the door.

CHAPTER 4

I didn't have to meet Lilith that first day. Rehearsal overran for hours, which seemed proof of a blessing upon me, not a curse. All in all, I was pleased with how everything had gone, and was able to reply truthfully when Philip came running in from the factory demanding, 'How was it? Are you all right?' I think he'd expected to find me bleeding like Doctor Faustus. The poor boy had been through so much. We all had.

We'd been forced to move further up in the house when Greg took our money, to the garret where the ceiling slanted and the windows were stained yellow. We owned one table, three chairs, various trunks and a cupboard full of crockery. A sheet, pegged to a piece of twine, separated Dorcas's bed from the boys'. I slept in an easy chair that smelt of must. In the corner, beside the fire, stood a washstand with a mirror. We shared a privy with the other families in the house. It wasn't dire. Many people had less. But now I'd be able to afford somewhere far better, and I resolved to do so sooner rather than later.

What was Oscar's unfriendliness or Silas's superstition, when all was said and done? I'd cope with whatever the theatre threw at me, even the actress Mrs Dyer dreaded, so long as I could keep my family safe.

I tried to remind myself of that determination on the next day, as I stood outside Lilith Erikson's dressing room awaiting her return.

I was all alone in the corridor, which struck me as eerily silent and still for a passageway in a busy theatre. The walls were hung with a deep red brocade, faded in patches around the lamps.

Scuffed doors lined the right side of the corridor: the first bore the name of the lead actor, Anthony Frost, in gold letters, yet Lilith Erikson's door was blank. Presumably they'd just erased the previous leading lady and were waiting for the new one to prove herself before stencilling on her name.

A mouse scuttled past my feet and disappeared into a hole in the skirting board. Moments later, a tabby cat slunk down the corridor with its tail raised. When it caught sight of me it mewed and changed course, nuzzling its head against my shins.

'Hello there.' My voice sounded too loud in the hush. The cat mewed again as I bent and petted it. Then I heard another noise behind me, a gentle *tap, tap*. My hand stilled. 'Is that another mouse, puss?'

There was a pause, followed by a low, guttural moan. The cat hissed and sprang away.

Something banged against the other side of the dressing-room door.

I leapt clear. The door bucked. A creature was scratching desperately, launching itself against the wood. I saw a flash of poor Eugene Grieves in his death throes. Silas's words came back. *There could be all manner of disasters unleashed by your loose tongue.* It couldn't be …

But I started to do it: to spin three times as he'd instructed me. The door flew open and a dark mass rushed out. I only had time to gasp before it knocked my legs from under me and I hit the floor hard.

Something foul dripped on my face. I closed my eyes.

'Eurydice!' A voice boomed along the passageway, carrying as only a trained player's could. 'Eurydice, stop that! Sit.'

When I opened my eyes, a long face was peering over me, upside down and surrounded by a cloud of black hair. 'Oh dear,' it said with a trace of amusement. 'Come on, let's set you back on your feet.'

I felt thoroughly stupid as I took the proffered hand and scrambled up. The woman who helped me was tall and willowy, more striking than handsome, with strongly marked features. She pointed at what I now saw was a poodle.

'In your bed, Eurydice.' The dog obeyed at once, traipsing back inside the dressing room with her tail between her legs. The woman shook her head. 'I didn't realise she could open the door. You'll have to forgive her, I'm afraid. Terrible manners.'

It wasn't much of an apology. 'Isn't the owner meant to teach the dog its manners?'

She followed in the poodle's steps and sat down at the dressing table, cocking an eyebrow. 'You're assuming I have them.'

So this was Lilith Erikson. Instantly provocative. I hated that she'd seen me sprawled in the dust. It put me immediately on the back foot.

'Well, *I do* have manners,' I said tightly, brushing down my skirts. 'I'm Jenny Wilcox, your new dresser. Pleased to meet you.'

Lilith laughed. 'No, you are not at all pleased! I can spot bad acting a mile off. Come inside for goodness' sake and stop this rigmarole. We both know this is a marriage of convenience.'

Entering the dressing room was like walking into a burial ground. Lilies bloomed from every surface: bouquets and single stems tied with ribbon. The scent was asphyxiating. Eurydice growled at me.

Lilith opened an enamel box and tossed a sweet to appease her. 'Don't worry. She's only dangerous when I want her to be.'

A bold-faced actress was bad enough; now I'd have to contend with her hostile pet. Usually I liked dogs, but this one was like the mythical Black Shuck. I swear it *knew* I was here to spy on its mistress.

'Nobody told me you had a dog.'

'Why would they? The Guvnor only gave me leave to bring her yesterday.' She waved the box at me. 'Humbug?'

I shook my head.

With all the flowers, the dressing room felt cramped. A wardrobe and a standing cheval glass took up most of the space. There was a small sofa, along with a dressmaker's dummy, but they were very much squeezed in.

'So you're my new dresser,' Lilith went on. 'Apparently I need one, although I always managed perfectly alone before. It's customary for an actress to select her own attendant, but

37

predictably Mrs Dyer stuck her oar in first.' She apprised me with her smoky eyes. 'Hmmm. You're her little protégée, aren't you? The Guvnor's launching me, she's launching you, and so we'll make our debuts as an experiment between them. What did you say your name was again?'

'Jenny Wilcox.'

'That's the one. I'm dreadful with names. You mustn't mind if I make up something of my own to call you.'

I gritted my teeth. 'Do you do that in the plays, too? Make it up?'

I'd expected her to glare, but she laughed again. 'No, no. I think that's the problem. My head is stuffed full of scripts and it hasn't room for anything else.' The gas lamps dimmed, then spluttered back to life. Lilith tutted and ate a humbug. 'They're always doing that. Speak to someone and get them fixed.'

Was that even my responsibility? I drew the tape measure out of my pocket. 'Actually, I'm here to make sure your costumes fit.'

Panic darted across her face. 'Oh, those wretched wardrobe people have indoctrinated you into their agenda already. They *have* my measurements.'

'They're over a year old.' I took a few steps and stood behind her stool. 'Figures change. Especially if you eat a lot of sweets,' I added pointedly.

Lilith clapped her slender hands. 'Bravo! I see what Mrs Dyer has done. She's heard I am allergic to cats, and so she has planted one in my dressing room.'

So she knew Mrs Dyer was against her; she was no fool. Evidently Lilith could give as good as she got.

'You're allergic to cats? How do you manage, with the mousers everywhere? I saw one outside just now.'

'It's nothing too dramatic; I can stand to be in the theatre with them. But it would be a problem if the wretched beasts came in here and got all over my things.' Lilith nodded at the flowers. 'Between Eurydice and the lilies, I keep them out. Now you can too.'

I watched her reflection in the triple mirror. She really did look like she could put a spell on you. She was perfectly cast as Lady Macbeth; you wanted to watch her, to see what she'd do next.

38

'Well, I'll make sure the cats stay away from your costumes,' I promised. 'But you need to let me measure you first.'

Lilith's mouth pursed as she sucked on her sweet. 'What a tartar you are! Can't I enjoy a moment's rest? A fine welcome home this has proved to be. I wish I were still in Southend.'

'It's hardly taxing to be measured, Miss Erikson. You just stand here and I do all the work.'

Grudgingly, she pushed back the stool. 'I see I shall have no peace until you are satisfied. This cursed week. First I hear that Eugene Grieves is dead, and now I'm at the mercy of a bullying dresser.'

I faltered at the name. 'Was he a friend of yours? That poor actor?'

She turned on the stool and tilted her dark head. '*Friend* is perhaps too strong a word. I used to be part of Eugene Grieves's troupe. I admired him greatly, but there's no working alongside a talent like that. You might as well not be on the stage.'

'No,' I admitted, casting my mind back. 'No, I don't remember any of the other actors at all.'

'Oh, you saw him play, then?'

I wet my lips. I hadn't wanted to hurt Mrs Dyer by telling her what I'd witnessed, but I had no such qualms about Lilith. 'I watched him die.'

Her grey eyes widened. 'No!'

'It was terrible. You should thank your lucky stars you changed theatres before it happened. I don't know how the troupe will go on working there, after that.'

She stayed silent for a moment. Something shifted behind her expression. It wasn't quite grief or sorrow. 'Tell me, Kitty,' she commanded.

'My name's Jenny,' I corrected her.

She waved a hand as if that didn't signify. 'Tell me, did you happen to see if Eugene Grieves was wearing a trinket when he died? A watch of some sort?'

Eurydice muttered in the depths of her chest. Maybe another cat was passing outside.

'Yes, he was wearing it.' Mrs Dyer had mentioned that watch too, the one with the muse, but that had been a different sort of conversation. It was odd for Lilith to jump straight to it without asking how her old colleague had spent his last breath, whether he'd suffered, all the usual enquiries a person with a heart would make.

There came a tap at the door. Eurydice barked. Before Lilith could call out, a gentleman entered. He wasn't a young man, but charm oozed from every pore. His attire was all the finest: a silk top hat and a Gladstone coat heavily trimmed with astrakhan. Silver hair grazed his temples.

'There she is, by Jove! My first lady, my leading light!' He caught sight of me and cleared his throat. 'You must be Miss Wilcox. We haven't been introduced.' He extended a ringed hand. 'Hugh Dyer at your service. They all call me "the Guvnor".'

I bobbed a curtsey as I shook his hand. 'Pleased to meet you, sir.'

It wasn't true; I was no happier to make his acquaintance than Lilith's. What did he mean by coming into a lady's dressing room and speaking to her in those flattering terms, when he had a wife and daughter at home?

'I was delighted to learn my wife had sought you out, Miss Wilcox. She is nothing if not charitable. After that nasty business with your brother and Georgiana … Well, let us say no more of that. You are very welcome here.'

'Thank you, sir.'

'No doubt my wife impressed upon you the vital importance of your role? Launching Miss Erikson here is the opportunity of a lifetime. She has great potential. Greater than any actress I ever saw before.'

Lilith neither thanked him nor demurred, she merely accepted his statement as fact.

I inclined my head in what might pass for agreement. 'I'm sure you're the best judge of that, sir.'

'I am,' he agreed. 'I have been in the theatre my whole life. My father was in the theatre, and my grandfather before him. Tragic plays are my bread and butter.'

'And … what is it we can do for you today, sir? I was about to measure Miss Erikson for her costumes …'

'Ah, of course, I have interrupted you. My apologies. You are not familiar with our ways, Miss Wilcox. Let me explain why I am here.' He smoothed his mutton chops. 'You may not realise, but I have been coaching Lilith – Miss Erikson – in her art for some time. She was trained, as all the actors are, but formal teaching can only carry an artist so far. I am her teacher now.'

'I see.'

'I am often obliged to visit her. Spend time with her in a private capacity, as it were.' He left a little pause. 'Nothing could be more reasonable than the regular interchanging of thoughts between an artist and her instructor.'

Anger pounded at my temples. He must have thought I was born yesterday. 'If you say so, sir. But right now I need to—'

'I beg your indulgence, Miss Wilcox. I shall try to keep my disruptions to a minimum. Yet I really must discuss Miss Erikson's performance in that last rehearsal. I have one or two ideas for improvement that the stage manager missed.'

I wasn't about to leave them alone together in the dressing room. If the Guvnor ordered me out, I'd have no choice, but until then I was staying put. I perched myself on the sofa, feeling like an unwelcome chaperone aunt.

A bell rang. Eurydice barked again.

'Time already,' Lilith sighed, rising to her feet. 'I must put off myself and become Lady M once more. Walk with me, Mr Dyer. You may tell me of your thoughts on the way.'

'A splendid notion.' He offered his arm. I watched her take it with growing unease. No wonder Mrs Dyer was suspicious.

'Make yourself useful,' Lilith called over her shoulder. 'Take Eurydice for a walk while I'm gone. Fill up my humbug box. Oh, and don't forget about those lights, will you?' I opened my mouth, but I was too slow to speak. 'Thanks ever so, Kitty.'

———————

I found Mrs Dyer's note waiting for me at home. The instructions were short and cryptic. '*Tomorrow. Box 6. Three of the clock.*' No signature, date or address.

Dorcas peered over my shoulder. 'She's a rum one, ain't she? Your new mistress.'

'They all are,' I admitted. 'Even stranger than the Fieldings were, and that's saying something.'

Box 6 was on the grand tier: one of the private spaces reserved for rich patrons. When I tried the handle of the gilt-framed door, it was locked, but Mrs Dyer opened it a moment later and glanced up and down the hallway, conspiratorial. 'One cannot be too careful,' she murmured. It struck me that she was enjoying playing the spy every bit as much as playing the grieving devotee of Eugene Grieves.

When she judged the coast was clear, she let me inside and turned the lock behind us. The interior of Box 6 was gorgeous, with shaded lamps, brass-studded velvet chairs and a Turkey carpet. Mrs Dyer spread her skirts and seated herself. She was still wearing black.

'And so, how do you find it? Are you pleased with your new position? I trust they are making you welcome in the wardrobe room.' She smiled as always – that ready, tremulous, wide-mouthed smile. But there was hunger in her eyes. She didn't really want to know about me. She wanted my gossip.

'They are, madam,' I said honestly. 'I enjoy working with them. A few of the other staff hold me at arm's length, because of my brother. But I have to expect that.'

'And … your actress? You have met her? Formed an opinion?'

I could be frank here, too. 'I don't like her.'

Relief broke over her face. 'Of course you do not! A smart young woman like yourself. You cannot imagine how I have longed to speak of that creature. Sometimes, I have feared I was running mad in my suspicions. But I am quite right, am I not? There is something … unnatural … about her. Strange, unfeminine. That clarion voice …' She shuddered.

It was hardly as bad as all that. Lilith was vain and self-assured, as I expected most women of her profession were. But she was also sly and provoking. She couldn't really believe I was called Kitty, even if she did struggle with names. It sounded nothing like Jennifer.

'She's giving me the run around trying to get her measurements. The wardrobe staff say she did exactly the same before the summer break.' I paused. Mrs Dyer had told me to speak without reserve, but she was a lady, after all. It felt crass to just blurt out an accusation of pregnancy. Maybe it was better to lead her with hints. 'That strikes me as suspicious. Why would she avoid being measured? Surely she'd want her costumes to fit well and look good?'

'How remarkable. She dressed herself before Hugh promoted her,' Mrs Dyer mused. Her eyes grew round. 'Jennifer, do you think she is hiding some monstrous secret beneath those clothes? Some terrible scar or abnormality?'

I'd been right, she was as naive as most of her class. My allusions had fallen on deaf ears. I'd have to be more explicit. 'Lilith *could* be hiding hives. I've found out that she's allergic to cats. But really I worried that, given what you've told me about her morals—'

'They used to say,' she interrupted, 'that witches carry marks upon their skin.'

This was going to be more difficult than I thought. I wet my lips. 'Maybe they did. But I'm thinking more of how Lilith flutters her eyelashes at the Guvnor, and how Silas says she's trying to charm Anthony Frost. Actually, Silas thinks she's trying to *seduce* Anthony Frost.'

Mrs Dyer swelled in her chair. 'No doubt. She is trying to ensnare Anthony as she ensnared Eugene Grieves. Did you know she upped and left the poor man's theatre, quite as suddenly as Georgiana left us? That was what first prompted me to keep an eye on her. If she betrayed Eugene Grieves, she may betray us too.'

I sighed. So she knew about that, as well. What more did she expect me to tell her? My observations would mean nothing if she couldn't connect the lines herself. And besides, I didn't have proof of what I suspected; only the cynicism bitter experience had brought.

'But Jennifer, there is another favour I would ask.' She retrieved her pocketbook and drew out a clipping from a newspaper. 'I hope you do not think me too presumptuous.'

The paper she handed me was a notice of auction. It announced that Eugene Grieves had died without next of kin and so his belongings were to be sold by lot. *Amongst the coveted items is an exquisite timepiece, in the possession of the actor for over twenty years and present for every stage appearance* ...

I shivered like someone had walked over my grave. 'You want me to go to an auction for you?'

'Do not look so alarmed! I would not dream of it; the auction house is no place for a young lady. No, I simply want you to put this in Hugh's office, somewhere he is sure to happen upon it. We are approaching an anniversary, you see,' she went on. 'Twenty years of marriage. I have been meaning to drop a little clue about the gift I would like to receive ... Perhaps you could help me nudge him in the right direction?'

It was hardly the height of romance. I'd heard of tourists visiting battlefields and taking home bones or teeth as souvenirs; this struck me as the same sort of thing. I couldn't stop myself asking. 'Do you really want a dead man's watch, for your silver wedding?'

A dreamy look came over her features. 'Ah, you do not understand. I met Hugh at a Eugene Grieves play. We fell in love admiring the talent of that actor, and my husband will buy me this watch to symbolise that our bond is timeless.'

Would she say the same, if she'd heard the endearments he'd called Lilith by?

'I cannot tell you what it would mean to own the item that inspired Eugene Grieves ... The very genesis of my love for the theatre, and then for Hugh! It is not so very morbid, is it?'

I wished she'd do this herself. Surely she had more excuse and opportunity to visit the Guvnor's office? But I was still new, I still wanted to please her. 'Not when you put it like that. I'll try to place this in his office, madam.'

'And you cannot imagine I would beg a favour without giving you something in return. Here.' She produced a cream calling-card and passed it to me. It bore a doctor's name and the words *Royal Orthopaedic Hospital*.

'For your brother,' she clarified.

This was the place we'd been saving up to send Bertie for his clubfoot. Medicine could work wonders these days, if you had the money.

'I do hope I have not overstepped my bounds in suggesting it. But I am fortunate enough to know one or two members of the board at that hospital. They shall have to perform an examination, of course. That doctor is expecting to hear from you. Once he has assessed what treatment is necessary, I should be very glad to pay for it.'

I couldn't speak. Obligation weighed heavy on my shoulders. It was kind – so kind – but I felt suffocated. 'I ... thank you, madam. Thank you so much. This is ... life-changing. How can I possibly accept—'

She hushed me. 'You are welcome. I do not see the purpose of wealth if you cannot employ it to spread joy.'

After that, I couldn't bring myself to tell her how the Guvnor had fawned over Lilith.

'It might be harmless,' Dorcas reasoned later that night, while the others slept. I scoffed quietly from my chair. 'Not harmless, then. You know what I'm saying. Lilith might be dancing your Guvnor on a string with no intention of tupping him.'

That much was true, but it didn't sit well with me. 'I hope so. I hope Lilith isn't pregnant. Mrs Dyer may be eccentric and obsessive, but she's kind. I don't want to see her broken and humiliated like ...' I trailed off.

Dorcas didn't remember much from the time Da left us, she was only five or six years old. Gregory and I had understood what was going on, saw how it tore our mother apart. I'd never shake the image of her, big-bellied and alone. We didn't say it out loud, but we all secretly blamed the upset for Bertie's foot. She'd been so wounded by Da that it had hurt the baby she was carrying.

'Keep your mouth shut until we've got Bertie fixed up,' Dorcas advised me. 'Tell Mrs Dyer the truth after that. From the sounds of this woman, she'll fly into a scene at the drop of a hat. We need her to keep her wits and sort out this treatment first.'

It was sensible advice. I stared into the dimly lit room. Philip snored, one arm curled round Bertie. This was my world, my cluster of people to protect. It wasn't worth risking their comfort for one rich lady who'd married a worthless man.

'You're right,' I whispered. 'You're right. I won't tell her. Not yet.'

CHAPTER 5

If I couldn't fulfil my duties of surveillance, I was at least determined to meet my responsibilities as a dresser. Obtaining Lilith's measurements became my mission.

Silas and I made our way down from the wardrobe department to the dressing rooms in time to catch the actors after rehearsal. I looped the tape measure round and round my fingers, like a pugilist binding his knuckles for a fight.

'Any tips?' I asked him.

He gnawed his moustache. 'My dear girl, I've been dressing Anthony for as long as I can remember. The man is as gentle as a lamb. I simply don't have the experience of difficult creatures like … that one.'

As he spoke, they appeared at the end of the corridor. Lilith's hand rested upon the crooked arm of an aristocratic, square-jawed man who must be Anthony Frost. The lesser players trailed behind them in the manner of a wedding party following the bride and groom. Lilith smiled winsomely up into her lead actor's face. He had none of the Guvnor's swagger. Anthony cast his eyes down, appearing proud, if rather bashful to be singled out. Then he caught sight of us dressers. His colour rose.

'Oh. Good afternoon. I wasn't expecting you so early, old chap.'

Silas sniffed. 'Evidently.'

Gently, Anthony disengaged himself from Lilith's grasp. 'These costumes are a bother, aren't they? I can't seem to keep my waist the same size from week to week. Which is it today, my good fellow? The silver-slashed doublet again?'

Silas nodded, stroking the garment arranged over his forearm. His expression was nipped and tight, as if he didn't trust himself to speak.

Lilith rolled her eyes at me. 'And you are here to torment with your tape measure again, I see. Well, do your worst. I am ready for you.'

I hadn't expected that. It was almost a disappointment, to have her yield so easily, but I mustn't look a gift horse in the mouth. I opened her dressing-room door. 'After you.'

Eurydice had been asleep. Her tail thumped against the wall as her mistress entered. I closed the door and began to unwind my tape measure. The scent of all the lilies was making me feel faint already.

'Stand up straight, please, Miss Erikson. I need you over here with your arms spread out.'

'Spoken like a true gaoler.' She unbent from stroking the dog, but folded her arms tightly across her chest. 'I can do it myself. Leave me your tape and your little chart there and I will note every inch down faithfully. Cross my heart.'

I baulked. 'Don't be ridiculous! This is my work. I'm paid to do it.'

'Then quite frankly I am doing you a favour.' The lights flickered. Lilith glanced up at them. 'Weren't you going to get those fixed?'

Maybe I wouldn't, now. Maybe I'd let them flash just to annoy her. 'I'll fix your lights when you let me measure you. Now come on, no more dallying. Unless you've got something to hide?'

She laughed, but it was brittle and false. 'Certainly not.'

'Then stand here and raise your arms.'

Reluctantly, she positioned herself before me. I passed behind her to untie the laces of her gown.

'We need to know what undergarments you'll be wearing to perform,' I told her. 'It'll affect the fit. We can put more boning into the gown if you're planning on short stays.'

'I shall be wearing exactly the same as I am today. I told you I was ready for you, Kitty.'

I tugged a lace sharply. 'My name is Jenny.'

'That may be. But you have claws and the mere sight of you brings me up in hives. What are you, if not a kitty-cat?'

Another day, I might have flared back, but I guessed what she was about. Distraction, deflection. It only inspired me to peel the layers away more quickly. Lilith wasn't a modest woman – she was an actress, for goodness' sake – her chariness meant she was definitely hiding something, and I thought I knew what.

I pulled her day dress off her shoulders and let it pool on the floor. Beneath, she was wearing a shift and a tightly laced steel corset. She'd bound something like bandages over the top, all around her waist and breasts. She reminded me of a mummy in the British Museum.

'What's all that?'

'It holds the silhouette,' Lilith said defensively.

I began to measure. Her legs were plumper than I'd expected. Spider veins wiggled across her calf. Had Mrs Dyer been there, she would've called these imperfections witch marks.

Lilith held herself stiff as I extended the tape and jotted down the numbers. Some had changed significantly from the previous records. The costumes would be too small.

Passing my measure around her waist, I noticed one of the bandages there had worked loose, but as I reached to peel it away she flinched. 'Don't paw at me!' she cried.

'I'm not! Calm down. This bandage wasn't secure.' I frowned at the number on the tape. Everything was confirming my suspicions. 'Are you sure you need this stuff round you? The corset should hold your shape well enough. All this binding's making your waist measurement much bigger.'

'I've had enough of this,' she declared hotly. 'I didn't come here to put up with your sauce and be called stout.' She tried to pull away but the tape measure was still wound around her waist.

I yanked her back by her shoulder. 'Wait! I'm not finished yet.' We were struggling, fighting for possession of the tape measure. 'Lilith, what are you doing? Give that to me! What the hell is wrong with you?'

The bandages started to unwind. Lilith snatched the tape from my hand and held it high above her head. 'You shan't have it,' she crowed. There was a wild look of desperation in her eyes. 'Go away! Leave me alone! Eurydice, come!'

The dog stalked forward, teeth bared. Temper got the better of me. First an actress had stolen my brother and ruined my life, now this one was trying to make me lose the best-paying work I'd ever had. She thought I was a cat, did she? I'd show her my claws.

I raked her chest with my nails. The bandages came away sopping wet. Lilith gasped and tried to cover herself, but it was too late. I had three younger siblings, I recognised breast milk.

'You're a mother!' I spat. It wasn't exactly as I'd thought; I anticipated she'd be hiding a current pregnancy, not an old one, but the disgrace was the same. 'You've had a baby and you're trying to hide it!'

Lilith's eyes sparked. 'Do you think I give a damn for your disapproval? People have been looking down their noses at me from the moment I was born.'

'Did you give them cause?'

That last thrust was a mistake. Lilith gripped my hand so tight that I felt the bones shift. She leant forward until her pale face was mere inches from mine. 'If you dare breathe a word of this … If you go running to Mrs Dyer …'

She looked like a witch, then, bearing down on me. Eurydice's growl rumbled in the background. Lilith squeezed tighter, tighter. It was my right hand. My sewing hand, my livelihood.

'You're hurting me!'

'I mean to. If you so much as hint at what you've seen today, you will live to regret it bitterly. Am I understood?'

Weakly, I nodded.

'I said, am I understood?'

'Yes!'

With a hiss, she dropped me and flung away. I clutched my poor hand to my chest.

'Good. Now get out. And take your damned measurements with you.'

Tears of pain and humiliation drenched my cheeks. How dare she? Fighting the instinct to fly at her, I kicked the dog aside and picked up my measurement chart. Taking the seams out would be agony with my crushed fingers.

'I won't tell the people in the wardrobe room you're a harlot,' I snapped. 'I'll just say that you got fat.'

A poor parting shot, but it was the best I could manage in my state. I nipped out of the dressing room before she could set her dog on me.

When the door closed, I leant my back against the panels. I had to tell Mrs Dyer now. I must. This was the exact reason for my employment. But what would Lilith do to me?

'Miss Wilcox? My dear girl, whatever has happened?' Silas was just emerging from Anthony's dressing room with the actor at his side.

I held out my hand. It looked crumpled, misshapen. I prayed nothing was broken. 'I had an accident,' I whimpered, hating how weak my voice sounded. 'I hurt myself.'

'Do tend to her, old chap,' Anthony urged. 'I can manage alone. Haven't you ointments and all that upstairs?'

'Yes, yes, I have them. Stars and garters!' Clucking over me, Silas wrapped an arm around my shoulder and began to usher me back to the wardrobe room. I wasn't used to sympathy. Usually I looked after myself.

'I wish you better, miss,' Anthony called after us.

'She did this,' I whispered to Silas as I leant against his shoulder. 'It was Lilith. She did it on purpose.'

His scandalised expression was everything I'd hoped for. 'If you ask me,' he murmured, 'that baggage needs to be taken down a peg or two.'

Mrs Dyer had told me to wait for another note, but I was tempted to peg it to her townhouse and blab the truth at once. Dorcas was taking Bertie for the assessment on his foot that very week, so maybe it was better to hold off? I couldn't decide. Scratching Lilith's chest like that hadn't only raked away the bandages; it had raised old feelings I'd hoped to put behind me.

For as long as I could remember, trouble had started with a pretty face. It'd been a neighbour, first, a woman I actually liked. She used to bring me barley twists, launder clothes companionably, side by side with Ma while we children played. Of course I'd noticed how Da smiled at her, but we all did. She was winsome, you couldn't help it.

Poor Ma could never compete. She seemed to sense that. After they left, she gave up entirely, wrote her life off as a bad job. Not even the adorable face of her newborn son could rouse her; in fact, his difficult birth depleted what little strength she had left. I'll always maintain that she died of a broken heart.

Never in a million years could I believe Greg would run off too, but I'd glimpsed his paramour Georgiana Mildmay and she was the same type: fair to the eye, sweet to the ear, casting a spell of charm. Like father, like son. And apparently the Guvnor shared their weakness.

It would destroy Mrs Dyer to find out. With her wedding anniversary coming up as well … Yet the thought of her remaining duped and ignorant made me furious. She'd been kind to me. There must be something I could do to help?

I found myself lingering around the offices, hoping for a sight of her. Instead, I saw Oscar slouch past, a coil of rope hung over his shoulder. He glared at me. 'What are you doing, lurking here? Why're you hiding round the corner like that?'

'No reason.'

He narrowed his dark eyes. 'I don't believe you. You're up to something. God knows why Mrs Dyer thinks she can trust anyone from your family.'

I caught my breath. Where was all this anger coming from? 'What have we ever done to you?'

'What have you done?' he repeated. 'You really have the nerve to stand there and ask me what you've done?'

I wasn't in the frame of mind to speak calmly. My own rage leapt to match his. 'Last time I saw you, you were Greg's friend. Now he's run off and you're acting as if you're the victim! He cleared us out without a penny left, do you understand? Thanks to him, I lost my place as a maid. I don't see how he could *possibly* have treated you worse, or why you should blame me for it!'

Oscar looked thoroughly dashed. Grabbing my arm, he pulled me a little further away from the offices, where we'd undoubtedly disturbed the work. 'You didn't know, then?'

'Know what?'

'I thought ...' He frowned. 'That jewellery. I thought you'd nabbed it for him. Snuck it off your mistress so he could sell it.'

I gave a ripple of horrified laughter. 'You thought I'd risk my neck, so Greg could go to America with his fancy woman? Greg stole the jewels from Miss Fielding, Oscar. He came to the house as my visitor, and that's how he served me. I'm lucky I didn't end up in prison. I'm lucky they couldn't prove anything against me.'

'Crikey,' he said, inadequately. 'I'm ... I'm sorry. I thought you were in on the scheme.'

'Well, I wasn't. I was duped like the rest of you, and kicked out of my place without a reference. Now I'm running round after Mrs Dyer, trying to get in the Guvnor's office to leave him this stupid note.' With my good hand, I pulled out the auction notice. 'And I really can't be doing with your accusations.'

Oscar grimaced. 'I'm sorry. I ... Wait. Why do you need to get in the Guvnor's office?'

I showed him the paper. 'I'm to leave this on his desk. Mrs Dyer wants to drop a hint so the Guvnor will buy her Eugene Grieves's pocket watch for their anniversary.'

Not that it would mean anything, now. What had she said? *A timeless bond.* That poor, poor lady.

Oscar gave a low whistle. 'There's no accounting for taste. I wouldn't fancy carrying that watch around. Did you hear about how Eugene Grieves died?'

'I *saw* it.'

'You never did!'

'We were up in the gallery when it happened. You can't imagine the amount of blood.'

'Crikey,' he said again. 'I've heard strange things about that man. He was talented but ... let's just say I wouldn't employ him, if I had a theatre.'

'And you wouldn't employ me either, that's understood.'

'Look, I really am sorry. I shouldn't have been so short with you. I've been on the defensive ever since ...' He trailed off, bit his lip. 'I'll make it up to you. Let me help you get inside the Guvnor's office. But you have to swear you're not stealing.'

'I'm not!'

'Good.' Oscar adjusted the coil of rope round his shoulder. 'I'll fetch him out of there and keep my eyes peeled while you nip in. It'll have to be quick.'

I nodded. I wanted to hear what he was going to say before he started talking about the office, but I couldn't pass up the opportunity of help. At least I could do *one* thing for Mrs Dyer, even if it meant precious little in the light of her husband's adultery.

Turning from me, Oscar approached the office and tapped on the door. I kept hidden behind the wall.

'Yes?' The Guvnor's voice.

'Beg your pardon, sir,' Oscar said. 'Miss Erikson's been asking for you.'

'Has she, lad? What seems to be the matter?'

'She didn't say. But she asked me to fetch you.'

So it was an open secret, then. Even Oscar knew the Guvnor would go running at Lilith's beck and call. Was Mrs Dyer the only one still in ignorance?

'I shall go to her directly.' I heard the Guvnor's polished shoes tapping over the floor, hurrying away. When I poked my head around the corner, Oscar stood there alone.

'Go on, then,' he said. 'Chop-chop.'

'I'll be as fast as I can.'

I crept inside. The office was inhabited by the scents of leather and ink. Letters, playbills and scripts were stacked haphazardly upon a roll-top mahogany desk. How did Mrs Dyer expect me to make sure he found the auction notice amongst all this?

A bolt of inspiration led me towards the coat stand. The Guvnor's Ulster hung in shapeless tweed folds. I slipped my good hand inside the pocket. There were other papers there, one of which felt stiff and thick like card. I pulled them out, thinking to sandwich my auction notice in the middle, but the photograph caught my eye immediately.

It was a vignette, about the size of a visiting card. A baby sat propped on the lap of a person I assumed must be its mother. She was swathed from head to foot in a dark sheet, even her face was covered. The effect was uncanny, like the poor infant had fallen into the clutches of the Grim Reaper. But it hadn't. The woman must be Lilith: the baby had a thatch of her thick, black hair. My stomach hollowed out. This was proof. Turning the card over, I saw the photographer's studio and date were stamped on the back. Southend-on-Sea, this very year.

Touring with a select group of actors? My eye.

Should I take this to show Mrs Dyer? I kept thinking of little Rachel, knowing only too well the pain of a separation from a child's point of view.

Outside, Oscar cleared his throat. I was taking too long. Hurriedly, I pushed the papers together and tucked them back inside the coat pocket. The photograph I put in my own.

'What kept you?' Oscar asked as I slipped out.

I shook my head. 'Nothing. Thanks for your help. I'll see you later.'

When Mrs Dyer first hired me as her spy, I didn't really believe I'd find anything. But now I'd have to give her this photograph and break her heart.

What would happen once she knew? Maybe she'd sack Lilith, maybe the play would be cancelled … and then what would become of my job? Mrs Dyer had vowed to protect me, but could she keep that promise if she left her husband? Or would she stick by him for appearances?

I wasn't paying attention. I didn't see the Guvnor coming in the opposite direction until he said my name. I stopped dead.

'Miss Wilcox,' he repeated, his voice prickling against my skin.

'Yes, sir?' I ground out.

'I was hoping I might find you. I have just been speaking with Miss Erikson.'

Rot me. She must have told him exactly what I'd seen when taking her measurements. I said nothing.

'Miss Erikson was concerned there may have been a misunderstanding between you, regarding a certain ... health condition.' There came his easy grin; so loose, so habitual, that it meant nothing. I wanted to wrench the fancy cane he carried out of his hand and beat him with it. 'But I told her there was no cause for alarm. "Miss Wilcox is a sensible young woman," I said. "She will understand the situation."'

'I understand perfectly,' I muttered.

He didn't even have the grace to look embarrassed. 'I would appreciate your discretion in this matter, Miss Wilcox.'

I scoffed. 'Exactly how much would you appreciate it, sir?'

'I beg your pardon?'

'If you had to give it a figure?' I kept my gaze steady on his.

'Oho!' The Guvnor's eyebrows shot up, as if he'd seen an impressive parlour trick. 'I see! You are a sharp one, aren't you?' He rummaged in his waistcoat pocket and offered me a small purse. 'I like you the better for it. A girl ought to have some spirit.'

Guilt needled somewhere below my ribs. I took the purse and stuffed it in my pocket beside the photograph.

'My wife was right about you, Miss Wilcox. I think you will prove to be *an asset.*'

That chafed. 'I don't think you ought to bring Mrs Dyer's name into this.'

The mask of joviality dropped. He looked almost wolfish with the silver at his temples. 'No. No indeed, it is my intention that she be kept from the business entirely. And if she is not ... If any rumours were to spread ...' He leant forward so I could smell the cigar smoke on his breath. 'I would know precisely who to blame. Eh?'

CHAPTER 6

I carried the finished costumes down as carefully as newborn babes. Mrs Nettles said gowns were never truly alive until they'd been worn; that a supple and dirtied dress played a part by itself. But I didn't want a puff of wind to blow on our beautiful creations. I'd spent so long making them bigger with my bruised hand. It was bad enough that they'd be sullied by the hussy who wore them.

'Jennifer! There you are. My, my, what excellent work you have done.'

'Mrs Dyer.' Of course she was here for opening night. I hadn't seen her since the awful discovery. She hadn't written, and God knew I was delaying the inevitable as long as I possibly could. Now the sight of her hit me like a fist.

She and Rachel were dressed in matching jade gowns. While the little girl's frock was simple, Mrs Dyer's revealed her shoulders and delicate collarbone. A choker of emeralds hid the fine wrinkles on her neck. Her toffee-coloured hair hung down her back in thick sausage curls. She looked so fragile, so refined, that I wanted to shield her just like the costumes.

'Forgive me for neglecting you,' she smiled, smoothing Rachel's hair. 'Business has quite overtaken me! All these preparations … But we have much to discuss.'

My gaze sought the ground. 'Yes, madam. We certainly do.'

'I shall not keep you now, I can see you are occupied. You will attend the after-party in the green room, won't you?'

'There's going to be dancing!' Rachel squeaked.

I tried to smile for the child. 'I don't know, madam. Bertie will be expecting me home—'

'Oh yes, young Albert! I had let it slip my mind. The doctor wrote to me, Jennifer, with excellent news. His examination confirmed that he can perform an operation to cut the Achilles tendon on the troublesome foot. It is not an instant fix; your brother will be obliged to wear corrective splints and retrain the muscles. But as far as I understand these matters, it will grant the little fellow greater mobility and the possibility of a near-regular foot in the future! Is that not wonderful?'

It would have been. It would have been an absolute blessing if guilt were not burning a hole in my chest. Such glad tidings she brought me – and what I had to tell her in return!

'I don't know what to say, Mrs Dyer. I never thought...' Cruel whispers had dismissed Bertie as a 'cripple' since the day he was born. Now he had a chance.

She nodded indulgently. She could see that emotion had rendered me mute. 'No matter, we shall speak more of this at the party. Do say you shall come.'

'Well...'

'Do come!' Rachel echoed, fixing me with her mother's eyes.

'Just for a half hour,' Mrs Dyer urged. 'Our anniversary is tomorrow and we are treating all the staff to Moët for the occasion. Come, the celebration would not be the same without you there.'

How could I refuse, with what she was doing for Bertie? 'All right. Just for a bit.'

Rachel applauded. She wouldn't clap if she knew my news and how it would blight her future.

I gestured to the costumes. 'I must be getting on.'

'Yes! Yes, of course. Your first show. Break a leg.'

I hoped I would. I yearned to turn an ankle, plunge through a trapdoor, anything to avoid going to this wretched party and having to speak the truth.

The conductor was in his pit. Strings hummed as the orchestra tuned their instruments. A gasman walked onto the apron of the stage, lighting the floats, whilst another ignited the chandelier with a long pole. Any minute now, they'd let the audience in.

Backstage was a muddle of dressers dashing to and fro, carrying paint saucers or flat irons. The supernumerary actresses brushed each other's hair; I heard Anthony Frost exercising his rich, bass voice.

As soon as I opened the door, Eurydice barked. Lilith didn't look up. She sat at her dressing table, her part spread before her, moving her lips to the words. The speech was the first big piece of the character, when Lady Macbeth fell on her knees and asked not for divine intervention, but the help of demons to achieve her ends.

'Apt, isn't it?' I sniped. '*Come to my woman's breasts, and take my milk for gall?*'

She glowered at me. 'I thought Hugh had paid you to hold your tongue.'

Hugh now, was it? No need to pretend and call him the Guvnor any longer. 'He paid me not to speak of your dirty secret outside this room. What I say to *you* wasn't stipulated.'

Lilith sniffed. 'This is my debut in a leading role. Do you have any concept of how hard I've worked to reach this moment? I won't have my triumph tainted by the jibes of a mucksnipe. Take the night off, Kitty. I would rather dress myself.'

I'd planned these outfits for too long to let the arrangements slip into another's hands. Lilith didn't know how to shake out the skirts, or the way the ruff should fan out like a halo at her neck. 'No chance. You're stuck with me and I'm saddled with you. That's the deal.'

She lifted her chin to the gaslights. 'Very well, then. Do your worst.'

'Let me paint your face while the curling tongs are heating up. I'll put the dress on last.'

Lilith pushed back her stool. 'I give you fair warning, I'll be scrutinising every detail. You won't slip any tricks past me, to make me look foolish on stage.'

I hadn't thought of that. I could've tucked her skirts up to expose her drawers, slipped a mouse inside her hat. But much as I loathed this woman, I wanted to do my job well. Lilith wasn't the only one trying to prove her worth tonight.

I cleaned her skin thoroughly. Lilith was young, about twenty-four, but the recent pregnancy had taken off her bloom. Her cheeks were dry. A spot studded her chin. I dipped the camelhair brush carefully in the saucer of paint and worked in strokes. Next, I darkened her brows with burnt cork and applied rouge to the apples of her cheeks. I painted her lips with cochineal until they blushed as red as Mrs Dyer's.

Lilith's hair wasn't in good condition. Up close it was matt, not glossy. I removed the curling tongs from their spirit stove and did the best I could.

Lady Macbeth's first costume was my favourite – the outfit she wore at Inverness, when she was only a thane's wife, clutching at his letter of prophecy: a damson, knife-pleated skirt and floral bodice. The petals were red, foreshadowing the spots of blood that would come to drive her mad.

Once the gown was laced and an attifet set at the back of Lilith's head, she looked glorious. I was proud of her; or rather, proud of my work.

Lilith stared deep at her reflection in the full-length mirror and drew her shoulders back. There was no tremor of nerves. 'This is my destiny,' she declared. 'Just you watch, Kitty. I'll set that stage on fire.'

Looking back, I think that was the night I fell in love. I'd always known that theatre could be powerful, magical even, but this performance touched me on another level. I'd been there from the start, seen how painstakingly everyone toiled to make illusion become reality. The enchantment felt deeper now I knew how many people had laboured together, muttering incantations before the spell could take effect.

I saw the backdrop Oscar had spent weeks painting brought alive under the careful rigging of the lights. Every tiny detail was perfect, from the choreographed sword fights to the papier-mâché battlements. Part of me had dreaded watching another play, after what happened at *Doctor Faustus*, but although this story was dark it didn't terrify me as I stood in the wings. I knew what to expect and when. I was acquainted with the real people beneath the paint and costumes.

Shy, gentle Anthony Frost transformed into an astonishing Macbeth. His mild persona disappeared beneath that of a warrior, lashed by ambition and guilt. Lilith was Lilith still: the same steely arrogance, only intensified.

We'd reached the part where Lady Macbeth was queen; I'd changed Lilith into heather brocade and a tight gold circlet of a crown. She sat at the end of a banquet table heaped with wax fruit. As Macbeth went to take his place, a blue medium passed across the lights. Violins made an unearthly whine from the orchestra pit. The ghost of Banquo lumbered onto the stage.

'That's brilliant,' I whispered to Oscar, standing beside me. The actor playing the ghost had a red ribbon about his neck to signify how he'd been murdered. His skin was chalked white and his doublet splashed with blood. 'I barely recognised him.'

The dead man sat in Macbeth's chair. A shiver ran over me to see his malefic expression.

'*Thou canst not say I did it,*' Macbeth pleaded to the man he'd sentenced to death. '*Never shake thy gory locks at me!*'

Oscar harrumphed. 'That's what happens when you betray a friend. It comes back to haunt you.'

Macbeth began to pace, his hands driven into his hair. The ghost of Banquo rose to his feet – and vanished, quick as a blink.

'How did they do that?' I gasped.

'Vampire trap,' Oscar answered.

I glanced further into the wings. The prompter was in his corner, studying the book and dispatching his boy to fetch the actors for their entrances. Horace, the stage manager, was watching with his hands steepled before his lips.

'I thought Lilith would make a better show of it,' Oscar observed. 'She's not bad. But I've seen her do more than this.'

I smirked. In my opinion, she hardly needed to act at all to resemble the evil Lady Macbeth.

Another actress appeared backstage, Clementine Price. She'd been brought in to replace Georgiana Mildmay. With her long-lashed blue eyes and blonde curls she looked like an advertisement for Pears soap, but she was clearly sick with nerves. She rocked ever so slightly on the balls of her feet, whispering her lines. '*Whither should I fly? I have done no harm. Whither should I fly?*'

My blood went cold. 'What ... what's she saying?'

'Can't you just shut up and enjoy the performance?'

'No, but those words ... I know them.'

'*Whither should I fly?*' Clementine murmured again. '*I have done no harm.*'

Oscar craned his neck to look. 'It's Lady Macduff, isn't it? She's killed at the start of the next act.'

I'd read the play. But that wasn't where my memory sprang from. 'Doctor Faustus,' I realised. 'He said the same thing. *Whither should I fly.*'

'What are you driving at, Miss Wilcox?'

I shook my head. I couldn't put it into words. 'I don't know. It just seems to ... follow me. I feel like I'll never be free of that play.'

Oscar's stance softened. He knew what I'd witnessed at the Helicon. 'Never mind all that,' he said. 'That's done with, now.' Gently, he placed a hand on my shoulder and pointed through the curtains. 'Look, you're missing it. The ghost's coming back for more.'

CHAPTER 7

Lilith wasn't content with the applause or the roses that sailed upon the stage. She tore Lady Macbeth's nightgown off so violently that she nearly ripped it.

'Careful! I worked hard on that!'

'Then you can share my disappointment, can't you?' she spat. 'I have laboured, made endless sacrifice, only to fall flat when it really mattered.'

I stopped to pick up the nightdress and straighten it out. Little as I wanted to offer Lilith comfort, I had to be fair. 'You were fine. The audience seemed pleased.'

'With Anthony!' She slammed a hand on the dressing table, making the bottles of scent chink. 'It wasn't good enough. I could have done better. It's in me to do better.' Her eyes narrowed. 'Maybe it was *your* fault, vexing me before I went on stage.'

One of Greg's phrases sprang to my lips. 'A bad artist blames his tools.'

She gave me her fiercest Lady Macbeth look. What the blazes did she want? She'd given a creditable performance, taken a curtain call. She hadn't astounded like Anthony Frost, but he had a meatier part.

'Well,' I said. 'You've undressed yourself. I'll put these bits in order then I'm going to the green room for some well-earned champagne.'

Lilith knelt by Eurydice and buried her fingers in the dog's tight black curls. I could feel her frustration buzzing round the room like a trapped fly.

Some people were never happy.

The green room resembled a fashionable, emerald saloon with divans, a piano and glass globes to shield the lights.

Polly and I stood in the corner clutching sticky flutes of champagne. Cigar smoke puffed and chatter muddled with the sounds of laughter and tinkling glass.

Silas waxed lyrical to anyone who would listen. He'd already emptied his drink. 'Did you see how Anthony made their hair stand on end? He is marvellous, truly marvellous. I have never felt so proud in all my days. That man is a paragon without equal. A true artist. This was the performance of his career. He is superior to Irving, to Grieves. I shouldn't wonder if a knighthood were heading his way.'

This was taking it much too far, but we let him drivel on. It was entertaining to watch Anthony pretend he couldn't hear. There was no doubt that Lilith caught every word.

She would have been arresting in her fashionable black evening gown, were it not for her sour expression. She looked like she'd sucked on a lemon. Her discomfort cheered me more than the champagne.

One of the musicians from the orchestra sat down at the piano and began to play a polka. Mrs Dyer danced little Rachel on her feet. With any luck, she'd be too preoccupied and I could slip out before she forced me to talk.

The stage manager, Horace, came and asked Polly to dance. She passed me her flute so I was stuck there holding two of them, looking like a lush. Plenty of couples were forming and joining in the lively steps. I wasn't really in the mood. But then I caught sight of Oscar, standing alone. All the other painters were dancing, yet none of the girls so much as glanced in his direction. Why was that?

Setting the glasses down on the piano, I crossed the room.

'Dance with me.' It came out more like an order than a suggestion.

Oscar eyed me warily. 'Why?'

'Because I'm asking you to.' Still he hesitated, reluctant to accept my pity. I swallowed. I hadn't really thought how stupid I'd look if he said no. 'Got something better planned, have you?'

Giving a reluctant grin, he shook his head and took my hand. I led him to where the others were dancing. He held me lightly at the waist. Up close like this, I could see that his fingernails were rimmed with colour. He smelt of linseed and calico.

The polka was a hopping, quick dance. Neither of us could stay self-conscious for long. Oscar trod on my skirt as I galloped backwards. I jolted against him and erupted into laughter.

'Sorry,' Oscar chuckled, grimacing. 'I'm out of practice with this.'

'It's me, I'm too slow and I always mess up the turns. Consider yourself warned.'

Over his shoulder, I saw Anthony ask Lilith to dance. She bristled, much as Oscar had when I approached him. But I was learning how her conceited mind worked. Lilith would accept despite, or rather *because* of, her envy. While she danced with the star of the show, at least all eyes would be on her.

I was right. She yielded.

I tightened my grip on Oscar's shoulder, putting him like a shield between us.

'I'm sorry,' he said again, more quietly. 'About before. Suspecting you and all that. Can you forgive me? I've not been myself lately. The whole thing's been a nasty shock.'

One of the carpenters I'd seen in the yard on my first day swept past us with a box-keeper in his arms. 'What's this, Thorne?' he sneered. 'Wilcox send you his sister as a sop, did he?'

Oscar's muscles turned rigid beneath my hands.

'Who's that? What's he talking about?'

For a moment he seemed too angry to speak. Then he said in a strained voice, 'I suppose I got … carried away. Put a few noses out of joint. They're all delighted to see me fall on my arse.'

'I don't understand.'

'I should've kept a level head. But you see what working here does to you. Dealing with fantasy, day in and day out ... anything seems possible. We used to talk, you know, about opening our own theatre. She'd be the star and I'd be the Guvnor ... I told myself it could happen. I told my mates, in no uncertain terms, that it was going to happen.' He shook his head. 'My dad says she played me for a fool and maybe she did, but I fooled myself plenty, too. Puffed myself up with all kinds of fancies about what would happen once we were married.'

My mind was scrabbling for a foothold. 'Married?' I repeated. 'Who were you going to ...'

And then it all made sense. Mrs Nettles had spoken of Georgiana jilting a painter to run off with Greg. I never imagined it could be Oscar; they were such good friends. Outrage constricted my throat; the feeling was becoming familiar. Whenever I thought Greg couldn't sink any lower ... No wonder Oscar had recoiled from the sight of me!

'Oscar, I didn't know. They said Georgiana broke an engagement, I didn't realise ...' His face contracted in pain. 'Damn their eyes,' I whispered. 'We're better off shot of the both of them.'

A fork tinged against glass. Oscar dropped me like a hot coal as a hush fell across the company. Everyone turned to face the Guvnor, who was climbing onto a divan and tapping his champagne flute.

'Ladies and gentlemen of the Mercury theatre, it gives me great pleasure to address you on this auspicious occasion! To extend, on behalf of my wife and myself, our heartfelt thanks.' He raised his glass to Mrs Dyer and she twinkled back at him. 'Twenty years of marriage, twenty years of joint labour, could not have been rewarded more richly than they were tonight. We are delighted with you all. I hope you will join me in toasting your most loyal patroness. I give you Mrs Dyer!'

'Mrs Dyer!' came the chorus.

She preened. She looked younger and more handsome when her husband's attention was turned upon her, like a flower raising its face to the sun.

He didn't deserve her. Who was he to speak of loyalty?

'And as for our company ... We all knew we had a great artist in our midst, but tonight's performance proclaimed it to the world. Tomorrow's newspapers will be writing odes to Anthony Frost's skilful portrayal of the Scottish usurper, better even than his Othello last year. Ladies and gentleman, raise a glass to Anthony Frost!'

'Anthony Frost!' Silas's voice rang prominent amongst the cheers.

Lilith's cheek twitched, as though a fly had landed upon it.

The Guvnor cradled his glass. 'It is a melancholy fact that as one sun rises, another sets. I have found great comfort witnessing the growth of new talent at this time of upheaval. The void left in our profession by the death of Eugene Grieves will not be easily filled.'

Mrs Dyer's smile wilted. Others hung their heads and murmured assent. My mind swerved an image of Doctor Faustus jerking in a pool of blood. When would that dreadful memory leave me alone?

The Guvnor reached into his waistcoat pocket. He produced not his own golden pocket watch, but something in an onyx case. Pearls blistered around the edge. I was close enough to see the engraving: a figure I recognised from Mrs Dyer's brooch: the Muse Melpomene, her lipless mouth distorted in grief.

Eugene Grieves's watch. He'd bought it, just as Mrs Dyer hoped he would. She could hardly stop herself from reaching straight for it.

'Yet we shall fill this terrible breach. From one generation to the next, the tragic muse lives on. This, my friends, is Eugene Grieves's iconic watch.' He held it up to the light. 'I deem it only fitting that this precious relic should pass into the hands of those who continue his work.'

I caught sight of Lilith; her eyes were enormous, like the theatre cats tracking mice in the dark. I couldn't understand the company's fascination. This whole spectacle felt strangely macabre to me, as though we'd cracked open Eugene Grieves's coffin and were peering at his corpse.

'It gives me great pleasure to present this watch to a lady who will cherish it above all things. A lady who will follow the call of Melpomene, wherever it leads.'

Mrs Dyer smoothed down her skirts, made as if to stand. I should be pleased. At least she'd have her little moment of joy before I had to open her eyes to the truth.

'Ladies and gentlemen, please join me in congratulating our new lead actress, Miss Lilith Erikson.'

No.

The sound of hands clapping together seemed to beat against my body. God knew my opinion of the Guvnor had never been high ... but this? How was he capable of such breathtaking cruelty?

He might have struck Mrs Dyer between the eyes. She'd half risen, but now she slumped back against the divan like a dead thing.

Lilith pushed to the front of the crowd, her hands raised in the manner of a supplicant seeking communion. The Guvnor dangled the watch into her palms and let the chain dribble in after it. She closed her grip instantly.

I couldn't, I *wouldn't* stay and listen to Lilith's speech of thanks. Without even bidding Oscar farewell, I made for the door.

I only glanced back once. The company resembled a series of tableaux, scenes from the play. Lilith portrayed wickedness triumphant: Lady Macbeth placing the crown on her traitorous brow. As for poor Mrs Dyer ... I'd seen a face like that once tonight, already.

She wore the forsaken expression of Banquo's murdered ghost.

CHAPTER 8

At least when Gregory had betrayed us, the blow was spread across a large area. Like a wall made of individual bricks, my family and I had braced together for impact. But Mrs Dyer had nowhere to turn. Her hurt could only burrow, deep within.

I found her alone in the luxury of Box 6, the queen of an abandoned court. Stealing across the carpet, I perched on the velvet chair at her left. Somehow it felt that if I made a sound or moved too fast, I'd break her.

'Oh,' she sighed, her voice pressed flat by sorrow. 'Jennifer. I am glad you are here.'

I knew from experience that platitudes would only rankle. 'I've been worried for you, madam.'

Slowly, she unfolded. Her eyes were puffy and red. 'I have not lived in society without learning the way of the world. Gentlemen's eyes will wander. But I really did believe ... with our romance ... with all that we shared ...' A sob escaped her. 'Did you read the play *Othello* in the book I gave you?'

'Yes, but—'

'I was Desdemona!' she wailed. 'I left everyone for Mr Dyer, and he has throttled me.'

Pity wormed its way into my chest. I could forgive her theatricals this once. 'Haven't you a sister, or someone you could go to?'

She took a gulp of air. 'My relatives, my so-called friends ... they did not understand my marriage. To them, the theatre was a "trade". Dirty and unrefined. They forsook me.' Tears streamed down her cheeks. 'I thought their behaviour cruel ... But perhaps they knew better than I. All he wanted was my independent fortune.'

She'd spoken of her wealth before, but I hadn't quite understood. The Guvnor was living on his wife's money. Buying Lilith priceless watches, paying for photographs of his bastard with Mrs Dyer's funds. Little wonder Greg should turn out rotten, with such a gentleman as his example. The 'quality' prided themselves on improving the morals of their workers, but this was what really happened.

Far below us, actors were rehearsing sword play on stage. Their rapiers made a harsh, metallic clash.

'Did you have the courage to confront him, madam?'

'Yes! I could hardly feign composure … He accused me of being hysterical. Ruining our anniversary and making Rachel cry.' She rubbed at her forehead. 'I began to doubt myself. Is he right, Jennifer? Should I be pleased that Eugene's watch may inspire another actor?'

'No,' I answered sadly. The time had come to tell the truth. It would add to her burden of sorrow, but I ached to see the Guvnor punished; in some twisted way, it would feel like getting back at Da and Gregory. 'Your resentment of Lilith is justified, madam. I've something to report. But … I really don't know how to tell you.'

Her eyes gleamed bottle green with fresh tears. 'Say it at once. Nothing could make me more desolate than I am right now.'

I doubted that. 'I've discovered … a photograph. And … bodily signs.' I screwed up my face at the memory. 'Things that show Lilith wasn't on tour this summer, after all.'

'Whatever do you mean? She took the train with all the rest. I waved them off from the station myself.'

I shifted in my seat. 'Maybe the Guvnor did take actors to a theatre in Southend. But Lilith went to the seaside for something else.' There was probably some delicate term that ladies used for modesty, but it wasn't in my vocabulary. She'd have to hear it in blunt language. 'To give … to give birth.'

Mrs Dyer's jaw fell slack. She was quiet for so long that I almost doubted she'd heard me.

'I'm so sorry, madam.'

No response. It reminded me of the blankness that had taken possession of Ma's face when Da left. My heart squeezed. What now? Would she blame me for the discovery? Would I even have a job tomorrow?

At last, Mrs Dyer drew a breath. 'But ... Jennifer, this is ... excellent.'

'Madam?'

'Why did you not tell me before?' Seeing my bafflement, she went on: 'This is the ammunition I need to beat the little witch! Hugh will not dote on her any longer, when he finds out what she truly is. A fallen woman! An illegitimate child! He will be revolted by Lilith now.'

Just when I thought the situation couldn't grow any worse, she'd assumed that Lilith kept a lover elsewhere.

'Do you have the photograph? You must bring it to me, as proof. At last, I will have something tangible to hold over her ... But why do you look so pitiful? Do not tell me you have acquired some sympathy for Lilith?'

I shook my head slowly. The sword fight ended; an actor released his death cry and I watched the truth sink into Mrs Dyer like blood into a rag. 'Merciful heavens. You cannot mean ...'

'I'm afraid so, madam. I found the photograph in the Guvnor's office.' I felt like a monster and resented the adulterers even more; why should I be the one saddled with the consequences of their guilt? It should be the Guvnor confessing this, having to look her in the eye as her heart shattered. 'I'm so, so sorry.'

'Oh.' She grabbed on to the partition of the box, her knuckles turning white. 'Oh.' A painful little trill of laughter escaped her. 'How foolish I have been. You must think me a great simpleton.'

'No, of course I don't.'

Weeping got the better of her then. I forgot my station and leant her my shoulder. Only a brute would refuse it.

I had no idea what she might do. She was too good for the Guvnor, but what recourse did she have? What happened with rich people who decided to separate? Divorces were costly and scandalous – I knew that much. Mrs Dyer might struggle to get back her money or custody of Rachel. That was, if she even decided to leave. She'd just told me she had no one left. Where would she go?

'She has stopped the very heart of me,' she wept. 'That evil woman ... But if she should alienate Hugh's affection from Rachel! If she should siphon all his love to her ill-begotten brat!'

I hadn't thought of that. I'd only imagined Rachel's distress, not the usurpation of her rights. 'What will you do, madam?'

'What *can* I do? Nothing, I believe, at present. There is no hard evidence. I must have something tangible to place before Hugh so he cannot dismiss me as hysterical again.'

I drew out the photograph and pushed it into her hands. A tremor ran through her frame when she saw what it was. 'There's this. And Lilith told the Guvnor I'd discovered her recent ... condition. He offered me money not to tell.'

Her mouth hung ajar. 'He did?'

'Yes. I haven't spent any, I brought it right back here for you today.' I passed the purse across hurriedly, as if it would make everything better.

Mrs Dyer weighed it in the palm of her hand. 'So this is all he believes our marriage is worth.' She heaved a sigh. 'Take it, Jennifer. I have more to give you besides for young Albert's operation.'

I gaped at her. 'No, madam, that's the last thing you should be thinking—'

'Hush, hush. You must go ahead with the treatment. Allow me to do this. If Hugh is squandering my fortune on harlots and their spawn, at least let me put an equal part of the money towards good works.'

That humbled me. In all her pain, she was thinking of others. 'Thank you. I don't know what to say. I've brought you such awful news, and you're still being good to me.'

'You have proved yourself faithful. Far more faithful than those I had reason to trust. I shall not forget it.'

What was the world coming to when an employee treated a lady better than her own husband? When a rich stranger had more compassion for me than my elder brother? The day Dorcas was born, Ma had told me that girls needed to stick together.

There was something in that. But then again, there were girls like Georgiana Mildmay. Like Lilith Erikson.

I'd better go and see Lilith now, although I could hardly stand to face her. 'I'm afraid I must leave you, madam. There's work to do ... God knows I haven't the heart for it.'

She patted my arm. 'Take spirit, Jennifer. Somehow we will vanquish Lilith between us. What is it the apparitions say to Macbeth? *Be bloody, bold and resolute.*'

I forced a smile and nodded. In her sorrow, Mrs Dyer had accidentally invoked the curse. It would be insensitive for me to remind her – what did it matter, now?

With all that had happened, it seemed impossible that things could get any worse.

There was a strange quality to the Mercury that day; a subtle change in the atmosphere that reflected the world outside. As autumn shifted to winter, as the sky darkened and leaves dropped from the trees, so the theatre moved from a place charged with magic to one pregnant with threat.

I told myself it was the tired, stale feeling that followed the exhilaration of opening night. But when I made my way down to the dressing rooms, I was aware of the gas lamps hissing louder than usual. Rather than trotting their rodent patrol, the cats lurked in the shadows, flashing their eyes at me. Even the walls seemed shabbier: peels in the crimson paper and scuffs on the skirting boards. There was a smell of worn stockings, unaired rooms.

Silas, Anthony and Clementine were gathered outside Lilith's door in whispered consultation.

'What's the matter?' I asked.

Clementine turned her big blue eyes on me. 'Nothing, exactly ...'

'Miss Erikson was acting distant and preoccupied all through rehearsal,' Anthony explained. 'We thought she might be unwell.'

'As soon as we finished, she locked herself inside her dressing room. She won't answer our knocks.'

Silas scoffed. 'Take my word, dear girl, it is all affectation. I have seen it with actresses a thousand times. The lamp of attention must always be turned upon them.'

'But what if it's not?' Clementine fretted. 'What if she's collapsed in there?'

'Then Miss Wilcox will dress you up and you may go on in her place. It would be no great loss, whatever the Guvnor says.' Silas turned to me. 'Can you credit it, Miss Wilcox? After the revelation of Anthony's performance last night, to bestow the great Eugene Grieves's watch on that ... that hamfatter! It is an insult. A degradation.'

'Not this again, old chap. What's done is done.' But there was tension in Anthony's strong jawline. Being overlooked had hurt him, even if he didn't want to show it.

For my part, I wasn't concerned about Lilith. If she'd keeled over, Eurydice would be scrabbling at the door and whining for help.

Pushing the others aside, I knocked once, then pressed my ear to the panel. Whispers. Lilith murmuring, snake-like, to herself.

'Miss Erikson?' Cool air stole beneath the door and touched my ankles. 'I can hear her running her lines.'

Silas's mouth twisted. 'As I thought. Putting on the airs of a prima donna. There will be no living with her now she's in possession of that watch. Do you think she'll deign to admit you inside to dress her?'

'She won't have a choice.' I pulled out the spare key Mrs Dyer had made for me. 'I'll see to her. You can all get along with your own preparations.'

'Oh gosh.' Clementine turned a shade of green. 'Is it that time already?'

'I'll fetch you the smelling salts and the ginger, dear girl,' Silas said, patting her on the shoulder.

I remembered her in the wings last night, rocking and repeating her lines. 'You'll survive,' I encouraged her. 'You did well yesterday. You didn't freeze or dry up at all.'

She twirled a finger in her blonde curls. 'No, I never do. It's only the thought that I might. I can't explain it.'

'It's a jolly odd experience,' Anthony said kindly. 'From the moment the call boy fetches you, as you walk through the wings ... that metamorphosis from yourself into the character. The process of change can be awfully painful.'

'Like a werewolf,' I put in.

Anthony raised his eyebrows and laughed. 'A werewolf! Upon my word, I like that.'

I slipped my key in the lock and opened Lilith's dressing-room door. Eurydice's nose appeared in the gap. She made a troubled sound, so human that it took me aback.

'What is it?'

Lilith sat before the dressing-table mirror, Eugene Grieves's watch held loosely in her hand. She mouthed her lines, the words tumbling one into another and breaking like waves against the shore.

'Too famous to answer the door now, are you?' No response. There was a vacancy, a glassiness in her expression. I closed the door behind me. Eurydice plastered herself to my side as I moved into the room. 'Lilith?'

'What?' she snapped, jerking alert. 'Can't you see I'm practising?'

'Your fellow actors thought you'd dropped dead. They've been knocking for you and you just ignored them.'

A frown creased her brow. 'I didn't hear. What did they want with me?'

'Not the pleasure of your company, that's for sure.'

Lilith tutted. 'It's no use, Kitty, you shan't vex me tonight. Everything is different now. I have a second chance.' She stroked the watch lovingly. 'Come and take a look. You didn't see it up close last night, did you? Have you ever beheld anything so wonderful?'

The artistry was fine, in its way, but that black case and the pearls put me in mind of mourning wear. Melpomene looked like she was coming for you with her pendulous club. The workings were loud. Something about the ticking found its way into my back teeth.

'My ma always said that pearls bring tears.'

'I don't suppose she ever owned them,' Lilith retorted. 'Besides, they're wholly appropriate. A tragic actress must be able to weep on command.'

I was thinking of Mrs Dyer's tears. 'People are saying the Guvnor should have given that watch to Anthony. Or to his wife. It would've been more fitting.'

Lilith pulled a face. '*I* was Eugene's pupil. The watch belongs with me, and no one else.'

I turned my back on her and passed to the wardrobe. She was a fine one to talk of ownership, when she'd stolen another woman's husband. 'It's only a gimcrack. Why does it matter so much to everyone?'

'Why does it matter?' she repeated, incredulous. 'This watch has been blessed by Melpomene herself.'

I spluttered with laughter. 'You don't really believe that? She's a legend. Melpomene is no more real than Spring-Heeled Jack.'

'She does exist,' Lilith insisted. 'Eugene saw her. She used to visit him and teach him. How else can you explain a talent like that?'

'Hard work,' I said, pulling the costumes out. 'Expensive training. Commitment.'

'I'm going to wear the watch tonight,' Lilith decided. 'We'll hang it from my girdle.'

I smoothed out the damson dress. 'That's an anachronism. Mrs Nettles won't like it.'

'I don't give a damn what Mrs Nettles likes.'

'You don't give a damn for anyone but yourself,' I muttered.

'I shall wear it all the time. Just as Eugene did.'

For the life of me, I couldn't think why Lilith would want to wear such a morbid item. Owning it was one thing, but having it about her person felt ghoulish. I'd be forced to look at it, too. To remember that man who had died so horribly while the timepiece swung from his waist.

Lilith rose to her feet, ready for me. There was no hesitation about being dressed tonight. She didn't even complain as the gaslights dimmed and surged. 'My time is finally here,' she said breathlessly. 'You cannot imagine how long I have waited.'

Not that long. She was still young. I pulled off her robe. 'Your debut was last night. You only get one chance to make a first impression.'

Lilith smiled, shook her dark head. 'I can see you don't believe me, Kitty. But it doesn't signify. Only watch. Melpomene will come.'

CHAPTER 9

If anything, Anthony was even better that night. He played the first four scenes with an intensity that made me hold my breath. Every movement portrayed the internal struggle of Macbeth: yearning to fulfil the prophecy of his greatness, yet reluctant to commit murder.

Silas and I exchanged a smile in the wings. Lilith had been certain Melpomene would visit her, but maybe the muse had called on the dressing room next door instead.

The curtain rose on Macbeth's castle in Inverness: candelabras, tapestries and battlements set the scene for Lilith's first appearance. The orchestra played Lady Macbeth's leitmotif. She strode on from the opposite side of the stage, Eugene Grieves's watch swinging to her step. There was no perceptible change. She spoke the opening lines as she always did, reading Macbeth's letter of prophecy aloud.

The messenger dashed on to tell Lady Macbeth that her husband had arrived with the present king. The scheming woman saw her chance to change the royal succession there and then.

A red medium passed across the lights. That was new. Lilith must have asked the Guvnor to make more of her first big speech. Violins played a skittering tremolo as she moved centre stage. The music crawled over my skin. I felt something coming; a tightness, a gathering, like static before a storm.

Lilith was taking her time. Making sure all eyes were upon her.

She dropped to her knees. The boards jolted. Spreading her arms in a cruciform, she threw her dark head back. '*Come, you spirits that tend on mortal thoughts, unsex me here, and fill me from the crown to the toe top-full of direst cruelty!'* The words bounced to the rafters of the house.

'That action's not in the prompt book,' Silas complained. 'She's meant to stand.'

A drumbeat started, low and ominous, from the orchestra pit.

'She's changed the music too!' Silas huffed. 'Why would they let her do that?'

I couldn't answer. My heart thudded in time to the drums as Lilith closed her eyes and swayed, like one in a trance.

It had always been a horrible speech. Now it felt sickening, ritualistic. Swells shifted uncomfortably in the orchestra stalls. A lady hid her face behind her fan.

'Come to my woman's breasts, and take my milk for gall, you murdering ministers, wherever in your sightless substances you wait on nature's mischief!'

Lilith slapped the letter against her chest. Someone gasped. She meant it this time, I realised. Lilith really meant the words: demons, murder, anything for success.

As I watched her, washed in that red light, I almost believed that Melpomene was on her way. Every beat of the drum was a footstep.

A tremor shook Lilith's frame. Her eyes flew open, fixed and staring at the gallery. The audience looked over their shoulders. Did she see something we couldn't?

'Come, thick night, and pall thee in the dunnest smoke of hell, that my keen knife see not the wound it makes, nor heaven peep through the blanket of the dark to cry "Hold, hold!"'

Her voice grew hoarse. The music was wild, maddening. Lilith held Macbeth's letter up to the crimson light. Then she tore it to shreds and ate them.

'What the deuce is she doing?' Silas cried.

Sounds of disgust rippled through the audience. I stared, fascinated and appalled. Lilith was out of her wits, but it was working: every horrified face in that vast auditorium was trained upon her as she stuffed the torn pieces into her mouth.

The red filter slipped away like a blood moon; the nightmare had passed.

'Well,' I gasped. 'That was ... different.'

Anthony Frost dashed in as the newly arrived Macbeth. He hardly mattered any more. Not after what we'd seen.

Lilith rose to her feet, altered. She had a poise, a presence that I'd only seen once before. The watch was a pendulum, moving back and forth across her thigh.

Anthony faltered for an instant. Beside her, he seemed a flimsy, mortal thing. '*My dearest love,*' he stuttered. '*Duncan comes here tonight.*'

I could see already how it would be. She was about to act him right off the stage.

———

Applause thundered through the auditorium. Shouts of 'Bravo!' came from the stalls; boys in the gallery stuck their fingers in their mouths and whistled.

Thanks to Lilith, it hadn't been a play. It was an assault on the senses, a feverish malady.

The cast reappeared to a wild ovation, but the curtain calls were for Lady Macbeth and Lady Macbeth alone.

She stood dazed on the apron of the stage, as if she couldn't comprehend what she'd done. A bullseye channelled the limelight full upon her face. She squinted and raised a hand to shield her eyes, a somnambulist roused from a dream.

She was still wearing the nightgown from the 'Out, damned spot' scene. It had caught on the sleeve. There was a rent in the arm that I'd have to sew up before tomorrow ... But I couldn't think of tomorrow. I couldn't think of anything except what I'd just witnessed.

The call boy handed Lilith a bouquet of lilies. Perspiration gleamed from her bone-white skin. As I watched, beads of blood formed at her right nostril and trickled in a stripe to her lip. I couldn't help remembering what had happened to the last actor who'd worn that watch.

'She's sick,' I told Silas. 'I think she's going to faint.'

At last, the curtain came down. Lilith tottered offstage and leant her full weight against me. I shuddered. She smelt of sweat and something else, something rotten.

'Silas, do you have those smelling salts?' I asked, but Silas was backing away, his eyes wary, leaving me saddled with the corpse of Lady Macbeth.

Blood was streaming now, dripping down her white night-gown. I pulled out my handkerchief and held it under her nose. Lilith draped her arm over my shoulder. Her eyes were glazed. I would practically have to carry her to the dressing room.

After Anthony's triumph last night, the other actors had gathered round and congratulated him, but no one approached Lilith. There was a frightened hush, at odds with the ovation beyond the curtain, as I dragged her away.

What had happened to her out on that stage? I couldn't get the image out of my head: Lady Macbeth, asking demons to fill her. Was it some invocation to her beloved Melpomene? Whatever she'd done, it had worked. And that terrified me most of all.

Eurydice whimpered as we entered the dressing room. Rather than rushing up to check her mistress was all right, she cowered in the corner with her tail beneath her legs.

I propped Lilith on the dressing-table stool. 'What on earth was that?' I cried.

She couldn't look up at me; she seemed to have difficulty fully opening her eyes.

The lights flickered.

I could leave her. Run away from ... whatever this was. I took a step towards the door. But it turned out I was like Macbeth: *too full of the milk of human kindness.*

I wanted Lilith out of this theatre; I didn't want her to die like Eugene Grieves.

She swayed on the stool, nearly collapsed. I ran to catch her. I'd get her changed into her normal clothes, at least.

The lights crackled. I ignored them, focused on my task. When I let down Lilith's hair, dark strands came away with the pins. There was a grey streak I hadn't noticed before ... or maybe that was the wavering of the lights.

I had to peel the nightgown off her slick skin. How was I supposed to get the bloodstains out before tomorrow night? All those drips from her nose and then the tear on the sleeve ... but that was bloody, too.

'You've cut your arm! How did you do that?'

The lights started to flash wildly. Our reflections blinked in and out of the mirror, as though we were caught in the middle of a stage effect.

Lilith just sat trembling. It was only when I detached Eugene Grieves's watch from her girdle that she snapped to life. 'Careful with that!'

'I will be. It's stopped ticking.'

'I'll wind it myself,' Lilith insisted, producing the key from a small box on the table. But her fingers were shaking too much. I took both items from her.

Now I had two horrible memories associated with this watch. I ran my thumb over the figure of Melpomene and remembered her painted eyes peering indifferently down from the ceiling of the Helicon as Eugene Grieves wheezed his last breath with no one to comfort him.

Flipping the watch over, I slotted the key into its hole. It turned with a grating noise, like fingernails across slate. There were words scratched into the back of the case. Not engraved by the jeweller; someone had carved them jaggedly with a nail or a pin.

Homo fuge

What was that? A name? Latin? I recognised it from some-where. I'd definitely heard it before ...

'Did you see this, Lilith? What do you think it means?'

She didn't answer. Her nose was bleeding again.

CHAPTER 10

There was a bite in the air, foretelling the season of dense coal smoke and fog to come. London carried a bittersweet atmosphere as the dregs of autumn dribbled away. But this winter would be better for me. There was enough fuel at home to pile the fire high. We all had new shoes and comforters. In a few days, Bertie would have the operation that started a new chapter of his life. My job had saved us.

When I considered that, the cloud of my fears dispersed, like my breath in the cold air. I convinced myself that the strange aura surrounding Lilith was just another theatrical illusion. All I had to do was dress the woman. It was a small price to pay for my family's comfort.

Still, I was reluctant to see Lilith again after that night. I dawdled on my way to work. A stall squatted on the corner of the street, where a man in a battered top hat was selling newspapers, pictures and books. I stopped to look. There were copies of *The Era*. I could buy one and read what was written about Lilith's animalistic Lady Macbeth ... But no. I was too angry over what she'd done to Mrs Dyer. Any words of praise for her would gall.

The streets seemed busier than usual as I approached the Mercury. Servants hurried by and clerks filed past me in their black coats and bowler hats. That was strange. Their offices in the city were in the other direction.

At first I thought there must have been an accident, an overturned cart that had blocked a road and caused a diversion. But the closer I drew to the theatre, the more tightly the pavement was packed. When I finally caught sight of Mercury on his pediment, the traffic came to a complete stop.

A queue looped from the gated entrance of the box office right round the street. I'd never seen anything like it. A swarm of eager bodies pressed forward, not caring who they crushed. What, exactly, had that review in *The Era* said?

I shouldered my way through. Huffs and curses followed me, shouts of 'Wait your turn!' One of the ushers appeared wearing the front-of-house uniform and hung a placard saying SOLD OUT upon the gate.

There was a universal cry of dismay. I didn't fancy staying outside for too long. This crowd could turn ugly at any moment.

'Let me pass!' I ordered. 'Get out of my way, I work here.'

Someone grabbed my sleeve. I tugged my arm away but the grip was insistent, pulling me to one side. 'Miss. Miss!'

I turned to see a young, clean-shaven gentleman with a green carnation in his buttonhole. He looked out of place in that tussle, his polished shoes rapidly losing their shine as others stepped on his feet.

'What?' I barked.

'Do you truly work inside the theatre?'

'Yes. I'll be late.' I went to move on, but his other hand seized my elbow.

'Please! Please, tell me if you work with Miss Erikson.' His eyes implored me.

'Might do. What's it to you?'

He released me and pulled out a pink, fragranced envelope. 'Be so kind as to pass on that letter. And …' He wet his lips. 'If you could obtain one of her … ahem … personal effects. Say, a stocking. I would be willing to pay you twenty pounds.'

My eyebrows raised. 'One of her *stockings*?'

'Fifty pounds,' he amended hurriedly, signalling for me to lower my voice.

Fifty pounds! The young swell was cracked. More money than sense. I could easily get a stocking, and Lilith would never miss it.

'Meet me at the stage door in half an hour,' I said.

Joy lit up his face. He clasped me again. 'Thank you. A thousand times, thank you.' He was getting too close.

'Miss Wilcox, is this man bothering you?' Oscar appeared beside us with his hands fisted on his hips. The gentleman dropped me at once, blushing furiously.

'I can handle it. He was just on his way.'

'Yes. Yes, I was. Good day.' Tipping his hat, he pushed back into the crowd and was swallowed almost at once.

Oscar watched him go. Then he scanned the churn of people, all ages, races and classes. 'Blimey,' he said. 'Have you ever seen a crush like this?'

'It's Bedlam.'

'Take my arm. We'll get through together.' It was handy to have Oscar at my side. He was taller and broader than me, good at elbowing others out the way.

'I hope it's not going to be like this every day,' I called over the hubbub.

'It might be. Miss Erikson wasn't half good.'

We fell silent for a moment, negotiating a woman with a perambulator. 'I didn't like her performance,' I admitted. 'It turned my stomach.'

'Yeah, but it was supposed to, wasn't it? That's the play. Lady Macbeth's meant to be horrible. But then her remorse with "Out, damned spot" … she was perfect there. That was the best scene performed since … I don't know. Maybe it was the best I've ever seen.'

I bit my tongue. I knew what Mrs Dyer would say about Oscar, about that young gent. She'd say they were under Lilith's spell.

We stumbled into the yard. They'd closed the gate to keep out the riff-raff, but Oscar had a key.

I slipped my arm from the crook of his elbow.

'Thanks,' I said, self-conscious. 'I'd better be on my way.'

He nodded. 'Take care.'

I wished he was going into the theatre with me, but he headed for the workshop instead. I shook myself. The Mercury was the same building as it had always been. Nothing about it had changed last night … Yet I found myself hesitant to enter. It felt like we were under new management, and that management was Melpomene.

No cats stalked the corridor that morning. Both they and the mice seemed to have jumped ship. Voices rose and fell in Anthony's dressing room; it sounded as though he was arguing with Silas. His door looked a little scratched, some of the gold paint had chipped away.

Lilith's door flew open at my approach and the Guvnor emerged, flushed and smiling. Nodding briefly to me, he closed the door behind him and set off in the other direction.

Bile rose in my throat. They were brazen with it now. Didn't he care who saw him? But maybe there were other people in there too, for I could still hear Lilith's laughter through the wall. Whoever sat with her was clearly very entertaining.

At least the presence of someone else in the room might help me to steal the stocking for that gent without detection. Fifty pounds! More than a year's worth of my already generous wage. For all my dislike of Lilith, I had to give her some credit: she was certainly paying my bills. I knocked once. When I entered, Lilith was alone. Just sitting before the mirror, cackling to herself. She'd draped the watch over the top, letting it hang beside her reflection. The minute marker crept forward.

There were more lilies than ever, in addition to confectionary, fruit baskets and piles of letters. Eurydice had her nose in a tin of Turkish delight.

'What's the joke?' I asked.

Lilith only threw back her head and whooped louder. I shivered. If the street outside was Bedlam, Lilith was one of its patients.

'Feeling better, then?' Moving to the wardrobe, I checked over the costumes. I'd brushed them down the night before, but I must have been distracted by Lilith's nosebleed. Smuts marked the hem of the damson skirt. There was something on the queen's dress too, a fine white powder like ash. Tutting, I wiped at them. The black marks smeared.

'Can't you keep anything nice?' I fretted. 'What's this, speckled all over? I haven't time to run these through the laundry and make you a new nightgown before this evening.'

'Oh, never mind that! Look at all this, Kitty! It worked. It really worked!' She grabbed a newspaper from the dressing table and waved it at me. 'Did you read it? Did you see what they said?'

'No. I watched the show myself. Why would I care what a critic thinks?'

She cackled again. 'I gave them the shock of their lives! Sent those fusty old journalists apoplectic. They called me unwomanly, said I ripped the Bard's poetry with my teeth. They ought to have known that wouldn't put the public off.'

I turned my back on her and tidied the wardrobe. The first stocking I came across was a woollen one, lightly worn. It wasn't quite clean – but I had a feeling that queer gent would like it better that way. My neat stitches made the initials L. E. near the top; I embroidered them on all of Lilith's things so there were no mix ups with the laundry. It was the closest to proof of ownership he'd get.

Grimacing, I slipped the stocking into my pocket. The commission was distasteful, but Lilith was hardly the modest sort. I would've felt much worse taking Clementine's things.

'Only see what they've sent me! Rimmel's perfume. Silver earrings, rose acid … I could set up my own shop.'

I closed the wardrobe and came to see what she was talking about. She was right; it was excessive. Piles and piles of gifts. My scruples disappeared. Lilith could spare me one stocking.

'Someone on the street gave me a billet-doux for you,' I said, slapping the pink envelope down. 'You've got enough admirers, now. Maybe you can give the Guvnor back to his wife.'

She dismissed my words with a toss of her head. 'They love me! I almost regret using a stage name. I want everyone to see this, every churl who curled their lip and said I couldn't do it. My uncle! Oh, my uncle will *spit*!' She clapped her hands in glee. 'Now, what's this? Oh, a little note. How sweet.' She opened it and giggled. 'Such drivel. They've fallen head over heels for Lady M, haven't they? Say what you like, the gentlemen want a nasty woman at heart.'

'Well, they're lucky they found you, then,' I sniffed. Beneath the perfume and the lilies, there was a hint of something sour. Rotten eggs. Sulphur. 'What's that stink?'

'It's gas. Mephitic vapours. The smell might go away if you get that light fixed, you know. Oh, blast.' Her arm was bleeding again, leeching through the thin material of her day gown. 'I bound it so tightly, as well.'

She was nothing but a mess of bandages beneath that dress. Bindings around her waist, her breasts and now her arm. The Lilith the audience saw was held together by lint. Utterly false.

'How did you even cut it?' I asked wearily.

She looked away. 'For all I know, you clawed me during a costume change.'

'Try to make it stop by tonight, will you?' I sighed. 'And don't, whatever you do, have another nosebleed. I won't remake this nightdress again.'

Speaking of which, I needed to be on my way: I'd struggle to drop the stocking off with the gent and run up a new costume in time, even with the sewing machine.

'Jenny, wait.'

I froze beside the door. She'd never used my real name before. 'What is it?'

Lilith picked up one of the ribbon-tied boxes and held it out to me. 'Take one. You were kind to me last night, when I was ill.'

'I wasn't. I was just doing my job.'

'So you say. But I think maybe you have a heart, after all.'

Awkwardly, I shook my head and left the room with Lilith still proffering the box. Perhaps she did mean well. But it reminded me of the barley twists from the neighbour who stole Da, and I'd been listening to Mrs Dyer for too long. I wasn't about to take sweets from a witch.

It was a mercy to escape from those cloying fumes. I strode to the stage door, which I rarely used, for it gave on to an alleyway where the theatre men smoked cheroots and relieved themselves. Frost diluted the stench that morning. A bone-grubber poked through a pile of trash with his stick. Broken glass sparkled on the cobbles. The gentleman in quest of a stocking would be even more out of place here.

Just as I was glancing about for him, a hand touched my arm. 'Jenny.'

I turned and the street seemed to be rushing, hurtling towards me. It was my brother. Gregory.

My first reaction was a surge of love. Uncontrollable, the instinct of many years. I hated myself for that; hated him for making me feel it.

'You look as if you've seen a ghost.'

I couldn't speak, but I reached out and slapped his face.

Greg recoiled, eyes wide. 'Ow! Well, I guess I deserved that.'

'Too right you deserved it!' I managed to grind out. 'What the hell are you doing back? How do you have the brass to show yourself here, of all places?'

He raked a hand through his hair. He'd always been the handsomest sibling, with embers of copper in his locks and flecks of gold in his hazel eyes, but he was looking worse for wear. His collar was dirty. Stubble shadowed his chin. 'I'm sorry, Jen. It all happened so fast. There wasn't time for goodbyes. Georgiana got this opportunity in New York and we had to go.'

Rage filled me so completely, I thought the force of it would lift my feet off the floor. 'You think I'm annoyed that you didn't say farewell? I couldn't give two straws for your goodbyes. What about Bertie's money? What about Miss Fielding's rings?'

He scuffed his shoe against the cobbles. 'I know. I'm sorry ... I was always going to pay you back.'

'It wasn't a bloody loan! You didn't even ask. You *stole*, from my employer too! Do you have any idea what I went through? I'm lucky I only lost my place. I could have ended up in prison!'

'I said I'm sorry! I made mistakes. Christ, Jenny, you know what it's been like for me! All that responsibility. Being the man of the house at thirteen years old! I saw a chance to have something good, all for myself, and I took it. I did what *I* wanted to do, for the first time in my life.'

I could've hit him again. 'Do you expect me to feel sorry for you? All that you've been through, I've suffered too. Bleeding hell, Greg. You betrayed your family and stole your best friend's fiancée, and you expect us to welcome you back with open arms?'

The bone-grubber was watching us with interest. I scowled at him.

Gregory picked at his nails. 'Anyway,' he went on, 'it's all worked out for the best, hasn't it? Look at you now! I could hardly believe it when I heard you were at the Mercury. And now Miss Erikson's made such a success …'

As if he'd done me a favour! My stomach dropped another rung. Greg had been a good brother to me, growing up, I never dreamed he'd hurt us. But I wasn't going to be blind like Mrs Dyer. I forced myself to stare his treachery in the face.

'That's why you're here, isn't it? You've turned up on the day of our triumph because you want something. So where's Georgiana? Licking her wounds now that Lilith's proved herself the better actress? Or did she pack you back off to England like a piece of unwanted baggage?'

Greg nibbled his lip. 'Don't be like that. She's my wife now.'

That surprised me. No doubt she'd compromised her good name by travelling alone with Greg, but I wouldn't have expected that to bother an actress. 'You got further than Oscar, then,' I said bitterly.

He ignored that. 'How are the others? I was going to visit them all at home today. I wanted to talk to you alone, first, but obviously that was a mistake.'

I didn't want him seeing the children, worming himself back into their confidence. Bertie idolised his eldest brother and Greg would only let him down again. 'You can't. We've moved. We've got our own house now.' It was only a white lie; we were going to find a new place soon. Besides, I wanted to rub it in his face, to show how well I'd coped without him.

'Where?'

'It's not your business any more.'

He took a step towards me. 'Damn it, Jenny, I've a right to see my own kin—'

The stage door slammed behind us. Oscar.

Greg visibly paled. My handprint stood out on his cheek, a livid accusation. 'There you are, Thorne. I was hoping to see you.'

Oscar balled his hands into fists. 'You've got a bleeding nerve.'

While Greg had expected me to be forgiving, he obviously didn't extend that optimism towards Oscar. He edged back a little. 'Thorne ... Thorne, you can't really be that shocked,' he stuttered. 'You must've seen it was coming! You didn't take Georgie's side over Lilith's promotion ... It hurt her, when you kept saying it was the right choice.'

'So I asked for it, did I?' Oscar spat. 'Me telling my fiancée she'd be better off at a comic theatre gave you the right to steal her?'

'No ... I'm not saying that.'

I crossed my arms. 'Turns out Oscar knew best, though. Lilith's the toast of the town and Georgiana's clearly made a mess of whatever chance she had in New York, if you've washed up back here.'

'I won't listen to you insult my wife,' Greg said, ironing out the tremor in his voice.

Oscar drew back his arm and punched him.

They began to scuffle. I leapt away, frightened now. One of them could get seriously hurt. Oscar had strength, but Greg was nimble, he pulled his former friend into a headlock.

'Stop that!' Lilith's voice rang as imperious as it did on stage. Even stepping into the alleyway, she carried herself with the poise of a queen. Eurydice flanked her, black hackles raised. 'You'll wake the dead with this commotion. Some people are *trying* to rehearse.'

The change in the men was instantaneous; they sprang apart, watching the dog.

I never thought I'd be glad to see Lilith, but I was.

'Jenny, I've warned you not to hang round the stage door. It attracts these unsavoury sorts.' She swept her disdainful gaze over Greg. 'People who have no business on this property.' At a touch from her mistress, Eurydice curled back her lips and growled. Her teeth were sharp and pointed, stained with the rose tint of Turkish delight. 'You had better be on your way,' Lilith warned him, 'before my dog removes you.'

Greg didn't need telling twice. He turned and fled, like the coward he was.

CHAPTER 11

Maybe it was poor form of me not to tell Dorcas that I'd seen our brother. But we were preparing Bertie for his hospital visit, cuddling him and telling him to be a brave boy. I didn't want Greg's name crashing into the room like a drunken actor, trying to steal the limelight.

The Royal Orthopaedic Hospital was a proud structure of red-brick and white windows. While Dorcas took Bertie inside, I paced the street alone, fretting. Mrs Dyer said it was a relatively simple procedure, but it was hard to dismiss dark thoughts. I imagined infections, accidents, braced myself for Bertie needing his whole leg amputated. After all that had happened in the past year, I couldn't allow myself to relax. I needed to be on guard, ready to cope with the next woe.

Finally, the door opened and Bertie emerged, hobbling on Dorcas's arm. The boot, brace and callipers were bigger than both the poor child's legs put together. He looked pale, but triumphant.

'Jenny!' he cried, spotting me at once. 'Jenny, they've cut my acky-lays tendon!'

Smiling at his pronunciation, I presented him with a bag of treacle squibs. 'Well, isn't that marvellous? What a good boy you are. And good boys get treats!'

'Hooray!'

'He didn't complain a bit,' Dorcas added as Bertie devoured the sweets. 'I was more scared than him!'

I patted her arm. 'You ought to have a squib too. The sugar will pick you up.'

'Can I go to the theatre now? Can I climb the steps?' Bertie demanded, his mouth full.

As if I'd let the baby of my family see Lilith's hideous Lady Macbeth! 'Not yet. Soon. I imagine there's a long road to recovery.'

'He has exercises to do,' Dorcas said. 'It'll take him a bit of time, especially since he's that much older. We need to guard against gangrene. But the doctor's hopeful.'

Tears pricked my eyes. It was such a relief to think that Bertie could have more independence as he grew.

'Well that's good news, isn't it, little man?' I offered Bertie my arm. 'Let's look out for a cab and get you both home.'

'I ain't half tired,' he agreed.

As we turned back towards the road, a familiar-looking carriage pulled up in front of us. A black horse stood between the traces, its breath pluming in the cool air.

I nearly lost my balance. It was the Dyers' growler.

Mrs Dyer let down the window, beaming her wide grin. 'Good afternoon, Jennifer. Why do you look so astonished? You can't imagine I'd let this little hero troop all the way home.'

'Mrs Dyer ...' I'd barely taken in what she'd said. 'This is my sister, Dorcas. Here's little Bertie – Albert. I didn't expect—'

Mrs Dyer held up a hand. 'I know perfectly well who these lovely young people are, there is no need for introductions. Any friend of Jennifer's, my dears, is a friend of mine. Now, young Albert. How would you like to celebrate by riding home in my carriage?'

Bertie looked like all his Christmases had come at once.

'We couldn't possibly ...' I began – but James the footman had already disembarked and was swinging open the door.

Mrs Dyer waited for the steps to unfold, then climbed out onto the pavement, no longer dressed in black but wearing a paletot jacket, a tight, bustled skirt of mauve taffeta and Moliere shoes.

'Up you go. You too, Miss Dorcas. I am sure your nerves have been tried sorely.'

Dorcas floundered. Little Rachel and her nursemaid sat on the squabs opposite. 'But we won't all fit inside.'

'Jennifer and I shall walk. We have business to discuss.'

I didn't fancy Mrs Dyer's odds of making it in those shoes, but maybe she only meant to accompany me part of the way.

Dorcas glanced at me for approval. I nodded. She clambered up, the apples of her cheeks pinking as she sat on the fine upholstery.

The driver cracked his whip and the growler pulled away. My heart sank. I didn't relish the thought of a tête-à-tête with Mrs Dyer. There could be only one subject between us.

'You shall have to lead the way, Jennifer. I am accustomed to let Lightfoot navigate for me.'

I set off slowly, making allowance for her short, mincing steps in that bustled skirt. An omnibus rattled past us, advertising cocoa powder. By the side of the road was a Punch and Judy show with a crowd of children gathered round. A few yards further down, an old woman had set up camp to sell peg dolls. Mrs Dyer followed my gaze and smiled indulgently. 'Ah. May God bless their little hearts. Such simple pleasures one has as a child.' I didn't reply. My childhood had been far from simple. 'Little Albert behaved impeccably. I fancy most children would be drenched in tears after undergoing the procedure he has faced.'

'Yes, madam. That's the way with Bertie. He never cries when you expect him to, but sets up a fuss about trifling things.' I paused. 'We really are very grateful to you for helping him. Especially after all your ... disappointment.'

She was silent for a moment as we crossed the street. 'As you can see, I have tried the utmost to pull myself into something resembling composure. Necessity has turned me into a thespian myself. Hugh has no suspicions that I am aware of his secret. He blunders on in ignorance, while I watch his every move.'

Always espionage with her. Was play-acting the only amusement carrying her through her sorrow? 'Have you decided what you're going to do about your ... predicament?'

'I steal into Hugh's library at night to read any correspondence he brings home. I am attempting to trace the child.'

This surprised me. 'You are? What for? Are you going to adopt it?'

'Heavens, no! I want to know where it is. Whether my husband is using my money to support the wretched creature. I must have all the information to hand before I broach the matter with him.'

A wretched creature. I remembered the infant in the photograph, its nest of dark hair, and my feelings softened. I hated what the baby represented, but at the end of the day, it was just that: a child that needed caring for, the same as any other. 'It's not really the baby's fault ...' I tried to remind her.

'I cannot see it as a baby, Jennifer. It is a *threat*. To my marriage, to our theatre's reputation, to Rachel herself. Suppose Hugh should make a will to favour this bastard child? Imagine if after death, all his money – which, you know, is mostly my own – should pass not to Rachel, but to the spawn of that ... that ...' She raised a handkerchief to her mouth.

Misgiving nibbled at my stomach. Only a moment ago, she'd looked at the children watching Punch and Judy with affection. Usually Mrs Dyer was generosity itself, but when it came to Lilith Erikson or Eugene Grieves, there was a whiff of the fanatic about her.

Would I be the same, faced with the offspring of my Da and the woman who'd stolen him? With a child of Greg and Georgiana's? I hoped not. But I couldn't say for sure.

'It's tricky,' I admitted. 'Even if you confront the Guvnor, he won't get rid of Lilith. No theatre manager in London would sack her now.'

'No.' Mrs Dyer shook her head and her earrings swung. 'No, the minx put us in a bind, as she surely meant to do. We have a full house booked every night of the run! Losing the ticket money would be nothing to me, but if we threaten to dismiss her ... She has some powerful blackmail to wield over us. Living, breathing proof of Hugh's shame.' Her lips wobbled again. 'I must protect my family! There has to be a way. Some method we are not considering.'

I mused on that. Remembered how queenly Lilith had seemed in the alleyway, how Greg and Oscar had stopped fighting on her command. 'It's her talent that's the problem, isn't it? It gives her power. Now people listen to her in a way they never did before.'

'Perhaps if she were to give one or two bad performances ... perhaps that would break the spell?'

I frowned. 'Maybe. But is she likely to?'

'There might be something you could do. Something to … throw her off.'

I sifted through my thoughts like the pages of a play. Lilith's star had only rocketed since she received that watch. If it went missing, somehow … That would shake her confidence for sure.

'Maybe …' I started, but Mrs Dyer stopped abruptly by my side.

'I have it. Gracious Heaven, Jennifer, I think I have it. A way to take her out of action, as it were. But it will all depend upon you.'

Warning bells began to clang inside my head. 'Take her out of action?' I repeated.

'In a manner of speaking. Do not concern yourself, I shall arrange all the details.' Suddenly she was beaming, radiant. 'Of course. Of course! Why did I not think of it before? But it cannot take place immediately. Let me see … It must be Sunday. A Sunday evening when the theatre is closed and no one is around.' Mrs Dyer linked her arm through mine and walked on with a new vigour to her step. 'That wretched actress thinks she is so clever. But the Mercury is my theatre. Hugh is my husband. I am the heroine of this play, and I shall write the ending.'

CHAPTER 12

Other theatres were planning pantomimes and Christmas spectaculars, but Lilith's notorious performance kept the demand for *Macbeth* sky high. We were still turning disappointed punters away from the box office each morning. It looked like the Scottish play would run until the New Year at least.

Maybe the sets and costumes weren't designed to last that long. Or maybe everyone was so busy keeping up with the new matinees that they simply didn't have time to clean. But it seemed to me that the Mercury itself wasn't thriving amidst its success. The more vivid and alive the action on stage, the more insipid everything else became.

I sat on the sofa in Lilith's dressing room, brushing out the queen's brocade gown for what felt like the hundredth time. Around the hem were little black-edged holes, the kind of singe a gentleman might make by accident with a cigar. Or had it touched the footlights, somehow?

Lilith wasn't laughing tonight. Her attention was focused on the watch. In the unnatural silence all I could hear was the mechanism, its whir and tick.

Now that I studied her reflection, I saw the mirror was foxed, speckled black at the edges although I cleaned it every day, and beneath the fug of the lilies there was still that rancid, carrion breath.

I glanced at Eurydice. Her coat was clean, her eyes bright; she didn't appear to be spreading dirt, but something was destroying all my hard work in this dressing room. What on earth went on in here when we left?

'Lilith?' I said. Silence followed. I gritted my teeth. It was often the third or fourth attempt before she deigned to reply to me. 'Lilith, we need to get you dressed.'

She kept her eyes down. 'Is it that time already?'

'See for yourself! You're gawping right at a watch, aren't you?'

Convulsively, she snapped the cover closed. 'I wasn't looking at the hands. I was ... listening.'

'To what?'

'To the muse. And there's no need to turn your nose up, Kitty. You might think I'm not quite the shilling, but my belief in Melpomene's carried me this far, hasn't it?' She sighed. 'Eugene taught me how to fail, how to bear myself gracefully if someone catcalled, how to face down bad reviews. There was never a lesson on what to do with ...' she gestured at the bouquets and gifts jammed on every surface, 'all of this. Success. He never thought Melpomene would call upon anyone but him.'

'Can't you just enjoy your good luck?'

'I *am* enjoying it,' she growled. 'But it's not luck. It's destiny. A higher calling.'

The lights blinked hectically.

'Well, this high and mighty thespian still needs someone to comb her hair and fasten her dress. Don't you forget it.'

'As if you would let me. Melpomene might be calling me upwards, but you, Kitty, are my siren, dragging me back to earth. You still haven't fixed those lights! What other star is forced to endure a thunderstorm in her dressing room?'

Our demanding schedule was taking its toll on Lilith's appearance. Her eyes were bloodshot, her skin drier than ever. That grey streak I'd noticed in her hair had widened to the thickness of a finger, and while I could colour it, or cover a multitude of sins with grease paint, it struck me that if this was any other person, I'd feel concern.

Scabs covered the wound at the top of her arm, near the shoulder. I'd stopped asking how she'd hurt it, but my mind still toyed with the puzzle. It wasn't a scratch that might occur accidently, brushing up against a scenery flat. This was a cut with jagged edges.

The call boy tapped on the door. A mask seemed to settle over Lilith's face. I thought of what Anthony had said about the transformation from actor into character; it really did feel as though Lilith herself had got up and left the room already.

'I'm not watching tonight,' I said. 'I've work to do.'

With a single nod, she rose and strode away.

Eurydice released a long, tired sigh. I watched her for a moment, waiting for a sign of mischief. Nothing. Whatever was causing the smell and the marks, it wasn't the dog.

Pulling out the dressing-table stool, I climbed up to examine the lights. The jets burned on steadily with no reek of gas. I stared, mesmerised by the gentle yellow dance of the flames. What Lilith didn't know was that I *had* asked one of the gasmen to look at the lights earlier that day. He said there was nothing wrong with them.

Nothing visible, perhaps. Instead, I followed my nose. The stench was worse to the side of the dressing table, and reached behind the mirror. All I could think was that a mouse had died and got trapped between the furniture and the skirting.

Climbing down, I grabbed the dressing table and pushed it aside. Bottles wobbled. For the first time, I could see the wall behind the mirror. I gasped.

Scorch marks were smudged across the pale lemon paper. Some were small and spiderlike, others large as the palm of a hand. There couldn't have been a fire, here. I would have known. Gingerly, I touched the wall. Some of the paper had blistered. I could almost feel it, bubbling away.

Voices rose from next door. This was the wall that stood between the dressing rooms of the two lead actors – surely if there were problems in here, Anthony would have them too? There was only one way to find out.

A tabby cat occupied the corridor, its narrow pupils tracking my progress. When I knocked on Anthony's door, Silas poked his pomaded head out.

'Is Lilith nearby?' he hissed.

I shook my head. Wordlessly, he took my arm and pulled me inside the dressing room.

Anthony stood by the cheval glass. He wore Macbeth's doublet, but the ties at the end of his sleeves were undone. 'It's nothing,

Silas. Don't get Miss Wilcox involved. Leave it be, there's a good chap.'

'Nothing!' Silas repeated, incredulous. 'My dear fellow, how far does it have to go before it's *something*? When she pulls your deuced arm off?'

'Oh, come now.'

I looked between the two of them. 'What's all this about?'

Anthony opened his mouth, but Silas spoke first. 'Your actress, Miss Wilcox, is simply out of control. She's run wild. Show her, Anthony, show her what that abominable woman did to you.'

Anthony massaged a hand over his lantern jaw. 'Really, old chap, I'd rather—'

He didn't finish his sentence, for his dresser seized his wrist and pulled up the sleeve. 'There! What do you make of *that*, Miss Wilcox?' My eyes widened. Anthony's arm was purple and black with bruises. Four scratches raked the skin near his wrist; one of them wept. 'And the other arm is just the same.'

I felt ill, remembering how Lilith had bruised my hand. 'Lilith did this?'

Anthony shifted uncomfortably. 'I doubt she means to. In the heat of the scene, during a performance … she rather jostles a fellow.'

'All this was the work of a moment! He only ran on to say the king was coming and she clutched at him like a vice!'

I'd seen her grab at Macbeth's arms, as she was directed to, but I had no idea she gripped so hard.

'Just patch me up, there's a good man. I've to deliver another monologue in a moment.' Anthony hesitated. 'Having said that, Lady M comes on after I speak. Better wrap something extra thick to pad me out.'

'I've bandages,' I said and dashed to fetch them. The same lint strips that bound Lilith's wound would have to serve for the ones she inflicted, too.

It was a mad rush to get Anthony ready in time. I didn't stop to absorb what I'd just learnt or consider how it made me feel. But once the call boy came for him, and Silas and I were alone in the dressing room, I realised I was afraid.

I'd warmed a degree or two towards Lilith when she sent Greg packing. Venom against my brother had blinded me to the warning sign. Surely the kind of woman who'd threaten a person with her dog was dangerous?

'Maybe we should tell the Guvnor,' I said quietly. 'That's twice she's hurt someone.'

'Dear girl, you know he won't hear a word against her.'

'There's ... something strange going on, Silas. Not just with Lilith. The lights keep flickering, and there are these burn marks on the wall ...' I moved to examine the wall between the dressing rooms. It was clean on this side. I pressed my hand against it, as I had next door, and felt only a vague heat. 'It all started when the Guvnor gave Lilith that watch.'

'Ill-gotten gains,' he remarked darkly.

'She thinks it's blessed by the Muse Melpomene but ... it feels more like a curse to me. And I've never been one to believe in that sort of thing.'

Thoughtfully, Silas fiddled with his lower lip. 'Hmm. There may be something in that, after all. The life of Eugene Grieves was successful, certainly, but his theatre was plagued with misfortune. A chandelier fell on the audience at a benefit performance once. And then there was that poor supernumerary actor in *The String of Pearls*. Can't remember his name. He got caught in Sweeney Todd's revolving barber chair.' He tutted, pained. 'Dreadful, dreadful business.'

This watch didn't just inspire tragic acting; it seemed to bring tragedy in its wake. 'Silas, there's something I've been meaning to ask. You know some Latin, don't you?'

'Yes, why?'

'What does *Homo fuge* mean?'

He turned pale. 'Wherever did you hear that?'

'It's scratched on the back of the pocket watch. I thought I knew it from somewhere.'

'Good God.' He subsided onto a chair. His lips pressed together so hard that they disappeared beneath his moustache. 'Let that be a caution to us all.'

'What's wrong, Silas? What have I said?'

'Those words, Miss Wilcox, are an injunction to flee. They urge any mortal to fly as swiftly as possible before disaster can overtake them. They are in the play *Doctor Faustus*. Have you seen it? The words appear in blood on Faustus's arm, crying against his pact with Mephistopheles.'

I had a horrible sensation then, like the skin was shrinking on my bones. I was back in the gallery of the Helicon with Philip's frightened voice piping in my ear. *Did that really happen, Jenny? Did the Devil come and carry that man off to Hell?*

'Maybe ... maybe Eugene Grieves carved them on the watch? Maybe he liked that part of the play,' I said lamely.

'Or maybe he was warning others against dealing with Melpomene.'

I pushed wayward strands of hair back behind my ears. 'No. No, there's no such thing as Melpomene. She's just a story actors tell themselves. Like that horseshoe they all touch before they go on stage. It gives them confidence.'

'My dear child, I've been working in the theatre since before you were born. Let me tell you, there is more to all this superstition than you would care to believe. Playhouses are not like other places. They are a portal, between our realm and countless others.'

Perhaps it didn't matter whether it was true, only that the actors *believed* it was true. Anthony's striking portrayal of Macbeth had stuttered and died over nothing more than the Guvnor failing to reward him. Lilith behaved as though she were untouchable because of her conviction Melpomene was with her. Maybe a good performance depended on the actor's state of mind, every bit as much as their training?

I remembered what Mrs Dyer had said about throwing Lilith off. She may have her own ideas for next Sunday, but I was the one working with Lilith day in and day out. I knew her. I knew what would work.

'I want to get that watch away from her. It would take the wind out of her sails. She'd perform differently and she might calm down a bit.' I looked hopefully at Silas. 'Maybe then, Anthony would have the chance to shine again?'

His eyes sparked with interest. 'Do not stop at half-measures. If what you've told me is true, it is not enough to simply take the watch. That contraption must be destroyed.'

As always, Silas went one step too far. I dreaded to consider what Mrs Dyer would say if her precious relic was damaged. 'I'm not sure that's possible.'

'Can't you "accidentally" smash it?'

'How? Lilith checks it before every stage entrance.' I rubbed my hand instinctively, feeling the ghosts of my bruises. 'You saw what she did to Anthony. If I broke her watch, I'm not sure I'd live to tell the tale.'

Planting his elbows on his knees, Silas propped his face in his hands. 'Of course,' he said slowly, 'you know what the Guvnor has planned for tomorrow.'

It took me a second to recall. 'Photographs?'

'Cabinet cards. They're all the rage, these days. People want a little piece of the actors to own. There will be separate portraits of Lilith and Anthony. But I have it on good authority that the Guvnor is planning one or two shots of them together.'

I didn't understand his point. All I could think was that poor Anthony would have to stand next to Lilith, after what she'd put him through tonight.

'You and I,' Silas went on, 'will be on hand to make sure they are absolutely perfect. The camera detects flaws that cannot be seen on stage. We shall have to re-powder their faces and tweak their costumes.'

'What are you driving at, Silas?'

'Lilith will wear her watch, but her focus will be on the camera. You say she checks the trinket before every scene, yet I doubt she'd go as far as to examine it between camera shots?'

'No ... probably not.'

'And so it is an opportunity like no other. You bend down, quite reasonably, to shake her skirt, to adjust the set of her hem, whatever you will.' He mimed the action from his chair. 'By a sleight of hand, you unclip the watch from its girdle and hide it in your palm.'

A cold, sick feeling crept over me. Could I do that without Lilith noticing? 'Then what?'

'Then, dear girl, you pass it to me. If she notices it gone, her suspicion may well alight on you, but a quick search will prove you innocent.'

That was some comfort. It still felt risky, though. 'And what, you'll take it for Anthony?'

'Certainly not!' He tossed his head. 'Anthony's brilliance does not depend on anything as ephemeral as a muse. He simply *has* talent. No, I shall make some pretence to go up to the wardrobe room. What I shall actually do is take a carpenter's hammer and break the hateful thing.' He smashed a fist down on his palm.

Silas made it sound so simple. Maybe it was. Just the idea of being rid of the watch, of never seeing those blistering pearls again, made me feel brighter. Mrs Dyer would be distraught, but at the end of the day she struck me as the kind of woman who would rather see the watch destroyed than in the hands of her rival.

'All right,' I decided. 'Let's do it tomorrow.'

A screech rent the air. I started, even though I'd heard it plenty of times. The sound of an owl. It meant that onstage, King Duncan lay dead and Macbeth would sleep no more.

Silas grinned at me. 'There is our omen, from the Mercury itself. Tomorrow the fiendish queen will fall.'

CHAPTER 13

Anthony had already posed for his solo portraits. He sat beside the Guvnor in the front row of the stalls, looking through the selection. He wore a royal blue doublet slashed with crimson and matching tights, but the man on the cards was reduced to shades of grey, black and white: Macbeth, crumbling to ash.

Now it was Lilith's turn to hold her 'point' alone on stage in front of the backdrop. I stood by the orchestra pit, clutching Eurydice's collar. She emitted a yip every time the powder flashed.

To me, it seemed like an excellent shot: Lady Macbeth in her purple brocade, placing the crown upon her brow. But the photographer kept disappearing beneath his hood and emerging with a sigh.

'What's taking so long?' Lilith demanded, trapped in her pose.

'We won't get a clear picture unless you hold still, madam.'

'I am!' Lilith barked.

The air was starting to taste of smoke.

Lilith appeared perfectly motionless, a statue, a pillar of salt. My eyes kept drifting down to the watch that swung halfway between her knee and hip. I *could* snatch it. I knew I could. Yet the thought of doing so gave me the same kind of nerves that fluttered through Clementine before she went on stage.

Eurydice snarled at another flash.

'Done?' Lilith asked through gritted teeth.

'I'm afraid not, madam. It's the muscles on your face. They blur on every plate.'

Huffing, she brought her arms down. 'Mr Dyer!' she called. 'Mr Dyer, this is unacceptable.'

The Guvnor glanced up from Anthony's photographs. 'What's this?'

Lilith stomped to the front of the stage and flung out an arm towards the photographer. 'I have been standing here stiff as a board, yet this fellow says I am blurred.'

'Come, that is simply not possible!' the Guvnor said reasonably. Handing the photographs to Anthony, he stood and walked over to where tailboard camera sat upon its tripod. 'May I see the supposed problem?'

The photographer and his assistant showed the Guvnor a stack of rejected plates. I crept closer for a look. The Lady Macbeth on the pictures had no clear outline. She was smudged, wispy at the edges. Her face looked doubled, sliding, caught in motion.

'No, no. This won't do at all.' The Guvnor stroked his side whiskers. 'But it is not Miss Erikson's fault. She knows how to stand for a photograph perfectly well.'

Inspiration struck. I saw our chance, and the fact that Lilith was flustered would only help matters. 'Perhaps, sir,' I suggested, 'we should take a break from this particular pose? Couldn't you take the photographs of Lilith and Anthony together? At least it would give her arms a bit of a rest.'

The Guvnor hadn't seen me creep up on him. He turned with surprise. 'Upon my soul, you are quite right, Miss Wilcox. A change of position will do the trick. Let us revisit this picture later on.'

I nudged Eurydice with my leg. 'Would you hold the dog, sir? She doesn't like the powder. I need to go and tidy up Miss Erikson.'

'Of course, of course. Come here, girl. You're not so bad after all, are you?'

Wearily, the photographer gave his orders on how the actors were to stand. Anthony traipsed up the stairs to the stage with Silas and me following in his wake. My heart was pumping like a piston.

'The thane is to stand gazing up and out to his destiny. Over yonder.' The photographer signalled the right-hand side of the dress circle. 'Perhaps a hand on his chest to show a stricken conscience. The lady leans on his shoulder. His left shoulder, madam. She is sinuous … slithering in to whisper her poison.'

'Oh, I see,' muttered Lilith. 'The man who commits the murder is wholly innocent, poor dear.'

'Wait,' I croaked. My vocal chords were pinched tight. I felt exposed there, up on the stage, the batten lights hot upon my head. 'Your face isn't even, and it folds your train to stand like that.'

'Yes, yes, let us work! Would you take photographs of these perfect frights?' Silas fussed round Anthony like a mother hen, nipping in to brush more powder onto his already waxen skin.

I didn't need to touch Lilith: she looked every inch the murderous queen. Still, I patted her hair and rouged her lips, all the while avoiding her eye.

Anthony planted his feet apart and stood as directed, noble chin raised. One hand rested on his scabbard, the other touched his heart. Lilith leant her weight against his shoulder.

Feeling sick, I bent and shook out her skirts. Even with the seats all empty, I had a sensation I was being watched. My hand didn't tremble; I detached the timepiece in one swift move without fumbling.

Blood rushed to my head as I stood up too fast, but Silas was at my side in an instant, palming the watch. I kept expecting Lilith to shriek, or for the Guvnor to raise the hue and cry, yet she held her pose, and he went on fussing the dog.

Together, Silas and I slid into the wings. His triumphant smile gleamed in the shadows. Of course, Lilith would notice her loss at some point and all hell would break lose. But, for now, we were conquerors.

The photographer took at least three shots. Then Silas heaved a sigh as dramatic as any actor.

'No,' he cried, walking out on stage. 'Something is missing. A vital element. Lady M should be holding the dagger.'

Lilith moaned. 'For mercy's sake. Mr Dyer!'

The Guvnor cocked his head. 'Actually, Miss Erikson, I believe he's right. Such an image would be striking: the dagger resting against his cheek. May we pause a moment?'

Anthony swallowed. I could guess what he was imagining, but the daggers weren't sharp. Lilith released him with a groan. I dreaded her glancing down, or moving and noticing that her girdle was lighter.

'It's up in the wardrobe room – I was polishing it earlier. Be back in the merest twinkle,' Silas tipped a wink at me and vanished into the opposite wings. I heard the ladder creak beneath his weight as he climbed.

Trotting down the steps, I took Eurydice from the Guvnor. 'Thank you, sir. I can manage now.'

Eurydice raised her eyes in silent reproach. Animals were canny; no doubt she could smell betrayal all over me.

The photographer scrubbed the lens of his camera furiously.

'What is it, man?' the Guvnor demanded.

'I'm sorry, sir. I've never had this happen before. There's some kind of speckling.'

'This is preposterous! Your camera is faulty. First it blurs and now it blots. Have you another?'

Silas had only been gone a minute or two. It already felt like a lifetime. I longed for the certainty that the deed was done, that the watch was smashed to pieces. Where was he now? Had he reached the wardrobe room?

Up on stage, Lilith placed her hands on her hips, listening to the photographer argue with the Guvnor. 'I will not swallow this nonsense,' she interrupted. 'We have been standing here for hours.'

'I shall handle the problem, Miss Erikson,' the Guvnor promised.

'No, show me. Show me my supposed mistakes.' She strode down the steps towards us. My heart froze in my chest. Surely now she'd miss the watch, banging at her thigh?

But she pushed past me and Eurydice without pause. Her head disappeared beneath the hood.

'There!' Her voice came out muffled. 'I am not blurred. I see the specks, but my outline is clear. I have been standing correctly all along.' She paused, her head still hidden. Too quiet. 'Wait just a moment. I cannot see … Where is my watch?'

That was when Silas screamed.

His cry rang through the flies, bounced into the auditorium. I looked up but there was nothing to see, all the ropes and pulleys were in shadow.

The silence seemed to stretch.

'Old chap?' Anthony called up, a hint of alarm in his voice. 'Everything all right?'

In answer, a windlass screeched. Something came plummeting down, fast. There was hardly time to blink before it smacked into the stage with a force that opened the trapdoor.

Anthony leapt clear. Eurydice barked and wrenched herself from my grasp.

The Guvnor dashed onto the stage and stood peering into the open trapdoor like a mourner over a grave. 'Good God!'

All reason deserted me; I pictured Silas caught by Melpomene, beaten with her club.

The auditorium erupted in utter chaos. I could hear shouts and footsteps from the cellar below the stage.

Picking himself up, Anthony made a lurch for the trapdoor. 'Silas!' The Guvnor grappled with him to keep him away. 'Silas!'

It couldn't be true. I hastened to the side of the stage, where a staircase led into the cellar. Men had come running up from the hoisting drum. Lanterns showed their faces blank with horror.

Blood fanned across the floor. Silas lay twitching in the centre, the back of his skull cracked open like an egg. His legs were the wrong shape. Bowed.

It didn't look real. It couldn't be real. It was just a stage effect.

'No!' I ran to try and help, but no bandages would fix him. He gurgled and moaned, blood pumping from him in torrents. 'Silas, what happened?'

He couldn't tell me.

No one could survive this. Warmth soaked through my skirts and I knew it could only be minutes before my friend died. I reached for his hand. It was rigid, clutched claw-like around Lilith's watch.

His eyes pleaded with mine, yet his mouth refused to work and when I bent down, all I caught was his final breath.

'No,' I sobbed. 'Please, no.'

Men approached and started to pull me away. 'Come on, miss. There's nothing you can do.'

'I don't want to leave him!'

'Best not touch him too much. We'll have to fetch the police, miss.'

Eurydice nosed past my legs. For the briefest moment, I thought the animal had come to offer me comfort. But instead, Lilith's dog trotted up to Silas's broken body, her paws soaking red, and calmly lapped at his gore.

CHAPTER 14

The coroner held an inquest at the local pub. Silas's death was analysed in a place reeking of beer and pipesmoke, while his body lay next door in the bagatelle room. We'd done our best to tidy him up for the jury and journalists to view, but the sight still turned men green. It wasn't fair. In life, Silas had been so dapper.

We witnesses squeezed around a circular table marked with rings from damp glasses. Anthony was unkempt without Silas's smoothing hand – his hair imperfectly greased, his necktie askew. He clutched a black-edged handkerchief, but he was letting the tears flow unchecked. I found I couldn't cry after the initial burst. My mind was a tangle of questions that needed answering before I could grieve.

The inquest did precious little to clear matters up. There was no damage to the bridge, no breaks in the railing, nothing to suggest why he fell. Not a single person had been there to see what happened.

And what could I report? That I'd once said 'Macbeth' out loud and failed to spin three times? That Silas had died holding a cursed watch? It was fiddle-faddle, and I knew it. Yet there was still a part of me that whispered these facts were pertinent.

It was Lilith who touched upon the watch during her interview, although not in the way I'd expected. She draped herself over the chair casually, as if this were only a matter of mild interest for her.

'Have you noted in your evidence that the unfortunate man had … How shall I put this?' She rubbed at her chin. 'That he was in unauthorised possession of my property when he died? I don't say this to besmirch his character. But it may be significant. If the deceased was in the habit of pilfering, he may have acquired enemies.'

Anthony stood up and left the room.

Shame laid its heavy hands upon my shoulders. It had been my idea to steal the watch, yet Silas was taking the blame, even in death. In a strange way, I felt I'd played the same trick on him that Greg had on me.

When Lilith returned to our table, she had the temerity to pull the trinket out of her pocket and caress it. There was not a chip, not a mark, on the onyx case. Lilith had simply wiped Silas's blood off and taken it straight back.

After less than an hour of consideration, the jury returned a verdict of accidental death. The Mercury was not guilty of any negligence. According to the jurors, Silas, who had climbed up to the wardrobe room for decades, had carelessly stumbled and plummeted to his doom.

No one was satisfied. But what else could the jury find?

The Guvnor leant in to address the little hoop of us around the table. 'This has been a trying day. Let's reconvene downstairs and raise a glass in Silas's memory.'

We plodded down the staircase and turned left into the main saloon, a room fitted with mahogany, brass lamps and etched glass. It felt far too brash and convivial, as if a corpse didn't lay in shattered pieces upstairs.

People stopped to watch Lilith pass. Whispers buzzed: 'Is it her?' 'Look who that is!' She pretended not to hear, only smiled her provocative smile. I itched to slap it off her face.

Other theatre folk were already there. They hadn't been witnesses, but wanted to attend out of respect. Mrs Dyer sat on a small sofa in conversation with Clementine. She was wearing black again.

I'd rarely seen Mrs Dyer and Lilith in the same room. I wondered what they'd do, but each seemed content to ignore the other, behaving as if she simply didn't exist.

Mrs Nettles stood at the bar, a hat covering her Titian hair. She was ordering a sherry but changed it to two when she saw me. 'You look as though you could use one, Miss Wilcox.'

I accepted the glass gratefully. The sherry's sweet, rich tang gave my senses a much-needed kick.

Mrs Nettles shook her head. 'Poor Silas. We worked together for such a long time. I never dreamed it would end like this! I used to complain about his little freaks and whims, but I was fond of him.'

'He knew that, Mrs Nettles. He considered you a true friend.'

It was easy to speak words of comfort to others – I'd been doing it most of my life – yet inside I was running over everything again. Could there have been someone up in the flies who pushed Silas off the bridge? Someone who ran away before they could be caught? It seemed the only logical explanation, although it was hardly reassuring to imagine a murderer at the Mercury. And who would want to hurt Silas?

I glanced over at Anthony, slumped in a corner, the table before him full of empty glasses. 'Poor Mr Frost. He looks like he's lost a limb. They were so close, weren't they, even with the difference in their ages?'

'Yes,' she replied carefully.

'I can't imagine being friends like that with Lilith.'

Mrs Nettles swirled her sherry. 'There was … maybe … a little more to it than friendship.' She glanced up swiftly. 'You won't say anything?'

I gaped at her for a moment. 'No. No, of course not. It's none of my business.'

She nodded.

Now I considered, it made a lot of sense. And Anthony's loss seemed all the more unbearable. Was it my fault?

Still cradling our sherries, we left the bar and claimed a table near the sofa. The Guvnor was standing behind his seated wife now. Lilith hung back a little to the side.

'I have announced that the Mercury will cover all of the funeral costs,' the Guvnor was saying. 'I hope I did right, my dear.'

'Perfectly. I would not hear of it being any other way. Silas must have the very best. We shall spare no expense. I shall arrange it all.'

Mrs Nettles and I exchanged sad smiles. He would have liked that. Silas always craved the finer things in life.

'Anthony Frost will probably wish to make the arrangements himself,' the Guvnor remonstrated. 'Silas had no family to speak of. Mr Frost and he were like brothers.'

'Pish.' Mrs Dyer waved a black-gloved hand. 'Only look at the poor man, Hugh. He is not in a fit state to arrange his own tie.'

'More importantly,' Lilith cut in, 'how is he to play Macbeth?'

Mrs Dyer took a sip from her drink as though she had heard nothing. But Clementine shifted beside her. 'Surely there's no question of that?'

The theatre had only been closed a few days while the investigation took place. They'd wanted to hold the inquest as soon as possible, before the body had time to moulder.

'No,' the Guvnor said heavily. 'No, the understudy will have to step in. It is only fair that Mr Frost be granted a leave of absence.'

'The understudy,' Lilith repeated with contempt. 'He doesn't have an eighth of Anthony's skill.'

It was the first time I'd heard her refer to anyone's talent except her own.

'Few men possess such a gift, but we must reopen all the same. It has cost me a pretty penny to refund the nights we have cancelled.'

Mrs Dyer gave a twitch of irritation. It was her money, really.

'Of course we must reopen!' Lilith exclaimed. 'We have wasted time. Respect is all very well, but failing to put on a play isn't going to bring the man back.'

Mrs Nettles gripped her glass. Even the Guvnor appeared embarrassed.

'The audience will all be there to see you, Miss Erikson,' he said in a conciliatory tone. 'It does not matter who plays opposite you.'

'It matters to me.'

Mrs Dyer rose calmly to her feet. 'Well, my dear,' she said, addressing only her husband. 'You manage these matters best. Let me know when you plan to recommence the play, and what I may do to assist with this funeral. I am at your service.'

I saw what she was doing: presenting herself as the amiable and reasonable wife beside the wilful mistress. It paid off; she certainly came away looking the best of the two.

Mrs Dyer crossed over to our table. 'Mrs Nettles. Miss Wilcox.' Her expression crumpled into sympathy. 'My condolences for your loss.'

We both murmured 'Thank you, madam' to our glasses.

'Miss Wilcox, I fear this sad occasion must put a halt to the little project we discussed. But rest assured I shall give it my full attention once the Mercury reopens.'

So she still cherished her plan. Good. We'd teach Lilith to take Silas's death so flippantly. I wanted her and that watch far away from the theatre, now more than ever.

'I'll wait for your instructions, Mrs Dyer.'

'Excellent.' Patting my shoulder, she turned back and retook her place beside Clementine on the sofa.

'What was all that about?' Mrs Nettles asked.

I didn't reply. Lilith was viewing me intently, her eyes two steel daggers pinning me to the chair.

CHAPTER 15

Mrs Dyer's summons came sooner than I expected, only a week after the Sunday we'd originally fixed upon. Maybe it was better to act while our nerve held. Given too long to reflect, I might start to worry that all attempts against Lilith were destined to end in death.

I fretted by the window, waiting for the growler to arrive. My guts were squirming like a barrel of eels.

'They're immoral, making you work on a Sunday.' Dorcas sat opposite Philip at the table, playing cards.

'It's not exactly work. It's complicated.'

Philip considered his hand before making a move. His expression remained grim. 'Does it have something to do with the man who died at the theatre?'

I glanced at Bertie, doing his exercises alone in the corner. I'd tried to downplay Silas's death at home, although I couldn't stop newspaper stories and gossip.

'Yes, that's it,' I lied. 'We're doing extra safety checks. Taking precautions to make sure it's all right for the play to start again tomorrow.'

'But who's making sure it's safe for *you*?' Philip demanded.

That was a good question. I tried not to let it throw me. 'Mrs Dyer will look after me. I have to help her out, after all she's done for us. She's not just fixed Bertie's foot; she's searching for a house we can move to as well. These rich ladies have connections. It's worth keeping them sweet.'

Dorcas laid a card down. 'I still think you deserve your Sunday rest. It's bad enough she makes you dress that actress you hate.'

I smiled and said it didn't matter. There was a time when I told Dorcas my secrets, but how could I explain what was going on here? She'd never heard of Melpomene, or the curse of *Macbeth*, she didn't even care for plays much since *Doctor Faustus*. Whenever I wanted to confide, the words melted like sugar on my tongue.

Finally, lights bobbed through the smeared glass. The growler pulled up with its lamps shining.

I grabbed my cloak and hat. 'Right, I'm off.' I kissed everyone rapidly in turn, my lips barely brushing their cheeks.

Mrs Dyer welcomed me into the carriage with a giddy girl's smile. 'The time is come at last! Here, take a hot brick. There is a chill in the air but the stars shine bright. They bless our endeavours.'

I hunched my feet against the brick gladly. She was right; it was freezing. 'What exactly *are* our endeavours, Mrs Dyer?'

She touched a finger to her nose. 'All will become clear. Lightfoot has orders to stop at the house of a friend of mine near Charing Cross. I hope you will not mind a short walk to the Mercury? I thought it best that the servants know nothing whatsoever. As far as they and Hugh are concerned, we are attending a philanthropic gathering.'

She liked to weave a tale, I reminded myself. It didn't mean what she planned was so bad that she needed an alibi.

Sabotage was easy when the owner of the theatre was complicit. Mrs Dyer slipped her key into the door to the main foyer and, for the first time, I entered the Mercury as a person of quality would do. I hadn't been inside since Silas died a fortnight ago. Uninhabited, it felt a different place. All the dreams and fantasies slept. I could sense them, charging the air, biding their time, watching us in their turn.

Our shoes clipped on the parquet tiles of the lobby. They looked dirty, but perhaps it was only shadows.

'Can you see?' Mrs Dyer hissed. Even her whisper echoed round the empty space.

'Barely.'

'We cannot light everything up, people will notice. I shall fetch us some lanterns. Keep them away from the windows.' She passed behind the ticket desk into an office, leaving me alone.

The bifurcated staircase rose before me, its tangle of iron bannisters stretching up like tree branches in the dark. The chandelier chinked gently. There must be a breeze, slipping through the joints of the windows and stirring the crystals. The air tasted strange, as though spiced with coal, although it could only be dust. Looking at the grand architecture, the stateliness of the place, I realised how similar the building was to a mausoleum.

Light cut in a beam across my feet. Mrs Dyer emerged with two dark lanterns.

'Here is yours,' she said, passing one to me. Shadows made her face look haggard. 'Now, where do you keep Lilith's costumes?'

'In her dressing room.'

'Excellent. Come along, then.'

Sweat ran down my neck, even though the theatre was icy cold. It was all too soon after Silas's death, I wasn't ready to be here again yet.

We stole silk-footed into Lilith's dressing room and coughed at the stench. The lilies had mouldered. I aimed my lantern at the wall behind the dressing table; the black patches had extended even further, eating through the paper.

'We will have to do it in the corridor,' Mrs Dyer decided, a handkerchief clamped over her nose. 'They must be able to smell the herbs. Fetch Lilith's costumes.'

'I don't understand, madam.'

'The cats. We are going to let the cats at her costumes.'

'But ... she's allergic.'

'Not excessively,' Mrs Dyer pointed out. 'If she were, she would not be able to work inside this theatre at all. Our aim is to make her uncomfortable. To entirely distract her from her performance.'

I remembered Lilith at the pub, bad-mouthing Silas on public record, saying the theatre need not close for him. I thought of little Rachel, caught between her parents. The dark-haired baby Lilith had presumably abandoned. My scruples dwindled until finally they winked out.

'Give me a minute.'

The hinges of the door creaked as I opened the wardrobe. I cast my lantern over the brocade, the knife-pleated damson skirt and a gown with inky, trailing oversleeves. Tampering with them felt akin to sacrilege. Then I saw the nightdress I'd hastily resewn, after the original was doused in blood. Bundling it in my arms, I joined Mrs Dyer in the corridor.

'Just this one,' I specified, spreading the costume across the floor in a white star. 'It's her last scene. "Out, damned spot." Everyone says it's her finest. That's the bit to spoil. And if she's taken ill then, it won't interfere with the rest of the performance.'

'How astute. Presuming it works. Should we not give the reaction more time to take effect? I do not wish for this outing to be wasted.'

'It'll work.' I spoke with more conviction than I felt. Silas had been so sure that our plan to destroy the watch would work, too.

'Very well.' Mrs Dyer produced a packet and began to sprinkle something across the nightgown. Soon the fabric was covered in little flecks.

'What's that?'

'Valerian root and a member of the mint family.' Mrs Dyer tipped the packet upside down, emptying it. 'You shall see its effect. Only wait.' She kissed her lips. 'Here, puss, puss.'

The influx started slowly. Two bright, reflective spots appeared at the end of the corridor. There was a mew, then a hiss.

A score of tiny lamps moved in the darkness. A fairy procession, weaving towards us.

The tabby cat approached first, bearing its sharp white teeth. A black-and-white tom followed quick on its heels, trailed by a slinking grey.

I never realised the theatre was home to so many cats. They flowed like liquid to the nightgown, where they rolled and twisted in ecstasy. The corridor vibrated with a low, resonant hum.

'Good kitties,' Mrs Dyer crooned. 'Good, good kitties.'

Her eyes glowed arsenic green in the lamplight. For a moment, my heart misgave me. I saw a woman with red lips, scattering her herbs and commanding an army of cats.

If it had been a scene in a play, I would've taken one look and called her the real witch.

Lilith had missed the stage. On the first night we reopened, she performed with an intensity that was almost painful to watch. The Guvnor had been right when he said it didn't matter if the understudy replaced Anthony. Nothing mattered, until Lilith made her entrances.

We burst back into the dressing room, fresh from Banquo's ghost scene. She was Lady Macbeth still. She may have worn Lilith's face, moved her body, hidden behind her pale skin, but it was undoubtedly the character standing there.

'Unlace me,' she commanded.

The next costume was her last, the contaminated nightdress. I folded my hands. 'You're not on again until Act Five. There's lots of time yet.'

'I said, unlace me. I didn't ask for your opinion.'

Supposing she reacted straight away? That would ruin Mrs Dyer's plan; all the irritation would happen off stage and Lilith would have time to recover. Or suppose her allergy was worse than we thought? What if I was stuck in here alone with a woman in crisis? I wished Mrs Dyer hadn't put it all on me.

'Are you deaf?'

Reluctantly, I approached and began to untie the knot at the small of her back. I'd go as slowly as I could. Lilith huffed and puffed in frustration. She was quivering, hungry, as though she were only satisfied on stage, as if she lived on Shakespeare alone.

'Hurry up.'

She was doing her utmost to extinguish any lingering feelings of remorse I might have. I teased the back panels of the dress apart, until her white shift and corset appeared through the weave of laces. Then I moved round to the front to pull the bodice forward and off her arms.

There was more resistance than usual. The fabric came away with a sticky, kissing sound. That was when I noticed the russet patches on her corset.

Horror held me rigid.

'Now the skirt!' she insisted.

'Lilith, you're bleeding.'

'What?' She glanced down.

'You're ... bleeding from your breasts.' The floor shifted beneath my feet. I couldn't cope with seeing blood again, not so close to Silas's death.

'Damn. Damn, damn.' She dabbed at her chest. 'Fetch my bandages.'

I'd never seen such a thing. Pushing down my gorge, I did as Lilith said and kept my eyes averted while she bound herself back up. I kept thinking of Mrs Dyer's descriptions of Lilith. Unnatural. Unfeminine. A woman whose breasts flowed not with milk, but blood.

'Fetch the nightgown.'

'But—' I started.

'Fetch it!'

Trembling, I approached the wardrobe. The hinges squealed again, crying out against me. Eurydice huffed when I drew the costume out. She must be able to smell the cat dander.

'Lay it on the sofa there and leave me,' Lilith ordered, still fussing around her corset.

I hesitated. 'Don't you need some help?'

'I won't have you mopping my breasts. I draw the line at that particular humiliation. Now get out. Off with you.' She made a shooing motion. 'Allow me a sliver of dignity.'

I was grateful to escape the scent of blood. Eurydice followed me with a baleful stare, her brown eyes full of mistrust.

I toyed with the idea of hiding in the green room, but if Lilith took ill on stage, my absence might seem suspicious. I should be there, on hand, for whatever might happen next. My insides were ragged and torn with fear as I made my way to the wings. Lilith was already sick. What if she had a reaction now, when no one was around?

The deed was done, I couldn't take it back. There was no remedy except to watch it play out.

The lights on the iron ladder swayed as I arrived in the wings. Oscar was there, appearing comfortingly ordinary in his painter's overalls; something real, when all around me felt mad.

'Is that you, Miss Wilcox? Should you be back at work? They told me you were here when ... when it happened.'

I swallowed. Silas's spirit had left his body just below our feet. Somehow I kept expecting him to plunge down from the gridiron again at any moment. 'Yes, I was. It was terrible, Oscar. Worse even than Eugene Grieves ... I can't think how he fell.'

'They've replaced the whole bridge,' he soothed me. 'There was no obvious fault, but some of the wood was a bit worm-eaten. It's safe now.'

I shook my head. I still thought someone must have pushed Silas. 'I don't know how I'll ever bring myself to go up there again.'

Oscar reached out and touched my arm. 'Wait for me tomorrow morning. We'll climb up together, the first time. You'll see it's nothing to worry about.'

That was kind. The sort of thing I would have expected from the man I knew as Greg's friend. I'd been so busy that we hadn't even spoken about our run-in with Greg or how Oscar felt to know his erstwhile fiancée was married. We should. Each of us needed a confidant. Oscar might understand the things I couldn't tell Dorcas – although I doubted he'd comprehend what I was doing tonight.

The first scene of Act Five was all set up. Tapestries and candelabra evoked an anteroom in Macbeth's castle. Two actors, dressed as a doctor and a waiting woman, made their entrance and consulted about Lady Macbeth's somnambulism.

I couldn't pay attention to their lines. I was as anxious as Clementine with her stage fright, waiting for the cue.

'*Lo you, here she comes!*'

A violin trilled in the orchestra. My gaze flew to the other side of the stage, where Lilith was due to enter.

There was no one there.

I swore beneath my breath. She never missed a cue.

The actress playing the waiting woman looked flustered, but was forced to carry on. '*This is her very guise; and upon my life, fast asleep.*'

Still no movement from the wings. A whisper buzzed through the orchestra stalls.

Oh God. What if Lilith was lying slowly wheezing to death in her dressing room? What had I done?

The waiting woman spoke as loudly as she could, clearly hoping Lilith would hear her catchword this time. '*Observe her; stand close.*'

A fraught second passed. Then finally, Lilith appeared, glowing a brilliant white in the gaslight.

Her feet made no sound upon the boards. Only the train of her nightgown whispered in her wake, secrets of tarlatan and tulle. She carried a single taper. Its flame played across her face, glistened upon slick tracks.

Her eyes and nostrils were streaming.

She drifted centre stage then forward, towards the floats, setting her taper on a stand. She raised a single palm and held it out to the audience. '*Yet here's a spot.*'

My throat tightened. There *was* a spot – or, more accurately, a patch of flushed skin, slowly climbing up her arm.

'*Out, damned spot! Out, I say! One, two, why then 'tis time to do't.*' She gave a bark of laughter that shifted quickly to a wheeze as she stumbled nearer to the footlights. '*Hell is murky!*'

The atmosphere quickened; a lady in the orchestra stalls drew back in her seat.

'What's wrong with her?' Oscar whispered. 'Was she ill in her dressing room?'

A suffocating pillow of guilt pressed over my face.

'*Fie, my lord, fie! A soldier, and afeard?*' Her voice sounded terrible, rasping. '*Yet who would have thought the old man to have had so much blood in him?*'

One of her eyes narrowed. She couldn't seem to open it again. Hives began to materialise on her face, blotching her white skin.

I thought I'd enjoy watching her suffer. I didn't.

Lilith clapped a palm over her red-raw face and sniffed. '*Here's the smell of blood still,*' she moaned. '*All the perfumes of Arabia will not sweeten this little hand. Oh. Oh.*' She swayed. The hem of her nightdress brushed the footlights. 'OH!'

She fell down in a heap.

Without thinking, I reached out and grabbed Oscar's hand. 'God help us,' I whispered. 'She's dead!'

The music stopped. The auditorium erupted: a bell rang, the curtain dropped. I ran out on stage. People surrounded Lilith, but

I was the only one who dared to kneel and touch her. She was still breathing, her pulse flickering faintly in her neck.

'It must be the cats,' I wailed, as if I didn't know perfectly well. 'She has an allergy, but she said it was mild.'

The stage manager ran for a doctor.

What had I done? Lilith no longer looked like a witch from a storybook: she looked more like a maiden caught in a wicked spell. Innocent. Defenceless.

I wanted the trapdoor to open and swallow me whole.

ACT II

The Duchess of Malfi

'Whether we fall by ambition, blood, or lust, like diamonds we are cut with our own dust.'

CHAPTER 16

After the nightmares I'd seen unfold at the Mercury, the bustle and push of Covent Garden came as a welcome relief. Christmas was imminent. The sky was a reliable, solid grey, the temperature invigoratingly chill. Costermongers passed with their donkey barrows creaking; women balanced baskets on their heads. The flagstones were slippery with cabbage leaves trodden underfoot.

Dorcas didn't work amongst the iron braziers and the stall-keepers. She'd been lucky enough to find employment in a little shop just off the market, which could be kept warm year round for hothouse flowers. A bell tinkled when I pushed open the periwinkle door. Wicker baskets and pots frothed with blooms of every colour. The scent was greener, fresher than the fug of lilies in Lilith's dressing room. My sister stood behind the counter, cutting stems. She wore a blue-striped dress and apron. Her hair was tucked under a white cap, but a single curl escaped over her ear.

'Good morning to you, miss,' I said in a false voice.

She glanced up, startled. 'Jenny! What brings you here?'

'It's all right,' I assured her. 'Nobody's ill. Well, except for Lilith. I'm going to visit her today. I thought I ought to take a tussie-mussie with me.'

Dorcas fixed me with a quizzical look. 'Really? You don't like her.'

'It's only polite, isn't it? And it would look a bit rum if I was the only person not to visit her.'

'I suppose.' Dorcas put down her scissors and wiped her hands on her apron. 'You're a funny lot, you theatre folk. All pretence.' I swallowed a wad of guilt. 'Even your mistress was in here earlier.'

'Mrs Dyer? You're not serious? What did she want?'

Dorcas shrugged. 'Flowers for Lilith too, I guess.'

'Not bloody likely!'

'Well, I don't know, Sally served her. But she came and found me when I was filling up the buckets out front. Asked me all sorts of questions, she did.'

There was a horrible creeping sensation over my skin, like the legs of an insect. 'What was she asking you about?'

Glancing around, Dorcas crooked a finger and beckoned me closer to the counter. 'She started quizzing me about my work here and asked if I'd want to open my own florist shop one day. She was talking like it could really happen! Do you think she might give me a leg up, Jen? Like she did for you and Bertie?'

There was no saying what Mrs Dyer might do. I realised that now. She'd stop at nothing. I didn't relish the thought of her calling on my family without me, crossing the boundaries between my theatre life and home life.

I avoided answering by turning to a bucket of carnations. 'Should I give Lilith these? I'm not used to making posies. Help me. You're good at all that: the language of flowers.'

Dorcas came out from behind the counter and began to select stems. 'Shades of pink will do the job best. Maybe some coral roses. They're for friendship and sympathy. See?' She held one towards me. 'Pretty. Chamomile for strength in adversity, chrysanthemum for condolences, mistletoe for surmounting all difficulties.'

I pointed to a bluish plant with bell-shaped blooms. 'What about those?'

'Hyacinths? No, that's not fitting. They're for begging forgiveness.'

I felt my cheeks heat. 'Pop one in there for me anyway.'

Shrugging again, Dorcas did as I said, arranging a lovely pastel bouquet. She tied it with ribbon, then wrapped it in paper. 'Here you go,' she said, holding it out. 'Still dripping with insincerity.'

'Very funny.' I hoped she was joking. I hoped that wasn't how I appeared now in Dorcas's eyes: false and artificial. But if I did, who was there to blame but myself? I'd gone along with being a spy, I'd hurt the actress I was supposed to help.

'Do you want a message?' Dorcas gestured to the counter, where there were cards of every shape and size, all edged in blue.

I hesitated. I didn't know what I'd write. 'No, don't worry. I'm going in person. I'll give a verbal message.'

'Wishing her well? I thought she was the actress, not you!'

I gave a hollow laugh. Was that really what I'd become?

The omnibus was packed full; I only got a seat inside because a policeman offered to climb up to the knifeboard and make room for me. The air was stuffy, flavoured with straw and damp wool. I wrapped an arm around my posy to shield it from the crush, but I could practically see the petals wilting as we jolted on.

I'd never been to Lilith's home before. It turned out she kept a villa in the suburb of St John's Wood, a fair ride out from the West End and its theatres – but perhaps that was the point. If the Guvnor paid for her board, as I suspected, he'd want to keep her tucked away, his visits screened from prying eyes.

Sure enough, when I alighted and found the little redbrick house, there was a growler waiting outside. I recognised the black horse with its one white sock. As I paused, debating whether to knock or go home, the Guvnor himself flung out of the door.

'Rascals! Dirty, rotten scoundrels!' He slashed at a rosebush with his silver-topped cane. The horse snorted and shifted its weight but Lightfoot, the driver, sat staring straight forwards.

Tentatively, I approached. 'Mr Dyer, sir?'

He swung round, his face red beneath his whiskers. 'Oh! Miss Wilcox.'

'Miss Erikson hasn't taken a turn for the worse, has she?'

His gaze followed mine, to the poor abused shrub. 'Oh. No. You must excuse me. I lost my temper. These infernal newspapers!'

I breathed a little easier. For a terrible moment, I thought I might have killed her. 'Have the critics been unkind, sir?'

He barked a bitter laugh. '*Unkind*? By Jove, that's putting it mildly. You would expect some sympathy for an actress of her calibre. But you know what journalists are like. They could not comprehend her talent, and so now they say she's given herself some kind of … fit, or seizure. An inevitable effect of behaving so *unnaturally.*'

I shifted in discomfort. That had been my first response to Lilith's strength, too: I'd thought her unnaturally bold. If I didn't know this illness had been brought on by my own treachery, would I be agreeing with the newspapers?

'Is she taking it hard?'

The Guvnor sighed. 'She laughs and says she doesn't care two pins for what people think of her, but of course she does. Deep down there is a sensitivity in her. That is what enables her to perform so exquisitely.' He closed his eyes, pinched the bridge of his nose. 'It is my own fault. With a talent of this magnitude … I should have been shielding her, keeping her safe like a diamond. Ensuring nothing of this nature could ever happen. There will be a change in the new year. Absolutely no cats.'

'But where will they go?'

'On the street, for all I care. Rachel may take one or two as a pet if she chooses, but they must be kept away from the theatre at all costs.'

Although it was light compared to my other sins, I felt bad that I was making the cats homeless. 'Very good, sir. Do you think Miss Erikson's well enough to see me now? I won't tire her. I just bought some flowers.'

He glanced at my bouquet and his jaw set. 'Flowers. That reminds me. I'll take the damned thing away, so it's out of her sight.'

Confused, I followed him back inside the house to a small parlour. A patina of dust coated the dresser and the mantelpiece. Other nosegays were dotted around, some turning brown already through lack of sunlight and water, but one floral arrangement stood out. It was a wreath. Something more suited to riding in a hearse.

The Guvnor snatched at it. 'You see what they are. Thorough blackguards. Who would have the gall to send this?' He ripped the card off and thrust it at me:

With commiserations on the death of your career.

I gasped. It was cruel, tasteless. But that wasn't what shocked me.

The card was edged with periwinkle blue. It had come from Dorcas's shop.

———

I found Lilith languishing in bed, propped up on a mountain of cushions. Eurydice lay curled at her side on top of a discarded newspaper. The chamber was all wispy curtains, jewel-coloured lampshades and patterned rugs; it would've been enchanting, if not for the clutter. Used teacups and dirty linen met me at every turn. Automatically, I stooped to pick up a garter from the floor. I'd grown accustomed to clearing up the chaos left in Lilith's wake.

'Ah,' she said thickly. 'It's you.' She clamped, of all things, a cigar between her teeth. Her eyes were bloodshot. It was hard to tell if that was from her allergy or from weeping.

'Should you really be smoking?' I asked her.

'Because it's unladylike?'

It was: I'd never seen a woman do such a thing. 'Well, yes, but mainly because the last time I saw you, you could barely breathe.'

'And whose fault was that?'

The guilty blush hit my face like scalding water. 'Listen,' I said haltingly. 'Lilith, I'm ... sorry. For what happened. With the cats. You're right, it must have been my fault. They must have got at your nightgown somehow. I should've been more careful. But I was ... distracted. What with Silas dying ...'

'And Mrs Dyer putting you up to it,' she added with a puff of smoke. I gulped, said nothing. 'Do you think I didn't realise you're her creature? I'm not blind.' She took a long drag. 'I don't hate you for it either. I understand that a woman does what she can to survive in this world.' Lilith adjusted herself against the cushions, wincing slightly. 'The truth is, Kitty, it wasn't only those beastly cats that made me collapse. You saw, didn't you? I took a lousy infection: milk fever, like a damned cow. So here I am with cabbage leaves under my shift and clover tea to drink.'

'You still feed it yourself, then,' I said awkwardly. 'Your baby?'

She shook her head. 'Let's not speak of that.'

Self-conscious, I set down my bouquet and began to tidy. I folded a petticoat and put it in the press. Lilith watched me with amusement.

'You're dreadfully *useful*, aren't you? No wonder Mrs Dyer chose you.'

I felt despicable. Only now was it dawning on me how truly disturbing Mrs Dyer's behaviour had been. She'd hired me to spy on Lilith, made me trigger her allergy and sent that deplorable wreath from my sister's shop. It was … hysterical. And God help me, I'd been swept up in her madness. 'I won't do it again. I should never have done it. Mrs Dyer may have cause to loathe you … but it's not my feud. I'm sorry.'

Lilith's gaze was inscrutable as ever. I remembered the bruises on Anthony's arm and how she'd squeezed my hand like a vice. Was she going to make me pay for my actions? Set the dog on me?

'You can serve your penitence by staying a while. I'm parched for conversation, rusticating out here in the suburbs.'

I nodded, trying my best to be meek. 'When do you think you'll be coming back?'

'Not until after Christmas,' she said tightly. 'It's not my choice. Hugh won't let me near the theatre until he's fumigated it and drowned all the cats.'

'He's not going to *drown* them.'

She gave me her saucy glance. 'He might.' She pulled her dressing gown closer round her. 'I would apologise for my state of dishabille, but you're used to seeing me like this, aren't you?'

I attempted a smile. 'Yes. I've probably dressed you more times than your own mother.'

Her face wavered like a candle flame. 'You have, actually. They cut me out of her, you know. She bled to death before I drew my first gasp.' Her tone was light, but she wasn't on stage. I could see the pain beneath her mask.

'I'm so sorry! I didn't know that. I never would have said—'
I imagined her as an infant, much like the child I'd seen in the

photograph, wailing for the mother that would never come. Orphaned before she could know her parent, as Bertie had been.

She waved her hand dismissively. The cigar shed ash over Eurydice, who grunted. 'It was for the best. Her life had effectively ended. I was my mother's disgrace, and then I killed her.'

Questions tingled on my tongue. Was Lilith telling me she was illegitimate? I didn't know what to say, so I started cleaning again. I'd never stopped to think of Lilith as a real person with a family, but she'd lost people, too. I remembered her mentioning an uncle, once, who didn't believe in her. What about her father? Did she know him? Or had he run away, like mine? It had been so easy to cast her as the homewrecker, as another Georgiana Mildmay. We might have more in common than I'd thought.

'It's probably good that you take some time off,' I said, stacking empty plates. 'I know you don't like to rest, but you've seemed unwell ever since you got that watch.'

The word acted strangely on her. There was a tightening, a sharpening, that I can't explain. 'Yes, Eugene's sainted relic. Bring it to me, will you?'

I faltered. 'Where is it?'

'In the top drawer, under the shifts. I had to squirrel it away there last night, the ticking was keeping me awake.'

I pulled the drawer open cautiously, as though something might leap out at me. In fact, the watch lay on top of the shifts. The material beneath was flecked with a fine, dark powder like soot.

I didn't want to touch what had once been bathed in Silas's blood, so carried it with the tips of my fingers. Lilith snatched it greedily.

Eurydice whined and leapt from the bed.

'Oh, Melpomene, I'm letting you down, aren't I?' Lilith's thumb traced the engraving. For a moment her expression looked as forlorn as the tragedy mask. 'Have they put Clementine on as Lady M in my place? How does she get along? I can't find a single line about it in the papers.'

I wet my lips. Poor Clementine. As if she hadn't been conscientious enough, they'd now put all this pressure on her. 'I think the fact the journalists haven't mentioned her says enough in itself. She's … not Lady Macbeth.'

'Ha! All that blonde hair.'

'I put her in a wig. I've tacked up your costumes so she doesn't trip over them. But she plays it differently. She's not a murderous, ambitious queen, she's … weepy.'

Wedging the cigar between her teeth, Lilith crumpled the newspaper with her spare hand. 'Yet *she* escapes a scathing review. They couldn't even leave me alone when I was at death's door.'

'But your admirers are loyal. I saw all their flowers.'

'They'll forget me in another week.' She scrunched a newssheet into a ball and flung it from the bed. Eurydice chased after it. 'I don't suppose you understand that, do you? You're too … loved.' The last word came low and deep, like a note on a piano.

It was true, I had people at home who loved me no matter what. A place I belonged. No amount of applause would serve to replace that. Who did Lilith have? There was the Guvnor, of course … but even he kept her hidden away here and denied their relationship in the real world.

'It's rotten luck. Silas told me *Macbeth* was a cursed play. I didn't believe him. I'm starting to, now.'

Lilith sighed. 'Poor old Silas. No one should die like *that*, should they? But he cursed himself. With all his superstitions, he ought to have had the good sense to leave my watch alone. Fancy interfering with Melpomene's work! I suppose he wanted her to favour Anthony instead …'

'Silas fell,' I said stubbornly. 'It was an accident.'

'Was it?' Lilith's cigar smouldered. She stubbed it out on a side table, heedless of the mark it left. I propped open the window to let out some smoke. When I turned back, she had the watch cupped in her hands. Now the room was quiet I could hear it ticking, ticking.

'It must have been an accident. Because if it wasn't, the only alternative is murder: someone pushing Silas. Who on earth would do that? They couldn't find anybody up in the wardrobe or the paint frame.'

'Nobody visible,' Lilith said darkly. She tilted her head to the side. 'I hear her, you know. She speaks to me.' Her eyelashes swept down against her cheek; she seemed to be listening intently. 'Every night I lay here and the lines are running through my head, over and over again. It's like … Lady Macbeth wants to exist. And she can't while I'm stuck in here.' She opened her eyes, caught the expression on my face. 'Well, you see how it is. I must get back to work. I'll go stark mad if Hugh keeps me off the stage.'

The watch felt like a living presence, its heartbeat thumping through our silence. 'You should get rid of it,' I said suddenly. 'Nothing good comes of that watch. I saw Eugene Grieves choke on his own blood while he clasped it. Silas fell to his doom with it in his hand.'

Lilith snapped the watch closed, clutched it to her chest. 'I can't do that. It means too much to me.'

'Aren't you even a little scared? I thought you actors believed in bad luck. Aren't you frightened something might happen to you?'

Her grey eyes slid over me. 'Something bad *did* happen to me, Kitty. But it wasn't caused by Melpomene. It was you and Mrs Dyer.' Her face twisted in dislike. 'Bloody Sylvia. She's as foolish and desperate over Eugene's watch as she was over the man himself. Is she really surprised that Hugh sought comfort elsewhere? That he'd pick the one woman who discarded Eugene and set out to make a name for herself?'

I bit my lip. She had a right to be angry at us, but it didn't justify her adultery. 'Did you tell the Guvnor what you suspected? That his wife was behind your collapse?'

She shook her head. 'What would be the point? He's dependant on her. Besides, I don't need Hugh to fight my battles for me. I have Melpomene now.'

The Guvnor certainly had strange taste in women. Both his wife and his mistress were cracked in their own way. 'You know,' I tried, 'it's probably the infection causing all these whispers. Making you hear and see things. You're a great actress, Lilith, but this Melpomene you hear … it's all inside your head.'

I wanted to believe it; I told myself I did. But as Lilith regarded me with a kind of indulgent pity, my fear ticked on in the background, steady as the rhythm of the watch.

CHAPTER 17

That was our first Christmas without Greg. None of us expected it to be so merry. We filled his place with all the trinkets and luxuries my wages could buy. We didn't have to choose between beef or goose; we had both, and a plum pudding as big as Bertie's head. Philip nearly broke his tooth on the sixpence baked inside.

I'd bought him his first good-quality cap. He spent his days making bowlers for gentlemen in the factory; he deserved a nice hat of his own. To Dorcas I gave a pair of Adelaide boots and enough material to make a new gown. Bertie received Chinese Roarers, which he wanted to set off inside, peppermint lozenges and a gutta-percha head. I wished I hadn't got him that. When he squeezed it, distorting the nose and mouth, it looked like Eugene Grieves in the throes of death.

Mrs Dyer sent me a present of teacups and saucers. 'For entertaining the neighbours,' I explained to the others. 'When we move to our new lodgings. She's found a place she says will be perfect.'

I'd grown wary of Mrs Dyer's judgement, but I was happy then, warmed by a coal fire and tipsy with wine. There were games and Waterloo pulling crackers, carols and sprigs of holly. Seeing the smiles on those beloved faces gave me a satisfaction like nothing I'd felt before. It was worth it, I thought. All the guilt, all the sneaking around; Mrs Dyer's instability and Lilith's whispers: it was worth any price.

My certainty started to fail in the New Year when Mrs Dyer's growler arrived and took us on a route I seemed to recognise, through streets I'd passed only recently. I told myself I was mistaken. Rain was falling steadily, drumming on the roof, obscuring the windows with mist and beads of moisture. I must be wrong.

But I wasn't. There were the familiar bare trees, the red bricks, the covered entrances. We pulled up in St John's Wood.

I turned to Mrs Dyer in disbelief. 'But this is—'

'Just down the road from Lilith's villa, yes.' She beamed from ear to ear. 'If Hugh can set his protégé up here, can I not do the same?'

The carriage seemed to be growing smaller, tightening around me. It wasn't kindness, after all: it was another task. 'Maybe ... maybe it would be better if I found my own place to live. Somewhere nearer to the theatre?'

Her laugh tinkled out. 'We have come all this way! Just view the house. I promise you will not regret it.'

She'd sent me some particulars, but that was nothing to seeing the place for myself. Empty of furniture and swept clean, the rooms seemed built for a giant. There was space enough for us all. Space to grow into the people we'd always wanted to be. The walls were hung with a Morris-style paper from the ceiling to the dado rail. Wooden wainscoting shone below. There were no carpets, but it didn't feel cold even on that January day. Downstairs consisted of a kitchen, a maid's closet and a parlour large enough for both a sofa and a dining table. A shallow set of steps led to the next floor.

'I believe little Albert should be able to climb these by now,' Mrs Dyer said. 'The gentle exercise may even prove beneficial. There is a nice sturdy bannister for him to grip.'

There were two rooms upstairs and a real flushing lavatory. I peered out of the window on to a very different neighbourhood to the one I'd known. 'We can't afford to rent this. The amount you quoted, that can't be right.'

She simpered. 'I may have had a little something to do with that. Your landlord found it difficult to haggle with a lady. His gallantry quite got the better of him.'

Why did it have to be so beautiful?

Outside, the pavement was dancing with plashing raindrops. If I leant forward, I could just see Lilith's house.

'You want me to watch Lilith all the time,' I said dully. 'To be a neighbourhood spy.'

Mrs Dyer tapped a finger against her red lips. 'I *had* hoped to prompt her to retire through ill health, but now Hugh has banished the cats ...'

I took a breath. I had to tell her. 'She knows, madam. Lilith knows what we did. I'm not sure I'll be of much use to you, now. She won't trust me again.'

Mrs Dyer clasped her hands, toying with her wedding ring through her glove. 'Well, that is unfortunate. But she can prove nothing. And if you are living here, calling upon her from time to time, might she not believe you have turned and become her ally?'

I closed my eyes briefly. I wanted this house. I wanted the future I could almost grasp, where I didn't have to sleep in a chair, where there were green spaces for the boys to play and Gregory would never find us.

'But ... to what purpose, Mrs Dyer?'

'We shall see. I have sent you the next play, but perhaps you have not had the leisure to read it yet. There are ample opportunities for sabotage there that have nothing to do with costume. At one point, the Duchess eats from a basket of apricots.'

I stared aghast. She was spiralling out of control. 'You don't mean ... we can't poison her!'

She flapped a hand. 'No, not *poison*, of course, what must you think of me? But some manner of purge ... that might be arranged.'

I imagined Lilith vomiting, loosing her bowels upon the stage. What would the newspapers write about that? 'No! It's too risky! We've already hurt her enough. Suppose we misjudged the dose? Lilith might die!'

Mrs Dyer's lips quivered, as they often did, but for the first time I realised it was not so much a nervous tremor as a kind of hunger. She *wanted* Lilith dead.

'Yes,' she said hoarsely. 'Yes, you are quite right. If there was an accident ... that would be a stain upon our souls.'

She'd been watching too much Shakespeare. I'd always thought her play-acting amusing, but this was beyond anything. Who did she think she was? Lady Macbeth?

Yet she'd done good too. That same impulsive nature had changed Bertie's life, was offering me this house. She might be brought round again.

'Mrs Dyer,' I said, as gently as I could. 'I understand why you want revenge, believe me. But Lilith isn't a witch. You mustn't let your hatred of her do this to you. You have a kind heart – look how you've helped me! Don't let your husband's betrayal turn you into something you're not. It's not my place to advise you, but I think … well, I think maybe the time has come for you to talk to the Guvnor about all this.'

She looked suddenly fragile. 'But what would I say? That he has made our marriage a mockery? That I realise I no longer hold his heart, or even his loyalty? If I speak those words to him … I will have to swallow the humiliation all over again.'

'I know. It's awful. You deserve better treatment than you've received, Mrs Dyer. But you can't go on pretending. Your marriage isn't a play. You can't cast Lilith as the witch and hope she'll magically disappear in a puff of smoke.'

Tears trembled on her lashes. 'You are wise, for one so young. But you do not know what it is to have a husband, a child …' She sighed. 'The balance of power is not equal, Jennifer. I do not have the ability to bring about change. Hugh will talk me round, despite my better judgement. He always does. He will convince me that Lilith *must* stay, for the good of the theatre, and I will yield to him because I love him, because I want to believe him, because I have no one else. I see it all, as though it were scripted for me.'

'But it isn't! You *can* persuade him to be a better man. And as for Lilith …' I scuffed the toe of my boot against the pristine floor. Even now, she was probably talking to her beloved watch. 'You don't need to make her ill. She's already unsound in her mind. She's a talented actress, but in the long run … I'm not sure she'll cope with this life. She'll flare bright and burn herself out like a match.'

'Do you really think so?'

'Yes. There's a phrase. I don't know if you use it in good society. "Give a man enough rope, and he'll hang himself."'

146

Mrs Dyer dabbed the tears from her eyes. They were shining like leaves after rainfall. 'I like that. I like that very much.'

With a heavy heart, I left the window. 'So perhaps it's better that I don't spy on Lilith and I live somewhere else. Somewhere smaller.'

'Oh no! You must take the house. It would be so beneficial to all your family. I have negotiated the deal.'

'But I won't be doing what you wanted. There's nothing in it for you.'

She came over and placed a hand upon my shoulder. 'You shall be happy. *That* is what I want. And it will not hurt to have someone keeping an eye upon Lilith, even if we take no further action against her. I have a saying of my own: *forewarned is forearmed*. Please. Say you will live here and watch. Simply watch. It is all I ask.'

I longed to trust her again. I longed for the house. Deep down, I was every bit as sentimental and self-deceiving as Mrs Dyer herself. For I wanted her to be the kind benefactor from a storybook, my fairy godmother. I wanted my happy ending.

'If you're sure, madam ...'

'I am certain.' She patted my shoulder. I felt uncomfortably like a pet. 'Stay by me, Jennifer. You shall get everything you deserve.'

Once the chaos of moving had settled down, once we'd explored the area, run about the rooms squealing with laughter at our good fortune, unpacked boxes and invited some of our new neighbours round for tea, I decided to visit Lilith.

Maybe she didn't deserve my consideration. But the call was relevant to our work. I'd read *The Duchess of Malfi* and longed to discuss it with someone who cared. To me it was better than any of Shakespeare's plays. The heroine was flirtatious, kind, brave and noble. I couldn't wait to dress her.

A charwoman opened the door. It only took one look at her stooped shoulders, the peeling skin on her fingers and her flustered demeanour to confirm I'd done the right thing. If I gave up my partnership with Mrs Dyer, this was what I'd become: a person who cleaned these houses for money rather than living in one.

'Madam's in the parlour,' the char said wearily. 'I'm not paid to announce guests.'

I heard Eurydice bark. 'Just as well. She won't have time to throw me out.'

Lilith was at least dressed that day, although her hair hung in a greasy black curtain over one side of her face. She was reading, her knees tucked up under her on the sofa.

It was clear to see why the charwoman was vexed. There were books and teacups piled everywhere, crumbs on the carpet, pawprints on the floorboards. Most of the flowers were still on display, wilting apace. A fly buzzed against the window, trying to get out. No guard or screen sat before the fire. There weren't even skirts on the furniture to protect it from smuts.

Lilith glanced up distractedly. 'Oh. I didn't expect to see you again.'

I thought it best to be honest. 'I live here now. Just down the road.'

She snapped her book shut. 'She's put you there to spy on me?'

'Yes,' I agreed briskly, moving a newspaper off the chair and sitting down. 'I shan't do it, though.'

She watched me for a while, her strong features marked with distrust. 'Do you expect me to believe that? After what you've already done?'

'Neither you nor I can afford the rent in St John's Wood. Mr Dyer pays for your house, Mrs Dyer pays for mine. Both of us have put some morals aside for that, haven't we?'

'So we are what? Partners in crime?'

'No. But we might as well be neighbours.' I pulled out the little sketchbook from my bag. 'I wanted to talk to you about *The Duchess of Malfi*. I've ideas to show Mrs Nettles already.'

Her interest sharpened at once. 'You've read it, then? And how do you like the Duchess?'

'She's perfect. Not like Lady Macbeth, at all! She has a good heart, a sense of humour and a strong will. I love how she dies defying the wicked schemes of her brothers.' I lifted an eyebrow. 'As you know, that's a topic close to my heart.'

She laughed then and rose up, beginning to pace, as though her feet were seeking the boards. 'You see, now, the beauty of tragedy? It has so many faces. Not all doom and gloom but nobility, honour and a hundred other qualities. You may laugh at a comedy, but you'll forget it in time. Tragedy has burrs. It sticks to your heart. You remember what it made you feel, always.'

There was no forgetting *Doctor Faustus*, that was certain. I spread the book on my lap. 'Come and look. I'm trying to capture what she goes through. Clothes that show her being stifled and crushed, yet that glimmer of indestructible beauty beneath.'

I showed her swatches of glacé silk, overlaid with gauze to obscure the sheen. Sketches of luxurious, champagne satin and a crocheted overdress that made it look as though the Duchess was caught inside a gold net. There was a material Polly had told me about that could be washed and tied wet with rope to achieve a crinkled, squeezed effect. I couldn't recall its name but I'd drawn it, clinging to the figure of a faceless woman with Lilith's dark hair.

'These are glorious!' she enthused. 'I have an idea – it came to me last night. Let me show you. Where are your pencils?'

I hadn't brought them, but she found one of her own and seized my sketchbook, leafing right to the back. 'Like this, with the bodice tight. A high neck and cuffs like, like manacles. But the sleeves puff, see?' Her frantic scribbles ripped through the page.

I stood and took the book gently from her. Her manner frightened me a little, but she'd been cooped up inside, away from what she lived for. 'That's good. Tell me about the colours.'

She held up a finger, bidding me to wait a moment. As she rummaged behind the cushions on the sofa I caught sight of a spider scuttling across the mantelpiece.

Lilith pulled out the Melpomene watch.

Flipping the case open, she checked the hands and nodded as if it had spoken to her. 'Regal hues. A deep amethyst. Virgin blue. Cardinal red – the colour of martyrs.'

I closed my sketchbook with a sigh. 'I think it will be good for you to get back to the theatre. Give yourself over to a new role, one a little less ... mad than Lady Macbeth.'

'*I'll tell thee a miracle, I am not mad yet to my cause of sorrow.
Th'heaven o'ver my head seems made of molten brass, the earth
of flaming sulphur, yet I am not mad.*'

'You know your lines already.'

'Of course. What else have I to do?' She glanced up. 'What
news of Anthony? Shall he be my twin, my Ferdinand? Shall he
order my murder and have his guilt turn him into a wolf?'

'I'm not sure,' I said, tucking my sketchbook back inside my
bag. 'The play's a bit macabre. He might not have the heart for it,
after Silas.'

'It's a shilling fine for refusing a part. I pity him, but there's
work to be done. He cannot ignore the muse forever.'

I rolled my eyes. 'All you talk about is the muse.'

My intentions had been good, but everything was relapsing into
its usual state. While my patience held, I'd try, at least try, to understand. 'What is it about Melpomene that obsesses you? I haven't
read the myths. Is she a wonderful character like the Duchess?'

'Eugene used to tell me stories,' she said, running her index
finger over the pearls that rimmed the watch face. 'Wild tales
about how he'd charmed her from Mount Helicon to dwell with
him. I have books. Sit with me a while and read.' She reached for
the bell, but then noticed the piles of dirty cups beside it. The top
one was growing mould. 'Oh dear. Better not ask the char for tea.
How does absinthe suit you?'

I thought she was joking, but she knelt beside the sofa and
retrieved a vivid green bottle. Yanking out the cork with her teeth,
she poured me a drink. 'Just a nip if you're not used to it,' she said
with her mouth full. 'It's got one hell of a kick.'

I sipped politely and nearly choked. The spirit was strong,
herbal and tasted like liquorice. Lilith spat out the cork and
grinned at me. 'Awake now?'

I chuckled in spite of myself. There was, at least, never a dull
moment with Lilith. I sat down on the sofa and tried another sip.
I liked it, but I wouldn't risk any more.

Removing two volumes from the bookcase, she sat beside me
and passed one over. 'Greek myths for you, Campbell's *Life of
Mrs Siddons* for me.'

I swapped her for the bottle of absinthe. 'I'm starting to think you don't hear Melpomene whisper; it's the green fairy instead.'

She gave a contemptuous snort and opened her book.

It was odd, how companionable it felt reading there together, considering I'd nearly killed her a few weeks ago. Perhaps Lilith was only tolerating me because of her loneliness, and I was only being forbearing because of my guilt. Still, it was a nice way to spend the afternoon, even if it was all pretend. Eurydice came to lay upon our feet and warm them, the fire blazed, and the stories held my interest. The single discomfort was the tick of Lilith's watch, punctuating my thoughts.

While I felt closer to Lilith, Melpomene still eluded me. She was a shadowy figure, always hiding behind that mask. The book said she'd been the muse of song and dance before her association with tragedy – I didn't understand how that could be. I hadn't heard of any other gods or patron saints that decided to switch.

I lifted my head briefly from the page, gazing at the Melpomene figure engraved on Lilith's watch. Why did she hold a club? Now that I considered, it looked worryingly like the shape of the cut on Lilith's arm.

'Don't gawp at me. It's off-putting.'

I went back to reading again. The author wrote that Melpomene charmed her listeners' souls. That much seemed to be true, if Lilith was anything to go by. Then there was a tale that she'd given birth to children by a river god, producing half-woman-half-bird creatures called Sirens. They sang too, but with a different purpose. They weren't telling stories; they were luring sailors to their deaths.

The ticking of the watch was growing louder. I flicked forward a few pages.

'*Thamyris the minstrel challenged the Muses and lost his eyes ... King Pyreneus tried to seduce them but was led to his death by leaping off a tower ...*'

I closed the book. I'd tried, but there was no inspiration here, only misery and gore. I'd endured quite enough of that.

'I have to go,' I said, rising.

She lifted her face to mine. There was a shadow of sadness, of regret, that I hadn't seen before. 'Come back another time. If you're going to spy, you may as well do it from my sofa.'

I smiled at the jest, but I suspected she'd only said it to sound less plaintive.

Was she really so desperate for a friend?

CHAPTER 18

The first sight to greet me as I entered the properties room was a corpse. Manacles bound his wrists. One of the hands was missing, leaving only a raw stump. His head drooped, the face obscured by a spill of blood-matted hair. My sickened gaze travelled down his torso to his calves, where three children slumped. The girl had died with her arms about his leg. The boy was more sprawling, his throat cut as he fought to shield a babe upon his breast.

'They've done a bang-up job, haven't they?' Oscar's voice made me jump. 'Looks like the real thing. No wonder it fools the Duchess.'

Of course I'd seen the stage direction when I read the play: *Here is discovered behind a traverse the artificial figures of Antonio and his children, appearing as if they were dead.* It was one of the fiendish ploys of Ferdinand to drive his sister mad. First, he gave her a wax hand bearing her husband's wedding ring, then he pretended he'd slaughtered her entire family. My imagination hadn't dwelt on the details. But now I saw the scene brought to life, my enthusiasm for the play suffered a sharp check.

'It looks like Anthony Frost. Is that his part: Antonio?'

Oscar nodded. A strand of brown hair fell across his forehead. 'There was a bit of a barny over it. The Guvnor cast him as Ferdinand, but he turned it down flat. He wanted to be a good character for a change.'

Lilith would be disappointed. Usually I'd take Anthony's side, but looking at this model I wished he'd chosen differently. It cut me to see him dead and dismembered, even in wax form. 'Poor

Anthony. I suppose it's an easier part for him. He didn't fancy the Cardinal?'

'He didn't want to be an evil brother at all.' The corner of Oscar's mouth quirked unpleasantly. 'Speaking of which, has Greg given you any more trouble?'

'We've moved,' I said stoutly. 'He can't find us now. Unless he comes back here, and I don't think that's likely, do you?'

Oscar rubbed at his brow, where a faint bruise still lurked. 'I don't know what to expect from him these days. I worried he might try it on with you over Christmas. Forgiveness and all that.'

'He'd get short shrift. I'm not a soft touch.'

His brown eyes warmed with something like affection. 'No. But you're kind. You can be tough and kind at the same time, you know.'

It wasn't an extravagant compliment, but I felt as embarrassed as if he'd gushed like the Guvnor and called me his leading light. I didn't know where to look.

'I did a bit of digging,' Oscar told me, 'to see what Greg and Georgie had been up to over the pond. I found out what sent them scurrying back on the steamer in such a hurry.'

'What was it?'

'Georgie caused a stink in New York, pitting the cast against each other, making all sorts of demands and then, when the curtain rose ... she couldn't deliver. The audience were having none of it.' He gave that bitter smirk again. 'I always told her she was better off sticking to music hall, song and dance, light comedy. Those were her strengths. But she never listened to me.'

'Artistic temperament,' I said dryly. 'You had a lucky escape. Imagine if you'd really set up your own theatre, and had to manage a prima donna like her.'

He chuckled, a warm, throaty chuckle. It made my stomach tense in a way that was both strange and pleasant. 'Ah, I was just as bad for a while. Caught up in her fantasies.' His face became serious. 'But you're right. I got off lightly. Greg's landed himself in a heap of trouble and you need to watch out for him.'

I still felt a swoop of anxiety on my brother's behalf; the habit of sharing in his emotions for so many years. 'What do you mean?'

'Georgie has expensive tastes. He already stole to feed them, now it looks like he's gambling too.'

I'd been forced to tell the Fieldings I suspected Gregory of taking their jewellery. His coming back to England could be dangerous, if they decided to pursue matters. Hopefully they were too rich and self-important to notice the movements of little people like us. But gambling was another matter.

'They left debts behind in America,' Oscar went on. 'If they start to run them up here too ... they might expect you to bail them out.'

'They can go whistle!' I flared.

'That's the spirit.'

I spoke bravely, yet I didn't trust my heart. I'd already softened towards Lilith. Could I really throw my own kin to the dogs, even if they deserved it?

Together, Oscar and I turned our backs on the bloody spectacle of Antonio's death and moved towards the door. The properties room felt like a museum of the Mercury's past. Books, candlesticks, rosaries and masks lined the shelves, whilst larger items such as weapons leant against the walls.

Some of the shelves were sagging, their contents slumping to the side. The blades used in *Macbeth* had mottled; there was a crack running down his wooden shield.

'Oscar,' I said hesitantly. 'Is it my imagination or does the Mercury look ... tarnished, to you?'

He examined the cabinets with a frown. 'I don't think the cleaners came in while we were closed.'

'But it's more than that,' I persisted. 'Even the scenery flats you're working on. The colours seem muted.'

'Cold, winter light,' he agreed. 'Wait until they're under the gas. They'll warm up, you'll see.'

I thought about the evening I'd spent in Eugene Grieves's theatre, how it seemed to wilt even as the action on stage came vividly to life. Maybe all playhouses suffered from wear and tear.

Bidding farewell to Oscar at the ladder, I headed towards the dressing rooms. I disliked weaving through the corridors without any cats around. Their presence had been comforting; even if I rarely saw them, I could sense them watching over us. Now the hallways felt colder. Scuttling came from behind the walls. It sounded larger than mice.

Anthony loped towards me from the other end of the hallway. He looked dreadful. Once his beard had been a neat door-knocker accentuating his chiselled jaw, now it sprouted in all directions. The skin round his eyes was as dark as if it had been painted with violet and ochre to play a villain. Never mind taking a lesser part; he didn't look as if he should be here at all.

'Miss Wilcox! Exactly the person I require.' He descended on me, hands outstretched, imploring. 'You can help. You must help. Keep her away from me!'

'Mr Frost, what's the matter? Of course I'll help you however I can. Just calm down. What do you need?'

'I need … I need …' He clasped a hand to his forehead. 'I need that indefatigable lady to leave me alone. She gives no quarter! She cannot know how she torments me.' His expression darkened. 'Or perhaps she does. Maybe she provokes me on purpose. She takes Silas's demise as though it were nothing. Nothing!'

It wasn't my place to soothe him with a touch or an embrace, but I wished I could. He resembled nothing so much as a child in need of shelter. 'I'll speak to Lilith. I'm sorry she's not been more considerate. She's so focused on this play and she'd set her heart on having you for her Ferdinand.'

'There is no need to inform me of that! It is all I hear from her, on and on, like a deuced harpy! How I must not go against the Muse. How I am displeasing Melpomene. Either she'll end up in Bedlam, or she'll send me there.'

'I'll ask her to stop,' I assured him.

'What does it matter to her who I play? We are all superfluous. The public would not care if you put monkeys in our roles, so long as she was there.'

'Don't talk like that, please, Mr Frost. What would Silas say? He believed in you and your talent more than anything. It would have broken his heart if you gave up.'

His mouth clamped tight. Of course he couldn't say it. He didn't need to say it: his own heart was already broken.

'Never mind Lilith,' I encouraged. 'You don't need her muse. You have one of your own. Do it for Silas.'

He blinked back tears. 'You truly believe he'd wish for me to carry on without him?'

'More than that. He'd want you to shine, to upstage Lilith!'

His brow cleared. It wasn't exactly an easing of tension. It was as though all his muscles had fallen slack. 'He would. You are right, Miss Wilcox. He would.'

'And you can do it,' I urged. 'Remember the opening night of the Scottish play, when you were the star?'

'Yes, yes,' he babbled, strangely excited now. 'I shall do just that: steal the show. Thank you, Miss Wilcox. Thank you.'

Before I could say he was welcome, he strode off, a new vigour to his step.

CHAPTER 19

I pomaded Lilith's dark hair into long curls that draped over one shoulder like brushstrokes of India ink. The makeup was light and girlish, but I added a beauty spot at the corner of her mouth. The Duchess was a bit of a flirt, after all.

When I stepped away, the woman sitting at the dressing table no longer resembled Lilith. I can't say why that bothered me – surely, it was the point of my job. But it was disconcerting to look at Lilith and see someone else staring back.

'Remember what I said,' I warned.

'Play nicely with Anthony,' she parroted back. 'I never meant to upset the poor man. I'm trying to help him. He won't astonish the crowds again if he keeps ignoring Melpomene's instructions.'

'You need to spend less time thinking about characters and mythological figures, more time thinking about people made of flesh and blood.'

Lilith pouted. 'Where's the fun in that?'

I busied myself with preparing the next costume: the dress tied up with rope. Silence reigned as I sat on the sofa to unpick the knots. I wished Lilith would return to whispering her lines, all I could hear was the maddening tick of that watch.

I tried to cover it with my own chatter. 'They say it's a full house tonight. That bodes well for your return, doesn't it? The journalists will soon be eating humble pie.'

Lilith sighed luxuriously. 'It's so good to be back. I don't live anywhere else. I go through the motions, but it's a poor imitation of life.' She observed my work. 'What are you doing with that?

There are no cats for you now, but you're resourceful. Lice in my wig? Firecrackers in the pocket?'

'I'm doing everything in front of you, so you can see it.'

'I *think* I can see it. What about sleight of hand? You might have been in training with an illusionist for all I know. Mrs Dyer would pay for your lessons.'

She wasn't wrong there. 'How could I hurt you,' I quipped, 'with the all-powerful Melpomene watching over you? If she's so mighty, why doesn't she just—'

The lights blinked out.

There was no warning, no hiss or flicker. Darkness swallowed us in an instant. Eurydice released a terrible howl.

There was a sound like ice breaking.

'Lilith? Are you all right?'

I couldn't see. The darkness pressed, thick as a hand across my eyes.

'Lilith?'

The lamps snapped back to full power. I squinted, blinded by the sudden burst of light. Lilith still sat before the dressing table. In front of her the mirror had cracked.

As I watched, a chunk fell loose to shiver over the paintbox and the hairbrush.

'Lilith, watch out! Don't cut yourself!' Throwing down the costume, I leapt to my feet and pulled her clear. 'Stand back, it might happen again.' The dressing table was a mess of jagged diamonds. It would take ages to clean. 'I swear this theatre is falling apart.'

Lilith rubbed a hand across her mouth, smearing the carmine I'd so carefully applied. 'It might,' she said thoughtfully. 'Eugene's whole place threatened to tumble about his ears. But that's the price you pay.'

'The price you pay for what?'

She grinned. 'For one hell of a show.'

―――――――

It took me so long to clear up the broken glass that I didn't make it to my spot in the wings until Act Two. I arrived just in time to see the Duchess gazing eagerly up at Bosola, one hand resting on the swell of her belly. I'd made that belly myself, a pouch of calico and wool, tied with tapes around Lilith's back.

'*Apricots, madam.*'

A boy brushed past me, touched the horseshoe and stepped out on stage. Like everyone else, his eyes were pinned on Lilith. He walked towards her in a kind of trance and offered the basket.

The audience tittered appreciatively as Lilith gobbled apricots, juice running down her chin. She had exactly the desperate air of a pregnant woman with a craving. She stopped abruptly, put a hand to her chest. '*I thank you, Bosola: they were right good ones, if they do not make me sick.*' She staggered. '*This green fruit and my stomach are not friends. How they swell me!*' Perhaps it was a filter cast over the light, but I thought I saw a touch of green creep across her face.

'*I am very sorry.*'

She winced – it was supposed to be the first pang of labour in the Duchess's secret pregnancy. '*Lights to my chamber,*' she said desperately. '*Oh, good Antonio, I fear I am undone.*'

Lilith tottered off the stage. But something was wrong. Her harried expression didn't lift. She careered right into me. 'Lilith?'

She was shaking, drenched in sweat. 'A basin,' she gasped. 'Get me a basin. I'm going to be sick.'

I half-supported, half-carried her into the wings. There was a man dressed as a soldier, wearing a round helmet. I snatched it off his head, just in time. Lilith folded and heaved out the contents of her stomach.

'Hey!'

'Mind the dress!' Mrs Nettles hissed from behind me. 'Don't let her stain the dress!'

It was shadowy with only the wing lights flickering on their ladder, but the liquid Lilith vomited looked the wrong colour. Too dark.

She swayed on her feet.

'I'll scrub your helmet out,' I promised the actor. 'Just … let me settle her first.'

Lilith started to shamble away, pulling me with her. For all her sweat, her hand felt deadly cold. I pushed aside the uncomfortable memory of Mrs Dyer, standing in my new house, talking of poison. She wouldn't. Surely she *couldn't*, without my help?

As we broke free of the billowing curtains, Lilith stopped and leant against a wall, running her tongue round her mouth.

'Are you going to be ill again?'

She parted her lips, reached in. A tooth came away in her fingertips.

'God almighty!' I cried.

Lilith regarded the molar, its long roots tipped in black. 'At least it's one from the back,' she shrugged, as though it were nothing. 'Come along, I need to change for my next scene.'

'You're never going back on stage?'

'Of course I am, Kitty. I'd rather die than miss another performance.'

Her vomit swilled in the helmet as we moved. Whatever that putrid smell was, it wasn't apricots. It was sulphuric, rotten, just like the stench in the dressing room.

CHAPTER 20

That Sunday I sat at home in our new parlour, with gentle light streaming in through the window, and read the newspapers. Each theatre column announced Lilith's triumphant return. They said she dazzled and shimmered as the Duchess, and she did. But I kept remembering that tooth.

I had a horrible feeling Mrs Dyer was behind Lilith's sickness, although the purges she'd spoken of couldn't rot a tooth in a matter of minutes. Lilith ate her fair share of humbugs, but her smile was even and white. It didn't make sense. Nor did the grey strands in her hair, the blood that occasionally dripped from her nose … It felt like she was going the same way as the theatre. Making the character rich and alive, while she faded away.

I shook myself. Between the separate influences of Mrs Dyer and Lilith, my mind was becoming clouded with all types of fancies. I should concentrate on what mattered: the reviews, and the money the theatre would bring in.

But while Lilith was lauded, Anthony Frost's performance suffered a drubbing. The critics complained of his 'hang-dog, dismal' Antonio and applauded the brothers in their quest to put an end to his misery. They wrote about Anthony as if he had no more feelings than a marionette. Didn't they understand that he was a real person, with real troubles that couldn't always be put aside for work? No one could pretend his was an inspired portrayal, but they could at least have forborne to mention it.

Wheels crunched outside. I raised my eyes with only the vaguest interest, for the parlour window looked straight on to the road and many carriages passed by. But then I froze. Mrs Dyer's growler had pulled up in front of our house.

I never dreamed she'd visit me here, so close to Lilith's home. Mrs Dyer would have read these reviews with very different feelings. If Lilith had succeeded despite her underhand plots, she'd be after my help again. And how could I deny it? I was living in her house!

I'd scarcely reached the hallway before the knocker banged. Dorcas emerged from the kitchen, red-cheeked and dishevelled from cooking, in no state to receive a lady.

'It's Mrs Dyer,' I whispered. Panic widened her eyes, she hurriedly wiped her hands upon her apron as I opened the door.

A wax doll of Mrs Dyer stood on the street outside. A perfect, bloodless copy. The only vestige of colour lay in her lips, which were painted red as a wound. Rachel stood beside her, stiff-backed and clearly terrified.

'Jennifer,' Mrs Dyer started desperately. 'Jennifer, I must speak with you.' Then she noticed Dorcas hovering in the background. The change was instantaneous; all her charm returned. 'Miss Dorcas, how delightful. I hope you are settling in well? Pray excuse me for intruding on your Sabbath day.'

'Not at all, we're honoured. May I – may I fetch you some tea?'

'Oh no, thank you. I shall not inconvenience you for long. I only crave a private word with Jennifer – it is quite urgent, I am afraid. Theatre business of the most pressing nature.'

My thoughts were leaping wildly. I stepped back and motioned them inside the house. Could Lilith's glowing reviews really have made Mrs Dyer look this ghastly? What if it was something worse?

'Dorcas, could you take Miss Dyer upstairs and show her the flowers we pressed? She'll be bored by theatre talk.'

Dorcas nodded, bending down to the child's height and extending a hand. 'Would you like that, sweetheart?' Rachel clung to her mother's skirt. 'Don't worry, I don't bite! I met you once before, d'you remember? I rode in your carriage from the hospital. Come on, let's leave your mama to her business. We'll go and look at pretty things instead.'

Rachel raised wary eyes to her mother, but seeing Mrs Dyer nod, she was persuaded to go.

'A thousand thanks, Miss Dorcas. I will only occupy your sister for a short period, I promise.'

But when she entered the parlour, Mrs Dyer closed the door and stood with her back pressed against it, as though she were barricading us in for a siege.

'Madam?' I said. 'You're scaring me.'

The look she shot at me was so wild, so desperate, that I took a step back. 'My heart.' She struck a hand against her bodice. 'My heart! I thought that there was none left of it to break. I have been in agonies, Jennifer, and unable to confide in a single soul. You are my only friend.'

'Then tell me what's wrong.'

Pain creased her brow. 'I have ached to! And yet ... I cannot bear the sound of my own voice, saying it aloud!' She sank down to her haunches, her gown pooling round her, the petticoats frothing beneath.

I was torn between exasperation and pity. Mrs Dyer was plainly in distress, but I didn't see why she had to express her emotions in this melodramatic style. She reached into her bag and groped around. Rather than producing the handkerchief I expected, she pulled out a piece of crumpled paper. I stooped down to her level, a similar pose to the one Dorcas had adopted for Rachel. 'May I take that?'

'Yes. Take it, take it. It burns me.'

I unfolded the page and frowned, trying to make sense of what I saw. There were neat, regular lines of writing in a copperplate script. It was a record, a ledger of some kind, full of names. The left side was torn. Mrs Dyer must have ripped it out of a book.

'What am I ...' I began. Then I glimpsed a familiar name. 'Where did you get this?'

'I have been to Southend-on-Sea. Frequently. It is not far, you know, on the train. I say that the air is beneficial to Rachel's lungs. Hugh is always reluctant to allow the trip, he urges me to try Margate instead. Well, you see why that is.'

'You shouldn't have this. It looks official. There are other entries here, someone might need to—'

'I could not leave it in the church! Brazen, announcing my shame to all the world! I wonder they allowed it. I wonder the vicar even consented!'

They'd certainly made no effort to hide the sin of fornication. Both parents' names were written on the baptism record, bold as brass. Hugh Algernon Dyer and Lily Fitzwilliams.

Focused on this, and the discovery of Lilith's real name, I didn't absorb the other information: the details of the child itself. But Mrs Dyer drew my attention that way.

'A son,' she breathed. 'A son. An heir. Hugh has all but acknowledged him as such. Do you realise what this means, Jennifer?'

My eyes raced along the entry. She was right. A boy, christened Algernon. I returned to my chair, smoothing the page over the newspapers. 'But ... where is this boy now?'

'With a nurse in Southend, since Lilith fell ill.'

'You've seen him?'

She looked disgusted. 'Gracious, no. But I have been watching my husband's correspondence closely. He remains in contact, although he does not visit in person.'

I couldn't think straight. I blamed the Guvnor – but I would have blamed him for not acknowledging the child and not monitoring its progress too. 'And he's said nothing? Absolutely nothing to you?'

She shook her head, spilling her hair from out of its pins. 'Not a word. For all I know he may have already changed his Will.'

Could he really do that? I thought there were laws against things like this: I knew there were laws against men taking their wife's money and packing her off to an asylum. 'But surely your money's protected? You had a settlement, or something?'

'We were married before the Property Act. None of my relations were there to advise me on a marriage contract or anything of that nature. I trusted Hugh. He has always given me an ample allowance to do as I will. I never dreamed it would be necessary to *protect* anything from him!'

The depth of the betrayal was stunning, but I saw a glimmer of hope. 'Don't worry, madam. The Guvnor won't abandon Rachel. He wouldn't leave her penniless! If anything, this proves that it isn't in his heart to just cast off a child.'

'Oh, Jennifer,' she wept. 'You are too naïve by half. You never thought your brother would abandon *you*, yet he did it all the same.'

How could I disagree?

'Besides,' she went on, 'an *adequate* provision will be of no comfort. Rachel is entitled to everything. It is her birth right. It is *my* fortune. That bastard has no more claim on it than the boy who sweeps the street!'

That was untrue. At least some of the money must have been the Guvnor's, or made through profits of the theatre. Lilith's talent had increased receipts tenfold. Little Algernon deserved something. But Mrs Dyer wasn't in the mood to hear hard truths. 'Do you want my advice?'

'Yes! Heaven knows I cannot think clearly.'

'All you can do is confront him. Threaten to expose the secret and ruin his reputation. Of course, you never would – but it might put the wind up him.'

I couldn't begin to imagine what all of this would mean for me. If Mrs Dyer twisted the Guvnor's arm and persuaded him to sack Lilith, would I even have employment? I liked to think Mrs Dyer would stand by me, move me to dressing Clementine or another actress, but I couldn't be sure. Recent events had proved her unpredictable.

'Yes,' she said, attempting to steady her breath. 'Painful as it is ... I must deal with Hugh.' Her emerald eyes slid to me. 'But you. You must help me deal with Lilith.'

Gooseflesh skittered over my skin. 'What do you mean?'

'She has taken everything I love, Jennifer. I want to take something from *her*.'

'I'm not sure what that would really achieve—'

'It would give me satisfaction!' she roared. 'Do I need any other reason? If I were a man, I would call her out and shoot her through the heart, but as it is ... I must use the weapons at my disposal.'

Mrs Dyer had let her emotions get the better of her, and I couldn't blame her for that. But she was going too far.

'I'm not your weapon,' I said quietly. 'I told you before that I wouldn't poison Lilith. Though I think you found someone else to do it.'

She regarded me coldly. It gave me a lurch of panic, to see her look at me like that. 'I am not asking you to physically hurt her. I wish only to break her spirit. To make her as wretched as she has made me.'

I lowered my eyes to the table, thinking furiously. I shouldn't have to make this choice. I was sick of Mrs Dyer talking as if Lilith had caused all the problems herself, without the Guvnor being a willing participant.

'If you do this for me,' Mrs Dyer said slowly, her voice like honey, 'you will not regret it. I shall set Dorcas up in her own shop. Engage a tutor to come here for Philip when he is not at the factory. You will want for nothing. You will be doing your family a great service.'

She knew where I was weak. I'd abase myself for them. Do anything so that I didn't have to watch Dorcas, Philip and Bertie feel the misery I'd experienced at their ages.

At the end of the day, Mrs Dyer had it in her power to keep me in employment, in this fancy house, or discard me utterly. Lilith could offer me nothing.

'If I did,' I said warily, 'this would be the last time. No more pranks, no more tricks. I've no reason to hurt Lilith. She's not harmed me.'

She smiled then, but there was something fixed and dreadful about that smile. 'Make no mistake, Jennifer. You cannot be both my friend and a friend to Lilith. It is one or the other. You must choose between us. You are not a stupid girl. I trust you to make the sensible decision.'

CHAPTER 21

Lilith was knocking them dead again. It was different, watching her succeed as the Duchess. Rather than creating Lady Macbeth, terrible to behold, she embodied someone you actually liked. I warmed to her through the character. I couldn't help it.

Which made what I had to do all the more difficult.

She'd come to change into her last costume. There was one farewell scene with Antonio, then the Duchess would be borne off to imprisonment, torment and eventually death. Of course, we had her die in white, but her underskirt burned scarlet, the colour for martyrs. No ruff or collar, so the audience could see the cruel noose looped round her fair neck.

Lilith didn't speak as I worked – at least, not to me. Her attention was entirely focused on the Melpomene watch. She monitored its hands obsessively, whispering, '*I am Duchess of Malfi still.*'

And just like the Duchess, she'd be betrayed. The sum was simple. I either turned traitor against Lilith, an actress I'd known for a few months, or against my entire family. Better to hurt one than to ruin three. My mind accepted that. My heart didn't.

There was a knock at the door. My stomach sank as the call boy announced Lilith's name. 'Break a leg,' I said, stupidly.

She offered me a thin, regal smile and left, taking the watch with her.

For once, the absence of that timepiece didn't lift the dense, oppressive atmosphere. I was painfully aware of the mirror, still unrepaired, and the stench twining its way round the flowers. Eurydice licked her paw as I tidied up the paintbox and put away the brushes. I wouldn't be able to delay my dreaded task much longer.

Sighing, I left the dressing room and made my way to the yard. It was quiet at this time of night, with only the usual noises of rolling wheels and clopping hooves from the street outside to penetrate the walls. Frost laced the cobbles. My breath plumed out like smoke as I reached beneath an old, broken piano. The bucket was there, as Mrs Dyer promised, covered with a piece of cloth. Shadows swarmed, making it look like there was something wriggling and twitching below. Even out here in the cold night air, the acrid, sour smell of the bucket's contents made me want to retch. How did a lady like Mrs Dyer dream up such a disgusting scheme?

She hadn't thought the matter through. Driven by malice and hurt, she hadn't stopped to consider what would happen if someone caught me. Just like the night of the allergic reaction, she was nowhere to be seen. She always left me to clear up her mess.

Passing back inside the theatre, I made a mental list of all the people who would loathe me after tonight. There was Lilith, obviously, and Mrs Nettles would never forgive me for ruining a costume. I felt hollow, thinking about Oscar's reaction. I'd be proving myself as Greg's sister: another bad apple.

I shouldn't lose my job, Mrs Dyer had promised me that. But she couldn't stop the glares and whispers of the staff.

No one questioned me as I went backstage and struggled up the ladder with the stinking bucket cutting into the crook of my elbow. Everyone was so focused on the play that they scarcely noticed me.

The bridge seemed so much higher, by night, than it had that day I passed over it with Oscar. Trembling, I stepped out onto the planks. They creaked beneath my tread. Most of the flymen were working around the gridiron and opposite Prompt Corner, oblivious of my presence. Why, then, did I feel watched?

The Duchess would enter soon, to see the coffin and be tricked into kissing a dead man's hand. I didn't have much time to cross the bridge and reach my spot before the lights went out.

Carrying the bucket slowed my step. I fought against the urge to look down; repressed the memory of Silas plummeting. The planks below me seemed to be moving, swaying in a breeze.

'He will kiss your hand and reconcile himself, but, for his vow, he dares not see you.'

It was too soon. I heard Lilith's voice, further away than it should have been. '*At his pleasure: take the lights hence.*'

Pitch darkness swallowed the auditorium. The audience gasped and murmured; this part always took them by surprise. All that filled the void were the voices on stage: the Duchess, clear as a bell, and Ferdinand's growl.

My fingers gripped tight around the bucket handle. It felt like the only solid thing left. I didn't dare to move in the dark. My eyes roved, desperate for a glimmer of brightness, and as I stared into the endless black, I thought I saw a shape. A human figure, standing directly above Lilith, where I should be.

Reason deserted me. Was this them? The person or thing that pushed Silas to his doom?

The figure raised its arms, then tested the rail.

'*Ha? Lights! Oh horrible!*'

My task. I'd been so occupied looking at the figure that I'd forgotten why I was up here. I'd missed my own cue.

'*Let her have lights enough.*'

Illumination flooded the auditorium; a lady in the audience screamed to see Lilith *en tableau* with a dead man's hand. But I wasn't looking at that. I was blinking against the light, struggling to understand that the shape I'd seen was Anthony Frost with a rope noosed around his neck.

He jumped.

It happened very quickly. Lilith only spoke two words of her speech: '*What witchcraft—*' before the screams erupted again.

It was a long drop, far higher than a gallows. Anthony must have realised the actors would try to save him by holding his legs if he dangled within reach of the stage, so he made the rope short. Too short.

It pulled his head off.

Lilith was covered from head to toe in a spray of gore. The torso flopped, still twitching to the boards, whilst the head remained tangled in the noose, its mouth open in a silent scream.

My knees unhinged. The bucket slipped from my hand, narrowly avoiding Lilith as it landed with a *thwack*, spilling maggots across the boards. She didn't scream. I don't think she was able to. She stood alone on stage, motionless amongst the chaos, her skin slick and red, the whites of her eyes huge. She looked like the Queen of Hell, still clutching the dead man's hand.

Shouts and screams made a wild cacophony in my ears. The curtain fell at an angle, only screening part of the stage, while the orchestra pit clanged with strings and drums as the musicians tried to fend off the falling maggots.

I crawled across the flies. Wood splintered my hands, but I kept moving. I didn't want shock to freeze me like Lilith; if it did, I'd have time to absorb what had just happened.

I'd remember telling Anthony to try and steal the show.

No one could doubt that he had.

For now, Lilith needed me. I reached the ladder and scrambled down. Horace was standing at the bottom, but he paid no attention to me as I descended. He was shouting, gesturing so frantically that a vein stood out in his neck. 'Get it down!' he hollered. 'Get it down!'

I thought he meant the curtain, but he was talking about Anthony's head. The stagehands couldn't reach it. It swung like a gruesome pendulum above their outstretched fingers, dripping, dripping, dripping.

All the while, Lilith was unable to budge. I'd have to go and get her.

Swallowing my gorge, I stepped out upon the stage. It was like walking into a nightmare: maggots writhing through puddles of claret. The incessant drip from the head sounded like the ticking of a clock. I tried to focus on Lilith, but there wasn't an inch of her unpolluted by Anthony's blood. It was on her lips, beading her eyelashes, pomading her hair.

I raised my palms, as I'd approach Eurydice. 'Lilith. You need to come off stage.'

Her mouth moved silently.

'I know. It's awful. Come away. Come with me.'

I had to touch her. I winced at the hot stickiness against my hands, the reek of iron.

'I've got you.'

172

She dropped the wax hand, which landed with a wet slap. 'It's Anthony, isn't it?' she whispered. 'That was Anthony.'

Was. The past tense made my vision tunnel. Of course, she wouldn't have seen: to her there was only bright light and a wave of blood.

'Yes.'

Lilith trembled. 'I warned him. I did warn him.'

I couldn't think what she meant. But at that moment, the men above succeeded at untying the rope; the head came crashing down and bounced to our feet.

Anthony's lifeless face stared up, frozen in the tortured groan of Melpomene's mask.

The costume was completely destroyed. It hardly mattered, but it was easier to mourn that than let the real, human grief creep in. Blood started to crust on Lilith's skin. It had soaked deep, right through to her petticoats, corset and shift. Only the Melpomene watch emerged spotlessly clean.

Eurydice licked Lilith's feet while I fetched water for the bath. Her muzzle had already taken on a russet hue. I led her away by the collar and tethered her to a coat peg with a belt.

There was a faint buzzing in my ears. My hands shook, rippling the water; I felt weak as a newborn. Somehow, I managed to fill the hip bath to the top, coax the sopping material away from Lilith's skin and guide her in. The dried blood twisted away in copper ribbons. I soaped her hair, thick and heavy to the touch, like it had been coated in tar. Soon the entire tub was red.

We were silent, each locked in our own hell. I wasn't aware I was weeping until my tears pattered into the water, soft as raindrops. If I'd seen him earlier, if I'd recognised Anthony up there, could I have stopped him?

Lilith tensed. Reaching down, she pulled a maggot off her stomach, held it up to the light and watched it squirm. 'Maggots,' she said in a hollow voice.

'Mrs Dyer,' I replied shortly.

She nodded as if my treachery didn't matter. All things considered, it really didn't, now.

Lilith flicked the maggot away and my thoughts flew at once
back to Anthony. What would become of the Mercury, after
this? His death, following not long after Silas's … there'd be
another inquest in that awful pub. I sobbed then, for what I'd just
witnessed, for the mind that could never be scrubbed clean.

Lilith shifted in the tub. 'No.'

I didn't pay much attention. Her brain was thawing from the
horror, she was unlikely to make much sense. But then she said
it again. 'No! It can't … surely it can't happen again, so soon?'
Her wet fingers latched on to my arm. I had a hideous flash of
Anthony's bruises.

'What are you talking about?'

'Feel, Jenny.' She grabbed my hand and pressed it flat against
her belly. I felt nothing. 'That fluttering,' she gasped. 'The
bubbling. I've felt it once before.'

'You can't mean …'

Her face crumpled. 'I can't go through that again. I won't!'

I just squatted there, my hand on her wet skin, past embarrassment, past everything. When Mrs Dyer found out … we were
doomed. The Mercury, Lilith, me and the Dyers.

Lilith's eyes sought the watch on the dressing table, as if it
could offer any help. 'Jenny, bring it to me.'

I shouldn't; she'd get water in the mechanism, but the thing
was hers to break if she chose. As I pulled away, I saw a note leaning against the perfume bottle that I hadn't noticed before.

'What's that?' she asked.

'It looks like a letter.' I picked it up. The paper softened in my
wet hands, but I saw Anthony's writing before it bled across the
page. His last words, scribbled and left for Lilith to find.

Perhaps your Muse has inspired me, after all.

ACT III

Antony and Cleopatra

'My resolution's placed, and I have nothing of woman in me.'

CHAPTER 22

The Mercury was closed as a mark of respect. They sewed Anthony's head back on as best they could and buried him in the same churchyard as Silas. We wanted them to be placed side by side, but that wasn't possible. Anthony had to go to the north with the suicides.

Suicide was the unanimous verdict; with the death of his dearest friend, the stinging reviews and the note to Lilith, the inquest barely stopped to debate it. I avoided all questioning. Nobody recalled seeing me go up to the flies: the image imprinted on their memories was of me leading a blood-soaked Lilith away.

Coping with my family's dismay was almost worse than my own.

'Like *Doctor Faustus*!' Philip cried. 'I told you the theatre's a wicked place!'

I sighed. 'I can't leave my position because of what happened to someone else. It's more important that we have food on the table and a roof over our heads.'

Bertie's eyes were like dinner plates. 'It made Greg disappear. Don't let it take you away, too!'

Only Dorcas came close to understanding. She stopped and squeezed my arm while we were mangling the laundry later that day. 'I know you, Jen. You'll swallow this down, you'll keep being brave and pretending, though it's killing you inside.'

'I'm fine,' I insisted.

I wasn't.

I didn't doubt Dorcas's capacity for sympathy, but I didn't want to sully her with the misery of what I'd witnessed. I'd save her from horrors, if I couldn't save myself.

Instead, I went to Lilith. We sat silently at the wrought iron table in her garden, watching birds peck for worms in the damp spring grass. Crocuses were pushing up, purple, yellow and white. Eurydice rested her head on Lilith's lap, poked her snout towards her mistress's stomach and growled softly. The bottle of absinthe stood between us on the table. Occasionally, we each took a nip. It chased the terrible images away.

'What are you going to do?' I asked at last. 'About the baby?'

She shook her head dully. 'My career ...'

'Well, that's going nowhere at the moment, is it? Not without a leading man.' I immediately wished I hadn't said that. I tried again. 'You'd better tell the Guvnor.'

Lilith rubbed her face. Her pale skin looked almost translucent in the spring sun. 'He's avoiding me. I expect the old dragon is avoiding you too. They're too busy coping with ... all of this.'

She was right; I hadn't heard from Mrs Dyer. After our last encounter, I wasn't about to seek her out voluntarily either. A breeze moved through the shrubs. It was still chilly, hardly weather for sitting outdoors, but we wanted the fresh air.

'It might be nice to have another baby,' I offered, thinking of Bertie's first smiles.

She snorted. 'Not to give birth. It was awful. And I haven't the time. Eugene Grieves ruled the stage for twenty-four years, but do you think a woman can do the same? I have to get all my best work done in the next decade or I'll be too old for a leading lady.' Her hand strayed to the watch. 'Even now, we're wasting time.'

'Anthony died. We can't put on a play.'

'He wouldn't be dead if he'd listened to me! Melpomene won't be silenced. She'll find a way out.'

I grabbed the bottle of absinthe and drew it away from her. 'I think you've had enough of that. Besides,' I added with sudden inspiration, 'the book you gave me. It said Melpomene was a mother.'

'To half-bird, dangerous creatures.'

'The thing is, Lilith ...' I took a swift gulp of absinthe for courage. 'The thing is: your career might come to a halt anyway. Mrs Dyer knows about Algernon.'

Her head snapped up. 'What?'

'She has the baptismal record. She's gone barmy: she ripped the whole page out of the register and ran off with it. She'll wield it over you. Threaten to expose you if you don't go quietly.'

Lilith gritted her teeth. 'Two can play at that game. She has every bit as much to lose if her husband is found out.'

So it would go on. The endless tug of war between them, poor little Algernon being wielded as a secret and a weapon. I drank again. Was there no way to persuade Lilith to bow out gracefully? 'I'm surprised you still want to go on stage, after what happened.'

'I don't have a choice. I told you before, it's a calling. I made a deal.'

I frowned. 'I'm sure your contract with the Mercury doesn't say—'

She reached across the table and snatched the bottle from me. 'That's not what I meant,' she said darkly.

Eurydice growled, her eyes still fixed on Lilith's belly.

I rose to my feet. Lilith was a comfort when we sat together in traumatised silence, but not in this mood. 'I'd better go.'

'Take some flowers,' she said, the bottle raised to her lips. 'There's a whole meadow in the parlour. Apparently the public think they'll make me feel better. Your sister is one for flora, isn't she?'

It touched me that she'd remembered Dorcas. 'Thanks.'

Inside, there were so many bouquets that it resembled a hothouse at Kew Gardens. On the walls, on the very tapestry of the sofa, small dark patches bloomed, marks worryingly like the ones I'd found in Lilith's dressing room. I only stopped to pull out some marigolds, asphodels and chrysanthemums, then set off home, the liquorice taste of absinthe on my tongue.

At least there was still our house, beautiful as a dream. Bertie and Philip had been making a kite ready to fly when the March winds came, Dorcas was growing seeds in her own little patch of earth, and none of us had to share a lavatory with another family. Good had come from the Mercury, too.

To my surprise, the door swung open before I'd made my way up the path: Bertie stood beaming on the polished white step. 'Jenny! You'll never guess who's here!'

Greg's frame blocked the light from the parlour window. This time he wasn't alone. Georgiana had dressed up as the perfect little wife to accompany him, a petite cap of blonde lace perched upon her hair and coral earrings that matched her painted lips.

'Poor darling!' she kissed the air beside each of my cheeks. 'What you must have *suffered*!' Then, catching sight of the flowers, she took them from my hands. 'You shouldn't have.'

My mouth hung open in disbelief.

Dorcas and Philip slouched on the sofa, arms folded, wearing identical scowls. 'Don't blame me,' Dorcas defended herself. 'Bert let him in.'

My brother hobbled up to me with glee. 'He's back, Jenny! Greg's come back!'

'I see that. Now he can bloody well go away again.'

Bertie pouted. 'But why?'

'We had to come, Jen.' Greg massaged the back of his neck. The stubble I'd seen on his chin in the winter had grown into a full beard. 'We read about what happened to Anthony. It's awful. Are you all right?'

As if he cared! 'No, I'm not all right! How the hell did you find us? I don't want you in my house. You'll steal anything that isn't nailed down.'

Georgiana ran her eyes appreciatively over the fashionable wallpaper. 'Don't be like that, darling. You seem as if you're doing very well for yourself, despite everything.'

I flushed hot then cold, remembering how Oscar had warned me about their debts. Then I noticed the diamond on her hand, bright as one of the chips that had fallen from Lilith's mirror.

'You've got a bloody nerve! That's Miss Fielding's ring! You're wearing stolen property in broad daylight!'

'Don't be silly,' Georgiana giggled, adjusting it. 'This old thing? – it belonged to my mother.'

She must have thought I was born yesterday. 'Get out. You're not welcome here. Get out.'

Bertie set up a whine, but Philip and Dorcas nodded.

'Be reasonable,' Greg complained. 'We came kindly. We were worried about you.'

Did he really think that would wash? 'I was fine until you showed up. Come on. Move your arse.'

Philip rose to help me. Georgiana gave a little gasp as I pushed her. I was determined to make them leave, but the damage was already done. They'd found us. Bertie might let them in again while I was at work. Each day they could wait for me to go, and sink their claws into him a little further.

And Oscar must be right about the debts. Although Georgiana was dressed well, they both looked thin and Greg had that strange softness about the mouth that came from heavy drinking. His eyes were threaded with crimson. I could imagine him playing cards until the small hours.

'I know we shall all be friends eventually,' Georgiana insisted as I shepherded her towards the door. 'We'll have to learn to get along.'

Greg ruffled Bertie's hair from the step. 'Don't worry, Bert. I'm sure we'll see each other again soon.'

'You don't deserve to see any of us,' I growled.

Philip snapped the door shut in Greg's face.

Bertie cried in earnest, pathetic as a calf wrenched from its dam. 'Phil was right!' he wailed. 'Your new job's made you wicked. You're a wicked, nasty sister and I hate you!'

'That wasn't what I meant—' Philip started.

I should have told Bertie then. I should have explained how Greg had stolen the money for his operation and a thousand other details I'd been shielding him from.

But Bertie could move faster now. He'd taken himself off up the stairs before either of us could stop him.

CHAPTER 23

It must have been a week later when the morning post brought a letter from Mrs Dyer, saying she'd send the growler for me early the next day. I viewed it with trepidation, and not just because it meant leaving Bertie unguarded. Last time we met, Mrs Dyer had been feral with rage about Lilith's son. Now her leading man had been decapitated and, unbeknownst to her, Lilith was breeding again; it hardly promised to be a happy reunion.

At least the weather turned in my favour with a glorious, warm morning, more like summer than spring. I angled my face up to the carriage window, garnering as much natural light as I could before the theatre swallowed me whole. Rather than travelling past the gated entrance and turning into the road where the yard opened further down, the growler stopped outside the Mercury's front steps.

Mrs Dyer stood there, waiting for me. 'Jennifer!' She waved her handkerchief to catch my attention. Considering all that had happened, she looked surprisingly cheerful. Feathers adorned the hat perched high on the top of her head and she wore a striped Dolly Varden dress.

I opened the door and slid out. 'Good morning, madam. I was surprised to get your note. Is something the matter?'

'Not at all. Quite the opposite.' Her smile and the flush in her cheeks were disconcerting. At least in plays, characters were consistent. In real life, people seemed to shift like fog. 'I must thank you. You acted as a true friend in your advice, and I am grateful.'

'You certainly seem a lot happier today.'

I closed the door of the carriage. At a signal from Mrs Dyer, it drove away.

'And so I am. That sounds heartless, in light of poor Anthony's demise … All I can say is that the tragedy presented me with an opportunity. I can wipe the slate clean now.'

'How so?'

'I followed your counsel and spoke to Hugh. It was immensely painful, but his remorse prompted him to grant me favours. I was allowed to select the new principal actor! You must come inside and be introduced. Mr Felix Whitlow is quite a name, you know. We are lucky to secure him.'

She started up the steps, but I hung back, my mind reeling. They were replacing Anthony so soon … Yet that was almost beside the point. Mrs Dyer had confronted the Guvnor, and she was beaming?

'What about Lilith?'

She paused, one foot on the step above her. 'It appears poor Anthony's death has achieved what all our tricks and stratagems could not. Hugh says Lilith is thoroughly indisposed. He will not hear of her returning for a good while yet.'

Indisposed. That was how he worded it. 'But she is coming back?'

Mrs Dyer grimaced. Checking quickly that no one was within earshot, she said, 'My husband believes she is a financial asset, which I cannot deny. And since he is halting all funds to Southend, he says Lilith must be allowed to earn bread for the …' She seemed to be struggling to find the appropriate word.

'Child,' I supplied.

A cloud passed across the sun. Her shadow lengthened down the steps. 'But here is my chance to prove him wrong. I am reopening the Mercury for a matinee performance of *Antony and Cleopatra*, in memory of Mr Frost. The proceeds will go to support his elderly mother. Hugh has put me entirely in charge.'

I'd read that play in the Shakespeare collection she'd given me. The fictional Antony was defeated and killed himself, too. I wondered why that hadn't occurred to her; it was inappropriate.

'Another actress shall play Cleopatra in Lilith's absence,' she went on. 'We must do our best to make her the darling of the public. I will fete her to such an extent that, when Lilith returns, she will find her place quite usurped! That will leave Hugh without a choice but to dismiss her.'

I tried not to let my cynicism show. 'Will that work? It would take a mighty talent to rival Lilith.'

She dismissed my concerns with a wave of the hand. 'Popular opinion can be manufactured. I have already arranged for a group of gentlemen to attend and give a standing ovation. I might just as easily pay another set to catcall Lilith.'

Thoroughly disenchanted, I watched her turn and trot up the steps. For someone so kind towards my family, she could be awfully cruel. At least Lilith's barbs were all on display. Mrs Dyer would smile serenely in your face while she stabbed you in the back. I followed her through one of the gated entrances and into the lobby. It appeared less sinister by day. The chandelier dripped crystals from a ceiling like sculpted meringue. I could see the pattern of the parquet floor and the veins in the Sienna marble pillars which bracketed the box office. The bifurcated staircase was no longer a shadowy tree but an edifice that rose majestically. Even so, sunlight revealed tatters; stains and chips that put me in mind of the Helicon. Would it be long before our theatre deteriorated to the same level as Eugene Grieves's?

The new actor lingered by the refreshment bar. He was more moustache than man, favoured with florid cheeks and small, hot blue eyes, which travelled up and down my figure before coming to rest upon my face.

'Jennifer Wilcox, it gives me great pleasure to present the Mercury's new leading man, Mr Felix Whitlow.'

'Delighted. Delighted! Upon my word, Mrs Dyer, how many charming ladies do you intend to produce in one day? My poor heart cannot withstand the assault.'

I didn't offer my hand to shake, but he seized it nonetheless, raising it to his lips. His facial hair prickled through my gloves as he kissed my knuckles.

It was a stark contrast to Anthony with his gentle manner and strong, handsome countenance. I drew back my hand and wiped it surreptitiously on my skirts. 'It's a pleasure to meet you, sir.'

I think that he smiled. It was hard to see, under that moustache.

'I know Mr Whitlow of old. He will be sure to draw an audience – we do so *need* a draw.' Mrs Dyer made a moue with her mouth. 'Society will not be eager to attend a theatre where a man was … where … well, you know what happened.'

'I think you underestimate the public, madam,' I said. 'A bloody death will only rouse their interest.'

Mr Whitlow chuckled. I supposed he would do for the Roman general Mark Antony. He looked like the sort of man who might call a troop up to muster. I had the vaguest notion that I'd seen his face somewhere before, maybe in another play. Mrs Dyer said she'd known him a while; perhaps he was in *The Corsican Brothers* or *East Lynne* when Greg brought me here, years ago?

'There is no accounting for taste,' Mrs Dyer replied carefully. 'But as we are undertaking a charitable enterprise, I do not much care what brings the crowds in, so long as they come, and we may keep poor old Mrs Frost in comfort through her old age.'

Listening to her speak, I almost believed kindness was her real motivation. I shifted my feet uncomfortably on the parquet floor. Had she fooled me like this, before?

'And so we shall,' Mr Whitlow declared. 'But my dear Mrs Dyer, how long are you to keep me in suspense? I have met Clementine Price and the ravishing Miss Wilcox here, yet I am still awaiting my queen. When shall I know my Cleopatra?'

For the first time that day, Mrs Dyer's smile slipped. 'In a moment, sir. Miss Wilcox dresses our leading ladies, and I intend for you to all meet together. I must just—' She made a little motion to me. 'I must just explain the brief to her first. Excuse us.'

Mr Whitlow inclined his head. Mrs Dyer had already started to retreat towards the box office. I walked quickly to catch up. Why was she putting so much space between us? Surely it didn't matter if the lead actor heard about the costumes?

When she stopped, her brow was furrowed. She wet her lips before she spoke. 'Now, Jennifer, I shall need you to be brave.'

'Madam?'

'You have worked with Lilith for many months now, so I know you are able to tolerate dressing women you dislike …'

I blinked. 'But why should I dislike this new actress? Who is she? I thought you'd give Clementine the part, although I guess her nerves might get the better of her in a lead role.'

'Ye-es,' she said uncertainly. 'You must understand that in my campaign against Lilith, I needed to employ someone who loathes her as thoroughly as I do. Who will not swerve from the mission. Were it not for that, I should have chosen differently... But we have a common goal. Better the Devil you know, as they say.'

I didn't understand. Who knew both Mrs Dyer and Lilith, yet was an enemy to me? She couldn't mean ...

Just then, a woman appeared on the landing of the staircase. She wore a day dress of powder pink silk festooned with ivory lace. As she descended the marble steps each footfall struck a new note of rage in my breast.

Georgiana Mildmay sashayed into the foyer as if she owned the place.

'I am sorry, Jennifer, but I am prepared to take any measures to fight for what is mine. As Cleopatra would have it: *Now from head to foot I am marble-constant.*'

I said nothing. Mrs Dyer needed to see her life as a play, to cast herself as the heroine. She never seemed to remember the final scene. Cleopatra didn't triumph. She was bitten to death by a snake. And if anyone was a serpent in disguise, it was the actress preening and simpering before us.

Georgiana gave me a little wave. 'Surprise! I told you we should have to get along together. Won't it be fun?'

I had to tell Lilith. I needed to vent my fury to someone who would be every bit as incensed as I was. Rot Mrs Dyer and her counterfeit charity. She'd once told me that she hated Georgiana, that she never rated her talent.

Georgiana as Cleopatra! It was an insult. Lilith had at least some of the sultry appeal of the Egyptian queen, she could make you suspend disbelief.

Maybe I should refuse to dress the woman who had split my family apart and treated Oscar like dirt ... Oscar! How on earth was he going to cope with Georgiana back in the theatre? Mrs Nettles and Polly would hate it too. Georgiana wouldn't have a single friend in the Mercury, although I didn't suppose she cared.

Clearly, this was what Mrs Dyer did. She found women down on their luck, desperate for a chance and gave them employment. She thought that her money could buy their souls and turn them to her purpose. She never really cared.

I'd been duped. But how could I extricate myself now? If I left the theatre, I'd never be able to keep up the rent. No; I'd stay. I'd stay and make sure both Georgiana's career and Mrs Dyer's plan failed utterly.

Rather than return home I went straight to Lilith's house. To my shock, the Guvnor opened the door. He'd removed his jacket, showing a brightly patterned waistcoat. His cravat was untied. 'Come inside, quickly.'

I obeyed without a word. The villa smelt stale. Where before there'd been a patina of dust, there was now a veritable snowfall. Bottles, play scripts and shoes lay scattered around. All the flowers had died since I'd been here a week ago.

'What's going on, Mr Dyer?'

The Guvnor subsided onto the sofa, heedless of the clothes and letters he sat upon. 'This is a bad business. A damnable bad business. And you, Miss Wilcox, must answer for your share in it.'

'Me? What have I done?'

'Do not act the fool. You know perfectly well that you have betrayed my confidence. I paid you for your discretion, but it seems that was money ill spent. Mrs Dyer knows all.'

I regretted that now, but I refused to feel ashamed. He was the one keeping a mistress; he was the one breaking sacred vows and concealing an illegitimate child – how dare he imply the aftermath was my fault.

'You underestimate your wife, sir. She has the mind and the determination to discover things for herself.'

His laughter was harsh. 'By Jove, doesn't she, though? It would be easier to part this dog from a bone than Sylvia from something she has set her mind to.'

On that we were agreed.

'Where's Lilith?'

'Upstairs. She has been in a devil of a state. Why weren't you here, caring for her?'

'I work at the theatre, Mr Dyer. I'm not her maid.'

He leant forward, clasped his hands before his face and exhaled into them. 'I've precious little reason to trust you. But it seems you are the only avenue down which I can turn. You're the only person Lilith will suffer to accompany her.'

I felt a stab of foreboding. 'Accompany her where?'

'I have made an appointment with a medical man. An appointment of the utmost secrecy. I cannot possibly convey Lilith there myself, but it is not right that she should go alone. She will need a person to care for her ... after.'

'After what? A medical examination?'

'A procedure. To clear up a ... female complaint.'

The floor seemed to tilt under my feet. 'That's ... illegal,' I gasped. 'Sir, if she's caught ... it'll be viewed as murder.'

His lips pressed into a grim line. 'I do not owe you an explanation.'

He was as bad as his wife, trusting me to jump at his word. 'Yes, you do! You're asking me to conspire in a crime, to risk my life. What makes you think I'll say yes?'

He ran a hand through his hair. 'You have taken Sylvia's side. No doubt you think she is innocent and wronged, but you do not see her at home. She was obsessed with Eugene Grieves. *Obsessed*, I tell you. He did not return her admiration, but it made me a laughing stock all the same. And then, when he died, to wear that ridiculous mourning ... She must make everything into a drama!'

I hadn't considered before how Mrs Dyer's infatuation with Eugene Grieves might have impacted on her husband. Had he taken up with Lilith as some kind of revenge?

'Your marriage is your own affair, sir. I don't take sides. But others shouldn't suffer for your quarrels.' I could hear how short and angry my breath came. 'Does Lilith really want this ... termination?'

'She wants to be back on stage, of course. Her career is everything. We managed to hide her condition last time, but now she is in the spotlight it will not wash. And to be perfectly candid with you, Miss Wilcox, I live in dread of discovery. Sylvia was wild when she found out about Algernon. Deranged. She vowed that if I didn't forsake my son, she would kill herself, or kill Rachel … And by God, I think she would. She'd throw herself and our daughter off of a bridge just to spite me.'

I shuddered. He had a point; there was no extreme to which Mrs Dyer would not go. I'd seen that myself this very morning. And getting Lilith back on stage was the clearest way to thwart her.

'I do not see how this could happen. I took the utmost care. We hardly … But it is of no matter. It *has* occurred. You will help Lilith, won't you, Miss Wilcox? I only ask you to act as a nurse. Watch over her until the danger is past. The procedure will happen with or without your consent … but I would rather she not be alone.'

It was an awful position to place me in, morally and emotionally. 'Let me speak to Lilith first. Make sure this is what she wants.'

The Guvnor nodded. 'Yes. By all means. Only … prepare yourself, Miss Wilcox. This ordeal, along with the great tragedy she witnessed, has taken its toll upon her. She is plagued, body and soul. The sight of her may shock you.'

I'd wiped her vomit, dried her breastmilk, scrubbed blood from her hair. I doubted any new developments could unsettle me.

Eurydice followed me to the base of the stairs but refused to go any further. The steps creaked as I climbed. I went to grip the bannister and saw that yet again there were those small, dark smuts, like pepper scattered across the wood. I pulled my hand back.

Crossing the landing, I knocked hesitantly at Lilith's bedroom door.

'It's me. Jenny.'

There was a smell. Deep and smoky; something burning.

No answer came, so I turned the handle and entered. Lilith was sitting cross-legged on the floor, staring into the fire. Although it was past eleven, she still wore her nightgown and her black hair was uncombed.

Eugene Grieves's Melpomene watch ticked in the palm of her hand. Below, I could see the web of blue veins in her wrist, pulsing to the steady rhythm.

'Lilith?'

Perspiration sat upon her brow and soaked her armpits. She was like one in the grip of a fever. She must have taken another infection since I last saw her. The change was pronounced, in such a short time.

'Lilith, won't you speak to me?'

Her head snapped in my direction. 'Have you come to take me back?'

'Back where?'

'To the theatre, of course! How much longer do they intend to keep me chained up in here?'

'You can't go back with a child in your belly.'

She groaned. 'Child, you say? I'm not sure it is one. It's like a ... a canker. A parasite. Draining my life.' Without warning, she leapt to her feet. I started back; there was a frightening energy about her. 'It's all going wrong, Jenny. *My laurel is all withered.*'

'Don't. Please don't quote *The Duchess of Malfi* to me. I never want to think of that play again.'

'Well, I haven't that luxury. I told you she *speaks*, on and on in my head.' She struck at her forehead with the heel of her hand. 'It's driving me mad. I won't have a moment's peace until I'm on stage again!'

I came forward, touched her shoulder. She was burning up. 'The shock of what happened to you, and now this baby ... it's making you ill.'

'Has he asked you?' She peered hungrily into my face. 'Has Hugh told you about the procedure to set me free?'

'Yes, but ... it's a big decision, Lilith. This is your baby, your own kin. And what if the operation doesn't work? What if you get caught? After all that heartache you might just end up in prison, or with a disfigured child.'

'I *told* you, it's not a child. It wasn't like this before. I was radiant at first, with Algernon.'

'Each of my ma's pregnancies were different.' I felt weak and strangely nerveless as I said it. Childbirth hadn't killed my mother, but she'd deteriorated fast in the weeks that followed. Bertie's arrival had been difficult enough. Lilith might suffer even more from inexpert tampering.

'Well, this one is a monster sent to torment me. I won't shelter it inside me any longer. Can't you see? I'm suffocating here. I'll shrivel away, and there will be nothing left except this damned *whispering* inside my head.' She grabbed the watch with both hands and seemed to steady herself. 'I need to act, Jenny. It's like taking an opium fiend away from his den. I was so close to establishing my name ... I'm getting better with every performance.'

I didn't like to upset her further, but she deserved to know what was going on behind her back at the Mercury. 'Mrs Dyer's putting on a play without you. A "benefit performance". She's cast Georgiana Mildmay as Cleopatra.'

She went absolutely still. 'Cleopatra! They're going to make you dress that chit, that milk and water miss, as the great Cleopatra?'

I nodded unhappily.

'When we played it before, I was Charmian. I wanted, I so wanted, I *burned* to be Cleopatra. I know her word for word. And that bitch has taken the part from me!'

'You might have other chances to play her?' I suggested tentatively.

'There are no second chances! I've gambled everything. *Everything*, do you understand? I've been given the talent, but not the time to use it.'

A slow, unnameable terror began to seep into me. 'What are you talking about, Lilith? You keep saying that. You'll have plenty of time ...'

'I'm going to this appointment as soon as possible. I'm casting this thing out of me whether you accompany me or not. But say you'll come. I'd rather have you there.'

I swallowed, wondering how I could possibly refuse. What would my siblings do if we were caught and I ended up in gaol?

'I'm terrified of this! You said the baby had quickened. That'll make the procedure more dangerous. It could kill you!'

'Screw your courage to the sticking place and we'll not fail.'

Another quote. 'Lady Macbeth went mad, Lilith. These characters on stage aren't people for you to base your real life upon.'

She gripped the watch, her fingers like claws holding a jewel. 'They're the only thing that's real to me, now.'

CHAPTER 24

We couldn't take the Dyers' growler that day. Every detail had to be inconspicuous. Both of us wore drab gowns and veils over our hats. The netting made it hard for me to read Lilith's expression. Her posture remained erect; shoulders back and chin raised, but that could easily be bravado rather than real confidence.

No physical hurt lay in store for me, yet I was queasy with apprehension as I hailed the cab that would take us to Harley Street. The doors closed over our legs, caging us in. The driver clicked his tongue and the horse lurched on. There was no crying off now.

It seemed to me that a layer had been peeled back from the world; sounds were too loud, colours too bright. Golden sun kissed the streets, petals of blossom drifted down from the trees and all of it felt as inappropriate as a laugh at a funeral.

Lilith pulled out her watch. As I saw the minute hand edge forward, a morbid thought struck me: it might be counting down the remaining time of Lilith's life.

'Have you met this doctor?' I probed. 'Are you sure he's reputable?'

'If he was reputable, he wouldn't be doing this.'

'You know what I mean. Can he be trusted not to ... hurt you?'

'Hugh made the arrangements. Hugh would not let me fall into the hands of a quack.' When I harrumphed, she turned towards me. 'You mustn't judge him too harshly. He has been a good patron to me.'

'Good?' I echoed, incredulous. 'Lilith, he's exploited you.'

'He has not. Hugh is the only person who has ever shown genuine and unshakeable belief in me. He cares.'

He cared about as much as Mrs Dyer cared for me.

We swerved round a gathering blocking half the road. A poor horse had collapsed in its traces. Its panicked, rolling eyes met mine; there was a painful jolt of understanding between us.

'No one wants to see you back at the Mercury more than I do. I can't wait for you to wipe the smile off Georgiana's face. But ... there are other options. You need to consider them. Couldn't you break your ties with the Guvnor? Keep the baby, marry and make your own family?'

'You green goose. Men don't just *let* you leave them. It was hard enough getting free of Eugene. Hugh would be so hurt and angry ... and he has it in his power to ruin my reputation with a single word. Talent or not, no respectable establishment wants to hire a fallen woman. Hugh's my patron. I've thrown my lot in with him, for better or worse.'

'Maybe you'd have to give up acting, then. But in the real world, you could be truly loved, for yourself.'

'Myself,' she mused quietly. 'No. That isn't a role I want.'

We continued in silence. All too soon we were approaching the circle of grass at Cavendish Square where we'd asked to be set down. Lilith paid through the hatch, the driver operated his lever and opened the wooden doors with a resounding clunk.

Few people were about. Other than the passing of a breeze, everything lay eerily still. We walked past iron railings, white-framed windows and arching doorways until we found the brass plaque we were looking for. I hesitated at the bottom of the steps. Anyone would think it was me, and not Lilith, who had to face the abortionist.

'Hurry up,' Lilith scolded. 'Lingering will draw attention.'

A woman answered the door. She opened it the exact width to admit us single-file and closed it almost on our heels. Her manner wasn't hurried, only efficient. Like us, she wore plain clothes. Her hair was parted severely down the middle and scraped back in a tight knot at the nape of her neck. 'Which of you is Mrs Williams?'

That threw me – but of course, the appointment had been made under a false name, a variation of Lilith's real surname, Fitzwilliams.

'I am she,' Lilith answered as boldly as she would on stage. I ached for her. How long would she be able to keep this performance up? Once inside a sterile room, with her legs spread … I dare not picture it. The image was too dark, it would swallow me whole.

'Give your things to your maid and follow me.' Her tone brooked no disagreement. 'You may wait in there,' she addressed me, nodding to a door on our right.

A shameful relief washed over me; I wouldn't be present for the operation. Lilith handed me her gloves first; they were damp with sweat. Next she pulled the pins from her hat and lifted it off, revealing a chalk-white countenance. She tried to keep the watch with her, suspended on its chain, but the woman tutted and said, 'No knick-knacks.' Lilith skewered her with a malefic glare. 'How can it signify?'

'If you want to keep the item safe, Mrs Williams, entrust it to your maid. I won't answer for any damage.'

Moments passed. Then slowly, as if it caused her great pain, Lilith unlooped the chain. The watch dangled from her hand. I had to prise her fingers apart to take it.

A trembling seized her afterwards. There was no time to express my sympathy. The woman turned and walked briskly down the hall, heels clipping on tile. Lilith shot me a desperate look before following her.

Grey spots began to interfere with my vision. I lurched into the room the woman had indicated, hardly noticing its dimensions or décor. My eyes snagged on a wingback chair and I aimed for it like a swimmer making for shore. Lilith was depending on me to be strong. All that was required was for me to wait here, and nurse her afterwards. I should be able to do something so simple.

Nonetheless, I kept thinking of Ma and panicking. She'd slipped away despite our best efforts. My only comfort was that Lilith had strength and wanted to live; maybe her steely determination would carry her through?

As the time passed, I began to feel more like myself. I folded Lilith's shawl and arranged her hat on my lap. The watch still ticked loudly. I flipped the case open and looked at the black dial. There was nothing remarkable there. Mother-of-pearl hands crept their way between Roman numerals. What was it that held Lilith captivated when she stared into this dark face; what made her so reluctant to let it go?

I strained my ears and concentrated on its mechanical heartbeat. Perhaps, if I listened close enough, I'd hear the whispers Lilith spoke of. But I couldn't. Just my breath and my pulse, steadying to match the rhythm. My index finger grazed the back of the timepiece, searching for the words *Homo fuge*. I felt them, rough and furious. Was it my imagination, or was the metal warmer to the touch there?

Lilith screamed.

The silence that yawned afterwards was somehow worse. I stared around the room, noticing for the first time how neat and comfortable it was, like a gentleman's study. The sound I'd heard was out of place, incongruous with these surroundings. Could there really be another room with stirrups for the feet and sharp metal instruments? I didn't want to think of that. It was easier to focus on the watch.

I observed the minutes pass, but I didn't really feel them. It seemed an age, yet also no time at all before the door creaked open. The woman ushered Lilith into the room with a gentleness that hadn't been there before.

Lilith shuffled along gingerly, her torso slightly bent; her grey eyes hazed with chloroform.

'Is she all right?' I stood up so fast that I nearly dropped her belongings. 'She looks dreadfully pale.'

'There was a minor complication,' the woman told me. 'A slightly unusual case.'

'Unusual how? Is she going to recover?'

'Really, I'm not a doctor. I cannot tell you.'

But she knew enough to plant that wrinkle between her brows. It struck me then that I hadn't seen the doctor myself; he'd used this woman as a mask.

Lilith parted her lips in a bloodless smile. 'It's gone.' She sounded husky. 'I'm free.'

She snatched the watch from me first, then leant against my shoulder while I wrapped her in the shawl. She smelt medicinal and sour. I perched the hat on her head and decided the gloves didn't really matter.

'I have sent for a cab,' the woman informed us. 'It's not advisable for your mistress to walk to the stand. Confine her to bed the moment she gets home. Nourish her as much as possible. Don't administer opiates for the pain until the chloroform is purged from her system, or it will slow her heart. Change the sheets regularly. She's bound to bleed for a day or two.'

It was too much to take in. 'Will she bleed a lot?'

'The amount varies. She must make it up by drinking plenty of wine and staying warm. Watch her. Be vigilant for signs of excitement, dizziness and vomiting.'

I had those symptoms myself. 'What shall I do if all that happens?'

She cast a glance at Lilith. 'Find a doctor to attend immediately. Don't mention that you came here. And pray for the best.'

So we were on our own.

How could the Guvnor leave Lilith in this state if he truly cared about her? She felt like a rag doll as I half-carried her out of the door to the waiting cab. She could barely lift her legs to climb in.

I told the driver the address and seated myself beside her. She clasped my hand. Her fingers were cold.

'I've got you,' I said as we pulled off. It was a shameful lie. None of this was under my control.

'Oh, Jenny. I do feel so terribly sorry for myself.'

'The worst part's over now.'

'Yes, yes. I'm glad of that. But it hurts when the wheels jolt.'

She closed her eyes and breathed heavily. It seemed to require every ounce of her concentration not to cry out as the carriage turned.

Don't let her bleed, I prayed. Don't let her bleed in the cab and blow the whole thing. How well had the doctor padded her up before letting her go? I imagined the warm trickle of blood on my lap at least a dozen times; so vividly that when the driver opened the doors I expected to see our skirts stained red. But there was nothing.

'Come on. We're home.'

Fear made me pull Lilith from the carriage too roughly. She yelped and startled the horse. All I could think about was getting her inside, away from prying eyes. The driver watched us dubiously, then whipped his horse and drove away.

Lilith was bent nearly double now. I propped her up against the wall and hunted for the door key in her pocket. There was a warmth there I didn't like, a hint of something pulsing beneath her many layers of skirts and petticoats. While I applied the key to the lock, Lilith threw up in the rosebush. That was one of the symptoms I'd been told to watch for. Yet didn't pain cause a person to vomit more often than chloric ether? I hurried her inside before the neighbours could stare.

Eurydice didn't run to greet us. She hunkered under the staircase, watching warily from the shadows.

Lilith groaned. 'It feels like he's thrust a red-hot poker through my middle and tied chains to my legs.'

'We'll get you to bed. They said to lie down.'

'But the stairs! Damn the eyes of whoever invented stairs! I can't, Jenny. I can't.'

I tried to bank down my panic. 'Then … the sofa?'

'I need the lavatory.'

'But that's upstairs!'

'I know.'

I cast desperately around. There were marks on the tiles behind us. Small drips of blood, falling from Lilith. I swore.

I'd seen Ma give birth three times. Those had been fraught experiences, but there'd been the hope of a happy ending to see me through. Now there was no baby to coo over and sending for help would be a colossal risk. Why on earth had I agreed to this?

'I'll have to carry you up.'

Lilith was taller than me. Her build wasn't heavy, but neither was mine, and we were both warmly dressed. There was only one way I could think of managing the ascent. Leaning her against the newel post, I stripped myself down to my shift and bloomers, freeing up the movement of my arms and legs. Then I started to undress Lilith.

Her skin felt so cold. She couldn't move much; she was curled in upon herself, tight like a fist, so I had to tear at the fabric in order to break her free. As the layers peeled away, I saw the doctor had indeed bound her up, and the bandages were saturated.

I choked back a sob. It was too soon after Anthony's gory death. None of my emotional scars had healed, and the sweet tang of the blood kept hurtling me back to that night. I saw his head unstitch from his neck, again and again. How was I going to carry Lilith when I was shaking so badly?

'Put your arms around my neck.'

She draped them weakly over my shoulders. I bent and lifted her legs. She released a sound like a cow being slaughtered at Smithfield Market.

'I'm sorry.'

Climbing the steps was more difficult than wading through deep water. I felt sure that I must drop her, must go tumbling back down. Clamping my teeth together, I summoned every atom of strength. We gained the landing.

'You'll have to stand now.'

I dropped her legs too quickly, exhausted. Lilith screamed again. Her warmth didn't depart from me; it was printed all over my front, the white stained with claret.

I wept as I steered her into the bathroom. There was a spike beside the toilet with papers for wiping, but I knew at once it would not be enough.

I sat her down on the porcelain seat and began to unbind her. She was still clutching that godforsaken watch. Her thumbprint shone upon the face in bright red.

There was a hot release as I pulled her drawers away. A wad of something like gauze dropped into the toilet, followed by a rope of slippery blood. I reeled back, sickened. The sound it made as it tumbled into the bowl was disgusting; raw meat hitting a slab.

I couldn't go near her again, couldn't touch her. She started to cry too. 'Help me, Melpomene,' she gasped, rocking slightly with the watch. 'Save me.'

It was no use appealing to a goddess of tragedy. I tore the pewter cross from my neck and threw it towards her. 'Try that instead. I'm going to … I'm going to burn all of this. Get water and fresh linen.'

'Jenny, don't leave me!'

'I have to. Just for a while.'

She scooped up the cross; she was already bent over so far that she was nearly touching the floor. Now she had them both, the necklace and the watch, one in each hand.

Escaping that room was a guilty relief. I leant against the wall and stared aghast at my hangman's hands, feeling every bit as sinful as Macbeth. I wished it was only a play; that I had a script. I was out of my depth here. What on earth should I do now?

I thought of sending for Dorcas to help me, but I didn't want to involve her in this horror. Maybe the Guvnor? How could he assist? He'd be of no practical use.

Tomorrow was the benefit matinee, when I was supposed to dress Georgiana for Cleopatra. I didn't see how I could possibly leave Lilith in this state. She'd need care for days.

I cried some more, washed in the kitchen and threw the stained clothes on the fire. They were past all hope of rescue.

By the time I'd found some wine and heated it up, a sort of torpor was spreading through my veins and I welcomed it. I wanted to be numb. Something had died inside of me, as well as Lilith.

Her eyelids fluttered when I returned to the bathroom.

'It's stopped,' she panted. 'I think it's stopped.'

'Drink this.' I pressed the cup to her lips and tipped wine into her pale mouth. She swallowed it greedily. A touch of colour returned to her face. 'Lilith, I need to clean you up and get you in bed. I think it will help stem the bleeding, if you lie down.'

'No! It hurts to move. Let me sleep here.'

'You'll fall off the toilet and crack your head open.' God knew I'd rather leave her there. The prospect of having to help wipe her, to wash the blood off all over again, was crippling. But I had to do it. Who else would? 'Come on, let's stand you up just a bit.'

Lilith handed back my necklace. Like everything else it was smeared and tainted; I set it on the floor beside the empty cup of wine. She'd gripped so hard that the shape of the cross was branded on her palm.

'Ready?'

She closed her eyes and nodded. She clamped one hand on my shoulder, still nursing the watch in the other.

'One. Two. Three. Up!'

Air hissed between her teeth. I grabbed some paper ready to stopper up whatever might fall from her as she moved. But then I froze.

It was black, tar like, splattered up the side of the lavatory and sitting darkly in the bottom of the bowl.

'Oh God, Lilith, this isn't right.'

'Just get me to bed before I faint.'

There was a good chance I'd pass out myself. Looping an arm around her back, I heaved her up and we shambled together into the bedchamber. Lilith collapsed onto the quilted comforter. The pulse flickered in her neck. Alive – for now. She placed the watch against her ear.

'Lilith, we should—'

'Let me sleep.'

I was scared to – frightened that she'd never wake up again – yet there was no doubt she needed rest. I took a blanket from the press and spread it over her. She shivered. Her odour was brimstone and treacle.

'I'll tidy the bathroom, but I have to wash you afterwards. You can't lie in filth.'

She didn't answer. She'd already lost consciousness.

Shakily, I left her. It was terrible to be alone with no one to care for, a prey to my own thoughts. I needed to keep busy. I forced myself into the bathroom again.

I'm not sure which was worse: the sight or the stench. At least the water closet could be flushed.

Grimacing, I approached it, hoping to prove my eyes had tricked me, but they hadn't. The basin was still filled with black, syrupy liquid.

Why was it *black*?

Black was threatening my vision now, obscuring it in patches. A rushing filled my ears. The tide I'd been holding back all day finally poured in. My knees buckled, I toppled forward, and the basin seemed to be rising to meet me. My forehead cracked against cold porcelain before I hit the floor.

I awoke pained and confused. A rotten, sewage smell filled my nostrils, yet at the same time there was daylight and a chorus of birds singing. Hazily, I tried to sit up. My head felt like it would split open.

With great care, I patted at my brow. There was a lump surrounded by tender bruises. My fingertips came back spotted with blood. The sight of it reminded me where I was.

There were subtle changes to the scene around me. I found my necklace tangled on my foot and the lavatory flushed. The stench lingered, floating back up the pipes, but at least that hideous black mass had gone.

'Lilith?'

I couldn't hear her around the house. Painfully, I climbed to my feet and wobbled out onto the landing. I'd never felt so disorientated. How long had I been passed out? Surely it should be dark by now … Or had I really hit my head so hard that I'd lost consciousness until the next day? I was supposed to be doing something that day … An unwelcome task. Every time I tried to remember what it was, the memory slipped away.

'Lilith?'

Her bed was empty, the blanket I'd covered her with thrown back to reveal a rusty imprint on the coverlet. Fear squeezed at my throat.

'Lilith!'

She wasn't downstairs either. Eurydice's long black tail poked out from underneath the sofa, but she refused to come out.

'Where is she, girl? Where did she go?'

A carriage clock on the mantelpiece chimed. I couldn't believe what its hands were telling me. I really had blacked out until the following morning. And I remembered where I was supposed to be.

The one place Lilith wanted to go. She'd drag herself there even if it took her last breath.

CHAPTER 25

I tidied myself and threw on some clothes. It was more than three miles to the West End, three miles I spent expecting to see Lilith collapsed in the kennel or hit by a cart. But she must have taken a cab, as I did. Thank heaven she was still lucid enough for that.

My stiff legs complained and my head shrieked as I ran all the way from the cab stand. People turned to stare; it wasn't decorous for a young woman to be pegging it through the streets, but after the horrors I'd witnessed such niceties had become laughable.

Oscar stood alone in the yard, one arm braced against a scenery flat. He looked as if he were using it for support.

Had he seen Lilith? Was she sprawled dead inside? I called out his name.

The face he turned up to me was set. 'There you are.'

'I know I'm late. I need your—'

'Why didn't you warn me?'

For a moment I didn't comprehend. How could I have known Lilith would do this? Then my spirits dropped another notch.

'They must have told you! The costumes have all been adjusted. "A nice, easy job," they said to me. "One matinee, a play we did a few years back, we've still got the set." You knew, and you didn't tell me. You were all laughing behind your hands, weren't you?'

No one had informed him Georgiana was coming back. He must've had the shock of his life. 'I meant to tell you. I'm so sorry, Oscar. Things have been ...' I trailed off. There wasn't a word.

It cut me to see the pain in his eyes. But then they travelled to my forehead and the expression changed. 'What the hell happened? Did someone hit you? Did that bastard Greg—'

'I don't have time for this!' Surprise silenced him. 'Lilith is sick. She's deadly sick, she's not thinking straight and she's run off. I need to find her before she hurts herself.'

Pushing past him, I hurried into the theatre. The commotion reached my ears at once; Lilith's voice always did carry. 'I have to go on!'

'It's *my* part. Mrs Dyer gave it to *me*' – Georgiana's shriller tones. 'My name is on the playbill.'

All the dressing-room doors stood open. Our new leading man lounged in the corridor, where he could observe the interior of Lilith's chamber. A smirk sat beneath his immense moustache. 'Now, now, ladies. Flattered as I am to have you fight for the chance to play opposite me, this really will not do.'

The room was full of bouquets wishing Georgiana luck, but the smell of sulphur hit stronger than ever. All Cleopatra's finery, her jewelled bodice, her peacock-feather fan and her elaborate headdress were tumbled in a shimmering heap on the floor. Lilith drew the skirt under her chin like a frightened child with a bedsheet.

Georgiana faced off against her, pink with rage. 'You haven't even rehearsed!'

'She doesn't need me to rehearse,' Lilith insisted. 'Don't inter-fere – don't interfere in her work!'

'Who are you talking—'

'Lilith,' I interrupted. 'Lilith, put that skirt down. You're not well. You shouldn't be here. Let's get you home.'

They both turned. Lilith's lips creaked up in a smile to see me.

'At last!' Georgiana cried. 'You're late! Will you get rid of her, please, darling? This is absurd. She's thinks she's going to take my part!'

'No,' said Lilith. 'Jenny's here to dress me.'

It galled to be on Georgiana's side of the argument. But there were dark hollows under Lilith's smoky eyes. I couldn't let her go the same way as Ma.

'I'm not,' I answered softly. 'I'm here to take you home. Come on, now.'

Lilith's fingers tightened on the fabric. 'I have to go on, Jenny. *You* know I have to go on.'

Oscar arrived in the corridor and exchanged a word I couldn't hear with Felix Whitlow. The actor chuckled. 'You're just in time for the show. The cats have got their claws out now, boy.'

I bit down on a spurt of irritation. Mr Whitlow could be dealt with later; I had to focus on Lilith. 'Let Georgiana play the part this once.'

'She can't do it.'

Georgiana bridled. I quieted her with a hand. 'No one's expecting to see you, Lilith. Not the audience, not the stage manager, not the Guvnor. It's just one special performance for Anthony's family. It doesn't even matter.'

Something desperate passed behind Lilith's eyes. Clutching the skirt to her chest with one hand, she reached the other into her pocket. 'Then tell *her* that. Stop her from pestering me!' She produced the watch and thrust it at me. I took an involuntary step back.

Felix Whitlow's chuckling stopped. 'What's that?'

'Nothing, just a watch,' I said.

But Lilith was still standing with her hand outstretched like a beggar woman. Felix could see what she held.

'He left it to you?' His whisper came out strained.

Lilith met his eyes. 'You know, don't you? You know what happens when we don't obey.'

Felix gulped. 'Georgiana, give her the costume.'

'What?' She rounded on him, incredulous.

'Just give her the costume. Let her play the part.'

'But—'

'Do not cross her!' Felix closed his eyes, trying to rein himself back from his outburst. 'Please … do as I say. It is for the best. Believe me.'

'It's not your choice, Mr Whitlow. Mrs Dyer decides who performs on her stage.' Georgiana had the nerve to bat her eyelashes at Oscar. 'Do tell him, Mr Thorne. They are treating me abominably.'

'That may be,' Felix cut in before Oscar could respond, 'but I will not go on without Miss Erikson. I dare not.' With that, he turned and hurried to his dressing room. The door slammed behind him.

I stood aghast. What did Felix Whitlow know? All colour had left his face when he saw that watch. *Homo fuge*. And he had – he literally fled from the sight of the thing. I remembered Mrs Dyer telling me she'd picked him for the company herself – was it possible that he'd known Eugene Grieves? Worked with him and Lilith in the past?

'This is outrageous!' Georgiana railed. 'I'll tell Mrs Dyer. I'll – I'll ...'

Oscar finally stepped forward. 'You'll get out and let the better actress take the role, Georgiana.' His voice was icy.

She gave him a downcast, flirtatious look. 'Now, Mr Thorne, we must be professional, don't allow personal resentment to—'

'You want my help? After all you've done to me? Fine.' He seized her slender arm. 'I'll help you to the door.'

Georgiana shrieked and clawed at him, but Oscar's grip was firm. He frogmarched her roughly out of Lilith's dressing room.

I might have been amused, if I wasn't so worried about Lilith. I sat her down on the stool, felt the temperature of her forehead. 'This is a disaster. You're barely fit to stand up. How on earth do you think you're going to perform for hours on stage?'

'The worst has passed now. I shall be well again.' Even Lilith's talent couldn't make these words convincing. When I stepped away, she nearly fell off the stool. 'Dress me for the part, Jenny.'

'This is madness,' I said. 'Utter madness. The doctor prescribed bedrest.'

'*I am fire and air, my other elements I give to baser life,*' Lilith quoted. She reached up and began to unpin her hat. A storm cloud of dark hair tumbled down. 'That bodice is so stiff with rhinestones, it'll hold me upright. Just make sure to pull the laces tight.'

'I won't!'

'Then I'll do it myself. I won't be gainsaid.'

The room shimmered around me as my eyes filled with tears. Desperately, I tried another tack. 'You're probably still bleeding.

Cleopatra's skirt is an Indian handweave, there'll be no getting any stains out.'

'You'll think of something. You always do. Either you dress me or I struggle on myself.'

I thought of taking the costume and locking Lilith in the dressing room. But then I remembered Felix Whitlow and his refusal to act without her.

I couldn't win. Lilith was going to do this with or without me.

I took a breath. 'I *do* have an idea. But it will take time.'

At least the mirror had been reglazed; it shone like a silver plate. I went to the wardrobe to dig out the false belly I'd made for *The Duchess of Malfi*. Lilith watched as I sat on the sofa and began to unpick the tapes.

'What are you doing?' she demanded.

'I'm going to pull out some stuffing and move the ties around to make you a sort of belt.' I held the cushion up. 'This bit will go between your legs and catch any blood. But it will probably make you waddle a bit. And that costume has a pretty slim silhouette; I can't guarantee it won't show lumps and bumps.'

'See, I *knew* you'd think of something.' Satisfied, she closed her eyes and slowly caressed the watch sitting in her left hand, seeming to fall into a kind of torpor.

My needle dipped up and down, a silver fish darting through water. As well as making the cushion, I'd have to let down the skirt and take in the waist; we'd fitted it to Georgiana's figure. My fingers couldn't move quickly enough, and I was still a little clumsy after hitting my head. I pricked myself in the thumb three times.

All the while, Felix Whitlow was running through my mind. The terror on his face. It reminded me of the look Silas wore as he spluttered blood, the rictus on Anthony's severed head. *You know what happens when we don't obey.* That was the same language she'd used when Anthony refused to play Ferdinand. But Anthony hadn't been punished by Melpomene, he'd killed himself.

Hadn't he?

I sewed on, lost in my thoughts, until the gas lamps flickered. Looking up, I saw Lilith was fluttering back to life. I needed to paint her face: kohl liner around the eyes and red lips, though I had no idea how I'd put enough colour back in her skin. Maybe I'd try to cover my own bruise at the same time.

'You look angry, Jenny.'

'I am. I'm furious. With all you've put me through this week ... I feel like – what's her name? Charmian? Made to fetch you snakes so you can kill yourself.'

She winced as I took the hairbrush and tugged it through her wild mane. 'The muse can use my body, whatever state it's in.'

'Have you *seen* the state it's in? You need to think less about the blasted muse and more about your own life.'

'That wasn't part of the deal.'

I cried out in exasperation. 'You keep saying this. What deal? What is going on?'

She shook her head.

Beneath her clothes, Lilith was in exactly the terrible condition I'd suspected: unwashed after yesterday's ordeal, a patchwork of stains and bruises. Mercifully the blood flow was now light. I dressed her as best I could.

'Leave me,' Lilith said peremptorily. 'Leave me alone to practise.'

'I'm not sure you *should* be alone—'

'Get out, Jenny. You know my routine.'

I knew she'd sit there in another stupor, whispering to her watch. A wave of exhaustion hit me. How could I help someone who wouldn't help herself?

'Fine, I'll go.'

Oscar was waiting for me outside the dressing room. We both stood there for a minute, dumb.

'I threw Georgiana out, but she'll go to Mrs Dyer,' he warned me. 'It's only a matter of time.'

'I don't care,' I blurted out. 'I don't care what she does. None of this should be my responsibility. I'm just a dresser! It's not my job to keep everyone happy, to keep all their secrets. I can't *do* this any longer.'

Oscar's expression softened. There was a scratch on his cheek; evidently Georgiana's fingernails had caught him. 'I'm sorry I shouted at you. It was the shock of seeing her here.'

'It doesn't matter. Not after what I've been through.'

He exhaled heavily. 'What the hell happened to Lilith?'

God knew I didn't want to peach on her crimes, but I needed someone. I'd been carrying too much alone for too long.

I took a deep breath. Then I told him everything.

We stood in Prompter's Corner as Cleopatra donned her robe and crown. A shaft of limelight fixed on her, brighter than a ray of sun. The very dust motes seemed to dance apart, as if they dare not touch her.

The audience sat spellbound. Our real monarch, dumpy Victoria, could never have held their attention the way Lilith did.

Somehow, she'd done it. She'd dragged herself up to give the greatest performance I'd ever seen. She didn't waddle, she didn't fall; she seemed to take on the bodily strength of Cleopatra herself.

The end of the play was drawing near. Cleopatra's lover was dead, her throne in ruins. She'd kill herself, rather than be taken alive to a future of servitude. She left her maid's embrace and approached the basketful of asps: black stockings with sequins that shimmered like scales. '*Come, thou mortal wretch, with thy sharp teeth this knot intrinsicate of life at once untie: poor venomous fool be angry, and dispatch.*' A cymbal crashed. The audience gasped as Cleopatra fixed the asp to her bosom. '*Peace, peace! Dost thou not see my baby at my breast that sucks the nurse asleep?*' Lovingly, she applied another snake to her arm.

A mournful tune rose up from the orchestra as she crossed the boards and folded herself onto a couch. Her dark head rested upon one outstretched arm. '*What should I stay—*' she sighed. Then she fell still.

Very still.

I barely marked the action on stage. I'd seen Lilith play dead plenty of times; never like this. She lay absolutely motionless. I couldn't even make out the rise and fall of her chest.

'Oscar,' I said in a strangled whisper.

'Bloody hell.'

213

How didn't the other actors notice? They kept on spouting their lines, and still Lilith didn't move. It was impossible. No one could hold their breath for that long.

'I should never have let her go on.'

Only a few lines more. The guards moved to either end of the couch. How were they so blind?

At last, the tag line came. The green curtain dropped and the audience erupted into applause. Stagehands rushed to move properties while the cast readied themselves for the national anthem. But Lilith didn't move.

Oscar swore under his breath.

Clementine called Lilith's name, touched her. No response.

'Keep the curtain down,' I shouted. 'For God's sake, keep it down.'

I ran out on stage and fell upon Lilith. I shook her, slapped her, ordered her to wake. Her lips were blue. Like Ma's had been.

Oscar was beside me in a moment. Together, we carried her backstage while the cast watched in horror.

We laid her gently on the floor. She looked dead. I was too angry to cry.

'Look,' Oscar breathed. 'There … on her arm.' The tight-fitting Cleopatra bodice was sleeveless. My eyes flew to her bicep. 'Isn't that where the snakes bit her?'

For a second, I thought Mrs Dyer must have smuggled a real asp into the basket, but then I recognised the cut. The scar in the shape of a club had opened afresh.

Doctor Faustus had bound himself to the Devil by cutting his arm. Lilith had spoken of a deal, a pact with Melpomene.

'Lilith, wake up!'

From out of her disordered skirts, I saw that hateful watch, still attached to her waist. I'd never loathed an object like a person before. This wasn't just a watch. It was … evil. Tainted. We'd paid the cost of one life for each marvellous performance it'd brought.

As instinctually as patting a choking man on the back, I reached down, snapped the chain and hid the watch in my own pocket.

Lilith convulsed and came gasping back to life. Her eyes were wild.

'Woah! Easy.' Oscar held out his hands. It was meant to be a soothing gesture, but it looked like he was trying to shield himself from her.

'What line was that?' she demanded. 'Is it time to make my entrance?'

'You already did,' Oscar fumbled. 'You were … brilliant. The best yet.'

'You nearly died,' I said bluntly.

But Lilith didn't listen to me. Her ears pricked to the audience, shouting her name.

'My curtain call.' Using my shoulder to lean upon, she winched herself up and shambled back on stage.

A roar of applause. How hollow it sounded, now. Oscar and I remained kneeling, in a state of shock.

'How did you do that?' he asked wonderingly. 'With the watch …?'

I could already feel it, burning a hole in my pocket. I remembered all too well what had happened when Silas had tried to take it.

'Listen, you can't tell Lilith I have her watch. She's obsessed with it. I need to take it away for her own good.'

Oscar frowned, looking beyond my shoulder. 'She only became a genius after the Guvnor gave her that watch.'

'She says it has powers,' I admitted. 'That it's a direct link to the tragic muse. But Oscar … it's bad. You *have* to believe me. It's bad for her state of mind and it's bad luck. I can't let her keep it.'

He bit his lip. 'Then what are you going to do with it?'

I listened to the whoops and the whistles, more enthusiastic than any I'd heard before. Most were genuine, but I remembered now who had paid to make them ring all the louder, thinking it would be Georgiana on stage.

'I know exactly where this belongs.'

CHAPTER 26

I didn't return to the dressing room. While Lilith took her curtain calls, I made my way to the front of house.

Swells were already leaving their boxes, eager to get out before the general crush. The whole walk was a blur of waving fans, silver-topped canes and perfume; all I could concentrate on was the beat of my footsteps, like the ticking of a clock. I kept remembering Silas, toppling from the flies when he tried to take this watch. I had to get rid of it. I had to get rid of it now.

The keeper of Box 6 frowned but let me in without comment. A wall of applause rose to meet me. The ovation was still going. Mrs Dyer and Georgiana sat rigid in their velvet seats, their faces bitter as crab apples.

'I wonder you have the boldness to show yourself.' Georgiana looked down her delicate nose at me. 'If it wasn't for your treachery, I'd be the one in that costume, taking that applause.'

I raised my eyebrows. Did she really believe that? Georgiana would only have received the ovation Mrs Dyer had paid for, not this spontaneous adulation. 'It was hardly my fault. Felix Whitlow refused to go on without Lilith. Now, if you don't mind ... I need to talk to Mrs Dyer alone.'

Georgiana huffed. There were people sitting in the boxes either side of us; she couldn't cause a commotion without attracting notice.

'Do not fret,' Mrs Dyer soothed her. 'We will resolve this situation.'

'You promised me ...'

'And I intend to keep that promise. Now go. By the time we meet again, I shall have formulated a plan.'

Glowering, Georgiana left in a rustle of skirts. Mrs Dyer raised her green eyes to me.

'Well, Jennifer. This is a disappointment.'

I nodded to the stage, now strewn with roses, and the audience conversing eagerly in their seats. 'It looks like a triumph to me, madam. Anthony Frost's mother will be provided for ... and *that* was the aim of the show. Wasn't it?'

'You know perfectly well what my ambitions were. You have worked against them. Against me.'

'Then why am I bringing you this?'

Her countenance altered the moment I produced the watch. 'Is that ...?'

'Yes. I stole it for you.'

She reached out hungrily. I dropped the watch into the palm of her opera glove. It landed with a soft, muffled thud. She stroked the figure of Melpomene with wonder. That expression she wore, it was the same as Ma's when we put Philip in her arms for the first time. 'It is finally mine.'

'So now we're even?'

'Yes,' she said distractedly. 'Yes, of course.'

It was done. Over with. The pregnancy was gone, the watch was gone; what more could Mrs Dyer resent? She'd wiped Lilith clean. I studied her for a moment, wondering if an iota of our partnership had been genuine. How could I ever know for sure? The only copper-bottomed certainty was that Mrs Dyer's jealousy of Lilith had twisted her into something horrible to behold.

I exited the box, leaving her alone with her precious trinket. She didn't notice me go.

After I'd taken a few steps back towards the foyer, the Guvnor appeared at the end of the corridor. He was dressed immaculately: a black jacket, white waistcoat and bow-tie. Rachel trotted beside him, holding an orange. She'd made a hole in the top and was squeezing the juice into her rosebud mouth.

There was nowhere to turn; we couldn't avoid one another.

'Miss Wilcox,' the Guvnor said haltingly. 'I trust you enjoyed the show. Miss Erikson's performance was a revelation ... and something of a surprise.'

'To you and me both, sir.'

His eyes asked questions his tongue could not. 'It seems she has bounced back from her ... indisposition with alacrity.'

Indisposition! He hadn't seen what we'd suffered. 'No thanks to you.'

He grimaced. 'My hands have been tied. The ... delicate matter is resolved, then?'

'Resolved.' My voice was the sound of a watch case snapping shut.

'Tonight, she was everything I knew she could be ... I would go and congratulate her ... it's a manager's duty ... but perhaps it would be better for you to pass on my regards.'

'Yes, sir. You've done quite enough already.'

He guffawed; my rudeness had shocked him out of his penitence. 'By Jove, you really are a little guard dog, aren't you, Wilcox? First my wife, now Lilith. You'll draw blood before you let a man near your mistress.'

I let my eyes linger on the child. 'There's nothing wrong with wanting to protect people, sir.'

His face seemed to drop, then. He took Rachel by the hand. Her big eyes, green like her mother's, stared up at me as she sucked hard on the orange. 'No,' he said sadly. 'No, you are right on that account, Miss Wilcox. Perfectly right. Protecting the innocent from these unfortunate events is the only matter of importance, now.'

When I reached the red corridor, a crash made me jump. There was a tearing sound; fabric ripping at the seams. It was coming from Lilith's dressing room.

Breaking into a run, I pushed past supers in their Roman solider costumes and threw open the door. A shoe banged against the wall, narrowly avoiding my head.

The carnage inside was absolute. The vases weren't just knocked over but smashed, littering the carpet with glass and water. Every flower lay decapitated.

Drawers hung open, rifled through. The wardrobe had been disembowelled of its contents. Even the sofa was haemorrhaging its stuffing through a series of long slashes in the cushions.

Lilith stood naked in a pool of silk and beads. A pocket knife quaked in her hand. It was a moment before I understood that she'd cut Cleopatra's costume to ribbons.

I swore, slamming the door closed behind me. 'What have you done?'

'Jenny! There you are!' She lurched forward; I had to sidestep to avoid the point of the knife. 'Do you have it? Tell me you have it!'

'Have what?' But I knew. Of course I knew. And a sick feeling of guilt poked its fingers down my throat.

'I've looked everywhere. *Everywhere*. My watch isn't on stage, it's not here, it's not ...' Her voice disappeared in wheezing, heaving breaths.

'Calm down. You're not well. You should be resting, you should be keeping warm.' Where could I guide her to sit down? The sofa was falling apart, her dressing-table stool lay overturned, and I didn't want to touch her bare flesh. Lilith drove her fingers into her tousled black hair. All I could do was watch her, as I did on stage. She hadn't shown fear and distress like this even at the abortionists'.

What had I done?

It was for her own good, I tried to remind myself. Once the initial shock had passed, she'd recover. Just like a lusher turning teetotal or an opium addict giving up the pipe, there was bound to be a reaction to the first withdrawal. But looking at her, naked and helpless as a newborn, it didn't feel like I'd done the right thing.

'I can't find it anywhere.'

'Where are your clothes?' I located the outfit she'd arrived in, a skirt and bodice of gunmetal grey. She'd ripped them apart too, but there was enough material left from the skirt to drape around her shoulders. Blood was still trickling down her left arm.

'Jenny, Jenny,' she moaned. 'What am I going to do?'

I righted the dressing-table stool. 'You're going to sit down and pull yourself together. Don't you realise what's happening out there? Your name is on everyone's lips. You've finally done it. Impressed every critic! This will be the time, Lilith, when you're invited to Henry Irving's Beefsteak Club! He'd hear people singing your praise even if he lived on the moon.'

Joy glimmered on her face for the briefest instant. Then it disappeared beneath the weight of dread. She dropped to the stool as if felled. 'I … I didn't think it would happen so soon.'

'Well, it has!' I said with forced cheerfulness. 'You can rest, now. Your reputation is assured. It's lucky for us both that the benefit was only one show.' I ran my hands through the tattered fabric on the floor. 'I'd never be able to stitch this back together again.'

'No … no. There's no fixing it now.'

'Let's find some clothes for you.'

She wasn't listening. 'It happened,' she said dully. 'All that I wanted. My crowning performance has been and gone in a flash. So quickly that I didn't even take the time to appreciate it and now …'

'It's all right, Lilith. Everything will be all right. You'll have a while to recuperate before the next run.'

She shook her head frantically. 'Don't you see? It's over. That's why it's vanished. My time is up and she's taken it back!'

'You're not making sense.'

'Melpomene took her watch back.'

Pity ached in my breast. No doubt there was something eerie about the watch, but her obsession was beyond that. People always said there was a fine line between genius and madness. Lilith had been walking it like a tightrope for too long. Perhaps I'd pushed her off the edge.

'Listen, Lilith,' I said gently. 'I'm going to speak to the Guvnor. I think you should see a doctor. You've spent years taking on the nature of other people for your work. It's alienated you from your own. There are men now who specialise in this kind of thing. Maybe one of them could visit you – privately, of course.'

She laughed. I'd never heard a laugh like that before. It was bitter, cold, terrifying. 'Oh, Jenny. There's not a doctor in the world who can save me now.'

ACT IV

Romeo and Juliet

'These violent delights have violent ends.'

CHAPTER 27

Summer heat had arrived early, yet left the sunshine behind. Rain splattered against the windows of the parlour. Inside, the glass was misting over.

I rubbed my tired eyes and returned to my sketches. The Mercury was due to reopen soon with Shakespeare's famous love story, and Juliet would be our best-dressed heroine yet. Everything was rosebud pink, layered with tulle, beautiful and delicate as a bubble. I adored every gown, but I couldn't picture Lilith wearing them. Lilith was good at strong, commanding roles. She wasn't girlish.

No doubt Mrs Dyer had chosen the play with that in mind. Although she'd taken everything from Lilith, she still couldn't bear to see her succeed, even when it made the theatre money. I wondered if she heard the watch, whispering, telling her of Lilith's weaknesses.

I should go and see Lilith again. She was like a song, always playing in the back of my mind. The Guvnor couldn't visit her now, couldn't arrange the care she badly needed, so I was the only person in the world watching over her. During my calls she'd sit like a statue waiting to crumble to dust. Only Eurydice's wagging tail raised a semblance of a smile on her wan face. She'd be all alone right now ... But I had my own family to think about, and there was so much work for me to do before the next show.

As the parlour door opened, I threw down my pencil and shook the cramp from my hand. Bertie came in. Things were still strained between us since I'd sent Greg packing. The way he looked at me had altered, as if he were viewing me through a lens of resentment. Greg had been the father figure in his life, the one to nurse a bruise or soothe him from a nightmare. Bertie was still too young to understand that it'd been me who'd made the greater sacrifice by leaving my home behind to earn more money for the family. I'd spent years slaving at the Fieldings', being treated like dirt by the gentry, just so I could send a decent wage home. But as far as Bertie was concerned, they'd only been years of absence. He never saw what I did for him.

'I'm bored,' Bertie complained. He came over to the table and shuffled through my sketches as though they were a picture book. 'What are these for?'

'Costumes. We're about to start rehearsing *Romeo and Juliet* at the theatre.'

'You'll take me to see *this* play, won't you?' he wheedled.

I deliberated, thinking of the script. There were plenty of references to carnal relations, but that would probably go over his head. 'I don't know, Bert. A lot of people die in it. You might get upset.'

'They really die?'

'No, it's not real. It's all an illusion.'

'Magic?' Bertie asked with interest.

'Not exactly. Just pretend. See, when Juliet dies, the dagger she uses is a gag. It's not sharp.' I grabbed a piece of paper and tried to sketch the prop for him. 'There's a spring in the handle, like this, so when you push on the blade it goes back into the hilt. To the audience, it looks like Juliet's driven the point into her chest. But really she's just pushed the blade back on the spring.'

'That's clever!'

I smiled. It was nice to share something with him again. 'It is.'

'I'd like to go,' Bertie repeated. 'I won't mind, now I know the gimmick. Please, Jenny?'

'Well ... I'll think about it.'

'Greg would let me go.'

I pretended not to hear that.

I'd need to see how things stood at the Mercury before I let the baby of my family step over the threshold. With all I'd witnessed, my instinct was to keep everyone I loved well clear of that building. But maybe the legend would prove true. Maybe taking Eugene Grieves's watch from Lilith had finally done the trick?

For all my bluster, for all my scepticism, deep down I was starting to believe along with the rest of them. I was hoping to get back to the theatre and find that Melpomene had gone for good.

There was a rap at the front door. Bertie limped to the parlour window and looked out. 'It's Greg! I said his name and he appeared!'

Just like the Devil himself.

I would've kept the house stubbornly locked, but as Bertie tapped on the glass Greg took a step towards the window and I caught sight of his face. One purple eye had sealed shut. His top lip was split, and snatches of his beard had been pulled out.

'He's hurt! He's hurt! Help him, Jenny!' Bertie rushed to open the door himself.

I followed slowly, my chest weighted with lead. Part of me had wanted Greg to get hurt. Now it had happened, I was afraid.

'Don't worry, Bertie, it looks worse than it is.' Greg's voice sounded strange and thick as he slumped over the threshold. 'I'll survive.' He concealed a wince when Bertie clung to his mud-splattered trousers.

'What happened to you?'

'I was robbed.'

Greg's eyes tangled with mine. I knew this was a lie, a sop for Bertie.

'We'll fetch the police!' Bertie decided. 'I can go to the station—'

I interrupted him. 'You'll go upstairs, Bertie, and wait in your room, there's a good boy.'

'I won't! Greg's hurt and …' He began to blubber, confused by all his strong emotions.

Greg placed a hand upon his shoulder. 'It's all right, little man. Do as your sister says. We need to talk.'

'But I want to stay with you!'

'Just give me a while to speak with Jenny. Please.' I could see what it was costing him to appear buoyant for Bertie's sake. As he gave a painful smile, I glimpsed a gap where a tooth was missing.

At last, Bertie was persuaded to clomp up the stairs. I took Greg to the kitchen and sat him down while I tore up lint for bandages.

'It's not my job to bind your wounds.' I ripped the material savagely. 'It's your wife's. What d'you mean by coming here in this state?'

He took a liquid, grating breath. 'I've been beaten enough for one day. I don't need your tongue-lashing too.'

I glanced at his hands. The knuckles weren't raw. If it was a fight, it was one-sided; more likely he'd been jumped by surprise.

'So what really happened?'

Greg looked away. His lips were puffed up, but I still noticed the lower one tremble. 'It's your fault, you know. That's why I came; to show you what you'd done.'

'My fault!' I shot back. 'How do you figure that?'

'They would have given me more time, if Georgie had gone on! If she'd got back on the cast list, like she was supposed to, before you and Lilith ruined it all ...' He stopped, spat out a mix of phlegm and blood.

I remembered what Oscar had said about Greg gambling. This was what happened when there were debts to collect and no money to pay them. 'What have you got yourself into?' I sighed. 'How many people do you owe?'

For a moment I thought he wasn't going to answer. Then he said softly, 'I thought it would tide me over, just until I found some work. And you know what? It did. For a while there, I really thought I'd come back home from America with Bert's operation money and then some. But it couldn't last. I pushed the lucky streak too far. Then I panicked. I didn't know when to stop. I kept thinking I could win it back ...'

'Cards are a fool's game, Greg.' Throughout our childhood he'd been wary like me, gripping tenaciously to everything we still had left. I couldn't imagine him gambling away a fortune, but that was what seemed to happen once the bug had bitten. Better men than him had gone by dogs, dice and cards. 'How much have you lost?'

'Don't ask me that.'

I wasn't about to give him a penny. Even if Georgiana had replaced Lilith, even if he had a steady income, he wouldn't be safe. A flush of luck and an addict would be back at the table, risking more.

'I don't like to see you hurt, Greg, no matter how much you deserve it. I'll patch you up. But bandages are all you're getting from me. You need to take responsibility for what you've done.'

He turned his one good eye on me, entreating. 'Just a few quid! Georgiana's missed a course. What if she's pregnant? That would be your own niece or nephew. You can't sit back and watch them starve!'

I felt myself wavering, flickering like the lights in Lilith's dressing room. But for all I knew, Greg was telling another desperate fib. I'd done enough to help others lately. I needed to start protecting myself.

'You've made your own bed, Gregory. I'm afraid you'll have to lie in it now.'

―――――

Maybe it was wishful thinking, but things did feel different when I returned to the theatre a fortnight later. As I sat sewing in the wardrobe room with Polly, the air seemed lighter and easier to breathe. Rather than perching on the edge of my chair, tense, I found it possible to lose myself in lines of neat, orderly stitches.

Everything was simpler on stage. Shades of blue for the Montagues, reds and pinks for the Capulets. I sat hunched over costumes until my back ached, my vision blurred and my fingertips turned numb. At last, I put away my needle and folded the gowns carefully into tissue paper.

'Do you think the theatre's changed?' I asked.

Polly was still bleary-eyed from sewing. 'Since when?'

'Well, since ... I mean, it felt terrible when Silas and Anthony died. I hated to be here. But now it feels ... settled. Don't you think?'

She shrugged. 'That's grief. Softens over time, don't it?'

'It's more than that.'

'Maybe it was Mr Thorne, throwing Georgiana out on her arse. Now *that* cheered me up no end.'

We chuckled and Mrs Nettles entered the room. She was carrying a stack of something carefully between both hands. 'Still here, girls? It's time you were on your way home.'

'We're just packing up.' Polly craned forward eagerly. 'What've you got?'

'Masks, for the Capulet ball. Aren't they fine?' Gently, she laid them out on the table before us. 'Here's Romeo.' It was silver, calling to mind a knight in shining armour. We could see our faces in its surface. 'Lord Capulet' – red edged with gold and a long nose that made Polly giggle. 'This one's Juliet' – hers was a simple white domino, painted with black teardrops.

My smile fell.

None of the masks had mouths; they ended clear of the tip of the nose so that the actors could speak their lines audibly. Why, then, did Juliet's make me think of Melpomene and that anguished face?

'I thought Juliet would have something prettier. Delicate and pink, to go with her gown.'

Mrs Nettles shook her red head. 'This one means more. Thematically.'

I didn't know how to object to that.

When the work was safely stowed away, I crept down to Lilith's dressing room. It smelt strongly of paint. A fresh coat of lemon covered the wall by the dressing table, obliterating all the dark patches. There was a new sofa to replace the one she'd mauled. Even the carpet had changed to a rich chocolate background patterned with golden flowers.

If I didn't know better, I'd say Mrs Dyer was renovating it for a new leading lady.

While Lilith had cherished the watch, it had felt as though Melpomene had drawn the life force from the theatre, from Lilith's very body, to make her art more vital on stage. But that night I lit the gas and sat determinedly for at least half an hour, watching and waiting. There was nothing at all. No smell, no creeping sensation. The lights didn't flicker once. Breathing a sigh of relief, I extinguished the lamps and left.

The auditorium lay blissfully still, its only illumination the Ghost Light that burned on a stand at the front of the stage. A man sat beside it, his legs swinging down into the orchestra pit, staring out into the darkness. Oscar.

I approached carefully so as not to startle him. 'What are you doing here?'

'Dreaming.' He patted the dusty boards by his side. 'Join me.'

I squatted down and sat in the Ghost Light's glow. Suddenly the stage was ours, not the actors'. A vignette world where the audience were nothing but a sea of black.

'When I look out like this,' Oscar mused, 'when it's quiet and no one's around, I can imagine anything I like.' He glanced lovingly at the gilded belly of the dress circle and the sweep of the gallery, the boxes that queued up to the proscenium arch. 'I can pretend it all belongs to me.'

'Would you want it? This place where Silas and Anthony died so horribly?'

Warm light licked over one side of his face. 'Well, maybe not *this* theatre. But in the darkness, if I try hard enough, I can forget that happened, too.'

I'd never forget. I wished that I could. Were it not for those memories, there'd be a deep sense of peace sitting here beside Oscar, watching the Ghost Light sway, waltzing with the shadows, dust drifting through its beam.

'How's Lilith?' he asked.

'She should be delighted. The ticket sales are through the roof and she has a stack of letters begging her to tour with other companies over the summer. She got everything she wanted but ... there's something missing. She doesn't even seem to care about the play. She looks ... depleted.'

Oscar kicked out his feet. 'Could it be guilt? Maybe she regrets that ... operation.'

Somehow, I didn't think it was the baby she missed. 'I hear Felix Whitlow's skittish too. A fine pair of lovers they'll make. *More courtship lives in carrion flies than Romeo.*'

'I talked to Felix, after what happened. You were right, he did work with Lilith and Eugene Grieves before.' He stared out into the auditorium for a moment before turning back. 'He said the watch changed Eugene, too. Made him throw over the woman he was meant to marry and become a bit of a recluse. But he got his success.'

How much people were willing to pay to satisfy their ambition. Eugene, Lilith, the Dyers, even Greg and Georgiana. They'd risked everything, and for what? None of them were happy.

'I know it sounds mad, but the watch is the reason I've stayed late tonight. I wanted to see if I'd made a difference, if Melpomene had gone. It's silly, isn't it?'

'I've heard sillier.' After a pause, he added. 'Don't forget you've given the watch to the owner of a theatre which specialises in tragedies. What if Mrs Dyer wants help from Melpomene too?'

I hadn't thought of that. The Muse struck me as something peculiar to actors, but why should it be? 'I hope to God she doesn't. I hope I never hear that name again. Whatever it was, whatever bad luck or curse that haunted us … it's left.' I looked pleadingly into his face. 'Don't you think it's left?'

Oscar put his hands behind him and leant back on the boards. 'No one really leaves the theatre.'

I couldn't tell if he was joking nor not. 'What do you mean?'

'That's what the Ghost Light's all about.'

'I thought it was to stop us from falling off the stage in the dark.'

He laughed. 'Well, yeah, it is. But it's also a mark of respect to all the actors who've gone before. Like a candle, burning in their memory. And some people …' He paused, peering deep into the darkness. Only the seats nearest to the Ghost Light were illuminated; the rows further back might have been at the bottom of a well. 'Some people think the dead actors come back and put on their own plays by night.'

I could imagine it; or rather, I could imagine Lilith. A servant in life and death, never free, forever saying words that were not her own. I shook the image off. 'Now you're the one who's being daft.'

'Maybe. You can't deny this place has a pull on people, though. Greg and Georgie left, only to come back again.'

Why did he mention them? It had been nice, just the two of us, alone in the soft lighting and the hush. Maybe I should tell him about Greg's wounded visit and the way he had stormed off afterwards. It would give Oscar a grim kind of satisfaction to hear.

'I'm sorry,' I said so quietly that the auditorium seemed to swallow my words. 'I did mean to tell you who was billed to play Cleopatra.'

He sighed. The flame dipped. 'Don't be sorry. That carry-on in the dressing room was exactly what I needed to see. All that time I'd built up a picture of Georgie, of how lucky I was to get her. It was cobblers. Watching her standing there, so false and affected, beside a woman who could really act, was an eye-opener. She's second-rate.'

'Well, they say love makes you blind.'

'It wasn't love though, was it? How could I marry someone like that? She didn't have an ounce of pity. Not for me, not for Lilith. I used to damn Greg's eyes, but now ... I think maybe he took a bullet for me.'

I ran my hand over the reflector covering one of the floats. I'd never noticed before, but it was shaped like a wing. There were feathered wings in the design of the proscenium arch too. Symbols of Mercury. Was there an inch of this theatre not steeped in myth?

'It's easy to lose your compass in a place like this. It's easy to start believing in things that aren't real.'

'You're real,' he said gently. 'And you're kind, and you've got spirit. Do you know, you might be the only part of the real world I actually like?'

I tried to laugh it off, but I could hardly breathe. Time stopped around us. I was so aware of how close he sat, how we seemed to be the only two people left in the world.

Slowly, he took hold of my chin and raised it so I looked him straight in the eye. His were chocolate in the lamplight. 'You *are* real, aren't you, Jenny? You're not a muse? You're not about to vanish in a puff of air?'

I could smell his breath, sweet as sugar cane. 'There's only one way to find out.'

I closed my eyes, leant forward. Our lips met.

It all melted away then. Melpomene, Lilith, Georgiana and Greg. All I could feel was the soft warmth of Oscar's mouth upon mine.

This was my scene, my moment in the limelight. I never wanted it to end.

CHAPTER 28

Summer in London is always dusty. That year, it was a sandstorm. The poor horses pulling the cabs and omnibuses plodded as if they were on their way to the knacker's yard. Under the heat of a mid-June sun, the stink of the dung piles intensified. Flies swarmed. Even the stone lions at Trafalgar Square seemed to pant, their tongues lolling for a drop of rain.

By contrast, the theatre was blissfully cool. My eyes took a moment to adjust themselves to the dark when I entered each morning. I was starting to relish the scent of beeswax and dust. Suddenly, the Mercury had become an oasis.

I'd fixed it.

All sense of threat had drifted away like a dark cloud passing in the wind. The costumes and scenery were beginning to take shape, and I was falling in love. But that was before the actors came back and started to rehearse. A few days served to make me realise that while I could repair the dressing room and I could banish Melpomene, I couldn't mend Lilith. In fact, I was worried I'd made her worse.

She sat as she had so often, reflected in the dressing-table mirrors. There were four Liliths – one in each glass and the original before me – but I couldn't see *her* at all. Something had gone. *Out, out brief candle.* Yes, that speech had got it right. Lilith was a walking shadow now.

Juliet's trick dagger rested in her hand. She kept pushing the point, in and out, with the flat of her other palm.

'You're not supposed to have that yet. It should be in the properties room.'

'I need it.'

The spring made a grating sound as it pulled back and popped on release. 'Why? To make a hole in your palm? To drive me mad?'

She let the dagger bounce back into position. Then she cocked her head. 'Listen.'

I did. There were the usual backstage noises before a performance: low chatter, doors closing and pulleys working in the distance.

'I can't hear anything.'

'Precisely. The silence is deafening.' She started again, making the dagger disappear and bound back.

Taking a deep breath, I shook out Juliet's first gown. Lilith had been through an ordeal. I shouldn't blame her for acting strangely. But her misery felt like a restraint on my budding happiness.

'There's no earthly use in primping that dress,' Lilith told me. 'It doesn't signify how I appear on stage. I shan't make a good show of it. I already reached the zenith. The only way from here is … down.'

'You have to try. We've sold most of the boxes, despite the heat. People are willing to swelter just to see you.'

Lilith laid the dagger aside. 'But Melpomene doesn't speak to me any more. She's gone.'

She *had* gone. We were free. If only Lilith could realise how wonderful that was. 'I thought Melpomene's whispers were driving you to distraction?'

A tear slid down her cheek. 'They were! But the only thing worse than the whispering is this terrible hush.'

Wearily, I took her in my arms. I never could have imagined embracing Lilith before, but things had changed.

'You'll be a perfect Juliet,' I soothed. 'You acted for years before you got that stupid watch, didn't you? You don't need Melpomene.'

She pressed her dark head into my chest. '*He that is strucken blind cannot forget the precious treasure of his eyesight lost. Thou canst not teach me to forget.*'

'That's not your line. It's Romeo's.'

'So it is. See, I'm already failing.' Her lips turned down, she looked just like the mask. 'It's going to be terrible. I'm so afraid.' I felt her tremble in my grasp. 'You remember what they did to the Sirens, don't you?'

'Who?'

'The Muses, Melpomene and her eight sisters?'

I exhaled irritably. 'No, I don't remember. You told me the Sirens were Melpomene's daughters.'

'They were! But they challenged the Muses to a singing contest. Of course the Muses won. They had no mercy on their own family. They plucked those poor Sirens of all their feathers and wore their plumage as a crown.'

'What does any of this matter? It's just a story.'

She wasn't listening. 'Do you think you could tell the difference between the Muse and the Siren Song? One a divine voice calling you to create and the other a lure, pulling you down to destruction? What if ... what if they sound precisely the same?'

'They're not *real*, Lilith. No more than Romeo and Juliet are real. They're just characters and stories to help us understand the world. The truth is, there are hundreds of people out there waiting for you to put on a show. You're being paid to do it, and you need to be paid to live and eat. So let me put this frock on you.'

She rose to her feet and stood slackly. She'd lost weight. The robe hung from her bony shoulders.

'I thought I wanted to be like Eugene,' she said. 'I wanted him to be proud of me. I thought I'd pay any price.'

'He *would* be proud of you. We all are. After your Cleopatra, the papers are comparing you to Siddons, Bernhardt and Terry. They're saying you're the greatest tragic actress who ever lived!'

'Yes. They do say that.' She picked up the dagger, pressed its point to her fingertip. 'It's strange how little it means, in the end.'

The Capulets' masquerade ball shimmered on stage. Candelabras and tall vases of flowers hid the wings from sight. A string quartet played on a platform above the two lines of dancers. Couples turned and weaved around each other in time to the music.

Felix Whitlow had shaved off his moustache to play the youthful Romeo. He lurked behind one of the false pillars, his eyes glinting through his silver mask. '*O, she doth teach the torches to burn bright!*'

I'd done my best. But the Juliet he spied on didn't live up to the words. The pale pink gown leant none of its rosy hue to her skin. She resembled a dressed corpse.

Romeo approached, touched her hand.

'*Good pilgrim, you do wrong your hand too much.*' The rest of Lilith's words were barely audible, her vocal threads had been pinched like a candle's wick.

Ripples of displeasure ran through the audience.

Felix replied to her speech even louder, compensating. '*Have not saints lips, and holy palmers too?*'

There was a long pause.

'Ay, pilgrim,' the prompter supplied.

'*Ay, pilgrim.*' Lilith's brows drew together, as if she were calculating an impossible sum.

'Lips that they must use in prayer.'

'*Lips that they must use in prayer,*' she repeated, without expression.

Someone let out a low hiss.

I could hardly look. It was so painful; I felt embarrassed for her. How was bold, strong Lilith reduced to this?

When he came off stage, Felix Whitlow seized me and dragged me over to the wing lights. 'What the deuce is wrong with that woman?'

Maybe I didn't need to lie to him. 'She's lost Eugene's watch. It's taken all her confidence with it.'

'Oh.' He adjusted his mask. 'Oh. Thank God.' The anger seemed to drop out of him. 'That's for the best. Yes. Better an acid review than ...'

'Than what?' I demanded, desperate to hear the truth at last. 'What exactly do you know about Eugene Grieves and that watch?'

Felix swallowed. 'More than I would like. I stood beside him while he died. I played Mephistopheles to his Faustus.'

So that's where I knew him from. No wonder he'd fled at the sight of the watch; it had been bad enough seeing Eugene die from the gallery, but Felix had a front-row seat. 'There was something special about that play, wasn't there? Eugene scratched the words from it on the back of his watch: *Homo fuge*.'

'*Doctor Faustus* wasn't just a play to Eugene. He had a fascination with the occult. Magic had ravished him, too. He told me,' Felix said slowly, as if each word cost him pain, 'that he'd conjured up a muse, more than twenty years ago, and bound her to his watch. He said she was the only reason he could act as he did. I thought him insane.'

'Melpomene,' I breathed.

'But *was* it? He may have asked for her, yet anything could have stepped into that breach.'

I remembered the language Eugene had spouted – guttural and demonic – and felt sick. 'What are you saying? Who else could it be?'

His silver mask shimmered and winked in the wing lights. 'How can I possibly know? I don't *want* to know. Even to speak of it seems absurd. But it was a dim and evil star that beckoned that man. Whatever he made a pact with ... it wasn't good.'

Timber creaked. My attention returned to the stage; the scene drop was down and they were moving the balcony set into place. Felix had to go.

'Take my advice, Miss Wilcox. However Lilith lost that watch, make sure it stays lost. I'd rather play opposite a lame duck than see another end like him.'

I nodded. I couldn't bring myself to confess that the watch wasn't lost at all; that it probably sat, at this very moment, clasped in Mrs Dyer's trembling hands.

Soon the scene was set for the Capulets' orchard with false trees and real potted plants. Lilith leant over a balcony twined with roses.

'*'Tis but thy name that is my enemy. Thou art thyself ... though ... though not a Montague.*'

The stage manager, Horace, sighed and pinched the bridge of his nose, as if Lilith's stilted delivery were giving him the megrim.

'*O, be some other name! What's in a name? That which we call a rose by any other name would smell as sweet.*'

I shifted my weight uncomfortably. It wasn't just Lilith's clockwork monotone; it was the words themselves. They echoed what Felix had said. We'd called the spirit in the watch Melpomene. But what if it hadn't been her whispering to Lilith and Eugene? What if it was something wicked that answered to her name?

A row of tipsy men sat grouped close together on a bench in the pit; they looked out of place, like they'd stumbled into the Mercury by mistake. One cupped his hands around his mouth and shouted, 'I've been with whores more convincing than her!'

A spatter of giggles. Lilith's shoulders went rigid. She took a steadying breath. '*Thou know'st the mask of night is on my face—*' An orange hit her square between the eyes. She stumbled, gripped the rail of the balcony for support. Harsh laughter swelled.

A second fruit followed the first, sailing wide and splattering against the scenery. Lilith gasped, struggled for her line, but before she could reach it an apple core smacked her in the chest.

I caught sight of Mrs Dyer sitting in her box, opera glasses raised. Her red lips grinned.

Soon it was a shower, a hailstorm of citrus rind and peanut shells. Felix Whitlow ran for cover opposite prompt side; Lilith crouched and raised her arms to shield herself.

'Do something!' I shouted to the stage manager. 'Bring the curtain down!'

Oscar appeared beside me. 'What's going on?'

Hoots rang through the auditorium; the audience were enjoying this game. The adoring crowd who had once tossed roses had turned into a sea of devils. A drunken clerk lurched to his feet and bowled his bottle overarm like a cricket ball. Liquid gleamed as it spilt, turning windmills in the air. Oscar swore. If alcohol fell on the gas …

The bottle shattered just above Lilith's head. Glass diamonds tinkled down into her black hair.

'Scene drop! Scene drop!' Horace roared.

Someone hauled on a rope and the curtain landed with a *thump*. It muffled but couldn't block out the ugly taunts.

I ran straight for Lilith, skidding on orange peel. She was cowering behind her balcony rails like an animal in its pen. I raised my arms to her. 'Climb down, Lilith. Come on, it's all right. I'll help.'

Her pupils flared. Just as when Anthony had died, she couldn't move.

Horace strode toward me, peanut shells cracking under his shoes. 'Miss Wilcox, go quickly and dress Clementine Price. There's enough time to get her ready for Scene Five. She'll have to be Juliet for the rest of the play.'

I kept reaching for Lilith. 'Find someone else.'

'It is your duty to—'

'I don't care,' I snapped. 'I'm not leaving Lilith in this state.'

He stormed off, shouting an order to the Prompt.

In the end, Oscar had to climb up to the balcony and carry Lilith down. From his arms, she turned her despairing eyes upon me. They used to spark like steel, but now they were ditchwater grey.

'Banished,' she whispered. 'Banished from the stage like Romeo from Verona.'

'Hush, now.'

Her head remained full of plays, yet something vital had gone, and I couldn't help but feel I was the one responsible for taking it.

CHAPTER 29

Citrus juice and glass were easier to sponge off than blood. Eurydice curled under Lilith's stool, licking her ankles clean. If only there were something either of us could do to fix the actress inside.

Lilith's performances didn't improve. Each play ended with an embarrassed trickle of applause. Crowds of people who had come to witness the rising of a star left disenchanted. Horace rotated her with Clementine, giving each the chance to play Juliet and Lady Capulet by turn, but it didn't help at the box office. Clementine's nerves had only worsened since she'd seen Anthony die and Lilith humiliated on stage. As for our leading lady, she was equally listless in every part.

Juliet's trick dagger had replaced the watch as Lilith's constant companion. She turned the hilt obsessively, keeping her fingers busy. All the while I knew Mrs Dyer would be sharpening her own dagger and preparing to cut Lilith's ties to the Mercury. The Guvnor had carried his point while Lilith remained a financial asset, but now he wouldn't have a leg to stand on.

'It's gone,' Lilith murmured as I dressed her hair. 'My art. All I worked for. Gone.'

'It'll come back. You've just lost your confidence.'

'I can't bear it, Jenny. To be diminished. To dwindle into nothing.'

I yanked the brush through her hair. 'You are *not* nothing! You're a person in your own right.'

She didn't even wince as I tugged. Her head bobbed back and forth limply, like a doll's. 'I don't know who I am if I can't act. It's defined me for so long.'

'You're Lily Fitzwilliams.'

'Lily Fitzwilliams!' she spat. 'She was nothing but a bastard, a disgrace. And now she will be again.'

Sighing, I stopped my ministrations. 'You're worth more than your art, Lilith. There are people in this world who care for you, whether you act or not.'

'Are there? Hugh isn't one of them.' She turned a baleful glare at the dressing-room door. 'You were right about him. He should be here comforting me, coaching me through my difficulties. But he wanted the talent, not the woman. He only really cared about Melpomene.'

I squatted down to look into her face. 'There aren't many performances left to get through before the summer break. You'll start afresh next season with a new play.'

The dagger clicked. 'It won't matter. It's all the same. My time has come to an end. There's nothing left to do now but ... wait.'

'Wait for what?' I demanded.

She didn't look at me, just ran her index finger up and down the blade. 'Eugene had twenty-four years. Twenty-four years, like the Doctor he died playing. I thought that might be the standard. A year for each hour of the day. But no. I've barely had twelve months. It turns out Lucifer was more generous than Melpomene. Who would have thought?'

A thin, sour chill crept over me. 'Lilith ... What did you do? Did you make a pact, like Doctor Faustus?'

Her silence was worse than an answer. At last she said, 'I've never been religious, you know. It isn't a hardship, to give my soul to the theatre. Where else would it go? It's always lived here.'

This wouldn't do. I needed to lead her out of the underworld of myths and characters from plays, bring her back to the land of the living. But how?

'Why don't you go down to Southend in August?' I suggested. 'You could spend time with Algernon.'

Her brows lowered. For a moment, she didn't seem to recognise the name of her own child. 'For what purpose? He doesn't remember me.'

'But he could,' I encouraged. 'It's not too late to be a family. You could leave all this behind, take your son back and raise him. You said you don't know who you are – well, you're Algernon's mother. No one can take that away from you.'

Her hands clenched around the hilt of the dagger as if in prayer. 'No,' she said softly, 'no, that wouldn't be fair. The truth is I'm a fallen woman now ... without success to perfume the stench. It's better for Algernon that he never knows his true origins. I'll find a good family to adopt him. They will pretend, right from the start. As far as Algernon is concerned, they will be his parents, he will be legitimate and he will belong. *That* is what I want for him.'

To Algernon she would forever be the lady in the photograph, smothered in a black veil. Until now, I hadn't thought that she loved her child, but this selflessness made me realise that she did, in her own way.

'It was a girl, you know,' she whispered.

'What?'

'The doctor said she never would have lived.' Lilith's chest heaved. 'There was something wrong. With her spine.'

She hadn't acknowledged the abortion before, hadn't told me a word of what went on in that room in Harley Street. 'She must have been very small,' I offered gently.

'Barely formed. They put her in a bucket.' Her eyes weren't focused on me, they seemed to be looking to some deep place of pain only Lilith could see. 'Her poor back. To me it looked like she had ... wings.'

I shuddered, remembering the black in the lavatory bowl. Something had clearly gone very wrong with that pregnancy. 'Then you made the right decision, Lilith. She's gone to a better place.'

'Gone,' Lilith repeated. 'Gone, gone, gone.'

CHAPTER 30

Bertie gazed about with undisguised awe. We weren't even in the lobby, just standing in the hallway opposite the stage-door keeper's desk. It smelt of perspiration and feet, and since the cats had been banished there were mouse droppings scattered about like a spill of peppercorns. A boy swept them, his broom scratching against the floor.

'It's magical,' Bertie whispered. He'd been forbidden from the place for so long he was determined to love it. Dorcas and Philip were warier. I couldn't blame them. It had been less than a year since we'd watched Eugene Grieves drop down dead. 'Will I have to climb lots of steps?'

I hoisted up a smile for him. 'No, love. I bought you all seats near the front of the pit.'

'I *can* climb steps, now.'

He could, and that was some comfort to me. I'd told him this visit was a treat before he started his first employment. Philip's factory had finally agreed to take him on for lashing and plaiting, and would promote him to blocking when he was able to stand for longer periods. Despite all the horror I'd witnessed, Bertie's life had been changed for the better. Now I was doing what little I could to help repair things for Lilith.

'Listen,' I said. 'Lilith is the lady with black hair playing Juliet. I need you to cheer extra loud whenever she comes on the stage. Can you do that?'

'Phil taught me to whistle!' Bertie poked two fingers in his mouth and made a strange, pained sound.

Philip pulled a face. 'I think we'll just clap really hard instead.'

'Please. And then you know what to do at the end? It would make her so happy to get just one curtain call. I appreciate there's only three of you, but do what you can.' I handed Dorcas the tickets. 'Thank you. It means a lot to me. Oscar and I'll take you to the refreshment saloon when it's over.'

'One ice cream per cheer,' Philip suggested.

I shepherded them through the stage door and back onto the street, so they could make their way round to the pit entrance. I remembered, suddenly, the odd gentleman who'd wanted one of Lilith's stockings. He never did come back; Oscar must've scared him off. Where were those fanatic admirers now? They'd all abandoned Lilith the minute she had a blip.

When I entered the dressing room, the lights were all off. Lilith sat in the dark with Eurydice's head on her lap. She gasped as I fired up the gas. Her pupils were dilated, as if she'd been at the absinthe, but they shrank to pinpricks in a moment.

'*More light and light, more dark and dark our woes.*'

I didn't answer. She was so full of quotes and cryptic sayings these days that I was learning to ignore them.

'Come on,' I said brightly. 'Last performance before the summer break. After this, you never have to think about Juliet again.'

She pulled Eurydice close. 'I've heard nothing about my contract. And why should they renew? Like Melpomene, they'll just let everything ... expire.'

After her astonishing portrayal of Cleopatra, I'd imagined her spending summer on tour, having her pick of the seaside theatres. It seemed like a distant dream now. 'You'll find something.'

She swallowed. Her throat was so slender. 'I'm afraid, Jenny. I must pay my pound of flesh ... and there is no Portia to save me.'

She was getting confused, again. That was from *The Merchant of Venice*. I gripped her shoulder. 'Just once more. I've got a good feeling about tonight.' I imagined my siblings in the pit; hoped they could cheer loud enough to drown out her pain. 'You're going to bring the house down.'

It was better. Nothing miraculous – she wasn't a spot on the Lilith of old – but compared to the rest of the season, this performance was a huge improvement. Bertie's enthusiastic huzzahs caught on, became a bit of a game amongst the costermonger lads in the pit, and although the house was half-empty a pleasant atmosphere pervaded. No one was about to turn nasty and hurl fruit.

I'd hoped Lilith might relax and start to smile, yet she became more highly strung with each change. Between Acts Three and Four I had to swap her costume speedily, transforming her from the newly awakened bride to the penitent seeking Father Laurence's cell. She was shaking so hard that I could barely tie the laces on her bodice.

'Where's the hood?' I scraped a brush through her hair and twisted it up, jamming the headdress on top. 'There. Now your prayer book …' But she was holding the trick dagger.

'Why do you have this?' I groaned. 'It should still be in the prop room. Romeo needs to have it on him when he dies … I'll have to run it back.' I snatched it from her.

'*My dismal scene I needs must act alone.*'

'Just three more scenes. Once Juliet's taken the poison, all you have to do is lie there until the denouement. You can sleep, can't you?'

'Can I?' she wailed. 'I do not know *what dreams may come.*'

I didn't have time for this. If I didn't get the prop back, it could spoil the ending of the play. 'The call boy will be along in a minute. Don't worry, Lilith, you can do it.'

As I left the room, I glanced over my shoulder. Her eyes met mine in the mirror, desperate. But I was in too much of a hurry. I sped away.

The properties room served as a painful reminder of my career so far. It still contained the model of Antonio and the dead children from *The Duchess of Malfi*, only partially covered with a sheet. I saw the witches' cauldron, Mark Antony's armour, the helmet Lilith had vomited into. Each object told a story of its own.

The props for *Romeo and Juliet* were nearer the door, everything neatly labelled with the scene they appeared in and to which character they belonged. Lilith always pulled the tag off her trick dagger; I hoped she'd left it tidily in its place where I could find it.

Yet as I squeezed my way between a chariot and a papier-mâché donkey's head, I saw someone else standing there, looking at the empty place where the dagger should be. Georgiana.

'What are you doing here?'

She gaped at the sight of me, but then she flashed her pearly teeth in a smile. 'Sylvia asked me to be on hand as an understudy. What if we were to have another orange incident? They might need an actress to step in at a moment's notice, and Clementine's not up to scratch.'

I didn't like to hear her calling Mrs Dyer by her Christian name. 'Well, *Sylvia* needn't have troubled you. Lilith's doing better tonight. She's a talented actress, she's just going through a bad patch.'

Her eyes became shielded, opaque. 'She's not the only one.'

Was Greg's situation really as dire as he'd represented? I assessed Georgiana's figure, trying to judge if she could be expecting a baby. Her gown remained tightly laced, but there was something about her skin, a sort of freckling that could be the mask of pregnancy. To judge by her fashionable outfit, she wasn't struggling financially; but then she could be using dressmaker's credit, running up more bills she couldn't pay.

It wasn't my responsibility; I wouldn't let them make it my problem. 'Will you stand aside, please? I need to put this back in its place.'

She made a great gesture of stepping out of my way. The property label for the dagger wasn't on the shelf. After a quick search, I was forced to give up and put the dagger back untagged. The stagehands knew what they were doing. The weapon Juliet used to kill herself was at least an obvious prop, not easily overlooked.

'I would have made a wonderful Juliet,' Georgiana observed bitterly.

Actually, she might have made a fair go of it; the role was more in her vein than Cleopatra had been, but I wasn't about to grant her any quarter. 'Juliet's loyal to the point of death. I don't suppose Oscar would say the same about you.'

She exhaled irritably. 'Oscar couldn't give me what I needed. He's a dreamer, darling. Hopeless. I had to leave him behind.'

'And what about Greg? Is he "giving you what you need"?'

A muscle ticked beside her eye. 'He was. But then he lost it all again.'

'I can't dally here all night. I've work to do.' I turned on my heel.

'I suppose I might as well come and watch the end of the play,' Georgiana sighed behind me. 'Sylvia won't mind if I avail myself of her box while it's empty.'

Warning bells chimed inside my head. Mrs Dyer's absence rarely portended anything good. With the cat allergy and the maggots, she'd taken care to remain out of sight.

The corridor to the dressing rooms was in its usual state of commotion. But amongst the various Montagues and Capulets, the wig-makers and the half-dressed dancers, there was something else running up and down. A black poodle.

'Come! Heel!' Eurydice bounded up to me then sprang away again, agitated, unwilling to stay still. 'How did you get out here?'

Lilith must have forgotten to shut the door behind her when she left with the call boy. It was closed now.

'Come on. There's a good dog.' I grabbed a curl of Eurydice's tight black coat and steered her back towards the dressing room. She came obediently most of the way. But just short of the door she whined and laid down. I couldn't move her.

Exasperated, I opened the door. Light blazed over the threshold. The lamps were burning brighter than ever; I screened my eyes with a hand.

As my sight adjusted to the stark, white light, a cold finger traced its way down my back. Lilith had rifled through the paint-box and brought out the carmine stick. Two words were scrawled on the mirror in large red letters:

Homo fuge.

My mouth hung open. None of this made any sense. But in a dreadful way, it did.

I turned and ran. The ominous lines Lilith had quoted rose up in my memory; I'd heard them but not really *listened*. Settling debts. Hamlet's monologue on suicide.

What could I do? Should I just pull Lilith off the stage? There was no plausible excuse. I thought of sounding an alarm, starting a fire and a thousand other mad ruses. Where was Oscar? Oscar could help.

The curtains billowed at Prompt Corner as I arrived and clung desperately to Horace.

'Miss Wilcox? Have a care!' He shoved me off; he hadn't forgotten my rudeness on the night Lilith was fruited.

'It's Lilith,' I gabbled. 'She's in danger.'

'From what?'

I opened my lips. What was I to say? 'From ... herself. Please, I know it sounds ridiculous. But you need to take her off stage.'

Horace gestured through the curtains. 'How can I?'

It was the final scene, the graveyard. Real skulls were piled in heaps. A stone angel overlooked tombs strangled by ivy. Felix Whitlow, dressed as Romeo, bore a torch in one hand. He drew back the lid of a sarcophagus, revealing Lilith on a bier. Roses lay on her breast and were scattered through her dark hair.

'Pull the curtain,' I urged. 'Or swap her out for Clementine while he fights with Paris.'

'Miss Wilcox, are you quite well?'

More action on stage as Juliet's scorned lover Paris tried to protect her grave.

'Please, sir. Let me go on and get her. It's the last performance of the season, what can it matter?'

Horace stared at me. 'And it is the final scene in the play. Don't ruin it now. This is the best run of Juliet she's made.'

'Her life's more important than a role.'

He scoffed. 'You are absurd! What harm can Miss Erikson possibly come to?'

A ball tumbled down the thunder run. Metal sheets clashed, imitating a storm of swords. Lilith was so close. If I could only reach her ...

'You were here,' I tried. 'You saw exactly what happened to Anthony Frost. We neglected him, but maybe we can save her.'

His face softened a little, or maybe it was just a shadow thrown by a wing light. 'There has been plenty to unsettle us this year. Go home, Miss Wilcox, and compose yourself. I promise to watch over your actress faithfully for the last minutes of the play.'

'But—'

'Now, if you'll excuse me.'

The stage manager could dismiss me but he couldn't make me leave. I hovered in the wings, a wad of fear in my throat.

Romeo had killed Paris. He laid him gently to rest beside Juliet. Limelight swept through a silver medium over her profile. With her white skin and red lips, she could be Snow White in the fairy tale.

'*Why art thou yet so fair?*'

One of the skulls caught my eye. It had no jawbone, yet it seemed to be grinning at me.

'Jenny?' Oscar arrived at my side. 'What is it? Horace said you were upset …'

'Something terrible is about to happen. Lilith was talking about death but I wasn't listening to her.'

He didn't dismiss me like Horace had. 'When? When did she say this?'

'Before … it was … just at the start of Act Four.'

'That was a whole act ago. She's been on since then. She's been great.' He gave me an encouraging smile. 'She's coming back to us.'

I shook my head. 'You don't understand. The mirror …'

'What about the mirror?'

'She wrote on it. The same words that were on Eugene Grieves's watch.'

Oscar frowned, trying his best to comprehend my babble. 'Lilith wrote on her mirror?'

'I hope it was her. But what if it was—'

'*The lady stirs.*'

Juliet started up from a nightmare, her hand swatting the air. I couldn't finish my sentence, couldn't explain what I feared to Oscar. The sight of Lilith held me transfixed.

'*O comfortable friar! Where is my lord? Where is my Romeo?*' It didn't sound like her.

'*A greater power than we can contradict hath thwarted our intents. Come, come away. Thy husband in thy bosom there lies dead, and Paris too.*'

She stifled a scream. Tears began to gush down her face as she cradled Romeo's corpse in her arms.

'See?' Oscar breathed. 'She's doing it. She's finally got Juliet.'

But something wasn't right. As she tried to suck the poison from Romeo's lips, the light darkened and changed hue.

'Who did that?' I asked, staring up into the flies.

'Must be a mistake.'

The blue medium. It usually went over the limelight when a ghost appeared on stage.

'*O happy dagger!*' Metal flashed. Juliet held the weapon aloft, casting its shadow over the boards.

The blood stopped in my veins. 'Oh, God.'

'What, Jenny?'

'*This is thy sheath.*' She plunged the dagger beneath her ribs with swift brutality. '*There ... rust ... and let me ... die.*'

Juliet gasped and coughed. For a moment, I dared to hope I was mistaken. But I'd seen that trick dagger hundreds of times. The hilt poking out from her chest was different.

By now she should have collapsed over Romeo's body. The page ran on from the opposite side, ready to say his line, but what he saw held him mute.

The blood spread slowly at first, blooming like a flower across her gown. Then it was gushing in carmine waves, bubbling from Lilith's lips.

Far off in the dressing room, Eurydice howled.

Nobody spoke. Nobody moved. Maybe they thought it a stage effect, something made of syrup and rouge. In absolute silence, Lilith crawled across the blue-lit stage, reaching out one bloody hand for the floats. She croaked a word I couldn't hear.

Her body landed with a thump, shaking the boards beneath her.

Time stood still. Dust motes drifted in the limelight as gory puddles formed.

Then somebody started to scream. They sounded an awful lot like me.

ACT V

Faust, Part One

'Of suns and worlds I've nothing to be quoted; how men torment themselves is all I've noted.'

CHAPTER 31

Their names were billed side by side again; in death as in life. Lilith and her leading man Anthony Frost kept each other company on the north side of the church. The Devil's side.

It didn't feel condemned there, just sad, with the unkempt grass and inferior headstones poking up through the earth. Sunlight seldom touched the graves. They were cool and dark in the shadow of the steeple; a place where slugs and beetles thrived.

Their monuments matched. The same stone, the same type-face, all paid for by the Guvnor. He hadn't skimped. Where most people sought to hide the identity of their hasty, unshriven burials, the Guvnor had given his actors their due, with the result that their names were the first you saw on this side of the church, proclaiming them king and queen of the suicides.

Spreading my skirts over the damp grass, I sat at their feet. Eurydice sniffed about while Oscar stood, leaning against a tree. We came at least once a week. The shade and the silence calmed me. I knew where Lilith was, here; I could keep an eye on her. Without the gravestone before me, I was apt to picture her bloody end, over and over again; or worse, dream of her being dragged to Hell by a demon wearing Melpomene's mask. But the graveyard was logical, formal. It wasn't so bad, to think of her here.

Dorcas's bouquet rested upon the soft, brown earth. Marigold for grief. Asphodel for regret. Willow and cypress for mourning. It was withering. Lilith spent her life seeking the limelight and now ...

'How's Bertie?' Oscar asked softly.

I shook my head. 'He still wakes up sobbing.'

'Dorcas? Philip?'

'I don't think they'll ever go to the theatre again.'

The bells tolled. A breeze moved the trees. Dappled light played across Lilith's name and vanished again.

Oscar watched me. 'What about you? Will you go back?'

A tear leaked from my eye. It was impossible to imagine a play without Lilith. That the summer would end and the Mercury would reopen as usual. Surely three deaths in one year were enough to shut any theatre down?

'We have to eat. But I don't even know if Mrs Dyer will still want me. What use am I to her now?'

Oscar sat beside me and wrapped an arm around my shoulders. Other mourners came and went on the good side of the church. Shadow brides with their bouquets of lilies, dazed children crammed into their Sunday best.

'I still think it was them,' he grumbled. 'Mrs Dyer and Georgiana. Lilith shouldn't even be buried here, she was murdered.'

Of course I'd told the police about Georgiana being in the properties room, about Mrs Dyer's tricks. I'd had to tell them about Lilith's behaviour too. There was more than one witness to me running around backstage that night, spouting that Lilith was a danger to herself. My own actions had helped settle the verdict.

'I want to believe it was murder. I really do. Because if it was suicide … I should have stopped it.' I let out one long, ragged sob. 'If Lilith killed herself, it was my fault.'

Oscar held me. Eurydice whined and nuzzled my ear.

'It's *not* your fault,' Oscar asserted fiercely. 'It's that bitch Georgiana. She'd do anything to get ahead. And you said it yourself: Mrs Dyer's not the full ticket. They killed Lilith.'

I tried to dry my tears. 'But the police said …'

'The police,' he guffawed. 'What do they know? Mrs Dyer will've paid one of the detectives off. She could have done it all, Jen. She could have pushed Silas, she could've worn Anthony down to despair. Where was she, when they died?'

I leant into him. Even in the summer, he still smelt of paint.

I'd been there for every death, felt the undercurrent running through the theatre and poisoning the air. I *had* sensed something evil at the Mercury. Could it really have been Mrs Dyer all along? 'You don't think … It couldn't be something to do with the watch?'

Oscar didn't laugh at me. He considered, picking at blades of grass. 'There's definitely something about that watch. The people who have it seem to get exactly what they want. But if Mrs Dyer sent someone to kill Lilith, I'll bet my eye teeth it was Georgiana and not Melpomene.'

My legs were going numb and ants crawled near my feet, but I didn't want to leave. How could I return to a house where I could glimpse Lilith's empty villa from the window?

Eurydice slumped down and raised her trusting brown eyes to Lilith's headstone. '*Lily Fitzwilliams.*'

The Guvnor hadn't consulted me about the memorial, but I liked to think I knew the reason for his choice. Lily Fitzwilliams, the unloved bastard child, could die like anyone else, but they'd never kill the legend that was Lilith Erikson.

She lingered on, immortal. A myth like Melpomene.

The letter came a few days later. It took all my resolve not to screw it up and throw it in the fire. But I couldn't ignore the inevitable; I'd have to face Mrs Dyer sooner or later.

I honestly didn't know what I wanted to hear from her. The thought of returning to work at the scene of Lilith's death felt like a prison sentence. Yet if Mrs Dyer told me I was no longer required, what would I do? Even if I found a new job, there was no way it would pay enough to keep the house. Bertie's eyes were already dark-rimmed from nightmares, and he'd be exposed to the rough world of the hat factory soon. I didn't want to tell him he'd have to leave his home, too. It was stupid of me to put myself in Mrs Dyer's power like this in the first place; I ought to have known it never could last. I'd had a run of luck, like Greg, and now it had come to a costly end.

We were well overdue for a storm. As I set out for the West End, I remembered with longing the rainy day of my first trip to the Dyer household this time last year. The heat was a yoke for everyone to carry, from the dogs that puffed like steam engines to the babies who wailed their distress.

The Guvnor stood at the second-storey window of Number 13, overlooking the gardens. The grass had dried brown and butterflies were flopping listlessly from one cracked flowerbed to another. There was no sparkle left in his eyes. He seemed a shadow of himself; a Pepper's ghost illusion. He signalled to me, but I ignored him; he deserved every ounce of guilt and agony.

I knocked at the front door this time. I thought I'd earned that privilege. At first there was silence, then feet pounded upon stairs. The Guvnor himself appeared on the threshold, gasping.

'Miss Wilcox,' he said hoarsely. 'Miss Wilcox I must speak with you.' Up high, behind the window, I hadn't been able to see his gaunt cheeks or the deep, harried sockets of his eyes. There were flecks of tobacco tangled in his beard.

'There's nothing you can say that will bring Lilith back.'

He caught his breath. Maybe he had cared for her in his distorted, faithless way. But not enough. 'No. Yet she's not entirely gone. She lives on—'

A door opened within, cutting him off. The Guvnor paled to see his wife issue from an inner room.

My hands curled into fists at my side. Besides the tattered Guvnor, she looked like a brightly painted character on stage, her lips redder than ever, her eyes glowing green. She thrived.

Instinct whispered that Oscar was right; she had orchestrated Lilith's death, though I had no solid arguments to ground this upon. I only knew what my gut told me, and it was telling me I wanted nothing more to do with this woman.

'Good morning,' she crooned. 'Miss Wilcox, do excuse our manners. As you can imagine, Mr Dyer has been quite unwell. Recent events have upset him terribly.' She sashayed towards us in a musky cloud of perfume and pushed the Guvnor's hair back behind his ears. 'My dear, what have we said about answering the door?'

He didn't appear soothed by her attentions. On the contrary, he squirmed beneath her touch. 'But I wanted – Miss Wilcox – I should—'

'Hush, hush. There is no cause to fret. I shall handle all of your business, my dear. Now you had better go back upstairs and take a little rest. James will ensure that you are comfortable.'

'No, but—'

'See to him, James.'

The Guvnor shot me an imploring look as the footman shepherded him back upstairs. I don't know what he expected me to do. If he couldn't command his wife, how could I?

Mrs Dyer's concerned manner evaporated the moment he was out of sight. 'Miss Wilcox,' she said coldly. 'If you would care to follow me.'

Once we reached the parlour, she stationed herself by the china dogs and leant against the mantelpiece. 'Well, Jennifer, as I am sure you anticipated, I have been restructuring the theatre company in light of Lilith's death.' She spoke the last words with relish, taking time to taste them on her tongue. 'Georgiana Mildmay will rejoin the troupe as our leading lady. For obvious reasons, she is not keen to retain your services.'

Georgiana, in Lilith's place. After all Mrs Dyer had said about her unreliability, her lack of talent, while pretending to sympathise with me. There must be something more to this: payment for a service rendered. 'Georgiana as your leading lady,' I repeated darkly. 'That's a turn-up for the books. How will you explain your choice to the company? They might think the two of you share a secret. That she's got something over you.'

I watched her closely, although if she had arranged Lilith's death, there'd be no hint of guilt; she thought Lilith deserved to die, like a villain in a play.

She offered a hard, fixed smile. 'I am sure you are disappointed to lose your position, but there is no reason for impudence.'

'There's plenty of reason! After all I've done for you … you can't just pick me up and throw me away again. I need this work, Mrs Dyer. You know I do, to keep the house. Please give me until Christmas at least. Give me time to find something else. Please.'

'It is not as if I have failed to recompense you for your services. You should not require more time. A prudent girl would have begun her search for work over the summer break.'

'I've been grieving,' I cried. 'I've been upset. I've just lost a ...' I stopped. I didn't know exactly what Lilith had been to me.

Mrs Dyer frowned, as though my distress was a mystery. 'Yes, it seems Lilith worked her spell on you, too. You have become quite a sentimental creature after all. Well, you know me, Jennifer. It is my pleasure to be kind. But really, my hands are tied in this matter. Georgiana has the final say.'

My heart stuttered in my chest. I only had one card to play. Did I really dare cross her? 'I hope you'll reconsider, madam. I think perhaps ... you'd have cause to regret letting me go so soon.'

She looked amused. 'Would I, indeed?'

'If I had to support myself by other means ... there's no saying what I might be driven to. What tales I might be forced to tell.' I fought to keep my gaze steady on her face. Slowly, her smirk began to wilt. 'Gossip columns are always looking for a scandal, aren't they, Mrs Dyer? And they pay. I think if I was put out of the Mercury before Christmas, I'd be obliged to entertain the theatre-going public in some other way ...'

The glare she turned on me could've pierced iron. 'You disappoint me, Jennifer. I had hoped to avoid descending to vulgarity.'

'Call it blackmail. That's what it is. And I don't want to use it, but you give me no choice.'

'The ingratitude!' she huffed. 'I had not thought you capable of this. After all my kindness! You will still rely upon me for a reference, at whatever point you leave. You ought to have a care how you speak to me.'

Looking at her, I couldn't believe she was the same person I'd first met. It was as though I'd dressed her for a part. Where was the patron who'd helped my family and sympathised with me? 'I never would have set out to hurt you. But you're not yourself any more, you've changed —'

'I have not changed,' she replied stiffly. 'I am the very woman who employed you. Do not deceive yourself. I told you from the first exactly what your role was and what I intended to do.'

I'd never agreed to murder. I put my hands on my hips. 'And what do you intend to do *now*?'

'I shall create the greatest playhouse in all of London,' she declared. 'The theatre Eugene Grieves could have possessed, if he had only taken up my offer.'

The grandfather clock ticked. At least, I think it was the grandfather clock; it might have been the watch. Mrs Dyer didn't wear it as Lilith had, but Melpomene seemed to have altered her all the same, brought every bad quality to the forefront.

She toyed with the ring on her finger, considering. 'I will not have you undermining my efforts, not when I have come so far.'

'Then let me stay a while. Keep me on until I find a place and I'll never breathe a word of what I know.'

'Very well.' She spoke through gritted teeth. 'You have won your point. You may stay until Christmas, but absolutely no longer.'

It was a relief, considering the alternative. And she needn't worry; I wouldn't spend any more time dancing attendance on Georgiana than was necessary. Even these few months would be a serious blow to my pride.

'Thank you,' I said tightly. 'What's the next play?'

She brightened a little at this. 'We are presenting a spectacular! I chose it myself: Bayard Taylor's translation of *Faust, Part One.*'

'Faust?' I was sure I'd misheard. 'That's not like ... *Doctor Faustus*?'

Her eyebrows raised. 'Goodness, Jennifer, your ignorance! Of course it is the same legend as *Doctor Faustus*, but a different play entirely. Goethe, instead of Marlowe. I thought it a fitting tribute to Eugene Grieves as we approach the anniversary of his death.'

Words failed me. Such a play wouldn't honour Eugene Grieves; only recall his awful death. And what of Felix Whitlow? Surely he'd refuse to take part? 'It seems in rather poor taste ...'

'I did not ask for your opinion,' she snapped. 'Do you require this work, or not?'

I did, although I wished to God I didn't. I should have done as Mrs Dyer said: pulled myself together and found a new place over the summer. I ought to have known Georgiana would demand her dues.

It felt ominous that my theatre career should end with the same story that began it: a deal with the Devil.

Homo fuge.

I saw Doctor Faustus's predicament now. The world became a place of torment when there was nowhere left to fly.

CHAPTER 32

I forced myself to read the play. Mrs Dyer hadn't lied; this version differed from *Doctor Faustus*. It was showier, more sentimental. We'd require twice the number of players for the choruses of angels and disciples, not to mention the peasants who sang and danced, the witches who circled on broomsticks and the fairy wedding. The effects were more elaborate than anything the Mercury had attempted before.

'Felix Whitlow wants to borrow our dog,' Oscar told me as we sat in the parlour with Dorcas the following Sunday. 'His character transforms from a poodle into a devil at the beginning. I think Lilith would have loved that, don't you, to have seen Eurydice on stage?'

Her ears pricked at her name.

I wasn't sure it was a good idea. 'Will Eurydice be safe at the Mercury now? Mrs Dyer isn't one to let a grudge lie. She'd hurt the poor animal just because it belonged to Lilith.'

'I'll keep an eye on her,' Oscar promised. 'She's our dog now. With any luck, I can train her to bite Georgiana.'

Our laughter was hollow. We couldn't relax enough for real merriment.

'I can't believe you're going back,' Dorcas said, seriously. 'I won't set foot in another theatre as long as I live.'

At least Faust didn't die at the end of this telling. Instead, Mephistopheles clamped his talons over the doctor's shoulders and bore him away on leathery wings.

'I don't *want* to go back,' I exhaled. 'Neither of us do.'

Oscar scowled. 'It's going to be hell. The memories are bad enough, but the lads in the paint frame will have a field day over Georgiana coming back.'

Dorcas placed her hand on mine and squeezed. 'Don't put yourself through it. Not for us. We can move house again. We can go back to how it was before.'

To me sleeping in a chair. 'I just want us to have one Christmas in St John's Wood. We deserve that much. And I need to line up a new place before I leave.'

'We'll save until Christmas,' Oscar agreed. 'Jenny will get her reference. Then we're both out of the Mercury for good.'

Leaving the world of costumes and plays would feel like leaving part of myself behind. I didn't want to be working at the Mercury any more – but I didn't want to give up the passion I'd found, either.

Dorcas frowned. 'What will you do, Jen? Service again?'

I shook my head. I'd have to break all ties with Oscar – there were no followers or sweethearts allowed in service. 'I don't know.'

'I'll find another theatre,' Oscar said. 'There are playhouses that would have me. Unless Mrs Dyer takes it upon herself to poison them against us.'

Dorcas sighed heavily. 'I used to envy you two with both your fancy jobs. Now I'm pretty glad to be a florist.'

In a story, this would be the time for a hero to arrive and save the day. But there seemed no chance of that. Oscar and I had made a career of lending our services to the tragic Muse, and Melpomene wasn't partial to a happy ending.

At least the costumes held my interest. Georgiana was playing Margaret, a wide-eyed country girl seduced by Faust. Mrs Nettles, Polly and I spent hours toiling in the wardrobe room trying to create outfits that perfectly symbolised her character's descent into sin. Margaret's many dresses began as simple, white affairs which then ranged through shades of pink until she became, literally, a scarlet woman. Each neckline edged lower, each hem had a thicker band of black, suggesting her wading through the mire.

Mrs Dyer spared no expense on her new protégée. The materials came from the House of Worth, Harrods and Morris & Co.

I couldn't detect any signs of pregnancy in Georgiana as I fitted her – so that had been either a false alarm or a desperate lie on Greg's part. If she'd become Mrs Dyer's creature to protect a child, I could understand it, but Georgiana was thinking only of herself. Still, I did exactly as she bid me; I didn't retort or complain when she asked for redesigns.

As she stood in Lilith's old dressing room, her hands on her small hips, I tacked up the front of her skirt. The train floated beautifully, like a cloud. 'At last you dreadful wardrobe people have got something right.' She primped her hair. 'I daresay Lilith never looked this good.'

Twirling a pin between my index finger and thumb, I imagined jamming it up her nose. Lilith would never have taken a stupid part like Margaret. The character was so naive she made Juliet look like a brothel madam.

'What a pity Mr Whitlow declines to play my Faust! I think he might change his mind, to see me now. Who could resist?'

'You look pretty, Georgiana,' I acknowledged grudgingly, 'but not tempting enough. You can't erase his memory of Doctor Faustus bleeding to death.'

She pouted. 'There's no need to be so disagreeable.'

Felix Whitlow was going to play Mephistopheles, as he had before. Maybe the role made him feel safe; he'd avoided harm in that part once. But I didn't envy him returning to the stage. Having one co-star die mid scene was bad enough; he'd witnessed two of them.

'Have you quite done? I need time to practise before I'm summoned to rehearsal. Horace wants us off-book this week. I can't work miracles, darling.'

I nodded. 'I'll go and make these changes now. Careful as you step out. Don't upset the pins.'

I helped her out of the costume and returned her to everyday clothes. Her skin smelt different to Lilith's, more powdery. I fought down a surge of grief.

'Don't forget to run me up that little gown we discussed for the church scene,' she warned.

'As if you'd let me forget.'

'It has to be perfect, darling. I'll make you do it over again until it *is* perfect. That is the scene they'll remember me for.'

Caustic remarks blistered on my tongue. I wanted to say they'd never remember a vapid doll like her, no matter what we dressed her in. 'Just worry about your lines,' I muttered and turned away.

With the frothy creation in my arms, I struggled to get through the dressing-room door and close it behind me: Georgiana's name had been painted in golden letters already. Anthony Frost had been erased by Felix Whitlow. Once more it hit me that my two colleagues were dead. I'd never see them walk through these doors again.

Battling tears, I made my way backstage and headed towards the ladder that led up into the flies. The rehearsal of a Faust and Mephistopheles scene was already in full flow: '*This was the poodle's real core, a travelling scholar, then?*'

I peered out on to the stage. New mahogany boards shone beneath a T-piece gas lamp; there was no indication of the place where Lilith had fed the theatre with her lifeblood. But she'd left something of herself, all the same. An essence. If I stared deep into the gloom of the orchestra pit, I could picture her long, white face, the brilliance of her eyes and the hair that flowed dark, like a river at night, over her shoulders.

Climbing the ladder had become second nature to me now, but there seemed a change in the noise of the rungs: a deeper groan of long-suffering. It was no better above the stage. The scene stretched over the paint frame was 'Walpurgis Eve in the Harz Mountains'. Black and shades of grey merged into whirling smoke, while a vivid slash of colour showed lightning splitting the sky. Flames licked through the heather; Oscar was adding sparks to them by flicking a brush.

He caught sight of me and left his post. 'How are you?' He'd got embers on himself as well as the canvas; his skin was covered in a fine red mist.

'I hate it,' I told him in a low voice. 'I hate ... all of this.'

'Me too. I thought it was bad when Georgiana ran away, but now she's back, it's worse. She's ruined the Mercury.' He worked his jaw. 'Couldn't they leave us with anything?'

'I don't think I can do this, Oscar. I can't work where Lilith died. She's still here. I ... sense her.'

Oscar gripped my hand; I didn't even care if he got paint on the dress. 'Of course she's still here. She gave so much of herself to this place.'

'That should feel comforting, but it doesn't. It feels like Lilith's trapped.'

He glowered. 'Maybe she is. Murdered spirits can't find rest.'

I fought back a sob. 'Where's the Guvnor? Have you seen him come in?'

'No, Mrs Dyer's taken over the whole office. She's got him well under her thumb. He can't help us now, Jen. The police won't help us either. We have to shift for ourselves.'

I couldn't accept that. I couldn't just do nothing.

'He wanted to talk to me,' I told Oscar. 'When I went to the house, the Guvnor tried to talk to me, but it was as though Mrs Dyer was keeping him prisoner. I was so upset at the time I ignored him. Maybe I should have listened. Maybe he's got evidence against his wife and Georgiana? I should go and see him.'

'Wait a minute. Mrs Dyer's got that footman, hasn't she? He'll spot you a mile off. What if ... what if I went instead?'

'Do you think the Guvnor would receive you?'

'I can try. I'll sneak out later, pretend to be carrying a message. If I knock on their trade door ... maybe they'll let me in. The Dyer servants have never seen me with you. It's worth a shot, isn't it?'

I squeezed his hand. 'Be careful.'

'I'll find a way, Jenny. I promise.' He peeked over his shoulder. 'I'd best be getting back to work, before I catch it.'

I didn't want him to leave. I felt my face crumple. 'I can't do this,' I said again.

'Yes, you can! You're stronger than anyone I know. Just one more play.' He put his hands on my shoulders, looked deep into my eyes. 'One more play and then you can thumb your nose at the Dyers. I swear it.'

———

Faust, Part One was Mrs Dyer's enterprise, through and through. She oversaw every detail. Horace, the stage manager, grew more harassed by the day. Not only did she demand perfection, but she'd bitten off more than the theatre could chew.

That morning was meant for rehearsal. Horace was letting the actors run their parts with minimal supervision; Mrs Dyer had brought us down from the wardrobe room to discuss costume requirements with him.

'Here's the problem,' Mrs Nettles said. 'You've got people dressed as monkeys, wearing long fur and grease on their faces. There's vapour and smoke from the cauldron, so they can scarcely see what they're doing. Then you want fire, coming down the chimney when the witch arrives! The witch can be dressed in wool, but I don't like the chances of those poor souls in the monkey costumes.'

'The animals need to look as convincing as possible,' Mrs Dyer demurred.

'Accidents have happened in other theatres, madam,' Polly put in. 'Ballerinas gone up in smoke because their skirts caught flame. They can't look perfect *and* be safe.'

Mrs Dyer waved a hand. 'We have the blankets and the sand buckets. There cannot be any real danger with our measures in place. Am I not paying the three of you to overcome these difficulties?'

Horace leafed through the prompt book. 'There's fire everywhere,' he said. 'Not just in this scene, Mrs Nettles. Jets spray out of the uncorked bottles. Faust opens a flaming book. You'll have to choose every fabric with this in mind.'

'I'm aware of that,' Mrs Nettles replied patiently. 'I've been trying to explain it to Mrs Dyer. To do the costumes she wants, we'll have to cut back on effects.'

'There will be no cutting back!' Mrs Dyer insisted. 'None. It is to be a *spectacular*. A different colour for every flame. Come now, the play has been staged before. It is not impossible.'

'But we don't even have an iron curtain. When you've got a flashbox attached to a bellows ...' Mrs Nettles began.

I couldn't feign interest any longer. Mrs Dyer would get what she wanted, one way or another.

Taking a seat in the orchestra stalls, I watched the actors. A group of supernumerary players milled about with their heads bowed. I recognised the church scene: Georgiana was obsessed with it.

Chairs stood in for the pews. The organ in the orchestra pit played a short dirge and everyone began filing into their seats. Georgiana took her place in the front row, a pout on her lips, irritated that Horace wasn't watching her.

A breeze dimmed the T-lamp and moved the curtains upstage. Part of the fabric seemed to detach itself, drifting slowly apart until it formed a figure. My mouth went dry.

It was a woman all in black. A veil covered her face, shoulders and hair. She floated slowly up the aisle to the organ's deep notes and took her place in the row behind Georgiana.

'*How otherwise was it, Margaret, when thou, still innocent, here to the altar cams't.*' The Evil Spirit. It was a scripted part – but no one else was in costume. We hadn't even *designed* the costume. Why was she wearing that?

I couldn't remember which actress was playing the Evil Spirit. Couldn't picture her face. All I could see was the photograph the Guvnor had kept in his pocket, the vanishing mother.

Georgiana clasped her hands as if in prayer.

The organ swelled, hummed right through the core of me.

'*Wrath takes thee!*' hissed the Spirit. '*The trumpet peals!*'

It must be a mistake; wax in my ears, background chatter muddling with the lines. But I'd heard Lilith speak a thousand times and this was her voice.

Georgiana started to her feet, backed slowly up the aisle, still facing the audience. '*I cannot breathe!*'

'*Hide thyself!*' The Spirit crowed. I sat nailed to my chair. It was – it *was* Lilith. How did nobody hear? The Spirit extended an ebony arm. '*Woe to thee!*'

I thought it was the rumble of drums in the orchestra pit. But then there came a whistling; wood splitting; shouts from

271

above. Georgiana raised her head, her lips parted to speak the next lines.

The backdrop of Walpurgis Night crashed down. It unfurled as it fell, flashing a blood moon. Georgiana threw herself forward just in time, hitting the boards stomach first, the canvas trapping her feet.

Everything erupted in confusion. Chairs were overturned, actresses screamed. Mrs Dyer rushed on stage to help her favourite out from amongst the debris.

The Evil Spirit had vanished without a trace.

Mrs Dyer's face was white and pinched with anger. 'Who is responsible for this?' she cried, searching the flies. 'What are you fools doing up there?'

But I think she knew, as well as I did, that it wasn't the painters.

Whatever she tried, Mrs Dyer would never purge her theatre of Lilith Erikson; it didn't matter how many doors she painted over, or which actresses she put on stage. Lilith lingered in the foundations, permeated the walls of the Mercury, insidious, like the scent of smoke caught in hair.

CHAPTER 33

Weeks of hot weather had bleached the grass even on the north side of the church. Leaves were falling from the trees with a faint brown whisper. There was mist in the mornings now; it clung low to the ground and cloaked the squirrels hopping to and fro. Everything spoke of change and decay as autumn took hold. It was all ending: the heat, my security and my time at the Mercury.

Oscar seemed troubled as we sat beside Lilith and Anthony's graves. Everyone in the paint frame had their wages docked for the incident with Georgiana; he was working long hours to repair the canvas. Still, I thought there was something else causing him to bend his head and focus on his shoes, barely conscious of me at his side or the corvids that squabbled in the branches above us.

'I went to see the Guvnor,' he said finally. 'Blimey, Jenny, you weren't wrong. He's in a real state.'

I swivelled round to face him. 'What? When? You never told me you'd been!'

'I know. I'm trying to tell you now. I turned up at the trade door and said I had a message for him. They let me in. I guess Mrs Dyer only told her lackeys to watch out for you. She wasn't expecting me.'

'What did he say?'

Oscar fidgeted. 'He's worried about Lilith's boy.'

'Algernon?' I'd thought of him often since Lilith died. It comforted me to think there was part of Lilith still living, somewhere out there.

'The Guvnor reckons Mrs Dyer means the baby harm. He thinks she'll hunt it out and – I don't know – poison it, or something.' He searched my face for a reaction. 'He's not wrong, is he? She's capable of that.'

I wrapped my shawl tighter around my shoulders. 'Dear God, she would. She'd throttle that poor little mite with her own hands and smile.' Had I caused this search with my blackmail? Was Mrs Dyer trying to make it so that I had no leverage over her, no secret to divulge? 'What on earth is the Guvnor going to do?'

The tips of Oscar's ears turned red. 'He wants Lilith's boy to have a real mother. Someone to protect him, no matter what.' He paused. 'He's set his heart on you.'

'Me?'

'The Guvnor says you're like a bulldog. You'd never let any harm come to Algernon.' A fond smile tugged the corners of his mouth. 'And he's right.'

My head was spinning. 'But ... but ...' Did the Guvnor mean to employ me as a nursemaid? Perhaps I *could* do that. It would be work, but I'd hoped to get free of the Dyers with my next position, and surely his wife would be peering over his shoulder ...

'Look what he gave me, Jenny.' Casting a glance to check no one was near, Oscar opened his jacket and pulled out a fold of banknotes. So many banknotes. 'The Guvnor wants to set us up. Pay for us to get married and run our own theatre. There's a place in the East End, he could get us the lease. Nothing like the Mercury, of course, it'd have to be a penny gaff or a music hall. But ... we could do it, couldn't we?' Excitement lit his face. 'Together. We'd be free of all those bad memories and *I'd* be the Guvnor.'

It was just like the first morning I'd sat in Mrs Dyer's parlour looking at the coins. A future beckoned me with open arms, and I didn't dare trust it. 'It's too good to be true. I've made a deal with the Dyers before, they always want something in return—'

'But this time, what the Guvnor wants is what we want, too.' For a moment his smile wavered. 'Isn't it? I mean ... don't you want to marry me?'

Unease trickled through my veins. I loved him, but it was happening so quickly. Could a happy marriage really be founded on a secret payoff? 'Oscar … this scares me. I don't trust the Dyers. Whatever they do … someone gets hurt.'

He fixed me with his liquid brown gaze. 'But you trust *me*, right?'

'Of course I do.'

'Then that's all we need.'

He kissed me. Sunlight played across my closed eyelids and the wind ran its fingers through my hair. I tried, tried so hard to absorb his optimism. I wanted to be happy. I really did.

When we broke apart he was grinning like a fool. I couldn't help but smile back. 'Our own theatre, Jen. We can do it. You, me and Algernon.'

Determination crystallised within me as I pictured the baby in the photograph with Lilith's big eyes and her dark hair. Algernon wouldn't sit on the lap of an anonymous woman any longer. I'd give him a face to lay over that black mask hovering in the background. He'd have the one thing Lilith had wanted for him, wanted for herself: a mother.

Maybe then she'd be at peace.

My dreams took me back to the Mercury that night. Not the theatre I knew, but a wasteland, a scene of rubble and ash. The bones of the building stood exposed, gradually being picked clean by the cool night air.

Cautiously, I crept across uneven ground. My boots stirred up clouds of powder. It moved restlessly, like a spirit, stinging my eyes and tickling my lungs, but I didn't want to cough. That dust was precious. I might be inhaling the costumes, the scenery or the plush seats that filled the boxes.

I might be breathing remnants of *her*.

I wound my way towards the place where the stage had been. Objects glinted at me from the ash: a helmet used by Banquo's ghost, cogs from machines in the cellars below. Everything stank of sulphur, as if the Devil himself walked two steps behind.

This was where Lilith stood for the last time. I planted my feet on the marks and tried to feel the power that had flowed through her veins. But I couldn't. I still couldn't find her.

Crouching down, I sifted through the salt-and-pepper ash with my fingertips. Something began to take shape. A face, an impression stamped into the soot: Lilith's features, drawn in a death mask. Her mouth gaped like an open wound. Her eyes were yearning, pitiful.

A soft pattering sounded in my ears. The wind moved again, scattering the image and blowing Lilith back to dust.

I snapped awake. My room was bathed in pale light and Dorcas's side of the bed lay empty. The mattress dipped in the place where she'd been.

Disorientated from my dream, I rose, splashed my face with water and dressed. I knew, rather than felt, that I was happy.

Only a fool would give herself over to giddy excitement in my circumstances. I was crossing Mrs Dyer, again. I had plenty of work ahead of me in starting a business and adopting a child. But the thought of waking up on some future morning and finding Oscar by my side filled me with warmth. I'd always wanted him for my own, even when I was just a maid. If only it were under happier circumstances.

As I descended the stairs, I caught sight of Bertie, still sat at the kitchen table, instead of at the factory. I quickened my step, alarmed. 'Bert? What's happened?'

But he wasn't hurt; he was defiant. 'I'm not going to work,' he announced. 'If you're leaving us, I'm going to go and live with Gregory and Georgiana. They'll let me stay home all day.'

I took a deep breath. I wasn't his mother, I couldn't stop him, but I knew how it would end. Either they'd turn him down flat or exploit him somehow; even if he wasn't at the factory, they'd make him work one way or another.

I bobbed down to his level. 'I'm not leaving you, Bertie. I promise. Oscar and I are getting married, but we won't be going far away. I'll still come and see you! Do you remember when I was in service? I didn't live with you then, but you still saw me.'

How would I manage, though? With the speed that things were happening, I'd overlooked vital points. Georgiana would spy for Mrs Dyer as I had; if she saw me with a child over a year old, she'd put two and two together. I imagined it progressing with horrible inevitability, a train stopping at stations on its way to Mrs Dyer. If Bertie knew about Algernon, he'd blab to Gregory, and Gregory would tell his wife ... Could I really go on seeing Bertie while keeping Algernon a secret? Would I have to choose between two poor, motherless boys?

Bertie must have seen the pain constricting my face. 'It's my fault, isn't it?' he asked in a rush. 'I kept saying I wanted to go to the theatre. Then when I got there ...' Tears filled his eyes at the memory. 'Everything went wrong.'

I hugged him fiercely. 'None of this is your fault. Do you hear me? If it's anyone's fault, it's—' I managed to stop myself in time. Blaming Gregory wouldn't dry his tears.

It was all such a mess.

The first person I saw at the Mercury that day was Mrs Dyer. An errand took me past the office and the door stood wide open. There was a new roll-top desk beside the Guvnor's, fancier and more elegant in design; Mrs Dyer hovered behind.

'Ah, Jennifer,' she called out. 'A moment, if you please.'

I stopped reluctantly. Somehow I was afraid she'd read the truth in my face, see that I was accepting her husband's money, *her* money, to raise Lilith's child. 'Yes, madam?'

'Come in.'

It was hot and airless in that office, like a public bath. 'You're setting up your own desk,' I observed.

'And why should I not? This is my theatre, as much as Hugh's. More so, in fact. I have sacrificed every inch of my pride for its sake.'

I looked over the contents of her workspace. Besides the usual pen stands, paperweights, inkpots and scripts was a cabinet card of Eugene Grieves. He wore a long black cape. His hands were raised, his fingers spread, one arm reached towards the camera. The lips were drawn back from his teeth in a snarl.

'Lord Ruthven the Vampire,' Mrs Dyer informed me. 'He was so young, back then.'

The muse's watch hung from his belt. His outline looked a little smeared, as Lilith's had the day that Silas died. I glanced away. There were no photographs of the Guvnor or Rachel, only an elaborate stand bearing the watch. How did it shine so brightly? After all the blood that had been shed over it, Melpomene only stood out clearer than ever.

Mrs Dyer caught me looking. Jealously, she snatched the watch up and locked it in her safe.

I scoffed. 'I'm not about to take it. I stole it *for* you, remember?'

'Once a thief, always a thief. One cannot be too careful. You have turned blackmailer already.' Passing back to her desk, Mrs Dyer drew out a sealed envelope from beneath a ledger. 'I have your letter of recommendation here. I presume you will need it, in your quest for a new position?'

I took it from her hands. Custom said I should thank her, but I couldn't do that. 'I might not take a new position, after all. I'm getting married.'

The surprise on her face was everything I'd hoped. 'Are you? Upon my word. I must give you credit for a fast worker. Who is the fortunate young man?'

'Oscar Thorne.'

'Ah, Georgiana's little cast-off. I did say that you should be begging for scraps without my patronage ...' I let the insult bounce off me. What did she know of love? The only way she'd got her husband back to her bed was to threaten him. 'But I shall congratulate you. Why not? I am feeling quite the philanthropist today.'

'Oh?'

Glowing with pride, she placed a hand on her stomach. 'Yes. I have reason to hope. Our heir will come at last and every penny of my money will be safe.'

Astonishment held me dumb. It was late in the day for a second child, but not impossible. I remembered Oscar saying the people who owned the watch seemed to get exactly what they wanted.

'I believe it is your turn to congratulate me, Jennifer.'

Maybe it was for the best. With a son of her own, she might stop looking for Algernon. I pushed away the images of Lilith's daughter, the black in the toilet, the spine and the 'wings'.

'I would, madam, but I don't want to tempt fate. These matters are fragile, aren't they?'

Her smile was bright and cold as ice. 'I have told you before, I am writing the script for this play. Everything shall turn out exactly as I planned.'

'But Melpomene's the Muse of tragedy,' I pointed out. 'Whoever owns your watch seems to end up dead.'

'I hope that is not some manner of threat.'

I spread my hands. 'Why should I threaten? I need nothing from you now. You need nothing from me. Our association is at an end. You've written my exit, and I'll go off when you bid me.'

'Yes, you will.'

'I'm glad,' I said. 'I'm glad I won't be here for the final act.'

With that, I turned and left the office.

CHAPTER 34

I ought to have known there'd be one last twist of the knife. What made me think Mrs Dyer would tolerate my frankness without punishment?

I sat alone in the wardrobe room, feeding Georgiana's church scene dress into the steady gallop of the sewing machine for what felt like the hundredth time. If I'd made all the alterations she required by hand, I would've left the Mercury crippled. My vision had been for an ox-blood skirt and sleeves with a white stomacher, symbolising that while darkness encroached around the character, her heart remained good. Georgiana was having none of it. She wanted gold lace trimming, embroidery all over the bodice. She'd rather look like a fashion plate than the penitent she was supposed to be. I left off caring. Let her preen and simper like a fool; she'd never be able to bring the character to life, so what did the costume really matter?

I'd just taken my foot off the treadle plate when Oscar banged into the room. 'You'll never guess what she's done now.'

'Georgiana?' I asked wearily.

'No, not her. The head of the coven, Mrs Dyer. She says I can't paint any more. I'm to spend my time watching over the dog.'

It didn't make sense. 'But isn't Eurydice only on for a short scene?'

'Yes! She doesn't even need training; she does exactly what Felix asks her to. This is personal. This is Mrs Dyer demoting me.'

I sighed and let go of the stupid gown. 'I'm sorry, Oscar. It's my doing. She's coming after you out of spite. I never should have told her we're engaged.'

Oscar scrubbed a hand over his face. 'No, don't say that. If you hadn't told her, someone else would have. The blokes in the paint frame think it's hilarious, like I've made some kind of trade with your brother. I hate them. I hate them all.' He looked up, inspired. 'Let's go now, Jen. What are we doing, letting them degrade us like this, while we've got all that money sitting at home? Let's just go.'

It was tempting. A large part of me wanted to cut this dress to ribbons and scatter it over Georgiana's dressing room. 'We can't. It would look too suspicious. We've said we're saving up to marry next year; if we left now, people would start to ask where we got the cash from, and Mrs Dyer might find Algernon.'

'We'll take him! Somewhere she can't trace us. Forget the music hall in Whitechapel; we'll do what Greg and Georgie did – go abroad.'

How I wished I could. But it wasn't in my heart to be that selfish. 'You know I can't do that. Bertie's already acting like Whitechapel is the end of the earth and he'll never see me again. I can't just leave. I won't be like them.'

His shoulders sagged. 'No. No, you're right.' He came over and sat down at the sewing table, stretching himself across the surface. 'It's not fair. How do you bear it? Waiting on her night and day, acting like she didn't murder your friend? It's not like you to be so … patient.'

'That's flattering.'

'You know what I mean. You've barely spoken a harsh word to her.'

Not aloud, perhaps. 'Here's the thing, Oscar. I've learnt a lesson from Mrs Dyer. Over the past year I've seen her hatred for Lilith consume her, twist her and make her into something awful. Georgiana's a first-class bitch, but I won't let her do that to me. I've got to be better.' I reached around the sewing machine and took his dry hand. 'I can see the other side. Our music hall, where you paint every landscape and I make every costume.'

'It doesn't eat you up that they might never pay for what they did to Lilith?'

'Of course it does. But if Algernon thrives, maybe that's a type of revenge in itself.'

We hadn't discussed what we'd tell the baby. My instinct was that I didn't want to keep Lilith a secret from her son. He'd be ours, he'd belong with us; the world didn't need to know, but Algernon should be proud of his heritage. He bore the blood of the greatest actress ever to tread the boards. I wouldn't let Lilith vanish into the dust, as she had in my dream.

'Maybe it's a good thing,' he admitted grudgingly. 'Me looking after the dog. I can make sure no one hurts poor Eurydice too.'

'Exactly. Mrs Dyer's trying to make you feel small, but don't rise to it. You're so much more than her. She's pathetic. Her family disowned her; her husband doesn't love her. All she has is that stupid watch and she's so scared of losing it that she keeps it locked up in a safe!'

'You don't think that watch will bring her good luck?'

I shook my head. 'It's a curse, Oscar. I've become superstitious enough to believe that much. Whatever power it brings, it comes with a cost. And I have a feeling that Mrs Dyer's going to get her comeuppance, one way or another.'

There's something about an opening night. The stir of anticipation, of witnessing a spectacle never seen before. The words might be old, but they emerge fresh with every new actor, reincarnated, again and again. It's a kind of magic. And like any magic, it comes with risk. *Faust, Part One* was more ambitious than anything we'd staged before. No one knew if we could pull it off.

Nerves were jangling, especially Georgiana's. 'It's too thick!' she fretted, pouting at her face in the mirror. 'You're too heavy-handed! Margaret isn't supposed to start off painted like a hussy.'

I bit back the insult on the tip of my tongue. 'It looks different under the lights,' I explained.

'If this is how we're to commence, I dread to think of the end. How shall I appear when Margret's virtue is lost? Will you paste me with a trowel?' Her eyes slid like a viper towards me. 'Is that how you caught Oscar?'

Gritting my teeth, I grabbed a handkerchief and started to dab the greasepaint away. Georgiana squirmed under my touch.

'No! Stop! You're smudging. It's worse than before.'

'Fine. I'll go fetch a basin of water and start again.'

Her brow wrinkled under the white streaks. 'Do we have time for that?'

'Lots of time. The curtain's not up for another half hour and there are six full scenes before you appear.'

'All the same, don't dally.'

I slammed the door behind me. Prissy little baggage.

A footstep sounded in the corridor. I glanced up, expecting to see another harassed dresser, but the figure was facing the opposite direction. It resembled a woman in a black dress.

A woman I knew well.

'Lilith?' I whispered, scarcely daring to believe.

She stood absolutely still. Then, without seeming to move, she drifted, sliding like a scenery flat in its track.

Fear roped around my throat. I rubbed a hand over my eyes. When I opened them, the figure was drawing further and further away.

I couldn't watch her slip from my grasp again.

'Lilith … wait!'

I stumbled in her path. There were sprinkles on the floor: a fine, white ash.

She wound effortlessly through the passages of the Mercury as though it was her natural element. A door swung open; I didn't see her push it.

'Lilith?' I said again.

The outline wavered, trembling like a cloud of flies. As I watched, astonished, the woman began to disperse before my very eyes.

'Jenny?'

My feet were treading upon marble.

'Jenny?'

I was standing at the top of the grand staircase, overlooking the busy lobby. It was packed with gentlemen in opera scarves and ladies with their shoulders bared. Fans fluttered like butterfly wings. I blinked, starting as if from a dream. The woman in the black dress was nowhere in sight. 'Where did she go?'

Gregory crossed towards me from the opposite side of the landing. 'Who are you talking about?'

'The woman in front of me. She looked like …'

He cast a glance around the lobby and shrugged. 'No idea who that was. It's a full house.'

My brain barely registered who I was talking to. I'd been so intent on following the woman in black that I'd simply accepted his appearance. But now I drew back. 'What are you doing here?'

Greg was dressed smarter than usual, his hair slicked back with grease. The marks of his beating had faded, but he was still missing a tooth. 'What do you think? It's my wife's debut in a leading part! I've got a seat in the stalls to watch her. Looks like she did pretty well for herself, in spite of you. You'll be apologising for all those horrible things you said about her, after tonight.'

'I'll apologise when she pays me back Bertie's operation money and returns Miss Fielding's ring. Or did she have to pawn that, to pay your debts?'

'Leave off, Jenny. Bert's had his operation now and you're getting married. It's all working out nicely. Why can't you forget the past and move on?'

Forget? I had to bank down my anger before I could speak. 'Once Oscar and I are wed, we'll never see either of you again.'

Something flickered in his hazel eyes, a shrewdness. 'Is it true that you and Oscar have signed papers to adopt the Guvnor's child?'

Blood rushed to my head. 'Who told you that?'

'It's a big secret, then?'

Laughter floated up from the lobby. Gazing down over the iron banisters, I could see Mrs Dyer at the centre of a small group. Her dress was an emerald sheath clinging to her body like a reptile skin. Black opera gloves covered her arms. She wore her Melpomene brooch right at the centre of her décolletage.

The Guvnor was merely her shadow. His cummerbund sagged about his waist and a carnation drooped in his buttonhole. Rachel clung to the tails of his coat.

'It's not true,' I said in a rush. 'I don't know who's feeding you such nonsense.'

Greg straightened his necktie. 'Just something I heard. I didn't mention it to Georgiana. Not yet.' He cocked his head. 'I don't think she'd be very happy with you going against her friend like that, do you?'

A bell rang. I cursed. I had to go and fetch water. Georgiana would be having kittens by now. 'It's not true,' I repeated. 'It's all lies. Don't you dare say a word, Gregory.'

His lip curled back, showing that missing tooth. 'Maybe I won't … if you and Oscar make it worth my while.'

CHAPTER 35

I changed Georgiana like an automaton, not caring what happened on stage. I believed it all now: that Lilith was here, watching over me. She'd led me straight to Gregory because she knew he was a threat to her son. Who in God's name could have told him about the adoption? What were we going to do? I wish I'd listened to Oscar. We should have taken the baby and run.

I tried to convince myself it didn't matter, that we'd find a way to protect Algernon somehow. But Mrs Dyer had the watch that gave her everything she desired. I had no doubt that she wanted Algernon's death. I couldn't let her win and wipe out Lilith's legacy. I couldn't bear it.

I was dressing Georgiana for her second-to-last appearance, an apparition of Margaret on Walpurgis Night. Her face was painted white and fetters trailed from her bare feet. The last touch was a red ribbon around her throat, foreshadowing Margaret's execution.

'Careful!' she choked, as I secured it. 'Are you trying to strangle me?'

Maybe I was.

'You haven't come to watch any of it, darling. Don't you usually spectate from the wings? You should see me knocking them dead out there!'

Saying nothing, I turned away and tidied up the paintbox. I didn't need their magnesium powder and coloured flames; I was in a hell of my own. There was only one scene left to dress Georgiana for after this. Maybe I could find Oscar and tell him to get ready. The second I put the dungeon rags on Georgiana, we could flee, get on a train to Southend and save the baby. It wouldn't be much of a head start, but maybe it would be enough?

I thought of Dorcas, left to manage the boys alone if I just disappeared. I thought of Bertie's trusting, elfin face and my promise not to abandon him. Could I really leave them? Did I have a choice?

'Well, I wish to see the spectacle, even if you don't.' Georgiana pushed back her stool and rose to her feet. The fetters clattered. 'This scene is the *pièce de résistance*. I shan't wait for the call boy.' Powder had turned her fair hair almost white. Georgiana was the reverse of Lilith as I'd seen her: ivory and clouds, instead of ebony and soot.

As the door snapped shut behind her, the lights flickered.

Strange. That hadn't happened in a long time.

Hurriedly, I pulled out Georgiana's last costume and grabbed the bits I'd need to fix her hair. Maybe I should try and pack some things for myself. There'd be no time to go home and gather my belongings. I found a satchel and threw in a few stockings, a comb.

Someone knocked at the door.

I jumped. 'Come in.'

The handle didn't turn. No one answered. Shrugging it off, I drew out a clean shift; Georgiana's would just about fit me. But then the rap came again.

Cursing under my breath, I pulled the door open. 'What do you want?'

There was nobody there.

Everyone must have gone to watch Walpurgis Night, because the corridor stood deserted.

'Hello?'

The lamps blinked out. Not just in the dressing room behind me but all down the corridor. There was a hissing, fizzing sound.

My heart began to pound.

'Lilith? Is it you?'

The light swelled back and I was no longer alone. She stood at the end of the hallway once more, staring directly at me. She wore the white domino from *Romeo and Juliet*, painted with black tears.

I pushed words past the fear in my throat. 'Lilith, I need your help. Algernon …'

She beckoned with a finger, moving as before, oozing down the hallway and through doors. I walked like Macbeth had, in a dream. *Is this a dagger which I see before me?* I didn't care if she was real or not. I'd follow her anywhere.

She led me to the manager's office. As I watched, the cabinet card of Eugene Grieves fell face down on Mrs Dyer's desk. A drawer slid open, the dial of the safe turned by itself.

My mouth went dry. The watch. Lilith wanted me to take her watch.

Could I do it? I thought of Silas, of Anthony; of Eugene and Lilith both gasping to death on stage while the mechanism ticked. What price would I pay? Would it be worth it to save her son, the boy who would become *my* son?

That was a mother's love: to make a deal with the Devil himself for the sake of her child. I didn't think I could, not after all I'd seen. Some costs were simply too high.

There was a clunk, then the safe door swung back on its hinges. I flinched, knowing I'd have to make my choice. Shining, metal walls reflected the watch on its stand. The tick echoed like the steady beat of wings. Warily, I approached. It felt as though she was calling me: Melpomene or her gaping mask.

My fingers trembled as I pulled the watch out. A blend of fear and longing raised gooseflesh on my skin. This wasn't like the other times I'd held it. I couldn't deny the feeling of power as the case rested in the palm of my hand, warm like a living creature.

Lilith raised a finger to her dead, black lips.

Stumbling back, I sat down heavily at the desk. I couldn't rip my eyes from the watch. If I listened hard, I could almost hear it now: a sweet, haunting voice …

Memories flickered: Lilith and the dagger, Eugene Grieves with his blood-red eyes. No good could come from this. I mustn't give in. I couldn't end like the others.

Unable to look away, I fumbled on Mrs Dyer's desk. Papers hissed together, an inkbottle fell. At last my fingers closed on a large, cool paperweight. My arm shook as I drew it back and poised the weight above Melpomene's impassive face.

This was either very brave or very foolish. Silas had died trying to destroy this watch. I'd read stories of those who pitted themselves against the Muses: Sirens plucked of their feathers, kings with their eyes gouged out. What made me think I was stronger than the myths?

'The show's over, Melpomene.' Closing my eyes, I gritted my teeth and brought the weight swinging down.

There came an ear-shattering crack. Someone screamed. I opened my eyes to see the watch in pieces and Lilith, twisting away into smoke. I could *taste* smoke, thick against my tongue.

Lurching out of the office, I was met by a grey pall swelling up the stairwell.

No. Surely not.

Covering my mouth with a handkerchief, I sped towards the auditorium and burst into the aisle through an usher's door. It was pandemonium. Colours and sounds raged around me; the battens were erupting in a riot of flame. Chunks of burning wood and metal dropped onto the stage, blocking the performers' exits. Chaos reigned around them. Stagehands scrambled in the wings, grabbing fire buckets, but the sand did nothing against the ferocity of the flames.

My conscience shrieked that I'd caused this, I'd unleashed Melpomene's curse.

The audience were on their feet, fighting to get out of the narrow rows. There was a bang then a cloud of fire, as tall as it was wide. The inferno climbed the curtains, one hellish hand over the other.

Georgiana howled under the limelight. The blaze snapped greedily at her skirts, devouring first her calves then her knees; she looked like a witch at the stake. Blind with agony, she charged offstage and into the orchestra pit.

Now the conflagration snatched at the gentry stampeding from the front row, igniting velvet coat-tails and tulle gowns. A lady's hand muff went up in flames.

Everything began to merge together, the shapes ghostly in smoke.

I had to get out.

The patrons weren't fine swells now: they pushed and scrapped for their lives. A lady shoved me violently to the side, crushing my feet under her heels. I screamed for Oscar, but I couldn't see him. I didn't recognise anyone in the mad churn of bodies, and they were pushing me further and further away from the stalls. Something boomed like a cannon, the crowd surged; I was slammed hard into the wall. I couldn't breathe, I couldn't move.

A bark cut through the uproar.

'Eurydice? Eurydice!'

The sight of a black poodle careering towards me with its teeth bared was enough to make people move. The crowds parted and I lunged for Eurydice, grabbing tightly on to her collar.

'Where's Oscar? Where's Oscar?'

He was meant to be watching her. Now she was alone; I didn't want to stop and think what that meant. He might be lying trapped under a fallen beam of wood ... But Eurydice dragged me on.

Heat was building fast. It hurt to breathe. I held on to the dog's collar for dear life as we stumbled out of the auditorium and down the wide, marble staircase. Beside us, an elderly woman slipped and fell. One minute she was there and the next she'd gone, as if someone had opened a trapdoor.

The lobby was a chamber of pain and reeling terror. I saw a gentleman with his topper ablaze, the frame melting and clamping to his scalp. Someone carried a child in their arms, its skin scalded lobster red. An usher I didn't recognise leant against the wall, overcome by a coughing fit. People kept treading on my skirts. I heard material rip, felt that I'd lost a good portion of my gown. Eurydice bit and gnashed to move us along.

Finally, finally, I burst onto the street. The air tasted clean, but it made me choke.

Shocked bystanders crowded the pavement and a fire engine blocked the road. Men were shouting, passing buckets of water. I couldn't focus on them.

'Jenny! Jenny, thank God! Are you hurt?' Oscar. Soot coated his face and white flecks were scattered through his hair. 'Jenny? Speak to me.'

My throat was too dry. 'What—' I began, and then the windows blew out.

Heat gusted over us. Oscar pushed me further back as the fire roared in triumph.

I scrubbed the grit from my eyes until I could see the Mercury shimmering, wavering, vanishing before us. I had the strangest sensation of watching myself burn; part of my own body, slowly setting on fire.

'We have to go back in.'

He blinked, his eyes lamps in his sooty face. 'What?'

'Greg's still in there!' Mortar started to crack. There was a shift, a sigh and the balcony collapsed into a heap of rubble. 'No!'

Oscar held me back. 'Shit.'

I strained against him. 'I have to—'

'You can't get in. It's too late.' He was right. The balcony had blocked all three entrances and twisted up the gates. 'I'm so sorry, Jen. He didn't make it.'

'Greg!'

He held me. There were no words.

My eldest brother was done for. I was in agony, and the pain wasn't all for me. How on earth would I tell the others? It would break Bertie's heart.

None of the Dyers had reached the street, either. I thought of little Rachel, so young, innocent in all this. Her parents didn't deserve my tears, but they had them all the same. Where was Polly? Mrs Nettles? Felix, Clementine … Had all these lives been lost?

'It's my fault,' I said hoarsely into the front of Oscar's shirt. 'It's my …' My voice croaked out. I'd inhaled too much smoke.

He was quiet for a moment. The flames rustled and cracked. Then he said, 'Lilith watched over us. She got you, me and Eurydice out.'

I didn't know if that was true. I didn't know what to think. Horace had spoken about the dangers of the fire effects used in the play, yet it seemed too strange that the blaze would ignite the moment I hit the watch.

That watch gave people exactly what they wanted. I'd held it for only a moment, but no one could doubt that my problems were now solved. Neither Mrs Dyer nor Gregory would bother us again. I had the bank notes, Oscar, and soon we'd have Algernon …

Had I really wanted this? Had I?

Charred flakes carried towards us on the breeze, soft and silent. I clung to Oscar while the Devil, or Melpomene, or whatever it was, claimed the theatre for its own.

I pictured the remnants of the watch surrounded by flames, melting, melding to the desk of Mrs Dyer who loved it so.

Homo fuge. That's what Eugene had scratched on the back. And I would. God help me, I'd flee this place and never look back.

Acknowledgements

In January 2020 I sat down at my desk to write a novel called *The Ghost Melody*. It wasn't going well, but then again my dad was seriously ill in hospital and I was still reeling from the sudden death of my beloved pet, Steve. Things will get better, I thought.

Over a year later, the world was in the grip of a pandemic, my father had just passed away, my husband suffered a life-changing medical event, and we had lost yet another pet. I had thrown away four attempts totalling over 144,000 words of *The Ghost Melody*.

I am inexpressibly grateful for the continued love and kindness which carried me through this dark time. My friend and agent Juliet Mushens proved herself an absolute hero yet again and I could not have coped without her. Dear friends Ally Whittle, Anna Drizen, Charlotte Wightwick, Louise Denyer and Nazmin Khan supported me emotionally, while my lovely parents-in-law went out of their way to ferry us between hospital appointments and funeral planning meetings.

The wonderful Katie Ellis-Brown was, at that time, providing maternity cover for my editor and found herself saddled with my chaos. To say she rose to the challenge would be an understatement. I honestly cannot thank her enough for her steadfast encouragement, insight and general sweetness. She made me believe in the project. She listened to me say, 'I've got an entirely new plot, a new title and a narrator who wasn't even in the other drafts,' and offered nothing but her support. *The Whispering Muse* is for you, dear Katie.

My delayed deadline meant I was also lucky enough to benefit from the expertise of my long-term editor Alison Hennessey when she returned from maternity leave. She hit the ground running, turned around a tight edit and her notes helped me to find the core of my idea. Thank you Alison, I am glad you got to be part of this book!

I would also like the thank my other key contacts at Bloomsbury Raven, Emilie Chambeyron, Amy Donegan and Francisco Vilhena, for their ongoing hard work and being a pleasure to deal with.

I am so fortunate in my whole publishing team. Let's hope the next book will be easier!

A Note on the Author

Laura Purcell is a former bookseller living in Colchester, Essex with her husband and pet guinea pigs. She is the author of six previous novels, among them Gothic novel *The Silent Companions*, which was a Radio 2 and Zoe Ball ITV Book Club pick and *The Shape of Darkness*, winner of the inaugural Fingerprint Award for Historical Crime Book of the Year. Her short story 'The Chillingham Chair' was included in *The Haunting Season* anthology, which was an instant *Sunday Times* bestseller.

A Note on the Type

The text of this book is set in Linotype Stempel Garamond, a version of Garamond adapted and first used by the Stempel foundry in 1924. It is one of several versions of Garamond based on the designs of Claude Garamond. It is thought that Garamond based his font on Bembo, cut in 1495 by Francesco Griffo in collaboration with the Italian printer Aldus Manutius. Garamond types were first used in books printed in Paris around 1532. Many of the present-day versions of this type are based on the *Typi Academiae* of Jean Jannon cut in Sedan in 1615.

Claude Garamond was born in Paris in 1480. He learned how to cut type from his father and by the age of fifteen he was able to fashion steel punches the size of a pica with great precision. At the age of sixty he was commissioned by King Francis I to design a Greek alphabet, and for this he was given the honourable title of royal type founder. He died in 1561.